FIVE WAYS
TO FALL

FIVE WAYS
TO FALL

a novel

K.A. TUCKER

ATRIA PAPERBACK

NEW YORK   LONDON   TORONTO   SYDNEY   NEW DELHI

ATRIA PAPERBACK
A Division of Simon & Schuster, Inc.
1230 Avenue of the Americas
New York, NY 10020

First Atria Paperback edition June 2014

ATRIA PAPERBACK and colophon are trademarks of Simon & Schuster, Inc.

For information about special discounts for bulk purchases, please contact Simon & Schuster Special Sales at 1-866-506-1949 or business@simonandschuster.com.

The Simon & Schuster Speakers Bureau can bring authors to your live event. For more information or to book an event, contact the Simon & Schuster Speakers Bureau at 1-866-248-3049 or visit our website at www.simonspeakers.com.

Cover design © Anna Dorfman
Cover photographs by Deborah Kolb/ImageBrief (woman) and Dave Allen Photography/Shutterstock (road and trees)

Manufactured in the United States of America

10 9 8 7 6 5 4 3 2 1

Library of Congress Cataloging-in-Publication Data

Tucker, K. A. (Kathleen A.).
  Five ways to fall : a novel / K.A. Tucker. — First Atria Paperback edition.
    pages cm
1. Man-woman relationships—Fiction. I. Title.
  PR9199.4.T834F58 2014
  813'.6—dc23
                                      2014003694

ISBN 978-1-4767-4051-5
ISBN 978-1-4767-4052-2 (ebook)

To Lia and Sadie

If you want purple hair, then have purple hair
(I will probably regret saying this one day)

To Sarah Cantin

For corralling those squirrels

FIVE WAYS
TO FALL

Prologue

Is it just me?

Or does everyone have a moment of "crazy" in their life—when raw emotion runs over your common sense like an eighteen-wheeler, compelling you to do and say things that make others stare in shock and shake their heads at you, wondering why you're acting so foolishly, why you won't just let go, why you can't see the truth.

Only, you don't care what *they* think or say because this is *your* life and this is *your* heart that has been swallowed.

That's what Jared did.

He swallowed my heart whole and then let my unwanted remains simply . . . fall.

Perhaps I'm being a tad melodramatic. Perhaps, when I figure out how to pick myself back up again, I'll laugh at all of this.

Until then . . . my remains will be here, lying in a pile of rejection.

Again.

~Reese

Chapter 1

∎∎∎

REESE

I've never seen that look on Daddy's face before.

*He's had it since he walked back from the pay phone. "Go on, now,"
he urges, his gruff voice cracking. "Go on inside."*

*"But . . . why?" I whine, casting wary eyes at the truck-stop diner,
empty but for a man with a Santa beard.*

*Daddy rests his hand on the steering wheel and turns his body to
face me. "Reesie, baby." I don't like his tone. It's that serious one that
makes my bottom lip wobble. "I need you to go back inside, sit down in
our booth, and ask that nice waitress for another piece of that pecan pie
you like so much," he says slowly, evenly.*

I swallow back my tears. "Alone?"

His face tightens, like he's mad. "Only for a little bit."

"And then you'll come in?"

*He squeezes his eyes shut and I'm afraid I just made him really
angry, but . . . I've never gone anywhere alone. I'm only five. "Remember that Daddy loves you, baby girl. Now go on."*

*Stifling back a sob, I slide along the old bench seat and push the
heavy old Ford truck door open.*

"Reesie," Daddy calls out as my red shoes hit the sidewalk.

Turning, I see his hand wiping at something on his cheek before he gives me a wink and a smile. The truck door makes a loud bang as I swing it tight. Holding my breath, I climb the steps and push as hard as I can against the diner door, the jangle of the bell ringing in my ears. I dart across the black-and-white checkered floor and climb into our booth—the one we were sitting in before Daddy called Mommy; it still has our dishes on the table—just in time to see the taillights of Daddy's truck disappear.

When the nice waitress with the big hair comes by, I tell her my daddy will be here soon and I order that piece of chocolate pecan pie with a please and thank you. I sit in that booth and gobble it up, thinking how lucky I am to get two pieces in one night.

And I wait.

With my chin resting on my palm, tucked into the corner of the booth, I stare out that window, watching for the familiar blue truck to reappear, checking the door every time that bell jangles. When the kind policeman sits down across from me and asks me where my daddy is, I tell him he'll be here soon.

■ ■ ■

There's no kind policeman to comfort me now. No nice lady bringing me a piece of chocolate pecan pie to combat the sourness in my mouth. But at least this time I wasn't abandoned.

I'm reminded of that the second I see my stepfather's face through the small glass window in the door.

His salt-and-pepper hair is more salt than pepper and he's gained at least ten pounds around his waist since I last saw him—nine years ago—but there's no mistaking Jack Warner. I don't think he recognizes me, though. The way his steely blue eyes wander over my violet hair . . . my piercings . . . the giant "Jared" tattoo that coils around my right shoulder, I think he's wondering if the police officer led him into the wrong room.

I'm lucky that I'm even in a room this time. Normally they throw you into a holding cell or make you sit in an uncomfortable chair next to a drunk named Seth who stinks of malt scotch and body odor. I'm pretty sure the female arresting officer felt sorry for me. By the lethal glare she threw at Jared and Caroline as I was escorted out of Lina's apartment, past *their* apartment door, on my way to the cruiser, the officer wasn't impressed with what she'd heard of the situation.

She didn't hear it from me, of course. Growing up around lawyers, I've learned not to say a word to the police without one present. It was my best friend and next-door neighbor, Lina, who declared that the apartment I trashed earlier today is still technically mine—even if my name isn't on the lease—and that they should be arresting the thieving, heartless bitch who stole my husband.

Unfortunately, I'm the only one sitting here now.

I hold my breath as I watch Jack take a seat, adjusting his slightly rumpled suit jacket on his large frame as he tries to get comfortable in the hard plastic chair. It's ironic—in this moment, it feels like he's both an integral part of my childhood and a complete stranger.

I can't believe I called him.

I can't believe he actually came.

With a heavy sigh, he finally murmurs, "Reese's Pieces." He's looking down at me the same way he did when I got caught rearranging the letters of a Baptist church sign to read something no nine-year-old girl—or twenty-year-old, for that matter—should have in her vocabulary. Despite the severe strain in our once close relationship, warmth immediately spreads through my chest. I haven't heard that nickname in years. "So . . . destruction of private property?"

I guess the cops filled him in. "I prefer to call it artistic expression." The canvas included Caroline's prissy clothes, her pretentious throw cushions, and that damn pornographic picture of them hanging over *our* bed. "Besides," I raise my hands, stained in crimson, and offer in a deadpan tone, "they can't prove it was me." When Lina found me sitting quietly in the dim kitchen light of her apartment, where I've been staying for the past two weeks, she let out a single yelp before realizing that I hadn't turned into a homicidal maniac and was in fact covered in red *paint*. I probably should have made the cops' job harder and showered before they arrived.

A tiny sad smile creeps over his face. I wonder if my attempt at humor adequately hides the crushing heartbreak and rejection that I'm drowning in after finding out my husband was having an affair with his high school sweetheart.

"I phoned Barry on my way here. Sounds like you've kept him busy these past few years." By his clenching jaw, I see that wasn't an easy call for Jack to make, even nine years later. Not surprising. Friends since they could barely walk, Jack and Barry were once equity partners together in his law firm. Until Barry had an affair with Jack's wife.

My mother.

All relationships instantly dissolved in a bath of bitterness that obviously hasn't fully drained yet. Glancing at his hand, I can't help but notice the absence of a wedding ring. I guess he hasn't remarried. After what my mother put him through, I don't blame him.

"And I understand why you called me now. You didn't have a choice, did you?"

"Not really," I admit, focusing on the stars and circles I'm finger-drawing over the table's cold metal surface. Barry is a high-priced, successful criminal lawyer who has gotten his unruly stepdaughter out of more than one debacle. The last incident was on my eighteenth birthday when I decided it would be funny to go retro and moon cars.

One of those cars was a police cruiser.

The cop was an uptight prick.

And I was drunk.

After helping me avoid indecent exposure and underage public drunkenness charges, Barry announced that my juvenile record was sealed, I was now an adult, and he was officially washing his hands of me. Three months later, when my mother left him for husband number four, it *really* became official.

"I'm surprised Annabelle's new husband didn't want this swept under the rug quickly."

"I didn't phone Annabelle. I don't want her to know about this." I stopped calling her "Mom" when I was eight. We both agreed it wasn't fitting for a woman whose true passions lay in exclusive club status and dirty martinis.

My doodling finger freezes suddenly. "*You* didn't phone her, did you?" That would be like handing her torpedoes for an effective insult air strike. She had called it after all. She'd said I didn't have what it took to keep my "blue-collar pretty-boy" husband happy for long.

Jack chuckles softly, though there's no mirth in it. "No, I definitely did not phone her. What would I tell her, anyway? You weren't exactly informative on the phone. Sounds like you're in some hot water, though."

My sigh of relief slides out and I'm back to doodling. "That's what they tell me." When the cops started throwing around words like "larceny" and "threats of bodily harm"—things that sounded excessive and unfitting, but permanently damaging to my fresh and clean adult record should they stick—I knew I wasn't going to talk my way out of this one. It didn't help that I used the picture of Caroline for target practice during my rampage, leaving a pair of scissors strategically placed through her eyes. "It's a good thing you still have that same law firm. You were easy to find."

Jack folds his arms over his chest and regards me with an unreadable face. A tiny part of me—the angry little girl lost somewhere inside—is ready to burst, to demand, "How could you have left me? I know why you left my mom, but how could you have shoved *me* out of your life so easily, too? *I* didn't cheat on you!" But I bite my bottom lip. Pissing off the one person who can help me right now wouldn't be smart. And I need to be smart.

Finally Jack leans back in his chair and says, "Okay, Reese. Start from the beginning and let's see how we can solve this."

I press my lips together to keep from smiling. Not because this is amusing. It's just that we've been here before. This really is starting to feel like days long since lost, when we'd meet up in the kitchen around midnight—after Annabelle had gone to sleep, when Jack was finally home from work—to contemplate my latest mischief over bowls of ice cream. He's even adopted the same hypnotic tone that always got me talking when my teachers, my guidance counselor, or anyone else really, couldn't. I'm pretty sure he uses it on all of his clients.

Twenty minutes later, after I've given him a rundown of my situation, I hear his disappointed sigh. "Working in a pet shop, Reese?"

"Not anymore." After leaving work early with the flu and coming home to *the big discovery* of Jared and *her* in the shower— oddly enough, the more it replays in my mind, the more it begins to resemble the shower scene from *Scarface*—I spent a week in Lina's bed, heavily sedated with Jim Beam and Nyquil. My boss fired me over the phone.

I don't care.

"And eloping in Vegas with a guy? At nineteen years old? After knowing him for *six weeks*?" I know that the chuckle that fills the room now isn't directed at me, even before his words confirm it; Jack's laughing at the irony of it all. "And you were always so adamant that you'd never get married."

I have no answer to that, except a quiet "I loved him," as the painful knot forms in my throat, as I fight the sob from tearing out of me. I did. I think I still do, despite how much Jared has hurt me. Since that day eight months ago when I stepped out of my best friend Lina's apartment and quite literally ran into her neighbor, a reincarnation of a mint-eyed Greek demigod, I knew that I had met my soul mate. Fireworks exploded, lightning struck, electricity coursed. All that love-at-first-sight bullshit that I didn't believe in—I instantly became a poster child for it. Common sense flew out the window with a cement block tied to its ankle.

Jared said he felt it, too.

And now, after six months of marital bliss, without a single warning sign, he's back with *her*.

That rotten illness festering inside me enflames with the thought, the humiliating reality a burn that doesn't want to subside.

"Look, Reese. I know you've always had a wild streak in you, even as a little girl. These choices you've made since I saw you last, though," his head is shaking, "possession of marijuana . . . trespassing . . . underage drinking . . . a fistfight?"

"It's not really that big a deal. A lot of people drink and smoke pot in high school," I argue, adding, "I'm just the one who kept getting caught."

"Drag racing?" He stares at me questioningly.

"Those were derby cars and that was totally blown out of proportion," I clarify.

Jack slides his glasses off and gives his face a rough rub, looking exhausted. It's a four-hour drive from Miami to Jacksonville and he arrived here five hours after I called, meaning he pretty much dropped everything to come. I can't help but wonder why he'd do that.

"At least I didn't get knocked up," I joke.

By the look of exasperation he shoots me, he doesn't find that remotely funny. "I had hoped you were too smart to get into this kind of trouble."

"I guess even smart girls can make a clusterfuck of their lives, can't they?" I mutter, though his words sting.

Because they're true.

There's a long pause, where Jack's mouth twists in thought as he regards me. "What are you going to do with yourself now, Reese? How are you going to make up for this?" When I was little, Jack always asked me for suggestions as to how I should be punished for my various childish misdemeanors. I think it was his way of getting me to agree on the outcome without looking like the harsh stepfather. I was pretty good at coming up with suitable penances and it was definitely preferable to sitting in a chair while my mother shrieked about what an embarrassment I was to her, the gin sloshing out of her martini glass with her mad hand gesticulations.

But I'm not a little kid anymore and Jack's not asking me to come up with a suitable punishment. He's asking me how I'm going to fix my *life*.

All I have for him is a defeated shrug.

Because that's how I feel right now. Defeated. "I don't know. Get another job, I guess."

"What about college?"

The eye roll happens before I can stop myself. Jack always hated my eye rolls. "My transcripts aren't exactly going to woo the administrative offices." Neither will the private school expulsion, earned when I broke into a teacher's office and stole a midterm exam.

"Because you *couldn't* do the work?" My arched brow answers him. "Because you *didn't* do the work," he answers for himself, shaking his head, his face a mask of extreme disappointment. "Is this how you want to live your life? In and out of police cars? Working minimum-wage jobs? In unstable relationships?"

"Does anybody ever really *want* that?"

Jack's right. I *was* smart. Some may say I'm still smart. But I've made so many wrong turns along the way, I don't know how many right ones it will take to course-correct.

I don't know if that's even possible.

I sit in silence, listening to the monotonous *tick-tick-tick* of the second hand on the wall clock above, watching Jack as he spends an exorbitant amount of time playing with the gold Rolex on his wrist, his breaths deep and ragged. I don't know that I can count on him. I mean, he forgot about me once. Looking at the twenty-year-old version of who he once knew, he's probably ready to stamp "lost cause" across my forehead.

And then he settles those kind gray eyes on me. "I honestly didn't know what to expect when I arrived, but I had a long car ride up to think about it." Folding his hands together on the table in front of him, a stern expression settles over his face. "I have a proposition. It comes with conditions, though."

A small exhale escapes me as I chew the inside of my mouth, relief and wariness dancing together. "Okay. I guess?"

"No more, Reese. Not even the harmless stuff."

"This is my first time here in years, Jack." Ironically, I convinced myself that meeting Jared was a turning point in my life, leaving me the sated and smiling wife who was happy hanging out at home and keeping out of trouble.

"Yes . . ." His eyes graze the walls of the police station room. "And yet here you are again."

He doesn't get it. He must not have heard me. "This was different, Jack! She *moved in*! I haven't even moved *out* yet! All my stuff is still in that apartment!"

He raises his hand to silence me. "You should have turned around and walked out. That would have been the mature, responsible thing to do. Instead, you let your emotions get the better of you."

I smirk as another wave of familiarity washes over me. "You always said I was too emotional for my own good."

"I did say that," he acknowledges with a sad smile. "And I'm still right. No more, Reese."

Picking at a loose thread on my sleeve as if the topic isn't cutting into my heart, I offer casually, "Well, I can definitely promise that I won't be getting married again. Ever."

That earns a soft chuckle. "You and me both, kiddo." A pause. "You remember Mason, don't you?"

My geeky stepbrother who used to spend half his time scowling at me and the other half staring as if my head were about to revolve on my shoulders. I recall that the day we moved out, he watched with a bitter smile, condemning me to follow in my mother's footsteps.

He despised my mother from the very first day that he met her.

My pursed lips at the mention of that name has Jack smiling. "Oh, yes. How could I forget? Your nemesis. Well, he's finishing law school this spring." Jack takes a deep breath and then holds it, as if he's hesitating. "Why don't you come and live with us until you get back on your feet."

What?

Jack continues, not addressing the bewilderment that must be plastered over my face. "I can get you into the paralegal program at Miami U. If you finish that, you can work for me. It doesn't have to be forever, but at least you'll have something solid to put on a résumé. It's a fresh start."

"I . . . uh . . ." Did I just hear all that correctly?

His eyes drift over my hair again. "You should think about a more natural color for an office environment and . . ." His focus settles down to the tiny diamond-encrusted septum ring in my nose and he cringes. "Maybe a few less piercings."

But . . . My tongue has somehow coiled itself into a useless ball inside my mouth as my mind grapples with this offer. It's far from what I had expected. "Why are you doing this, Jack? I mean, it's great and all, but why?" He really doesn't owe me anything. It's enough that he came all the way out here to bail me out.

"Because I shouldn't have turned my back on you, Reese. I let—" A flash of pain betrays his otherwise calm demeanor. "Let's just say I'm making amends." He pauses. "What do you say? I need to get out of this town. I can feel Annabelle's shadow looming." He shivers for effect, making me snort.

"Well . . ." My fingers rap across the table as I give my current situation—that of a police station room—another once-over. I have no job, no home, a shattered heart, and a pending criminal record. I should probably make the first smart choice I've made in a long time. But . . . "Not sure the cops will let that happen, Jack."

"You leave that with me."

Another pause. "I'm riding my bike down."

His mouth twists with displeasure. "I assume you're not referring to one with pedals."

"No pedals," I confirm with a small smile. I got my motorcycle license when I turned eighteen and bought a bike a few months later. Another element of my "badass" self that Jared loves.

Loved.

Jack heaves a sigh. "That shouldn't surprise me. You always did threaten your mother with getting one. Anything else I should know?"

"I'm a slob," I warn him. "And a certifiable bitch in the morning."

"Well, I guess some things just don't change, after all." Reaching up to give his neck a slow scratch, he mumbles, "Mason will be thrilled."

■ ■ ■

Six months later

"Could we have picked somewhere more commercial?" I ask dryly, draining my fourth margarita in record time as my gaze drifts over the beachside bar, complete with canopies, twinkling Christmas lights—in July—and too many happy, laughing people. Even with the sun setting and the light ocean breeze passing through, a light sheen of sweat coats the back of my neck. It's a typical summer night in Cancún, Mexico—hell-hot.

"Commercial is safe," Lina answers in her distinctive flat tone. She always sounds bored to tears.

I roll my eyes. "You're safer in this country than you are in our own nation's capital—you do realize that, right? That's all just media hype."

"Tell that to the American couple who just had their heads lopped off a month ago."

"If I were going to tell them anything, it would be to not run drugs for the cartel," I retort.

She acknowledges that with a lazy shrug as she sips on some frothy calorie-laden pink thing with an umbrella sticking out of it.

"Why don't we put on a pile of diamonds, jump into a random cab, and get the guy to drive us through the quiet, dark back streets of Mexico City?"

Lina's thin lips purse together tightly as she regards me. "It's never fun to discover your best friend has a death wish."

With a snort, I wave the server down for another drink. "But it *would* be fun to watch someone try to take Nicki down."

As if hearing her name from across the lounge, Nicki—who I met when I answered a "roommate wanted" ad in the newspaper—and the third member of our little "Reese is turning twenty-one and is still bitter as hell so let's go to Cancún" entourage, turns her head to catch our gaze from her seat on a swing by the bar. She winks as she downs another shot of tequila.

"How does she make that work so well?" Lina mutters with a hint of envy. I know exactly what she means. All around us are flirty girls in pastel barely-there dresses and sun-kissed skin. Not Nicki, though. She sits by that bar like a femme fatale in a skin-tight leopard print dress and four-inch black heels, her platinum-blond hair coiffed like Gwen Stefani's, her red lips glaring against her pale skin, and sparkly chandelier earrings dangling from her ears. All that femininity oozing from her is counterbalanced by a full sleeve of ink and the muscular physique she's honed through her latest passion: dead-weight lifting. The tall guy talking her ear off right now? She could bench-press his two-hundred-odd pounds without breaking a sweat. That, coupled with her three-year stint cage-fighting before she switched hobbies, makes her one badass twenty-five-year-old woman.

"It works so well because she's beautiful and mysterious and she's not stupid enough to run off and marry some guy she met in a hallway who's still in love with his ex," I mutter around my straw, catching the wince flash across Lina's face. It's the first time I've made any open reference to Jared since leaving for Miami, perfecting the art of denial while I impatiently waited for my heart to freeze.

Our waiter places a fresh margarita on the table next to me with a wink. I force a smile and I'm sure it's altogether hostile by the way he hightails it back to the bar. I can't help it. He has dark, shaggy hair and olive skin. Just like Jared.

"You *have* to let it go, Reese. It's been *six months*. You—" My flat glare makes her voice falter, her words a dishonor to the very real, very raw pain I still feel. Especially today, on what would have been our one-year wedding anniversary.

And is instead Jared and Caroline's wedding day.

Because karma hasn't been cruel enough.

She quickly changes tactics. "You've started a whole new life. New city, new home. Soon, a new look . . ." Her free hand reaches up to flip strands of my hair, reminding me that the purple will be gone the day that I return. "You've got that great new job."

I roll my eyes.

"It's not cleaning up puppy shit and getting bitten by snakes." She taps the puncture marks on the meaty part of my thumb. A physical reminder of the day I made the idiotic mistake of sticking my mouse-scented hand into a cage to freshen the aspen chips and ended up with a two-foot-long ball python's fangs embedded in my flesh.

That happened the exact same day my sky fell. A very fitting scar.

"Not literally. But I'll be working in a law firm, Lina. Plenty of snakes."

After we made our agreement, Jack quickly went about throwing all kinds of legal jargon at the cops. In the end, it was unnecessary. Given the epically huge lack of judgment that Jared used sending me into that apartment unprepared to collect my things, he convinced Caroline not to press charges. So I walked out the police doors without any record of my moment of crazy.

Jack let me wallow in his spacious Miami house for one week, wearing my pajamas and gorging myself on Ben & Jerry's Butter Pecan ice cream out of the tub for twenty-one consecutive meals, before he tossed a bunch of application papers my way. He said, "It takes four to six months for most students to get through, depending on how hard you work. You can do it all online if you want and I have a paralegal spot waiting for you when you're done. Decent pay, good people. It's just a start, Reese."

I've never had any interest in working at a law firm—especially the one tainted by my mother—but I had made a deal with Jack and I *am* smart enough to see a good opportunity. So I immersed myself in the program, using it as a distraction. Once I got into it, I actually didn't mind the course work. It took me five months to complete and I ended up finishing with a near-perfect score.

I start my new job the Monday after I get back from Cancún.

"Oh, no. You're having doubts. You're going to bail on Jack. If you do, you're dead to me," Lina says.

"Oh, ye of little faith." Surprisingly, as unreliable as I can be at times, the thought of bailing on Jack has never crossed my mind.

"Fine. Let's talk about happier things. How's Annabelle?"

"Okay, see this?" I gesture to my face, which has contorted into a mixed pucker of disgust and loathing. "Sour face. Do not speak of she who must not be named."

"Do you want me to break into her place while she sleeps and turn her fans on? Guaranteed death, according to *my people*." Lina was adopted by a lovely Korean couple as a baby and raised to fully embrace their culture, including all of their death-by-fan superstitions. The fact that she's a five-foot-eleven-inch willowy blond who towers over both her parents means nothing in the Chung household. Her name is actually Li-Na, but she Americanized it in high school to make life easier. She speaks Korean fluently—throwing more than a few people off—and can shovel food into her mouth with chopsticks like the best of them.

We've been best friends since sophomore year, when I discovered Lina crying in a bathroom stall after Raine Higgins and her posse of bored and bitchy juniors had been bullying her. I did what any naturally spiteful high school kid who hates bullies would do. I spray-painted Raine's car with Korean expletives that I found on the internet. That, along with a picture of her giving her boyfriend a blow job in a parking lot that I covertly took—after stalking her at a party—and glued to the inside of the windshield of her *locked* car with Krazy Glue, was enough to keep Lina from ever being bothered by her again.

The tightness in my chest suddenly lifts with Lina's attempts to sway my mood. "Are you sure you and Nicki don't want a third roommate?" Lina and Nicki moved down to Miami about a month ago, into a condo that Lina's parents bought for her as a college graduation present.

"Absolutely sure," she confirms without missing a beat, her focus intent on the little pink umbrella twirling between her thumb and index finger. Lina's living habits are about as opposite to mine as the Arctic Circle is to the Sahara Desert. Everything in her apartment—from her linen closet to her pasta jars—is tidy and labeled accordingly. Those two weeks that I sought refuge in her apartment after breaking up with Jared nearly destroyed her.

"Okay, enough about bad stuff. Didn't we talk about finding you a fling?"

I groan as I survey the crowd. "I remember you talking about it and me ignoring you. I've tried. Three strikes is enough for me."

"You have *not* tried, Reese. Admit it."

Either there's an influx of douchebags or Lina's right and I'm subconsciously sabotaging myself. First there was Slick Steve, a senior at Miami U who showed up to our date with perfectly coiffed hair and an outfit right off the set of *Grease* the musical. Then there was Metrosexual Mark, a blind date from Nicki's work who picked his teeth with his fork and had a weird habit of adding "if it were me" to 90 percent of the sentences that came out of his mouth.

The final straw, though?

Emilio. Good ol' Spanish I-look-enough-like-your-ex-husband-that-if-you-dim-the-lights-this-might-actually-work Emilio. I might have been willing to see where it went had he not opened his wallet and laid it out on the table to proudly display his collection of extra-large Trojans, and then propositioned me in Spanish.

I shudder with the memory. "I'm starting my harem of cats."

"You hate cats."

"True. But I also hate limes, and look at me now!" I hold up my glass. "Besides, I've already found my Cancún fling. Lina, meet Mr. Cuervo. Mr. Cuervo . . . my best friend, Lina." Leaning in, I waggle my brow and whisper, "If you're nice, he'll let you call him Jose. I plan on spending the next six nights with this naughty little Mexican." I wave a hand at the server as he whizzes by, letting him know that I need another drink by pointing to my nearly empty glass, as I add, "He can be a bit of a whiny bitch in the morning but he makes up for it by dark."

"Great. Because you're not emotional enough when you're sober," she mutters, adding with a sigh, "Well, an incessantly drunk Reese should make for an interesting trip, at least. Just try not to get arrested. I hear the cells here aren't as nice as the ones you're used to back home."

Nicki must have been monitoring my drink levels from her perch by the bar because she saunters over with a fresh margarita in hand, either oblivious or ignoring the attention she naturally garners. "Here you go, *señorita*," she offers in a deceptively soft voice as she flicks her tongue piercing. I automatically roll my tongue, sensing the absence of mine. Jack hasn't outright demanded that I remove my piercings but I knew, by the way he kept cringing, that the barbell through my tongue was truly freaking him out. I removed that one out of respect, but I'm holding out on the others until the last possible moment.

"Jose isn't complaining about my level of intoxication," I respond to Lina, giving the rim of my glass a slow, sultry lick. I have a high tolerance for alcohol, borne from years of underage partying. It would seem, though, that lame, tourist-trap Cancún serves strong margaritas and the warm and fuzzies are *really* kicking in.

"Who the fuck is Jose?" Nicki asks, her pretty face scrunching up.

"It's Mr. Cuervo to you."

She finally clues in and that musical laugh of hers rolls out. "Oh . . . oh, buddy! No! That's so sad. We need to fix that." Her curious eyes scan the lounge. "You promised me you'd exorcise Jared from your vagina if you met a hot guy . . . There. The one in front. Perfect." She raises her inked arm, signaling someone as if she knows him.

Oh, God. I suck back a large gulp. "Seriously, Nicki. After the tooth picker you set me up with, I think I'm done. And exorcisms take at least two days to prepare for. Can't I just drown myself in frozen green goodness for tonight? I'm not even dressed for it." I'd thrown on a pair of shorts and an old faded rock concert tank. I don't even have makeup on.

"What do you wanna be this time? Architect from L.A.?" she asks, ignoring my opposition completely. Her eyes twinkle as they flash to me. "Stripper from Pasadena?"

I nod with appreciation. "That was a good one." Before Jared, the three of us used to head out to the bars on the weekends—Lina and I with fake ID. We'd make up identities: jobs, cities, sometimes names, and see how long we could keep it going while guys bought us drinks. Once, I had a guy completely sold on me being a goat herder from Iowa. He was as dumb as a bag of bricks.

The shuffle of approaching feet stirs an anxious flutter in my stomach. I *really* don't want to carry on a conversation tonight, fake or otherwise. "Helloooo boys," Nicki purrs playfully. I feel the eyes of women around us as they sit up to take notice, their rays of envy scorching my skin. I decide I can't play disinterested just yet. I need to know what type of fiend Nicki has targeted. As casually as five margaritas will allow, I turn and . . . slide right off my chair, my shorts providing my ass with little protection against the hard tile floor.

"I have shamed Mr. Cuervo," I mutter, ducking my head, the night air carrying mocking giggles my way as I accept that it's only eight o'clock and I'm way more drunk than I realized.

A large hand appears in front of me, palm up. "Well, *I'm* impressed." I hear the smile behind the masculine voice and I can't decide if I like that or not. Accepting the help—because the sooner I'm off the floor, the better—I'm pulled to my feet and into the broad chest of a blond with a big, obnoxious grin.

Wearing a fucking red shirt.

Chapter 2

. . .

BEN

I love the angry ones.

Of course, anyone who knows me would argue that I love any and all women, and I can't exactly disagree. But I love the angry ones the most. They're a challenge to be conquered, the reason for their fury usually fitting neatly into three buckets: insecure, scorned, hormonal.

And this chick gazing up at me with fire in her caramel eyes? I'm betting on bucket number two.

"My, what an awfully bright *red* shirt you have on," she pushes out between gritted teeth, as if she's trying to be polite but can't hide her disdain.

I didn't know what I was walking into when the punk-rock chick with the crazy-ass muscular body waved us over, but her friend with the purple hair and her back to me had me intrigued. Now that I'm getting a good look at her face, I know who I'm spending my last night with in Cancún. She's not what some would call traditionally "pretty." Her eyes are slightly too big and far apart, her nose is slightly too long and slender, and her lips—though nice and wide—are on the thin side. Yet something about all of that put together makes her sexy as hell. Maybe it's the little nose ring. Or maybe it's the way her decent-sized tits are pressing up against me, her low V-neck tank top—a casual shirt, telling me she's not trying to pick anyone up—giving me a fine view of her cleavage. Whatever it is, my dick is certainly pleased. "You like it?" I ask.

An irritated glare flickers to the material. "No."

I can't help but chuckle at her candor. "Will you at least give me a head start before you gore me?"

Those thin lips curl into a condescending smirk. "Bulls don't see color. That's a myth."

The only thing I love more than an angry girl is a *smart*, angry girl.

This is going to be fun.

"Well, how about I solve the problem for you." I take a step back from her and swiftly yank my shirt off, exposing six days of suntanned skin and an upper body that I know looks damn appealing because I work my ass off to keep it that way. The random catcalls from the tables around confirm it.

And then I simply stand there and grin like the cocky ass that I am as Angry Girl can't keep her eyes from scanning the muscles I've honed since my college football days, her lips parting ever so subtly. I see the shift in her, the moment where she realizes that, though she'd prefer to castrate the entire male species right now, she can't ignore her attraction to me.

At least, that's what I want to see.

"Sir. Excuse me, sir." A glance over my shoulder finds Angelo, the short Mexican waiter who's been serving us all week, standing there with a tray of beers for my friends and me. We didn't even have to ask. Hell, I love Cancún. I could live here forever.

"Angelo! Why the fuck are you calling me 'sir'?"

"Uh . . ." He licks his lips as his eyes dart to the tile floor. "Please. Management requests that you wear proper attire in the lounge area. Please."

"No worries, pal." Poor Angelo is probably ready to shit his pants, as afraid as he is to offend me, the guy who has lined his pockets with a month's worth of rent in tips. Snagging a beer off his tray, I take my time sucking back a few mouthfuls, feeling her eyes riveted to my throat.

Yeah, I've got this one in the bag.

With an easy smile, I place the bottle down on the table and pull the shirt back over my head. "Though you may have to deal with Angry Girl in front of me, now. She *hates* my shirt."

Angelo casts a polite smile her way as he hands out beers to my friends, and I know exactly what he's thinking. He's seen me walk out of here with a few different women this week.

What else can I say but . . . I'm on vacation.

I *was* planning on just hanging low tonight, going to bed solo. Now, though, getting this purple-haired chick naked sounds like more fun.

"Angry Girl will try to restrain herself, Angelo," she purrs, draining the last of her drink and placing it on his tray before scooping up a fresh one. She still has a full one sitting on the table, too. "But only if you come back with another one of these in under five minutes. Otherwise, there's no telling what she'll do." Narrowed eyes glimmer with secret amusement.

"*Sí, señorita.*"

I smoothly tuck a twenty into his shirt pocket and pat his shoulder. "For causing you any trouble with management." Angelo nods and quickly heads off as I stick my hand out. "I'm Ben. And you are . . ."

Angry Girl accepts it, the skin of her hand soft and cool within mine. "Jill." Thumbing to her left, she adds, "Sabrina. And that's Kelly over there. She's Korean."

What? My brow furrows as I regard the cute girl-next-door blond sitting across from us, trying to make sense of that strange introduction. A skillful distraction, it would seem, because it gives Jill a chance to slither into her seat, her back to me once again. She props her feet up to rest on the only vacant chair at the table, her long, shapely legs all the more visible thanks to the tiny shorts she's wearing.

"Travis, Kent, Murdock," I toss out with a lazy gesture toward the guys, three of my roommates from Miami. They can take care of themselves. I'm on a mission. I waste no time seizing an empty lounge chair from the table next to us. Flashing a big smile at the cougar eyeing me, a redhead who is definitely hot enough to fuck should this thing with Jill go sideways, I swing the chair around and take a seat so close that my knee—the one that cost me a guaranteed NFL career and still throbs in damp weather—rests against Jill's bare leg. She doesn't shift away. "First night in Cancún?"

One of her perfectly shaped brows arches. "You're persistent."

"A persistent fool," I correct her with a grin, earning the non-Korean girl's laughter. "First night in Cancún?" I repeat.

"How can you tell?"

Finally. An open door for a conversation. I jump through it like a circus dog. "Because you're way too tense, you're downing those drinks like you're on a mission to wake up naked on the beach, and you have no tan lines."

"Huh . . ." She ponders that for a moment while I inhale her perfume. She smells like strawberries and cream. I wonder if she tastes like strawberries and cream. "What are you, a detective?"

"Bouncer at a strip club."

Her head falls back and she starts laughing, a deep, throaty laugh that I want to record and play back again at a later date. "Of course you are."

I shrug. "It pays the bills." I could kill whatever assumptions she's making about me by telling her why I'm really here in Cancún: to celebrate finishing law school and taking the bar exam.

But I don't.

I simply watch her tongue curl around the salty rim of her glass. Dirty thoughts flash through my head and I'm forced to discreetly adjust myself. If she notices, she doesn't comment. Hell, she probably knows exactly what she's doing to me. There are no innocent vibes coming off this chick.

"And what do *you* do?" I ask.

She purses her lips. "I'm a marine biologist. From Seattle."

"A Doogie Howser marine biologist?" The girl could pass for twenty-three. Twenty-four, tops.

"I'm twenty-nine."

"Sure you are." I jut my chin in her friend's direction. "And she's Korean, right?"

In response, her friend spews off a string of something that sounds a hell of a lot like Korean, followed by a smug smile, and I'm left with my mouth gaping wide.

Okay. *Still . . .* "Marine biologist? Really?"

She takes another long draw of her drink and licks her lips before she announces, "I love me some big fish." *Yeah . . . lying. Fine. I'll play along.* "How long are you here for?" she asks, feigning disinterest, as the guys find chairs and pull her friends' attention away.

I let my eyes skate over her features again, silently counting seven piercings—two in her nose and five in her ear—and wondering how many more she has hidden under those tight little shorts and that tank top of hers. And I suddenly find myself wishing I were just starting my vacation today. "This is my last night."

"Really . . ." An unreadable look passes through her eyes as they quickly flitter over my features, landing on my mouth. "The exorcism needs more time," she mumbles under her breath.

What the fuck? Wouldn't that just be my luck to land a nut job for my last night. Not that that couldn't be fun. I'm always up for something different. "Maybe we should start right away then?"

The heated look she shoots me with—like she's deciding between jumping onto my lap or filleting me—makes me give this a moment's pause. Maybe I *should* be more careful about who I bring back to my room. I take another look at her frame—she's probably too small to cause any real damage without weapons—

and notice the giant name inked into her arm. As much as I want to trace the letters, I keep my hands to myself. It's like petting a strange dog; you don't even reach out until you know it's not going to lunge at you. So I point at the tattoo instead. "That would suck if it were an ex."

"Yeah, it *would*." The bite in her tone is suddenly back, and this time it comes with a sheen just barely glistening in her eyes. She quickly blinks it away, trying to keep the tough act going. *Dammit.* I groan inwardly as disappointment settles in. She's not just scorned. She's still *raw*. She's going to be one of those drunk chicks who suddenly erupts in tears. Probably during sex.

Nothing worse than a girl crying halfway through sex. A definite limp dick maker.

She clears her throat. "I don't see any tattoos on *you*."

Okay, at least she's trying to steer the conversation away from her and her current situation. I can roll with that. "You haven't seen all of me yet." I know I sound like a cocky bastard, but it somehow works for me.

A tiny sly grin curves her mouth for just a moment before she stifles it, as if she didn't mean to let it slip out. "Any hidden ones?"

"Nope. Hate needles," I answer truthfully.

"Wuss."

I shrug. "*You* obviously don't mind them. Any tats or piercings besides the ones I see?"

All I get is a taunting smile in return. *Fuck.*

A sudden burst of Rihanna pumps out over the speakers as the regular lights dim down and the dance-floor lights kick in, indicating that the hotel lounge is turning into a club as it does every night at this time. Jill's cringe tells me she's not impressed.

"Not your kind of music?" My gaze immediately drops to her tank top, a faded Pearl Jam album cover printed on the front of it.

She shakes her head. "I'm more into classic rock and nineties alternative."

Seriously? "Were you even alive for that?"

"I can play every single Aerosmith song ever recorded on the guitar," she says, as if that answers my question.

Sweet Jesus. Stretching my legs out as I try to picture her rocking out with a guitar strung over her shoulder—naked—I offer, "You know, girls who play the guitar are fucking hot. You any good?"

Another cunning smile behind her drink answers me. Yeah, she's good. And, damn it, so sexy. In a loose-cannon kind of way. The only kind that snags me like a trout on a shark hook. Just like Kacey, one of my best friends, did. That girl had a self-destruct button affixed to her chest for the longest time. I saw it a mile away and I still fell for her hard.

Angelo chooses that moment to swoop in and place a drink in her hand and a shot of tequila on the table for everyone. Jill doesn't even wait. She lifts the glass to her lips and downs it. No salt, no lime.

"Am I going to have to carry you home tonight?" I offer with a wide grin.

She smacks her lips as she drops the glass onto the table rather loudly. "I think I'm going to aim for waking up naked on the beach."

"I have some experience with that. I can give you a few pointers."

Her hawkish eyes roll over my body slowly before landing on my face, fixing a hard gaze on my mouth. "You're not my type."

I've heard this before and I don't believe her. Hell, I'm everyone's type! Eventually. "And what is it exactly about me that you don't like?"

A wicked gleam in her eyes tells me she thinks I'm going to regret asking. Little does she know, I don't give a shit. I have a thick skin and an easy sense of humor. This should actually be amusing.

"The womanizing mama's-boy football-player part who spreads the charm on like peanut butter and has had a different girl in his hotel room every night this week."

"Not *every* night."

She rolls her eyes. "Oh, and you're blond. I'm not into blonds."

"You're completely wrong about me." She's pretty much nailed it, actually.

"Really?" As if to prove her point, she taps the ring on my finger. The one I earned taking my team to the national championship.

"I don't play anymore."

"Not good enough?"

I chuckle. She's good at the hits to the ego. "Too good, apparently, because some guy felt the need to wreck my knee." Between the dislocated joint, the torn ligaments, and the nerve damage, I'm surprised I can even run anymore.

Those caramel eyes soften for just a flash, so fast I almost miss it. "I'm still not sleeping with you."

"Well, I don't know what *you* had planned, but I'm just here to hang out and make some new friends," I offer, feigning innocence.

This one's going to be a bit more challenging than I thought.

But she'll change her tune eventually.

Chapter 3

■ ■ ■

REESE

"You know they rob you blind when you rent a room to yourself at these places," I announce as I stumble into Ben's hotel room. It's the cookie-cutter design—two queen-sized beds covered in tropical floral bedspreads and adorned with swan towel creations, the walls plastered with tacky mass-production artwork.

I hear the door lock click behind me. "Yeah, but it's worth it on nights like this. Wouldn't you agree?"

"You've got this all figured out, don't you, Don Juan." I half-fall, half-lean against the wall to balance myself as I kick off my flip-flops. Once I got past the whole red shirt issue—I hold a special kind of grudge against that color—I realized that Nicki may have called forth the perfect exorcism candidate after all. As if his dazzling blue eyes and deep dimples weren't enough to win me over, the second Ben pulled his shirt off in the middle of the lounge and stood there like an arrogant bastard, that incredibly ripped body of his on proud display, I knew there would be no pretenses with this guy. No confusion. No false promises of a life together. Or even a phone call.

But what makes Ben the most compelling candidate is the fact that he has effectively distracted me from all thoughts

Jared. I mean, he's about as opposite as you can get. Ben is rugged and blond, whereas Jared is "pretty" and dark. Jared's chest and arms are covered in tats, while Ben's body boasts a naked—and appealing—canvas. And where Jared is quiet and introverted, Ben is as outgoing and obnoxious as you can get.

An interesting bonus? He's had me laughing all night long. Granted, I was usually laughing *at* him, but still.

Thanks to Ben, I've had several hours' respite from excruciating thoughts of my ex-husband and his elaborate wedding to *her* in Savannah, Georgia, happening at this very moment. I only know about the wedding because I stalk Jared's Facebook profile daily. While he has never been good at posting status updates, Caroline could join an Olympic Facebook team the way she plasters pictures and wedding plans and "I love you's" on his wall like unsightly graffiti.

Unfortunately, even a guy like Ben couldn't cure me of all thoughts completely and the second they crept out from the dark recesses—the moment I felt the drunk-girl tears about to erupt—I told Ben that he was bringing me to his hotel room.

Wandering farther in, I throw an arm toward the bed not covered in his clothing and suitcase. "You sleep in this one?"

Heavy footsteps approach behind me. "Yep."

"Okay then." I lean forward to shove everything from the unused bed.

"What are you doing?" Ben asks with a chuckle.

"I'm assuming you've had your other *conquests* over there," I mutter, his suitcase making a loud thud as it hits the ground, the contents spilling out. "I want an untainted bed."

"Hey, you're the one who grabbed me by my belt and demanded that I bring you here. I was just as happy hanging out by the bar."

I snort. "Yeah. I don't think I've ever seen as bad a case of eyeball static cling as tonight." If his eyes weren't on my boobs or my legs, they were glued to my face. I'll admit, his undivided attention on me felt damn good. A real ego booster when I needed it most.

Strong hands grasp my hips and pull me back toward him. Even in my drunken state, it's impossible not to notice Ben's prominent erection digging into my ass. "How long have you had that problem?" I joke as heat rushes to my thighs. Am I actually going to go through with this? I've had only one other one-night stand before and I don't even classify that as such because I knew the guy. I just didn't particularly want to date him. He was arrogant. Just like this one.

He chuckles softly. "Since I watched you fall off your chair. And I don't consider it a problem as long as it's dealt with before the morning." A large hand curls around to my abdomen and starts sliding up along my rib cage, guiding my body upright. "I don't fly out until eleven, so we've got lots of time." Spinning me around to face him, he lifts my arms to settle on his shoulders before his hands fall down the length of my arms and farther, his thumbs running over the contour of my breasts on their way to wrap around my waist. His eyes rest on my mouth. "So . . . invertebrate zoology? Biotechnology?"

"Your dirty talk is going to make me lose control." *What the hell is he talking about?*

"Why'd you lie, Miss *Marine Biologist* from Seattle?" I can tell by his smile that he's not angry, or even annoyed. Amused, if anything.

Oh . . . I shrug. So he figured that much out. Doesn't seem like he's picked up on the fact that we've been using cast names from *Charlie's Angels* all night. I'm actually surprised. I could see him being the type of twelve-year-old boy to jerk off to reruns of a young Farrah Fawcett. "I don't know. I like to role-play." Adding coyly, "Sometimes I like to play dress-up, too." I actually fucking hate costumes, but judging by the spark of excitement in Ben's eyes, his imagination is taking that and running to all kinds of filthy places.

He's fun to toy with.

That's exactly how I ended up here.

That and too much tequila.

He leans in. His lips—so contradictorily sweet next to that obnoxious mouth—land on the nape of my neck, eliciting an embarrassing groan out of me as I tip my head back and coil my arms around his head. It's not Jared's mouth, but it will work.

The room is beginning to spin, but this feels so good that I force myself to ignore the revolutions as I lean farther into him. I continue to ignore them as his fingers slip under the hem of my tank top to pull it up and over my head. Tossing it aside, his hands quickly find and unfix the clasp to my bra.

"Damn, I knew it." He shifts back to get a good look at my bare chest as cool fingers graze the silver hoop through my left nipple. He gives it a skilled tug, just enough to elicit a gasp and a burn in my lower belly. With a devious smile, he murmurs, "What else you got?" He has my shorts and panties on the floor before I know what's going on.

"I thought there was no rush?" I mutter, grabbing Ben's arm to stop myself from toppling over as I step out of them, a spike of nervousness jumping in me as I acknowledge that I'm completely naked in front of this fully clothed and fit man who works at a freaking strip club. I have a small waist and decent boobs, but the package comes with a tiny abdominal "bump" and an ass that's a tad fuller than I would like.

I hope he's too drunk to notice.

A frown mars Ben's forehead as he peers down at my face. "You okay?"

"Yeah. Why wouldn't I be okay?"

"Because your eyes just crossed. That's usually not a good sign." The crease deepens. "Are you sure you haven't had too much to drink? Because I don't like to—"

I answer by grabbing the front of that red shirt and yanking him down into my mouth for what I hope is not a sloppy-drunk-girl kiss. But probably is. That seems to be all he needs, because his arms snake around my body to crush me against him. It may just be the alcohol but, damn, does this obnoxious bouncer have some skill. I hadn't expected it. In truth, I thought he'd be the "no kissing on the lips" kind of guy. Now, though, I find myself mesmerized by him, letting my hands crawl all over his chest, ready to find out exactly how skilled he is.

If only this spinning would stop.

And this uncomfortable feeling in the pit of my stomach . . .

Oh . . . no.

Call it gut instinct, an ounce of good luck buried within a pit of bad, I don't know . . . but I intuitively peel myself away from Ben's lips a second before a night's worth of margaritas rushes up my throat and shoots out of my mouth.

All over the front of Ben's red shirt.

Oh my God.

Did that just happen?

I'm temporarily frozen, staring at the streaks of green-tinged sludge all over his body.

"Oh, man . . ." Ben groans, the disgust plain in his tone.

Yes, that just happened.

I don't even have to look at Ben's face to know that all thoughts of getting laid have vanished from his mind. They've certainly abandoned mine, leaving me doused in an icky coat of mortification. That alone has my stomach churning more. I sense an encore performance coming. The hell if I'm puking anywhere in front of or on him again! Clamping two hands over my mouth, I turn and make a run for the bathroom. Unfortunately, something jumps out and trips me and a second later I find myself sprawled across the floor, the cool tile chilling my completely naked body, a dull pain beginning to ache in my toe.

"Shit, are you okay?" I hear from behind me.

I'm going to puke. I'm going to puke doing a facedown starfish if I don't get up *right now.* The bathroom is no more than six feet away and I know I'm not going to make it all the way back to my feet. So I do the next best thing.

Scrambling to my hands and knees, I crawl toward the bathroom.

The bellow of laughter from behind me—oh God, the view he must have of me right now! I didn't think this through!—only makes me pick up speed, until I'm crossing the threshold, slamming the door, and flipping the lock. I lunge for the toilet just as another wave of green shoots out, filling the bowl.

When I've purged my stomach of its toxic contents, all I can do is lean my forehead against the toilet seat and relish the cool porcelain as my rib cage throbs and my body breaks out in a sweat.

A soft knock sounds on the door. "You okay in there?"

I don't answer. I can't answer.

Why! Why did this happen to me? I'm not a puker! Lina is the puker!

"You know, if you hated the shirt that much, you could have just asked me to take it off. I was about to anyway." I don't know how he could possibly be making jokes about this. He's the one covered in vomit. Just the thought has me shuddering. "Look . . . Some chick just puked on me and I really could use a shower. Can I come in?" The door handle jiggles and I thank baby Jesus for having given me the good sense to lock it. The last thing I want is to have him come in here and see my naked body hunched over his toilet. I need to get my clothes and get out of here without facing him. Ever again.

"You're alive, right?" There's finally a hint of worry in his tone. "I don't have to bust down this door?"

That's the last thing you have to do. "I'm good." I pull myself up to the sink to splash my face with some cool, fresh water. Reaching for his mouthwash, I dump a mouthful in and begin gargling.

"Come on, Jill. We've all been there. I'm sorry I laughed."

I've never been so happy that I used a fake name. The story will go down in history as a puking purple-haired girl named

Jill who crawled to his bathroom, her naked fat ass wiggling the entire way. I'm fine with that.

There's a long pause and then I hear his heavy sigh. "I'm leaving some bottled water next to the door for you. Don't drink the tap water or you'll be spending the rest of your vacation in the bathroom." His footsteps move away just as another wave of nausea hits me, courtesy of my minty-fresh breath.

I dive for the toilet again.

Chapter 4

. . .

BEN

Two months later

"Not an ocean view, but it's all yours," Jack Warner offers, leading me into an empty office the size of a closet, with a window overlooking the small parking lot.

"Ocean views are overrated," I throw back with a grin.

That earns a chuckle as my new boss slaps a strong hand over my shoulder. "Glad to have you joining us, Ben. My son credits you as the reason he graduated law school with such high grades."

"Your son's a smart guy, Mr. Warner."

"He says you're smarter. That's why I hired you. And call me Jack."

I'm liking my law school buddy's dad more and more. After a rather intense interview, I was convinced he was an uptight prick and I had no hope in hell of getting hired. I was surprised when he personally called with the job offer a few weeks ago. What a fucking relief that call was! Given that I've been too busy making solid money as a bouncer at a strip club to try for an intern position somewhere, I have zero experience. So many firms won't even look at you without experience, even if you graduated near the top of your class, which I did.

I've obviously pegged Jack all wrong. I mean, here he is on a Monday morning, the sole equity partner of a Miami law firm employing about forty people, taking time out of his jam-packed schedule to show me around.

"Speaking of sons . . ." Jack smiles at someone behind me. I turn to find a tall, lanky guy in nerdy, thick, black-rimmed glasses edge into my office. I offer him a smile of my own as our hands find each other in a strong clasp.

"How was your summer?" Mason asks, adding, "Kent said Mexico was good?" Aside from some texts and emails, Mason and I haven't talked since the day we took the bar exam in July.

"Mexico was great."

By Mason's little smirk, I know Kent gave him some highlights that shouldn't be elaborated on. Especially not right now, in front of my new boss. Mason was supposed to come down with us, but he decided to start at his dad's firm right away. I told him he was a fucking idiot for doing that. I mean, we're not even "associate lawyers" until we get our exam results, which are coming in a few weeks. And then what? A lot of fielding client case update phone calls and proofreading briefs and motions for who knows how long before we're actually trusted to take on our own clients. Why not enjoy the summer?

"Mason, I'll let you help Ben get familiar with the firm. I've got a nine a.m. and court this afternoon. How about the two of you meet me in my office at noon and we'll go out for lunch," Jack says, tapping a thick folder. "Some paperwork for you to fill out and hand in to the HR department today, Ben." With that, the man swiftly exits.

I stroll around my desk and ease myself back into the burgundy leather chair with a big grin. "This place is pretty sweet."

Mason nods slowly, running a hand through his curly dark

hair and then, as if realizing that he's just made it even messier, he quickly tries to smooth it back down. "I've got a call I need to make and then I'll come back, okay?"

"Yup." In the three years that I've known him, the guy still hasn't learned how to carry on a casual conversation.

"You'll be shadowing Natasha in family law for the foreseeable future. I'll introduce you two when I come back."

"Natasha?" I raise a suggestive brow.

"She's engaged," he quickly throws out.

"But the more important question is, is she hot?"

Mason rolls his eyes. "I already told you about the policy against office romances here, Ben."

"Who said anything about a romance?" *What is it about these fucking cock-blocking employers? First Cain, now Jack?* Dropping my hands onto the oversized mahogany desk in front of me, I give it a good pat. "Always wanted to see what a hot lawyer looks like spread out on one of these." I'm not serious, but I like watching Mason go through his various stages of awkwardness, where he gets all agitated and starts fiddling with his glasses.

And . . . man is he ever fiddling with them right now. I smile. The two of us couldn't be more opposite if we tried. Standing there in his plaid short-sleeved shirt and black tie, the guy looks like he's heading for a seventh-grade chess tournament. I didn't wear a tie today. Dress code states business casual is fine unless you're going to court or meeting a client and I'm doing neither, so why would I dress like an office monkey?

I let him twitch for another few seconds before relenting. "I'm kidding, Mace! I promise. I'm turning over a new leaf."

"As of when?" His tone screams doubt. He's known me for long enough and has seen me in action with our friends more than once, so his skepticism is fair.

"As of my going-away party at Penny's this past weekend. Nothing's going to top that. I think my dick could use a break anyway." I shake my head as I laugh to myself. Mercy and Hannah sure know how to send a guy off.

"Oh." A small, knowing smile curves his lips, but it vanishes just as quickly. "Well, good. Just don't forget that. Especially around my stepsister."

Whoa. "Hold up. You have a stepsister? Working here?" This is new information. He's never mentioned her before. Then again, he's a private guy. "Is she a super geek like you?"

"She's *nothing* like me. There's probably a pot of fresh coffee in the break room down the hall and to your left." He starts shifting on his feet. The guy can't handle being late for anything.

"Go on, Mason. And thanks for the hookup."

"Sure, Ben. I'll be back in"—he checks his phone—"eighteen minutes." And he will. On the nose. I watch him take off at a brisk walk and I shake my head. The guy still lives with his father. Most days he's wearing mismatched socks on account of being completely color-blind. If I hadn't sicced Kyla from our first-year contracts class on him and witnessed her drag him into a bedroom at a frat party, I'd bet money that no woman besides his mama has ever seen his dick. Knowing Kyla as I do, though, she not only saw it, she made good use of it.

A yawn escapes me and I taper it off with a loud groan and a mutter of, "Yes to coffee." It's going to take time to adjust to early morning starts. After years of crashing with the sunrise and taking only afternoon classes, my body is suffering right now. First things first, though . . . I pick up the phone and punch the keys without thought. I memorized this number when I was four years old and I've been dialing it every day for years. Normally around dinnertime, though.

I'm hoping she's on the back porch, drinking her cup of Earl Grey tea and checking her email on her iPad. I smile at the memory of teaching my fifty-one-year-old mama how to use that thing.

Unfortunately, it's not she who answers.

Knots instantly spring into my neck. "Hey."

A grunt responds.

"Is Mama around?"

"Out in the grove."

She should be back by now. She's always up at the ass-crack of dawn to do her rounds, checking the trees. "Have you gone out to make sure she's okay?" Ever since that mild heart attack seven months ago, I've been worried about her being alone out there for too long.

"She's fine."

"All right. Let her know I called." He won't. I guess I'll have to call back later anyway.

"Where are you calling from?"

I wonder what the caller display says. Hell, that's probably why he answered in the first place. Because he didn't know he'd be talking to his son. "Warner—the law firm I'm working at now." Mama probably didn't bother to tell him that I finished law school.

"Never heard of it."

I bite back a sigh of exasperation. Despite its small size, Warner is one of the most reputable law firms in the state. Five generations of Warners have owned it, holding some prime real estate in the downtown Miami core. According to my research, Jack brought in a partner—his best friend—and for ten years, they worked together as Warner & Steele, exploding the client list by more than double. They parted ways some years back when he bought the other partner out.

In any case, I wouldn't expect my dad to know a law firm from a donut shop. He's just trying to needle me. "Later." I hang up and head out in search of that cup of coffee before he has a chance to put me in a bad mood. He's the only person capable of doing that.

The Warner office itself is a mix of new and old—modern light gray walls, mahogany wall-to-wall bookshelves and desks, open-concept desks in the center of the room, fishbowl offices lining the outskirts. It's as if someone decided to redecorate but ran out of either money or creativity. Jack did mention something about renovating in the winter. The place seems fine to me, but I'm a twenty-five-year-old who lives with five other guys and would come to work in board shorts if he could.

The office isn't huge or complicated and it takes no time to find the break room, though I play the "first day" card and let an adorable law clerk lead me there, smiling and blushing at me the entire way as I watch her curvy ass sway. I have an appreciation for the many shapes and sizes of the female form. The old me—as in two days ago—would probably have her number by now. The new me is trying something different. Specifically, he's trying *not* to hit on every female he finds attractive.

Heading back to my office—a coffee mug in one hand and someone's homemade muffin in the other—I survey the desks out in the open where the administrative staff sits. From the looks of the pictures and knickknacks, it's mostly women. Mostly married with kids. Many in their forties or beyond. Man, what a different world this is from Penny's, where I was taunted by bare tits and ass from every angle! At least that makes it easier to keep my pants on around here and try to act like a responsible adult.

Because that's what I am. Ben Morris, Esquire. Well, almost. Either way, I like the sound of that.

Passing by a small office almost directly across from mine, a picture on the wall catches my attention. My feet falter as I smile fondly at the framed Pearl Jam album cover, thinking back to that crazy purple-haired fake marine biologist, Jill.

Damn, that girl was something else.

After stripping off my puke-covered clothes and tossing them over the balcony, I stretched out on the bed and waited for her to emerge from the bathroom, dying for a shower. I even considered going over to Kent's room, but I didn't want to leave her alone in there. I guess I passed out because the next thing I knew, the sun was beating down on my face through the window and Jill was gone.

Not even a note.

At least she didn't rob me. Or kill me.

I tried finding her, but after charming one of the front desk girls into searching the hotel guest list, no one by the name of Jill came up. It was obviously registered to one of her friends and I didn't remember their names. The resort was too damn big to go searching, especially when I had to rush to repack everything she had scattered before catching my plane home.

I'm not gonna lie—for a couple of weeks after, I searched for a purple-haired girl named Jill on Facebook. Partly because I wanted to say sorry for laughing. Mostly because she was a lot of fun and I wouldn't have minded hooking up with her again. Minus the puke. I didn't tell the guys what really happened. As far as they know, it was balls-deep as usual for me that night.

The cotton-candy-pink sweater hanging over the back of the chair makes me think this is a female's office, but everything else disputes that. Folders sit in piles on the desk, on the floor, on boxes, on the spare chair. Where there aren't folders, there's scattered mail and junk. Multiple Starbucks paper cups sit by the desk phone, next to an open box of Oreo cookies and a bag of beef jerky. A crumpled bag of chips and crushed cans of Red Bull surround the trash bin.

A computer monitor—decorated in no less than a hundred multicolored Post-it notes—is on and displaying a screensaver of a rusty old blue truck in a field.

I'm intrigued, to say the least. I can't imagine what kind of female this sty could possibly belong to, and part of me is afraid to find out. It's not dirty, per se. It's just messy beyond anything I've ever seen. I step forward and begin scanning her desk, looking for a nameplate or something to identify her.

And that's exactly what I'm doing when she walks in.

"Is there a reason that you're snooping through my things?" a crisp voice calls out.

Pulling on a smile that usually takes the edge off even the

moodiest of women, I turn around. A blond in a short green dress and cowboy boots stands in the doorway, a tall coffee cup in her hand and a deep scowl furrowing her forehead.

I open my mouth to introduce myself but falter as panic flashes in those eyes.

Those caramel-colored eyes.

"Holy shit!" *I don't believe it.* There's really nothing I can think of to say except, "You owe me a new shirt!"

Chapter 5

...

REESE

I've been eviscerated on a Monday morning. My guts are splayed all over the dark gray office carpet for all to see.

And I can't breathe.

What the hell is *this guy* doing in my office?

He's as shocked as I am, obviously. That loud boom of "holy shit!" that probably carried through half the floor and has all the little old hens peering over their bifocals at us can attest to that.

And now he's staring at me with wide, disbelieving eyes. "Jill? Is that you?"

"You don't recognize your one true love?" That might have sounded witty had my voice not been shaky and my cheeks not been burning hot. For a pro player like this guy, the fact that he remembers my fake name says something. I was *definitely* memorable.

"You look so . . ." His voice drifts off as those baby-blue eyes roll over my all-blond hair and land on my face. "No more piercings?"

Not trusting myself to speak again, I tap the pinhead-sized diamond stud in my nostril. I've taken the septum ring and the majority of my ear piercings out, though. Part of this whole "new me" thing I'm trying.

Ben's head bobs up and down slowly as if still trying to process this. Then his focus drifts down to my chest and his eyes narrow. I swear he's trying to make out the outline of the metal ring that's hidden there.

And I'm trying to control the hyperbolic flashback that took weeks to suppress—there's just no way vomit shoots out of a person like a fire hose!—as the walking, breathing proof of one of my most mortifying nights stands in my office.

I waited a good two hours to creep out from the bathroom that night, to find Ben stripped down to his boxer briefs and snoring in bed. Quickly pulling my clothes on, I hightailed it out of there.

And now my botched exorcism is leaning against my desk, his muscular arms folded over his chest. The playful smile that stretches across his face tells me he's found his bearings and is back to the cocky guy I was one vomit away from sleeping with two months ago. "What are you doing here?"

"Working," I manage to get out without sounding weak. Easing farther into my office, I replace one of the many empty cups littering my desk with my new one, trying to act nonchalant when, really, I'm fighting the urge to turn and run somewhere where I can regroup. "I think the bigger question is, what are *you* doing here?" How did I *not* know he was from Miami? Oh yeah . . . I didn't bother asking. I was too busy deciding whether I should have sex with him. And now, as I steal a glance at how well that black button-down and those dark gray dress pants look on his strong frame, I remember what swayed me. Well, the tequila certainly didn't help.

Heat engulfs my cheeks.

I *puked all over* this guy.

And then he watched my bare ass crawl across the floor to his bathroom.

Mr. Cuervo and I—and all of his Mexican cousins—are no longer on speaking terms.

"Mr. Warner offered me an attorney position."

"I . . ." *What?* Ben's going to be *working* here?

"I finished law school in the spring."

Gritting my teeth against the pain as I suck back a mouthful of burning-hot coffee—I'm going to regret that later—I mutter, "You failed to mention that."

He twists his mouth in thought. "I was too busy trying to figure out what kind of marine biologist you are."

"Recent career change."

"Right." His eyes are twinkling as he watches me, amused. *Jerk.* "Is this going to be awkward?"

"No . . ." I say, tossing my purse on the ground, "because you're going to resign immediately."

He heaves a sigh. "It's not a big deal. So you—"

"Shh!" My hand flies up to stop him as heat flares into my cheeks again. That's the last thing I need floating around work. "Don't!"

We lock gazes for a long moment and I can't read what his says. Is he regretting that night as much as I am? Because, for all the stupid things I've regretted doing—and that's a long list— that night is sitting on top of the mountain waving an "idiot" flag.

A sudden voice behind me interrupts us. "There you are, Ben. Natasha's waiting."

My eyes do an involuntary roll, both in response to the sound of my stepbrother's mind-numbing tone and to the mention of Natasha, the thirty-year-old type-A law bot who's trying to kill me with divorce depositions. Ben catches my reaction and doesn't even try to hide his grin as he offers, "Hey, Mason. I was just on my way back to my office."

"There's no cleaning staff here on weekends. You're inviting infestation with this mess," Mason mutters, and I know that's directed at me. Mason couldn't sound more apathetic with me if he tried. We may live and work under the same roof, but we're no more friends now than we were before I moved in eight months ago. I actually wish I had caught his reaction on video when he came home from class and found me in the kitchen, drinking straight from the chocolate milk jug. Jack hadn't given him any warning that I was back in their lives. I thought his head was going to explode.

"But I have pets to feed," I retort. Everything about Mason—except the unruly mop on his head—is pristinely neat: his pressed shirts and pencil-leg pants, his Subaru hatchback, the office next to Jack's that I've seen him disinfect with Lysol wipes every single day. The only time he has anything to say to me is when he's pointing out how pristinely neat I am *not*. Needless to say, we don't cohabitate well.

"You don't want to talk to her this early in the morning. She hasn't had her first feeding yet and she's more abrasive than usual," Mason warns Ben.

"Listen to Jiminy Cricket. He knows things." It has taken almost two months of snarls and glares, but I have everyone trained. Even Jack knows not to attempt conversation with me until this giant cup of coffee is empty and I've opened my office door, after spending an hour cursing the sender of every new email that has filled my in-box. I'm relatively pleasant after that. Of course the lawyers tolerate it because I run circles around all the other paralegals here, even the ones who've been here for years. Clients agree to flat rates for paralegal work and then I deliver on it in record time, freeing me up to work on more cases and generate more profit. They leave the heavy clerical shit to the others and give me work that requires research and analysis and critical thinking, stuff that has always come naturally to me because I'm inquisitive and willing to test boundaries. I guess it helped that, while I was sailing through the paralegal program, Jack was passing on all kinds of books on statutory and case law, stuff they teach you in law school. Looking for ways to drown my spare time, I devoured them. No one would believe that I've been here for only two months. It feels good. For the first time in years, I feel smart.

With a chuckle, Ben begins making his way out, stepping around me extra slowly. "Maybe abrasive is what won me over before."

"Wait a minute . . . You two *know* each other?" There's definite wariness in Mason's voice now.

Ben's wide grin doesn't fill me with ease. "Yeah. We met in Cancún."

Mason pushes his big, geeky glasses up with an index finger as he looks at me. "When were you in Cancún?"

I shake my head at him. Of course he wouldn't remember. As tidy and regimented as Mason is at work, he can be scatterbrained when it comes to regular life. He kind of reminds me of a mad scientist, without the lab coat and test tubes. "July. My birthday. Remember? You gave me tickets to see U2?"

Mason's eyes ignite with a spark of anger. "I didn't *give* you those tickets. You stole my credit card number and ordered them!"

I make a point of holding my hands up to my chest in mock insult. "I was merely ensuring you got me a memorable gift for my twenty-first birthday."

"I thought you were twenty-nine," Ben pipes in with a wry smirk.

"And I thought I'd never see you again," I snap.

Understanding seems to hit Mason then and, when he shifts his focus to Ben, I see something that looks an awful lot like revulsion pass over his face. "Please tell me Reese isn't the purple-haired girl Kent was talking about?"

"Reese?" I hear Ben's voice somewhere in the background, but my brain is too busy processing key words.

Purple-haired girl. Kent. Talking about. Mexico.

For the second time in under five minutes, I feel the blood drain from my face as I'm hit with my own level of understanding. And horror. Ben isn't just a new employee. "Oh my God. You're *friends* with my *stepbrother*?"

Ben's eyes cut to me, his brows shooting high up his forehead. "Your *stepbrother*?"

"Oh, fuck!" Mason starts shaking his head. "Seriously, Ben?"

I steal a glance at Mason, who *never* swears, before settling daggers on Ben's face. "Yeah, Ben. *Seriously?*" I hiss through gritted teeth. "What would Kent have said about the purple-haired girl, *Ben*?" I haven't admitted to that night to anyone except Nicki and Lina, and that's only because I came back to the hotel limping. If Ben told his friends . . . and Mason knows . . . I'm going to die. Mason will totally use that against me one day. He'll tell everyone at the firm and they'll talk about it behind my back. I'll walk into meetings to the abrupt end of giggles. And then I'll be forced to kill everyone.

With wide eyes panning back and forth between Mason and me, Ben looks torn between exploding with laughter and bolting out of my office.

And that's the perfect time for Natasha to poke her head in. "This must be Ben," she chirps in that high-pitched voice that has grated on my nerves since day one, offering him a bright smile and a hand. "I'm Natasha. You and I will be working closely together."

"Looking forward to it, Natasha," Ben offers casually, scanning the female attorney's body in front of everyone and grinning while doing it. He's not doing it in a leery pervert way, but *I* still find it exceptionally annoying. If there's an ounce of luck left for me in this world, Ben will get himself fired for sexual harassment.

Unfortunately, it doesn't look like Natasha will be sounding any alarms. Flipping her long apricot-colored hair over her shoulder, she giggles like a complete airhead—which she's not; she's actually quite sharp, though I'd never boost her ego by telling her that—and says, "Great. Well, we should get started. I'm buried with cases right now. Fortunately I've had Reese here to help me with a lot of the legwork." She flashes her brilliant white teeth my way. "Speaking of which, did you have a chance to get through that file?"

I knew I'd be supporting the lawyers in this job. What I didn't know is that I'd basically be doing all the work so they could sign off and collect their hundred thousand–plus a year. I swear, I wouldn't be surprised if one of them asks me to wipe their ass soon.

"You mean the forty-two-page contract I was working on until two a.m. last night? Or the sixty-page deposition I just found sitting on my desk?" I match her giant smile, only mine is so fake and rabid that a blind dog would know to shy away. Her olive-green eyes flicker to my full cup of coffee. "Ben, how about we go to my office and let Reese get settled?"

Brilliant idea.

She and Mason waste no time exiting my personal space.

"Extra-large for that shirt . . . *Reese*," Ben whispers as he passes by.

I hold my breath as I watch him exit and then I rush to throw my door shut. I hide behind it, the only place that isn't visible to the outside world, thanks to the wall of windows. But I'm sure everyone hears the thump as my head connects with the hollow wood.

This has to be karma, coming to take a giant bite out of my ass.

Chapter 6

...

BEN

"Nothing happened."

"That's not what Kent said."

"Well, Kent wasn't there, so how the hell would he know?" I sigh. "She was loaded."

"Since when is a girl too drunk for Ben Morris?"

"Dude." I shoot a glare at Mason as we find a park bench in the shade to help ward off the September midday heat, drinks and lunch in hand. Jack had to cancel plans due to a client emergency. Apparently that happens a lot.

He holds his hands up. "Sorry. I know you wouldn't do that."

I watch him as he carefully unfolds and smooths three napkins over his lap and then surgically unravels some weird veggie-tofu-wrap shit, careful not to let so much as a shred of lettuce fall out. We've all teased Mason about his chick diet for years, but the guy's so particular about things, he can't even be shamed into a greasy burger. I kind of like that about him. "Are you going to eat that or marry it?"

"You saw her office, right?" he asks, ignoring me. "She's a slob. Living with her is a fucking nightmare." That's two f-bombs dropped by Mason today. Swearing is another thing he doesn't do, which tells me that either the idea of me screwing around with his stepsister or his stepsister in general really gets under his skin.

A flash of my trashed hotel room in the morning hits me and I smile to myself. "And yet she sure cleans up nice." I get an eye roll in response. "Look, I know she's your stepsister, but she's fucking hot." As much as I liked the "I don't give a shit" wild-girl look she had going on in Cancún, this new look—with her pretty blond hair and her little dress and her boots—is a huge turn-on.

"And certifiable." He fixes me with a look. "Seriously. Her nickname around the office is Rancor."

Coke shoots out my mouth as I stifle a laugh. "Does she know?"

"I guess you missed the life-sized cardboard standee in her office? The day she heard Nelson from contracts slip and call her that within earshot, she rush-ordered it from some *Star Wars* website. She sets it up beside her door on the mornings when she's *extra* annoyed." He shakes his head at me as I explode in laughter.

For everything else about her that was a lie, I'm glad to see that biting sense of humor is genuine. I like a woman who can make me laugh. "If she's so difficult, why would your father keep her there? I mean, don't get me wrong, I'm glad he has. I'm looking forward to working with her."

"You won't be for long," he mutters. And then sighs heavily. "Even though she's highly unprofessional and will likely get the firm sued on employee relations issues at some point, I'll admit that she's *really* good at what she does. All she has is a high school diploma and a paralegal certificate and yet she's telling half the associates how to do their jobs, quoting laws and statutes. And she's usually right. It's disturbing, how fast she picks up on things."

"So you're saying she's a genius," I say around a mouthful of food.

"Yeah, maybe," he says with a hint of resentment in his voice. "She's also selfish, reckless, unreliable, and impulsive." He downs his Perrier and mutters dryly, "All signs of a sociopath."

"Oh, hell." I roll my eyes. I forgot that Mason did his under-grad in psychology. "Give me a break. Your sister's not a sociopath, Mace! You just really don't like her, do you?"

"Stepsister," he corrects, his tone sharpening a little. "It's not that I don't like her. Well . . ." He half-shrugs. "I'll admit, I'm not overly fond of her. But really, I just don't trust her. My dad didn't hear from her for nine years, and then out of the blue she calls him to bail her out from a Jacksonville police station back in January?" Shaking his head, he adds, "He dropped everything and drove up there. He almost lost the firm's biggest client that day because of it."

Hmm . . . What was she doing in a police station? "Does she have a record?" Not that I really care. Unless it had anything to do with performing exorcisms on guys who are trying to get laid.

"Juvenile. It was sealed when she turned eighteen. Mostly stupid stuff, from what my dad told me. Fights . . . pot . . . drag racing."

My eyes shoot up at that last one.

"This last time was pretty serious, though. She vandalized her ex-husband's apartment."

My sub freezes midair to my mouth with this new informa-tion. "*Ex-husband?* Didn't she say she just turned twenty-one?"

Mason's head bobs. "Married at nineteen. She knew the guy for all of six weeks before they eloped in Vegas. Tell me you're surprised that their marriage didn't last."

"Shit . . . That tattoo on her arm. Was that him?" It has to be. And I made that boneheaded comment about it.

"Yeah, I think so. Apparently when she went back to move her things out, she splattered red paint all over the apartment." His eyes widen knowingly. "Do you get the symbolism there? *Red* paint . . . ?"

"She's feisty." Again, something I knew. Again, something I like. I can't help but note her choice in color and start to laugh. That shirt never stood a chance.

"Sounds like the divorce was ugly."

"The guy cheated on her."

"Shmuck." If you can't be monogamous, don't get into a committed relationship, let alone a marriage. That's my philosophy. Which is exactly why I don't commit to anyone. "So Jack decided to bring her to Miami with him?"

Nodding slowly, Mason admits, "My dad always really liked Reese." He snorts. "More than he liked me. But how do I know she's not out to con him? Her mother already bled him dry once."

I chew my sandwich silently, waiting for Mason to elaborate, surprised that he's telling me this much to begin with. "He and Reese's mom were married for five years before he found out she was having an affair with Barry Steele."

Pieces start clicking together. "Warner and Steele . . . Old partner?"

Mason nods.

"That's cold."

"Yeah, well, Annabelle is an opportunistic, self-centered whore. She nearly destroyed my family's legacy. It cost my dad a fortune to buy Barry out and then she tried to swoop in to pick at his bones like a vulture, but Barry wouldn't let her. Dad's still recovering financially. That's why he hasn't been able to finish the office renos." Mason pauses for a drink. "Apparently she left Barry about three years ago and moved on to a U.S. senator."

"Is she hot?"

"Yeah, I guess. But so was Grendel's mother," he mutters, making me shake my head. Leave it to Mason to reference *Beowulf*. Folding up the wrappers from his sandwich, careful not to spill crumbs on his pants, he goes on to say, "My dad's not stupid, Ben." Mason's eyes look that much bigger behind those big glasses as he peers at me.

"What's that supposed to mean? Hell, he can't possibly blame me for that night! I wasn't even hired here yet."

"He knows your type and he knows where you've been working the last four years. He almost didn't hire you because of it. He made me promise him that you'd be able to keep your pants on before he made you an offer."

I chuckle. "Well, you may have your work cut out for you, Mace."

"I'm not kidding. Look, he just finished dealing with a lawsuit against Warner from three years ago. A guy from litigation was dating a paralegal. When they broke up, it turned sour. Apparently she got pretty hostile and brought it into the office. Jack eventually had to let her go and she sued for wrongful dismissal. He doesn't want to deal with that again. That's why he has these rules. Rules that are meant to be followed."

Mason is a rule follower, through and through. Black-and-white. That's what will probably make him a very good lawyer. I'm a big "gray area" kind of guy, always looking for ways to bend and reinterpret the rules. That's what will probably make me a damn fantastic lawyer.

"If it means anything to you at all . . . he thinks you've got a lot of promise, Ben, but he won't think twice about firing you if he catches you screwing around with anyone," Mason says.

Getting fired right out of law school would look terrible. Good luck finding another job in Miami after something like that, and I'm stuck here for the foreseeable future. My mama needs at least one of her children to stay close.

"And if he caught you with Reese . . ." Mason goes on, shaking his head.

Slapping my buddy on his shoulder, I promise, "Point made, and don't worry. I told you, those days are over. Plus, something tells me that girl's pride won't let her give me the time of day." Getting puked on isn't something I strive for when I bring a girl back to my hotel room, but shit happens when you're pounding booze. Hell, two days ago I was on a stage with Mercy's thong on, my nut sac hanging out for all to see. Not one of my finer moments, but I'll survive. Something tells me stuff doesn't slide off Reese's shoulders as fast, though. And maybe it's not even the puking. I did watch her crawl naked across the floor, too. And I laughed at her while she was doing it. I don't think most women would appreciate being laughed at in that situation. Even Kacey would probably beat me senseless, and she takes it like the best of them.

Mason's mouth opens but he hesitates, a sour expression twisting his face. "What'd you do to her?"

I lift my hands in surrender. "It's not about what *I* did to *her*."

He's on his feet and marching forward, shaking his head. "Just don't tease her, Ben. You'll regret it."

Shit. Not teasing her about this is going to be really hard for me, seeing as that's what I do best. Besides, I owe her for not letting me shower in my own damn bathroom. "Hey," I call out and ask on a hunch, "what'd *you* do to piss her off so bad?"

His feet slow and I hear his heavy sigh as he turns, a guilty look plastered across his face. "I said some stupid stuff about her father."

Chapter 7

•••

REESE

"You really should try the key lime. We're famous for it," the waitress suggests with a smile as she places my order for a slice of chocolate pecan pie in front of me.

"I'll keep that in mind," I answer, just like I've answered a dozen times before, eyeing the perfectly intact pecan halves that decorate the top of my sliver. It isn't easy, finding a chocolate pecan pie. Sure, everyone's got a pecan pie on the menu. It's the chocolate that makes it unique. The pie is the reason I started coming to the Bayside Café six months ago. Remembering my borderline obsession for this particular flavor, Jack introduced me to it. The place has quickly become my safe haven.

And since starting at Warner—only a few blocks away—I'm here several times a week. It has a beautiful waterfront patio with teakwood tables and royal-blue umbrellas, crammed with palm trees and plants of all sizes, enough to make it feel like a jungle that you can hide in. Which is exactly what I'm doing tonight, with my newspaper crossword puzzle and a law textbook.

I couldn't bear being in the office anymore. Natasha kept poking her head around my door, Ben in tow, asking for this deposition or that contract. And as much as I kept my eyes averted, I still managed to see him at least a dozen times today.

I'd be lying if I said that Ben's not an *extremely* attractive guy. Now that I'm sober, I can attest to that wholeheartedly. My only saving grace is that I'm too busy trying to block out my embarrassing memories to be in any danger of tripping over myself like half the women seemed to be doing today. It was pathetic. Even Natasha seemed more bubbly than normal. And the dimpled smiles he flashed each one of them tells me he loved every second of the fawning.

The first forkful of pie is sliding into my mouth when my phone comes alive with the sound of minions singing the banana song.

"Happy Monday," I mutter into the phone.

"I hate numbers."

"It's a good thing you won't be dealing with them on a daily basis for the next forty years, then." Lina finished her undergrad degree last spring and passed her CPA exam with flying colors. Now she's working at a small accounting firm down the street to collect a year of experience before she can apply for her license.

"What are you doing?" she asks.

"Hiding from karma at Bayside."

"Don't drink the coffee," she warns.

"Too late," I mutter, swirling the last bit of the toxic substance in my mug. Every time I come here, I order a cup to go with my chocolate pecan pie. It's habit, I guess. There's no other explanation. The coffee is weak, it has a salty aftertaste, and there's always a weird film at the bottom of the cup. No one with taste buds would like this crap.

With a heavy sigh, I divulge the horror of my day.

"So Mason is friends with your botched exorcism," she states flatly. I can always count on Lina to lay it out like it is. No beating around the bush. No softening the blow. "What did the guy say to you?"

"That I owe him a new shirt."

She snorts. "Well, he's got you there."

"Thanks."

"Maybe I'll take a break and swing by. We can mock people together," Lina offers. Another plus to this job: having my best friend only four blocks away from me.

"Don't bother. I've been here for two hours. I actually have to go back to the office. The law bot dumped three new cases on my desk today."

"Fine. Do you want to come over for dinner sometime this week? Nicki's cooking."

"Does it involve turkey bacon?"

"All unconventional meats have been banned." Since Lina owns the small two-bedroom-plus-den condo that they moved into, she is well within her power to stop Nicki from inflicting others with her strange dietary preferences.

"Then I'm in."

"Okay, good." There's a pause, and then Lina sighs. "Look, there's something I need to tell you."

"Well, this doesn't sound promising." I shove a large piece of pie in my mouth.

"It all depends on whether you want your best friend, the one who sticks up for you, has lied to the police for you, has gone along with all of your harebrained ideas, to be happy."

"You've never lied to the police for me."

"Senior year. The bottle of vodka in the trunk when we got pulled over."

"Fine. One time," I heave with exasperation. "What has that earned you today?"

"Well, I've started seeing someone that you may not . . ."

Lina's voice blurs as I watch a ginger-haired woman flounce through the patio, her purse swinging on her arm, as happy as any home-wrecking husband thief could possibly be.

"Oh my God!" Chunks of piecrust get sucked down my

throat with my gasp, stirring up a cough that I struggle to suppress. "It's her!" I hiss.

"Her who?"

I watch my ex-husband's new wife sit three tables over with what I assume is a friend.

"Her!" I hiss even more sharply, dipping my head so I'm not so obviously staring at her.

There's only one "her" that I could be talking about with such venom in my voice, and Lina catches on quickly. "What? Here in Miami?"

"No. In *hell*! Because that's where *I* obviously am today!" First Ben, now Caroline?

"Has she recognized you yet?"

"No, but she hasn't looked this way." Without my purple hair and piercings and in professional clothes—minus the cute and trendy cowboy boots that I'd normally never wear but Nicki insisted must be worn with this dress—Caroline *may* not recognize me. I hope not. Just in case, though, I open the menu and prop it up, ready to duck behind it if necessary.

"I'm coming down."

"No, you're not, because she *will* recognize you." With Lina living next door to them for months, it was impossible to avoid her in the hall completely. Knowing Lina, she would have been skewering Caroline with her eyes at every single chance. "Why is she here?" A second, smaller gasp. "Did they *move* to Miami?" Jared always wanted to get a ship-welding job down here.

"I dunno. What does his Facebook profile say?"

"I haven't been on it since Cancún." As hard as it was to wean myself off that addiction—my only connection to Jared—I couldn't bear seeing the proof of them married. Just the idea still feels like a knife plunging into my stomach.

"Okay, just a sec. Let me see if we're still friends on . . ." I hear the clatter of a keyboard on the other end. "Yup. They just moved to Miami. Two weeks ago."

"Shit," I mutter more to myself, a strange, unpleasant feeling stirring in my chest, adding softly, "I guess he got the ship-welding job." We used to lie in bed at night with the lights dimmed and Muse—his favorite band—playing softly while he doodled ships all over my body, explaining the different parts and what his work would entail. I couldn't care less about ships, but I'd lie still and let him get it out of his system. I knew it was only a matter of time before he'd get distracted by the naked canvas.

"What does she do again?"

"Besides destroying marriages and tearing out people's hearts?" I've found it helps to paint her as the villain here, though I know I should be directing at least some of that hatred at Jared.

Ignoring my acidity, Lina offers, "Well, at least Miami's a big city."

"And yet it's a fucking small world, obviously."

"Deep breaths, Reese," she coaches calmly. As though she's afraid of what I may do. I can't blame her. I've never been above punching a girl when she deserves it.

"I'm fine," I snap, watching the key factor in my heartbreak a fork's launch away, in her gingham dress—really? Outside of Disney World and *I Love Lucy*, who the hell wears gingham anyway?—and her straight hair stretching down her back. A strange, perverse pleasure blossoms inside of me as I watch the woman who had no issues stepping in to rip my life right out from under me giggle away with a friend, unaware of my presence.

I've never actually spoken to her. Aside from a few details Jared provided me in the beginning of our relationship—they were childhood family friends who turned into high school sweethearts, though she lived in Savannah—he never talked about her. I thought she was long gone from his life. Clearly not.

What made him want to marry her? Sure, I guess she's pretty, in that average, boring way. She appears to be bubbly and sweet and probably never curses. I'm guessing she knows how to wave a pom-pom and I'd bet money she was part of some Delta Fuck You sorority. But what does he see in her? What about her makes sense to him?

Jared always said he couldn't stand those kinds of girls; that I was fresh air to him, after years of being suffocated by what his wealthy parents wanted of him, of his life.

That he and I made sense.

That he couldn't breathe without me.

I watch her run a hand through her hair, the sparkle from that diamond I know Jared can't afford on his salary catching my eye, reminding me that it doesn't matter what I *don't* see. All that matters is what Jared *does* see.

I guess he found a way to breathe without me after all.

I unconsciously find myself twirling the simple yet beautiful vintage sterling silver and pearl ring on my finger that Jared surprised me with the morning of our spur-of-the-moment trip to Vegas five days shy of my twentieth birthday.

That turned into the best day of my life.

And clearly the worst mistake of my life.

I've switched the ring to my right hand, but haven't had the courage to stuff it into the wooden box of the past under my bed just yet.

"Reese?" Lina's voice interrupts my thoughts.

"Seriously, I'm over it. I've gotta go or I'll be stuck in the office all night. See you tomorrow." I hang up the phone and hunch down slightly, eyeing my half-eaten pie—there's no way it's going to be finished.

I think about leaving as I continue watching her. The patio is unusually quiet, enough so that that annoying southern twang of hers carries over to me. I listen to her chatter on about how she and her *husband* just moved into a condo down the street and she'll be coming here a lot because they have the *best* coffee.

I sit at the café for another hour, breaking off squirrel-sized bites of my pie though I can't taste any of it. When she gets up to leave, I quietly pack my things, wait for her to exit, and then duck out of the café. To do what any sane ex-wife would do.

I tail her for five blocks, to a condo building.

And now I know where my ex-husband lives.

■ ■ ■

Great. Because today isn't bad enough.

My humiliating one-night stand—a six-foot-three-ish smirking blond—is sitting in my chair, his feet propped up onto my desk, when I return from the bathroom.

Reese, zero. Universe . . . *I hate you.*

"Why are you still here?" It's almost ten at night and, aside from Jack and Mason, everyone has gone home.

Making a point of opening and closing the two side drawers of my desk, he says, "I was looking for that beef jerky."

"I ate it." I push my door shut with my foot and toss my purse onto my desk.

His eyes roll lazily over me from head to toe, not even bothering to hide it. "I thought we should talk." And then he abruptly slides his legs off and stands, giving me a full view of his solid frame, which I try not to get caught noticing. Ben doesn't over-dress—not like Mason, who would wear a three-piece suit to bed if it was considered appropriate—but he's got one of those bodies that everything hangs from well.

We trade places, Ben wandering around to the front of my desk, while I keep my distance by circling around the other side to take a seat in my now vacant chair.

"I never told Kent about what happened in my hotel room. I let them think I scored."

An odd sense of relief swarms me. And surprise. I figured Ben was the type to tell a good story at others' expense. But . . ."Mason?" I'd imagine that the disgust I feel with the idea of my stepbrother having sex goes both ways. Fortunately, I've never seen him so much as second-glance a female.

Ben dismisses that with a slight wave. "Oh, *he* knows what really happened, but he won't say a thing."

"Oh my God!" I cry out, my previous relief burning up with the sudden fire in my cheeks. I lay my forehead down on the cool desk. *Mason won't say anything, my ass!*

"Relax." I hear footsteps approach and then a hand settles on the back of my neck. It has the opposite effect on me, my body going completely rigid. "I left out the part about the puking. And the crawling. I'm guessing you're still a little sensitive about that." I hear the humor in his voice. "How were you feeling the next day, anyway? You hit the ground pretty hard."

"*Now* you're concerned?" I spent the rest of my Cancún vacation with bruised knees and a cracked nail from where my toe must have caught the bed frame.

"I didn't mean to laugh." I look up in time to see a giant grin stretch out across his face, making his words hard to believe. "And if it's any consolation, you have a phenomenal ass. I should know. I got a *really* good look at it."

I groan inwardly. "Today's not a good day for me, Ben."

His hands lift in surrender. "Fair enough. I wanted to say that I'm sorry." He rounds my desk again—it's as if he's circling his prey, but in a very casual, nonthreatening way—and stops in front of the personal pictures I've hung on the wall.

His finger swings to the picture of the rusted old blue Chevy. "What's with you and vintage trucks?"

"I like them," I say simply, not willing to elaborate further.

I quietly watch him evaluate things for another few minutes, until he suddenly asks, "Hey, do you want to go for lunch tomorrow? Seeing as you do a lot for Natasha and I'll be working with her over the next few months, maybe we should start over." He turns to peer at me with earnest blue eyes, his voice cracking under its sudden softness. "What do you say? Truce?"

Jack is always telling me that I need to make decisions based on common sense and not emotions. After spending a few weeks with Ben, my mortification will disappear.

Right?

So making peace with Ben now would be win-win.

Right?

I open my mouth.

And then I see that devilish twinkle and the corners of his mouth twitch. "They make extra-strong margaritas at Amigos, down the street. Just like you like them. I'll bring a change of clothes, for after, of course."

"Get out." This is going to be hell.

"We could take a nice long *crawl* down the boardwalk, and then—"

"Fuck. Right. Off." I hate him.

He grins, completely at ease, his attention grazing over my life-sized cardboard cutout of that stupid alien thing I ordered online a few weeks ago as a "fuck you" to Nelson, the annoying contracts lawyer down the hall. "Oh, come on, Reese. It's not that big a deal. You need to learn how to laugh at yourself."

Maybe if reality—in the form of a troll in a gingham dress—hadn't just stuck its spike heel into my heart again, this wouldn't bother me so much. But I walked in here already feeling pathetic. Now I'm beyond livid.

I feel the wicked smile stretch across my lips as I turn my attention to my monitor. "Enjoy your first few months here. I imagine June will be helping you out, seeing as her caseload is light. I think you'll enjoy working with her." He won't. June talks to herself and has permanent pastrami breath. Her caseload is light because she's every lawyer's last pick. She's slow as molasses.

He closes the distance until he's hunched over the front of my desk, a frown flittering across his forehead. "I thought *you* were working for Natasha?"

Closing and piling Natasha's case folders on top of each

other, I push them to the edge, gesturing for Ben to pick them up. "Sorry, but Nelson came by earlier today, begging for my help, and I agreed. I'll be tied up with him for the foreseeable future. Didn't you know? I go where people need me the most."

The thing I love most about Jack is that he has never assigned me to specific lawyers. He lets me go where the work is and my interests lie, treating me kind of like a freelance paralegal. I'm the only one who gets to do that and I'm pretty sure the other paralegals hate me for it, but I don't care. I'm not here to make friends.

As irritating as Natasha can be, I tend to work with her most. She's busy, her cases bring in a lot of money for the firm, and there's usually a fight involved. I love a good fight.

When Natasha came by my desk this afternoon, she came ready to stroke my ego, telling me what a valuable asset I would be to her because she's super busy and doesn't have the extra time needed to help a new lawyer. Apparently the learning curve is steep and regardless of how smart Ben is—according to the chatter, he graduated near the top of his class—he's in for a rude awakening.

And now, Nelson and I are going to be attached at the hip, whether he likes it or not. I've just decided.

"Huh." Ben's lip curls into a smirk. I think he just figured out what's going on here. That he has royally fucked himself.

"But I'm sure you'll do just fine without me, seeing as you're so clever," I offer with mock sincerity.

"I'm not worried, Reese. Disappointed. I think you would have enjoyed working with me."

Fighting the urge to roll my eyes, I call out, "Close the door behind you."

He leaves it wide open and strolls past my window, winking at me as he passes.

Chapter 8

...

BEN

My mama is always warning me that I have no common sense when it comes to women.

I've proven her right, yet again.

Why did I have to be such a jackass?

If I had just listened to Mason and shut my big mouth, Reese would be helping me figure out some of this shit. Now I'm stuck with June, a fifty-year-old woman who wears the same blue cardigan every day, constantly mutters under her breath, and has turned me off of luncheon meat forever.

Two weeks into my job at Warner, and I'm buried in paperwork. The number of ugly divorces and custody battles in the state of Florida only solidifies my resolve to stay the fuck away from anything that looks like a marriage. I haven't left my office before midnight once this past week, and here I am on Saturday morning, dragging myself through the trenches, feeling less like the guy who finished near the top of my law class and more like the village idiot who should have stuck with kicking drunks out of Penny's.

A knock pulls my attention to the door, where Jack looms

with a coffee mug in one hand and a plate of muffins in the other. "I hear you're a fan of Mrs. Cooke's baking." He sets the plate down on my desk. "God love the woman, but I wish she'd stop bringing this stuff to the office. I blame her for my weight gain." He pats his soft belly for effect.

Mrs. Cooke, Jack's assistant, is a heavy forty-five-year-old woman with short brown hair, a giant mole on her upper lip, and Coke-bottle glasses, who sweats profusely and probably won't live past her sixtieth birthday if she doesn't start eating better. But damn, can the woman bake. She's almost as good as my mama.

Jack's gray eyes survey the stacks of files on my desk. "How is everything? I see Natasha is keeping you busy?"

"She is." I nod slowly. My office is starting to look like a storage locker and my fingers are covered in paper cuts. "Who knew there'd be so much paper in a digital world?"

"How are you liking it so far?"

Besides wanting to shoot myself in the head at least once a day? "Nothing I can't handle."

Jack smiles sympathetically. "I remember my first year. It was hell. I wanted to quit. But don't worry—it'll get better. Half the battle is having the right team behind you so you can focus on what's important."

First *year*. Great. "I'm going to hold you to that," I chuckle, just as the rumble of a bike engine sounds outside my window.

"Ah, good. She came," Jack murmurs, taking a sip of his coffee as he wanders over to look out on the Warner parking lot.

She? "Who?" I ask, curiosity getting the better of me. I join him at the window just in time to see this "she" slide her helmet off, her long blond hair spilling out over her shoulders. "Holy shit," I blurt out, staring down at Reese as she straddles a Harley in a pair of jeans and a tight leather jacket, a rare tranquil look on her face as the engine idles, completely at ease, as if she were born to ride a motorcycle.

Looking hot as hell.

I feel Jack's gaze on the side of my face and I realize I'm ogling his stepdaughter in front of him. Swallowing, I add quickly, "Those things are dangerous."

Shaking his head as if in defeat, Jack mutters, "I know. You should have seen the piece of junk she was riding before I co-signed for this one with her. It's the best one on the market for women."

"You *let* her ride that?"

He snorts. "There's no 'letting' Reese do anything. That girl has been making her own rules for as long as I've known her. At least this way I was able to get her to agree to some basic safety in return. She's usually more agreeable when she feels like she's making the decisions."

Noted.

I wonder if that's why he gives her free range over the cases she's going to take on. Wandering back over to my desk, Jack picks up the framed picture of me. It's Mama's favorite—me at fourteen and in a blue-and-white football uniform, standing on the field next to her after having won my first freshman game as quarterback. "You play at all anymore?" Jack knows the basics about my football career from my interview.

"Here and there, for fun. I help my old high school coach out sometimes but I can't run like I used to, with the pins in there." I sigh. "It was good while it lasted." I have buddies in the same boat as me, permanently benched from concussions and torn ligaments. Years later, they're still not taking it well, hung up on the "what ifs," depressed about their monotonous day jobs and their one-car garages. I try not to think like that. If I do, I'll be a helluva lot more depressed than those guys. There were no "what ifs" for me. With my ranking and the scouts circling, I was a guaranteed draft into the NFL. All it took was one tackle to destroy my right knee. Took me right out of the game. Out of what I loved.

My dad nailed it when he said what goes around, comes around. And man, did he ever enjoy saying that right to my face.

"I'm sure it was," Jack agrees, setting the frame down gently. He strolls over and pokes his head out just as the elevator dings. "Reese?" We're the only ones in the office, so the name echoes through the open space. There's no doubt she heard him. The sound of footsteps approaches. My stomach does a weird flip of excitement as she appears in my doorway. During the week she wears nice office stuff. Today she's in ripped jeans that hug her thighs and that nice round ass of hers. Beneath her unzipped jacket, I can see an old Mötley Crüe T-shirt that stretches across her tits. I'm not even sure if she ran a brush through her hair. Maybe that's from the bike ride. It doesn't matter, though. I like this look.

Of course, she doesn't so much as glance in my direction, though I'm sure she knows I'm standing right here, staring at her. It *is* my office, after all.

She hasn't spoken a word to me in two weeks, since that first day. She's made every effort to be excessively busy on cases for Nelson, who, according to a very annoyed Natasha, she once declared she'd rather peel her fingertips off with a grater than work with.

"You got my note?" Jack asks.

"That's why I'm here," she says, her voice much softer and friendlier than anything ever directed at me. "What do you need help with?"

"I need my best paralegal to help my newest lawyer get on his feet. Natasha told me that Nelson's been monopolizing your time. She and Ben are struggling to keep up with cases, so I've told Natasha that family law can have you a hundred percent for the next few weeks, if you don't mind."

I watch as she turns those shrewd eyes on me, narrowing slightly, clearly thinking I had something to do with this. I have to press my lips together tightly, fighting the urge to laugh. If I laugh, she'll hate my guts. I need her to *not* hate my guts. Ideally, I need to find a way to make her love my guts. I get the impression she doesn't even *like* most people, so this may be a challenge.

Jack pats her shoulder, his voice softening, as if coaxing a frightened animal out of a corner. "Help the poor guy out in whatever way you can. He's practically sleeping here."

Chapter 9

. . .

REESE

"You really should try the key lime pie," the waitress suggests as she slides my usual order in front of me.

"Maybe next time." I impale a pecan with my fork. If I keep this up, my ass is going to start spilling over the sides of the brand-new Harley SuperLow that I found sitting in the driveway when I came back from Cancún. It was a birthday/graduation present from Jack. After a brake line snapped in my old Honda Shadow, he had deemed it unsafe and shipped it to the junkyard while I was away. He made a sizeable down payment and I'm making modest monthly installments to cover the rest. I think it's all part of his plan to turn me into a responsible twenty-one-year-old woman. Who rides a motorcycle.

I gladly accepted it, unable to contain myself the first time I cranked the engine and got lost in the distinctive rumble deep within my chest. I was planning on getting lost in that rumble all the way down to the Keys today, until I found the note from Jack on my bedside table, asking for my help in the office. After all that Jack has done for me, he's one of the few people who I'll go out of my way to please, so of course I changed my plans. Had I known that the law bot and Ben had bid for my undivided attention, I might not have come so willingly.

Having a smirking Ben sit there watching the ambush, his arms folded over his chest, certainly didn't help my mood. He knows exactly why I've been working on mind-numbing corporate contracts for the last two weeks. Honestly, I don't think driving a knife into my ear would be as painful as listening to Nelson's nasally voice drone on about this clause and that amendment and blah, blah, blah . . . But as agonizing as it has been for me, I've taken some pleasure in knowing that Ben's overinflated ego may be taking a hit.

I agreed to Jack's request, of course—through gritted teeth— and told them I'd be back in an hour because there was something important I had to do.

That was almost three hours ago.

And that's why I'm not at all surprised that Ben is now standing in front of my table with a big smirk on his face, like he's caught me red-handed.

"This *does* look very important."

"Food quality control," I mumble as the vacant metal chair drags along the patio stones and he takes a seat.

"Well, I hope you failed the coffee because it tastes like ass," Ben says, helping himself to my glass of chocolate milk.

My mouth opens to say something about that but I quickly shut it. I don't really want to think about where Ben's mouth may have been. And does he talk to everyone like this, or just me?

"Jack told me you'd probably be here."

"I'm highly predictable when it comes to food." I eye the boxed pie he just set down with a raised brow. "Hungry?"

"It's for a pregnant friend who I want to visit later, if I ever get out of the office."

Trying to guilt-trip me. Nice. Unfortunately for him, I grew up with a master manipulator and I don't generally fall for it. "Good for you, keeping your baby mama happy."

That loud, bellowing laughter of his carries through the patio, turning heads. "I can't wait to tell her you said that." Yanking my fork out of my hand, he stabs at my plate and shovels a piece of my pie into his mouth. "Damn, that's good pie. You should try the key lime next time, though."

"I hate limes."

He shakes his head and says in a slightly exasperated tone, "No you don't, Reese. You're just being difficult."

"Says who?"

His gaze roams around, stalling at a table of young women. "Says the margaritas I ended up wearing."

I grab my fork out of his hand and pull my plate closer, my free hand wrapping around the outside of the plate as if to protect it. "I actually do hate limes. That night was about me embracing change."

"And how'd that go?"

"Well, now I'm positive that I hate limes *and* change."

Ben's head tips back to take in the blue skies with a smile, and I can't help but notice his Adam's apple protruding from his neck. He has a really thick, strong neck, but not like one of those gross no-neck guys. Quite the contrary. "Tell me something . . . is suffering through Nelson's contracts for the past two weeks—which *everyone* knows you hate—really worth it?"

"I love working with Nelson," I lie. "His voice is enchanting."

Leaning back in his chair, relaxed, he watches me quietly for a moment. "Mason warned me not to piss you off."

"See? Jiminy Cricket knows things."

"Yeah, I guess so."

Washing the last bite down with my chocolate milk, I offer in a patronizing tone, "It's a good thing that you don't need me."

"Oh, but Jack thinks I do, so . . ." He stretches those arms above his head—the sleeves of his loose black T-shirt falling to reveal how much time Ben must spend in the gym—and smiles proudly. "I guess you'll be helping me whether you like it or not."

I heave a sigh as my gaze roams the patio, knowing that I'm stuck. Jack never steps in to dictate who I work with. He always says he's just happy that I'm working so hard and keeping out of trouble. If he has done it now, it's because he thinks it's necessary.

"Look." Ben rests his elbows on the table as he stares at me with that penetrating gaze that probably enraptures many women. "If I promise to never mention anything to do with Cancún again, can we start over?" He dips his head a bit, his big blue eyes full of sincerity. "What do you need me to do? Cry? Grovel? I'll do whatever you want. Please."

I like this side of Ben. I'm sure it doesn't happen often, and I'm sure he has this conversation well planned out, but still. I like listening to him beg.

"Come on. Anything. Do you want something embarrassing to hold over my head, too?"

The spark of interest—not so much about balancing the scales as curiosity about what could possibly embarrass this jackass—must be evident in my face because he quickly pulls his phone out of his jeans pocket. "Here, look at this. At least there's no concrete evidence of *you* ass-up on the ground." Not sure what to expect, I take the proffered iPhone, acutely aware of his fingers grazing mine in the exchange, and turn it around to see a guy climbing up onto a stage of some sort, with a scrap of what looks like a pink bikini riding up his ass and a set of—"Oh, my God! Is that . . . ?" With a cringe, I zoom in on the screen to see a very unflattering angle of Ben.

"Yup. I keep waking up to texts of these pictures from my friend. She must have taken about fifty of them. Thinks it's hilarious." Ben smoothly grabs the phone out of my hand as I burst out in laughter.

"I need to meet this friend. I like her already."

"Yeah, you'd probably get along well with Kacey. You're a lot alike." Pausing to drop his phone back into his pocket, he suddenly turns serious. "Look, I'm drowning in this shit, Reese. And

June . . . holy fuck!" His enormous hands cover his face, dragging down to reveal his frustration. "If I have to sit in a room with her for one more hour, I think I'll slit my fucking wrists. I can't be spending every weekend in the office. My mama runs a citrus grove and she's gonna need me there when the season opens, and I just need help. Please help me."

I heave a sigh. Maybe he did learn his lesson. Maybe . . . my thoughts trail as I watch the hostess lead two people to a table on the other side of the patio. I recognize that swagger in the guy's step; the curly wisps of hair around his ears and down the back of his neck are longer, urging fingers to swirl them.

Waves of emotion crash into me as I watch Jared slide into a chair. He's wearing his usual dark blue jeans, hanging off his hips provocatively. I'm sure that if I lifted up that soft gray T-shirt, I'd see the elastic band of his Calvin Klein briefs—he won't wear anything else. His naturally dark skin is darker than normal, as if he's been spending more time in the sun. He probably is, if he's working outside. His arms also seem bigger than they . . .

"Earth to Reese?" I hear Ben call out, adding, "What is it with chicks gaping out?"

I manage to turn my attention back to Ben's waiting face for all of three seconds before I'm compelled back to Jared.

And I watch. Like a lunatic who deserves a sedative cocktail and a padded room, I watch Jared for the first time in almost nine months, as he entwines his fingers through hers and brings her hand to his lips, kissing it softly, mouthing something that looks like "I love you."

He used to do that with me.

"Shit," I mutter, swallowing the rising sickness and jealousy as I angle my face away, trying to discreetly block my profile with my hand should Jared glance over in this direction.

"What is it?" Ben begins, turning in his seat.

My hand flies out to land on his cheek, slapping it as I push his face back to me. "Nothing. I'm ready to go."

He easily overpowers my strength, his bright blues quickly scanning the tables. Somehow he zones in on the right one. Or wrong one, depending on who you're asking. "Who are they?"

"Who is who?" Playing dumb has never been my strong suit.

"That smokin'-hot redhead and the dude?"

"She's not that hot!" I snap, and then grit my teeth as the grin hits Ben's face. He was baiting me and I failed. I can't help my attention from wandering over to their table again. My stomach constricts as I watch her flip her hair over her shoulder and giggle as he says something, his smile radiant. Try as I might, I can't stop staring at him, as the hollow ache of betrayal throbs inside my chest, remembering his pale green eyes . . .

And suddenly those pale green eyes are focused on me.

I freeze like a squirrel caught within the sight lines of a car as the various stages—meaninglessness to recognition to shock to worry—flicker across his face, as Jared realizes that his crazy ex-wife is sitting only a few tables over. And when Caroline realizes that she has lost her husband's undivided attention, she turns to see what could possibly be more important.

Thankfully I manage to break eye contact before her gaze lands on me, and now I'm back to staring at Ben with what I imagine looks like panic. "Keep your eyes on me, *please*," I beg.

"That's not hard to do." I think that was flattery but right now, it's not working on me.

Shit. I knew that one day fate would play a cruel joke on me. The world is too small and cold-hearted for it not to. But it wasn't supposed to happen so soon and like this. Not in my faded jeans, and ratty old T-shirt and black boots, and with helmet-head hair. *I* am supposed to be the smoking-hot one.

My ears begin to burn as I feel their eyes shift from me to each other and back again, no doubt discussing what to do. Ben must have picked up on my anxiety because he reaches over and clasps my hand with his. I don't even try to pull away. Leaning in slightly, he murmurs, "You okay?"

"No."

A mixture of surprise and concern flickers within his eyes. "Do I need to hurt someone for you?"

Despite the situation, I feel my heart melt a little. It's kind of sweet that Ben's taking on a protective role. I guess years of being a bouncer have developed those instincts. "Yes, but not in the way you're thinking." From my peripherals, I see Jared shift out of his seat and start heading my way, Caroline on his heels.

Oh shit. "We're dating, okay?" I blurt out without really thinking.

Ben's face stills for a moment. And then a smirk that is nothing short of victorious spreads across his lips. "*You* want *my* help?"

"Please, just—" I don't have a chance to beg before I find Jared standing next to the table.

"Reese? Is that you?" The smooth cadence in his voice is just as alluring as it was the first time I met him, when he ensnared me in his trap. Caroline wastes no time roping her bony arm through his, indiscreetly positioning her hand so that her rings are front and center in my line of sight. In case I didn't already know that they were married. I force myself to take a slow, calming breath, only to sense the rattle in my chest.

"Hey, Jared." I'd love to sound indifferent or flippant, but I can't keep the softness from my voice. Jared's very presence has always had a tranquilizing effect on me. From the corner of my eye, I notice Ben's eyebrow spike as his gaze shifts to my arm, where the noticeable tattoo remains.

"Wow, you look so . . . different."

I flick a few strands of my hair. "New job requirement." A wobble in my voice belies my casual answer. I hate it.

Jared's attention turns to Ben, quickly scanning his upper body, before moving back to me. "What are you doing in Miami?"

"I live here. I moved nine months ago." *Right after you ripped out my heart.*

"Huh, Lina didn't say anything about that." *That's because she would have tortured you if she could get away with it.* My straight-laced friend has a mean streak just waiting to be unleashed, probably worse than mine. "We just moved here about . . . uh . . ." He frowns, seemingly flustered.

"Two weeks ago," Caroline finishes for him in her heavy southern drawl, adding, "into a fantastic condo by the water." Her cheek rests against his shoulder. "Right, honey?"

That seems to snap him out of it. "Yes. Right." He bites his lip. "I got a welding job down here. Working on ships."

"Just like you always wanted," I murmur, hazarding a direct look into his eyes. They're still as piercing as always.

"Exactly." A small, quiet smile touches his lips. Jared's never been a big grinner. Not like Ben. He's naturally reserved, choosing to sit back and take the crowd in rather than lead the charge.

There's a long pause during which Jared simply stares at me and I grit my teeth and Caroline seems intent on molding herself to his body. This is beyond awkward. The only one who seems perfectly at ease is Ben. By the wide smile on his face, the bastard is enjoying this.

He sticks a hand out. "Hi, I'm Ben."

With a slight nod, Jared accepts it. "Jared."

"The ex-husband, right?"

Jared's face twists with a hint of displeasure. "And this is Caroline."

Ben winks at her. "The mistress."

With a slight pucker, she tucks her hair behind her ear and offers, "*The wife.* Jared and I have been together since we were twelve." As if that justifies everything. I hear the hidden message clearly. My marriage to him was a frivolous blip in their planned life of happiness.

"Right." The dryness in Ben's voice is rare but unmistakable. He obviously doesn't care if he offends anyone and he's happy to pet the elephant in the room. Part of me wants to kiss him. The other wants to punch him square in the nose.

Thankfully, he changes topic and tempo in a heartbeat. "Great place here, down by the water."

"I know, right?" Caroline's eyes lighten up and I wonder if it's all an act. If she's really this cheerful and sweet. "I just love their coffee. I come here every morning."

I know this already. I know because last Tuesday I sat out on a park bench and waited almost an hour for her to appear. She comes in for her morning coffee at eight thirty. Then she walks four blocks west to an old renovated house where she's an administrative assistant for an insurance brokerage. I know this because I followed her from the café to her place of work.

And I am well aware that what I did is entirely unhealthy.

"So you must have *just* gotten married. Congratulations."

Does Ben not miss a damn thing? Men are not supposed to notice these things. And men like Ben are *definitely* not supposed to notice these things. I shoot a "way-to-bring-that-up" glare his way but he ignores me, keeping his eyes on the happy couple.

"Yes. Back in July, in Savannah. It was the most beautiful, *classy* wedding."

A perfectly targeted knife through my back, directly into my heart. As if that weren't enough, I catch her thumb worm its way under the sleeve of Jared's T-shirt, playfully drawing circles as she pushes the material up to reveal a new tattoo. A cloaked figure holding up a welding torch.

Right where my name used to be.

I close my eyes against the painful lump in my throat and the dull ache swelling inside my chest, wishing I were wearing a long-sleeved shirt or my riding jacket right now. Anything to cover up the tattoo that I *haven't* rid my body of. I don't doubt for a second that the move was completely intentional on her part. Caroline isn't the sweet little Georgia peach she pretends to be.

This is just too much to handle. I always knew that actually facing Jared for the first time since our appalling breakup would be difficult. I just never comprehended the magnitude of the ripple through my carefully guarded heart, seeing the very real and very painful way in which he has moved on and, in so many ways, I have not.

Jared clears his throat and lifts his arm over Caroline's shoulder, effectively hiding the tattoo from my line of sight. "So, where are you working these days, Reese?"

I'm still trying to find my voice when the sound of Ben's chair scraping pulls me from my silent hell. "She works at my law firm," Ben answers for me. He stands and takes my hand, hauling me out of my chair. I follow blindly.

"Law firm?" Jared's eyes spike with disbelief as Ben throws an arm over my shoulders. Now that Ben's standing, the difference in size between the two of them is staggering. I always thought Jared was big, but he's on the lean side in comparison.

"One of the smartest women I've ever met. She has half the attorneys there running in circles to keep up, including me." Peering down at me with that mischievous smile of his, he murmurs, "Isn't that right, babe?"

I offer him a tight-lipped smile.

"In fact, she's going to be stuck in the office helping me all weekend. But she's amazing. She *never* complains about it. Right?" Ben's eyes are on me, waiting expectantly.

He's got me in a corner and he knows it. I heave a sigh. "I do what I can."

He winks as if sealing our silent deal. And then the cocky asshole pulls me against him, close enough to lean down and kiss me right on the lips. He doesn't even attempt to make it appropriate for the middle of a café and an audience, his tongue sliding in leisurely before finally breaking away.

Under normal circumstances, that might have been a pleasant surprise because, despite having convinced myself that it was just the tequila, Ben actually is an incredible kisser. Right now, though, I'm just trying to come to grips with the first significant aftershock of the quake that rocked my world.

I don't know what the hell I'm feeling.

All I know is that I'm a little light-headed, Jared is staring hard at me, and Caroline is staring at her husband, an odd, stony expression on her face.

Ben's free hand reaches back to get his wallet. He pulls out a twenty and tosses it onto the table to cover my bill. Grabbing his pie box, he offers, "Nice meeting you two. I need to get my girl back to work. We have a *long* weekend ahead of us." Swiveling my stiff body around and toward the exit, he sticks a hand into my back pocket, getting a good grip of my left ass cheek that he emphasizes with a squeeze, and adds in that loud, obnoxious voice, "You know, I think you should help me paint my office red."

The air vanishes from my lungs as my cheeks burn.

I'm going to gut him.

And Mason, because Ben obviously found out about the red paint "incident" and my failed marriage from my stepbrother, who was just looking for a way to make me look bad, no doubt.

Whistling softly, Ben guides me toward the exit. I don't dare turn around. All I can focus on is putting one foot in front of the other and try my hardest not to cripple Ben with a sharp elbow to his ribs. "Thanks for reminding them about that!" I hiss between clenched teeth.

"About what, the paint?" He lets out a loud snort. "You honestly think they don't remember?" His hand escapes my pocket, freeing his arm to drape over my shoulders again. "I was just letting him know that *I* don't care if my girlfriend is a complete whack job. I want to hear more about it sometime, though. I'm betting it's a good story."

"Way to take advantage of the situation. Ten points for being a douchebag," I mutter as we stop on the sidewalk and wait for the light to change.

"I just helped you make your ex-husband jealous, so you're welcome. I don't do pretend boyfriend shit. I'm normally Switzerland. I went rogue for you, so be grateful."

"All out of the kindness of your heart?"

"Definitely for an organ of mine," I think I hear him mutter under his breath, and then I catch the crooked smile as he says more loudly, "Exactly. Don't be a chick and read anything into it, okay?"

The arm around my shoulders slides off, allowing him to reach up and grasp my chin. He pulls my face up to meet his crystal-blue eyes. "You still have a thing for him?"

"No."

Obviously not believing me, he adds in a much softer timbre, "You know it took both of them, right?"

"I know."

He sighs, and for the first time I don't see humor anywhere in his face. "You're not stupid, Reese. So don't be one of those stupid girls who pines over an asshole. Especially one who's married."

I hear him but I don't, latching onto something he said earlier. "Do you really think that made him jealous?"

"Damn straight it did. I saw the look on his face and so did that little tart wife of his. No way a guy who's been in you wouldn't be bothered watching someone else stick his tongue in your mouth."

"I think you should send that straight to Hallmark." Ben sure knows how to boost a girl's ego, I'll give him that. If I weren't so distraught over seeing how Jared permanently erased me from his arm, I might actually be capable of a smile.

Ben's typical charming, dimpled smile is back as he stares at me. "And thanks for not biting off my tongue back there." There's a pause, and then his eyes flicker behind me. "They're coming out right now—No, don't." His fingers tighten their grip on my chin to keep me from turning back, keeping my eyes locked on his. "Too obvious. Want to *really* get under his skin? And hers, because I can guarantee you she didn't like seeing the way he gawked at you."

The urge to irritate Caroline is impossible to ignore. My single nod is all the invitation Ben needs. Setting his boxed pie on top of a newspaper stand beside us, his hands find their place on the back of my neck and my ass as he pulls me into his body, this time with a kiss that should be reserved for behind closed doors. It even earns a few honks and hollers as cars drive past.

When Ben finally releases me, it takes me a moment to remember why he was kissing me in the first place. "Are they still watching?" I whisper, a little breathless.

"Shit. That wasn't them after all. I should get my eyes checked." His frown lasts two seconds before it twists into an impish grin and I know I've been duped.

I pick up the pie sitting on the newsstand beside us.

And I smash it into that broad chest.

■ ■ ■

"How are you and Mason even friends?"

Ben looks up from his file at me, his eyes glancing off my socked feet that sit on top of his desk. If that's a hint, I don't take it. If I'm going to sit in his office all weekend, I'm going to be comfortable. "What do you mean?"

I answer with an eye roll. "You know exactly what I mean."

He leans back in his chair and stretches, giving me an appealing view of the ridges in his chest and shoulders. "What can I say? I'm a friendly guy. People like me. Especially hot little purple-haired chicks."

"Did you meet a lot of those in Cancún or did you branch out?" *Great.* I was just thinking how nice it was that Ben honored his promise not to bring any of that up, and now I've gone and mentioned it.

His eyes narrow slightly as if he's assessing me, deciding what to admit to. "I think most of them were blond. Except for the one from Spain. Oh . . . and a redhead."

Awesome. I'm not at all surprised. Not for one minute did I think I was anything except his night's target. Puking all over this guy was probably my saving grace. "You must have been awfully tired after that," I say with mock concern.

He flashes those devil dimples at me. "Two of them were best friends, so . . . I was after that night."

I struggle to keep my jaw from dropping, because I have a gut feeling that Ben couldn't be bothered to make things like that up. I may consider myself adventurous—Jared certainly thought so—but I don't think I'd have the first clue about keeping up with a guy like Ben. He worked in a strip club, after all. "Have you always loved yourself this much?"

"I had an awkward year in 'ninety-nine, but I got over it quick," he offers with a chuckle, turning his attention back to his computer screen. It's been hours since we came back from that disastrous run-in with Jared and Caroline, and Ben and I have sat in his office the entire time. I've kept myself busy going through the caseload, making notes on next steps and important dates, things I can knock off quickly, paperwork we can hand off to June and the other paralegals that don't require much thought or interaction to complete. Between that and the light conversation, I've managed not to feel too down about Jared after all.

Ben hasn't cracked a single margarita or crawling joke. He hasn't mentioned the public fondling he did of me on the street corner—thank God Jack wasn't looking out his office window at that particular moment.

It's as if it didn't even happen.

I study his tanned, handsome face. That chest-constricting smile. After sitting in here with him for this long, as much as I hate to admit it, Ben's not the bad guy I convinced myself that he'd be. Yes, he's still cocky, obnoxious, and downright infuriating sometimes, but he works hard, he seems to genuinely respect Jack, and he's nice to everyone. Even my nerdy stepbrother.

So, maybe Jack forcing us together was a good thing. I have enough to be on edge about, without playing Mission Avoid Ben at Work. And now I won't have to sit in Nelson's office, thinking of ways to shank him and get away with it.

"I was right." I reach over and pick up the picture of a much younger Ben on a field, in his football uniform. A tiny brunette woman—his mother, I presume, though he looks nothing like her—stands beside him, a proud smile on her face. "How old were you here?"

"Fourteen."

Really? I would have guessed at least sixteen. "You were a big kid." And gorgeous. Even at that age, I can see that Ben would have had all the little girls batting their lashes. "You said you were injured, right?" I think I remember Ben saying something about that in Cancún. When he nods, I ask, "What made you become a lawyer?"

"Honestly?" He pauses, tapping his pen against the pad. "I was going pro. There was no other way about it. Then some jackass plowed into my knee. Everything about the hit was dirty. The ball was out of my hand a good five seconds before that. The guy wanted me out for good. It wasn't the first time he had done something like that. He shouldn't have even been on the field." He leans back in his chair, and a rare morose expression passes over his face. "The NCAA got involved, suspended the guy for *one* fucking game. I was pissed, but there wasn't much I could do. Once the NCAA rules, they won't change it. Still, I had to try. So I built a case against the guy myself—with specific names and dates and witnesses. His history." I can see the spark of passion in Ben's eyes. "I appealed the suspension. It didn't change anything for me, exactly like I had expected. But when the idiot took another player out the next year, the case I'd built made sure he was out for the year." Ben shrugs. "I couldn't play anymore, but I figured sports law was something I might be good at. I know the ins and outs of this profession, beyond just the game—how to spot future talent, all the top schools, standard contract requirements and terms, and all that bureaucratic bullshit. I figured with some luck, I could do well."

"But Warner doesn't have a sports law department, Ben," I say slowly, not wanting to dampen the sudden excitement in his voice with the obvious.

He grins. "I know it doesn't, Reese. Not yet, anyway. I was actually offered a job at a sports law firm on the West Coast, but I need to stay in Miami because of my mama for now. And, Jack's willing to let me try to build one here, after I've put my dues in."

Ben turns his attention once again to his work as I feel the small smile curl over my lips. Jack is always looking for ways to help people out. I wonder if he's taking a chance on Ben because he's a good friend of his son's and Mason doesn't have a lot of friends. Jack's the kind of guy who would do just that.

"What else did Mason tell you about me?"

I see the dimples appear, even at this angle. "That you're certifiable."

"And?"

Ben's gaze lifts to me. "And I like certifiable."

"Well, sorry to disappoint," I offer with a heavy sigh as I bite into an apple that Jack dropped off earlier, before heading out. "I'm completely sane. He's just had it out for me since I jumped out of his closet and made him piss his pants." Of course I leave out the part where I was wearing a clown costume and had a very realistic-looking cleaver in my hand. And I was eight. Because those details actually might make me sound a tad unstable.

Ben bursts out in a roar of laughter; a genuine, chest-warming sound. "Okay, are you going to help me with this work or just sit there and look tempting all day?"

I roll my eyes—though I secretly bask in his words.

■ ■ ■

I don't believe it.

Eight hours after that ridiculous public display at the café, I'm straddling my bike outside a Chick-fil-A and inhaling a sandwich, while staring at a private message on my Facebook account from my ex-husband.

> Was great seeing you today. You're more beautiful than ever.

I reread the message at least twenty times as bitter nostalgia consumes my insides. Jared always greeted me with a groggy, "Hey, beautiful," as soon as my alarm went off. The first time he said it was especially jarring because I hadn't heard it since I was five years old, when my father was still around. Growing up with a mother that looks like Annabelle—and me looking nothing like her and everything like my father—I know what beautiful is and I know that I am not it. Sure, there's *something* about me. Something that *sometimes* grabs *someone's* attention.

But, Jared always made me feel beautiful.

My appetite has suddenly vanished. Wrapping up the rest of my dinner and sticking it back in the bag for later, I type out with shaky hands:

> Great seeing you, too.

Simple.

And highly untruthful. Was it "great" to see Jared today? Was it even remotely pleasant? No, it wasn't. Yet I feel a spark of something inside me that convinces me otherwise. And as much as I want to be a bitch, as much as I want to lay into him with my litany of "whys"—*Why did you leave me? Why did you lie to me? Why did you break my heart?*—I find myself staring at my screen, waiting for the little "read" indicator to pop up, hoping for a response.

I'm still staring at it when I hear a woman's heels clicking behind me. "Do you have a light?"

I turn to find espresso brown eyes drifting over my frame, probably in the same way I'm now assessing her. She's beautiful in a very seductive way, her long black hair poker-straight and sleek, her lips full and pouty. Her breasts *way* too swollen and round to be real.

"Sorry, don't smoke."

She lets out a loud sigh of exasperation as her hands drop to her sides, a cigarette perched between two fingers. "Why does no one fucking smoke anymore?"

"Because it's highly uncool. Plus I already have a black heart. Black lungs would just be overkill."

"You and me both," she mutters under her breath, studying my bike. "Yours?"

"What gave it away?"

She dissects me through narrowed eyes for a long moment before jutting her chin toward the Harley next to mine, the one with the red and yellow flames on the body that I was admiring earlier. "My boyfriend's. He's on his way out soon. Hey!" She waves down a guy walking by on his way in, holding up her unlit cigarette. He seems only too happy to dig into his pocket for a lighter, his eyes trained on this woman's cleavage as she pulls a flame from it. "Thanks, babe," she says in a low, husky voice, giving him a wink as she blows a puff of smoke directly in his face. "Now keep moving before my man comes out here."

What a bitch. I kind of like her.

My phone chirps again and, unable to stop myself, I check the message.

Seeing you with that guy today was hard. Is it serious?

"Are you fucking kidding me?" I mutter, my eyes widening with shock. *Really? Him* seeing *me* with someone else was hard on *him*? And why is he asking about Ben, anyway? Is he . . .

Holy shit. Maybe Ben was right.

"Bad news?" the woman asks between inhales.

I feel the scowl creep over my face. "No. I don't think so." I pause to process this turn of events, as a strange, giddy urge rises up. "I think I made my ex-husband jealous today."

If it was hard on him, then . . . he still cares.

And I had worked so hard to convince myself that he didn't.

Those first two weeks after I found them together in the shower, I was delusional. At first I thought there must be some sort of misunderstanding, that I didn't see what I thought I saw, that I didn't hear what I thought I heard. And then one morning I woke up from the haze—puffy-eyed and emotionally exhausted—and accepted that it was real. From that point, my thoughts morphed into a desperate hope that Jared would quickly realize his mistake, that he was simply confused, that it was just the one time, that maybe he had been drinking. Heavily. At eleven a.m. on a Tuesday. I wanted so badly to believe anything that resulted in him crawling back to me, begging me to forgive him.

And I knew that, if he did, I *would* take him back. As strong and independent and stubborn as I am, I would have caved in a second. Because that was the only way to stem the agony coursing through my heart all conscious hours of the day.

When Lina found a note from him tucked in her mail slot asking for a divorce, denying my delusions, proving to me what a fool I was, a toxic bitterness took over to stanch the vacuous hole left. That was it. It was over.

I've clung on to that bitterness for months, allowing it to morph into indifference. It has been a motivation of sorts, to prove that while Jared doesn't want or need me, I don't want or need him either. That I wasn't humiliated by him, too blind to see what was going on under my nose.

But now he's given me this new feeling to hold onto—a sick sort of satisfaction, knowing that there may still be a shred of *something* left in his heart for me. Like hope rekindled. Or maybe it's just my battered ego getting a steroid shot. Whatever it is, it's altogether intoxicating.

"You're trying to win him back?" she purrs through an exhale, watching me carefully.

"No . . . he's married. To the woman he cheated on me with." *Win* him back? Could that even happen?

"Why are you even talking to him then?" She puts her cigarette out with her heel, having finished it in record time.

"I don't know." I don't know this woman and don't care if she judges me. Maybe that's why I admit out loud, without giving it too much thought, "Maybe I still do want him back." I pause and then add, "After I hurt him." After I make his heart ache, let him feel lost, make him regret his choices. And then, when he has cried and groveled and suffered . . . maybe I'd take him back.

Get back what we once had.

"And then you could live happily ever after." I can't tell if she's being sarcastic or not. But then her sour mask slips for just a moment, revealing a kind of sympathy behind it that tells me she knows something of my pain. "I spent years waiting around for someone, hoping he just needed time. It was stupid."

"I haven't been waiting around for him," I argue.

She shrugs as a tall guy wearing a leather jacket, torn jeans, and heavy black boots exits the restaurant, heading our way.

"Yours?" I ask, nodding toward him.

A soft smile flitters across her hard face and I can tell it's rare to come by. "Me and Fin have been friends for years. He's always been there for me. I just finally noticed how much he means to me."

When he reaches us, he wastes no time swooping in for a quick kiss, which she grants, tugging on his beard playfully. To be honest, he's not at all what I'd expect a girl that looks like this—who could be a stripper or an escort—to be attracted to. But, to each her own.

"How do you like it?" He eyes my bike with a reverence unique to fellow riders.

"I could use a bit more power, but I love it." When Jack surprised me with the offer to co-sign, he had already done his research. Apparently I'm less likely to kill myself on this "starter" model.

"I was thinking of getting China one of these," he admits, following up with a grin and, "But I like having her on my back."

"Wow. Bike talk. Thrilling," the woman mutters dryly. "Ready to go, babe?" She pulls her helmet on and gives him a playful smack on the ass as if telling him to go. He complies, throwing a long leg over the seat of his bike. She uses his shoulders to balance herself as she follows suit, straddling the bike behind him. Then she settles those sharp eyes on me. "Word to the wise: if you have to fight over a guy, he's not worth it. Go for the one who's waiting for you." She coils her arms around her boyfriend's waist as he starts the engine.

I watch them swiftly pull away together.

■ ■ ■

Lying on my bed with one arm nestled beneath my head, still fully dressed, I stare at my phone, deciding on how to best answer Jared's question about Ben. I finally settle on:

I haven't married him yet.

Humor. When in doubt, always use humor.

And yet, it's still cutting.

As I wait for his response—which I may not get tonight; Jared was always terrible with responding to texts—I roll onto my side to reach beneath my bed. My fingers latch onto the smooth wood of my little treasure chest—the box that holds my past.

The scent of cedar tickles my nostrils as I open the box up and study the wedding picture hidden inside. The crisp white costume of the Elvis impersonator who married us can't eclipse the wide beam on my face as I stand tucked into Jared's side, my flirty violet dress complementing the color of my hair. The way the camera is angled, the diamond in my nose ring sparkles against the flash. Jared is looking as casual and sexy as usual in faded jeans and a fitted Kings of Leon T-shirt that hugs his beautifully sculpted body as if it were designed for him and him alone.

I used to think that Jared was designed for me and me alone.

We understood each other. More importantly, he said he loved me for me. All of me. My bitchy self in the morning, my sarcastic self at most other times, except for when I melted into something soft and approachable—almost vulnerable—in his arms. He loved that I ride a motorcycle and that I know how to play a guitar and can belt out Joni Mitchell and Eddie Vedder while making scrambled eggs, one of only a few things I can actually cook. He loved that my hair was purple and my body was pierced and that I didn't balk at the idea of matching tattoos. Not even for a second.

He loved that I was independent and emotional and that I was "different" from all the other girls.

I, in turn, loved that he didn't care about his parents' money and chose welding because he loves to work with metal. I loved the way he didn't look twice at other girls while I was sitting around with him. I loved the way he'd tell me to invite my friends out with us. I loved the way he couldn't go a whole night apart from me. He even tried, once. He came down to Miami for a friend's stag and ended up driving all the way home that same night to curl up in bed with me at five a.m.

I loved the way he chose me in an instant. How he *wanted* me in his life. He was the only man who seemed willing to commit to forever with me.

I loved the way he loved me.

With a sigh, I tuck the picture in and pull out the creased sheet of paper beneath it, the note that Jared delivered to Lina's door.

Reese—

I'm sorry you had to find out this way. Caroline and I ran into each other and . . . I still love her. What you and

I had will always be special to me. I'll pay all the fees.
Please, just sign the documents so we can all move on.

I'm sorry.

Jared

I never thought that a flimsy sheet of paper could have the power to impale a human being. It came with one of those "do it yourself" online applications for a divorce from the State of Florida and colorful little Post-it tags indicating where I needed to sign.

I knew that Jared didn't put those there.

I've kept this note to remind me of how badly Jared hurt me and how I want nothing more to do with him. And yet, now that he's here in Miami, now that I've had a taste of what it feels like to have his attention again . . . I don't know that I can just walk away. I certainly can't stop thinking about it.

I heave a sigh as I check my phone once again. Is it really worth it, though? That Chick-fil-A woman is probably right. Or, at least, she *may* be right.

It's been a while since I opened up this box. Digging deeper, I find even older memories. Even more painful ones.

A picture of a little girl with pigtails, her hands stretched as far as they could to reach the handlebars of her daddy's Harley while she pretended to ride it. I pull that one out and study it intently, just as I've done for years, until a light knock on the door startles me. Jack pokes his head in, ducking it slightly as if tentative about my reaction. "How was working with Ben today?"

I can't help but smile. He's worried that I'm mad at him for pulling the boss card. And making me work on a Saturday, no less. "Fine. We got through a lot. I told him I'd meet him at the office tomorrow."

"And he's been . . . professional?"

I stifle a snort. I know exactly what Jack's asking. "You don't have to worry, Jack." I think that's all Jack does regarding me.

Worry.

Worry that this new-and-improved Reese he has helped create is only temporary. That it's only a matter of time before I fall off the law-abiding wagon, so to speak, or he has to bail me out of some jam, or I run off and get married again.

I notice Jack's shoulders droop as if relieved of a weight. Walking into my room, he reaches for the picture in my hand. "You used to fall asleep with this. I always put it away before your mother found you with it. She would have burned it."

"Good thing Annabelle was never one to tuck me in, then," I mumble dryly, though I feel the warmth spreading in my chest over Jack's admission. I actually never realized that I hadn't secreted the picture away, myself. Or that Jack had come to check on me at night.

He harrumphs, studying the picture for a minute before handing it back.

"Hey, are you really never going to get remarried, Jack?" I ask, tucking it away and pushing the box under the bed.

"Oh . . ." A deep frown furrows his brow. "I figure twice is enough for me."

"Is it because of Annabelle? Did she screw you up that bad?"

"It's because of a lot of things, Reese's Pieces." He smiles sadly. "I let go of that hurt a long time ago. Holding on to people who don't want your love is never healthy." He heaves a big sigh. "Maybe if I meet the right woman, things will change."

"Well, you've certainly caught Ms. Sexton's attention," I tease with a smile, knowing I can get away with it. Jack's a real easygoing, tolerant guy.

He cringes. "I prefer someone a little more . . . refined." Despite what her last name may suggest, with a chronic case of black roots and a cigarette always hanging out of her mouth, Ms. Sexton is about as far from the sexy single neighbor as you can get. Divorced twice, the Boston native's nasally voice makes her accent decidedly unattractive. You can usually find her watering her lawn. She's the one wearing lime-green spandex leggings, a sports bra, and Crocs. The fact that she has birthed four kids and has an old-school Cesarean scar running vertically down her stomach doesn't dissuade the fifty-year-old from flaunting what she *may* have had at some point, twenty-five years ago. I'm surprised there haven't been official complaints from the community. It's an upper-middle-class neighborhood of sizeable detached homes and landscaped properties.

Jack leans down to place a soft kiss on top of my head. "Good night."

"'Night, Jack," I mumble, but then call out, "Jack?"

He stops and turns, a questioning look on his face.

"Do you believe in fighting for something you want?"

"I'm a lawyer, Reese. All I do is fight," he acknowledges with a grin, but then frowns. "Why?"

"No reason. Just curious."

With a hand on my doorknob, he studies me for a moment. "You're staying out of trouble, right?"

I rest my head down against my pillow. "So far."

There's a pause and then a sigh of exasperation. "Good night, Reese."

"Good night, Jack."

As soon as the door clicks, I roll over and grab my laptop to do something I haven't done in months.

"Good ol' Facebook. Helping people stalk since two thousand and . . ." I mutter, pulling up Jared's profile page, gritting my teeth in preparation.

Just as I had expected. Picture after picture of flowers and bows and a giant fucking white dress plaster his wall. All posted by Caroline. Really? A church wedding? Jared's an atheist. There must be five hundred people filling this place to watch the atheist get married. Jared hates crowds.

He's smiling in every single picture; I can't deny that. And he looks just as knee-buckling handsome in a tux. Still . . .

A new post pops up as I creep his profile. Surprise, surprise. She strikes again!

> My big sexy man is going to protect me here, tomorrow morning! What should I wear?

There's a link attached to an extreme paintball park north of Miami.

My stomach tightens. I love paintball. Jared and I used to go *all the time*, usually dragging Lina and Nicki along. I even have my own camouflage outfit and a semiautomatic paintball gun.

I click on the link to read about the establishment—family-owned and operated for twenty-five years. That's always a plus. It means they know how to run things and they'll have enough referees. It's a huge field north of the city, with a wooded area. I much prefer those to the inner-city ones, where you're crammed into a warehouse building. This also means that there will probably be a lot of players. With all the protective gear and masks on, it's hard to identify a person . . .

I can't go alone. I mean, I'm not above crazy, but that's a little bit too much. No, I need to go with my people. I quickly text Lina and Nicki:

> Paintball. Tomorrow. Nine a.m. You bitches are with me, right?

I'm not going to tell them why. It doesn't matter. We'll have fun either way.

Nicki responds immediately with a simple "in." Lina takes a few minutes longer, even though I know she has read it.

> In, as long as I can bring the guy I'm seeing.

After I agree to that, because I really don't care who she brings as long as I have a chance to nail Caroline in the head with a splatter of red paint, we figure out logistics and sign off of our group chat. I lie back in my bed and sigh.

Shit.

I forgot about Ben. By the time we get out there and back, shower, eat, and all that . . . I'm not going to want sit in an office all freaking afternoon.

I scroll to find Ben's number, thankful that we exchanged contact information before heading our separate ways today:

Sorry, can't help you tomorrow. Something came up.

And then I shut my phone off.

Chapter 10

■ ■ ■

BEN

"Something came up"? What the fuck does that mean! No way am I letting her ditch me. We got so much accomplished today.

Hell no.

I'm lying in bed as I quickly type out:

> You can't bail. You still owe me for today and I need your help.

No response. She hasn't even received it. She must have shut her phone off. Scanning my contacts, I dial Mason. He picks up on the second ring.

"Go tell Reese to check her damn phone," I demand, a rare hint of irritation in my voice.

"Uh . . ." I picture him fiddling with his glasses. "I'm not at home at the moment."

"Shit," I mutter to myself. "Where are you? The library?" Mason's a predictable guy. It's either Warner, home, or the library.

"Why do you need Reese?"

"Just . . . she's supposed to help me at the office tomorrow and she's trying to ditch me."

A hiss sounds into the receiver, followed by a low female

giggle in the background, making me double-check the display to make sure I actually dialed Mason Warner. I did.

This can't be right. I recognize a sated female giggle when I hear one. "Dude, are you getting laid?"

With a heavy throat clearing, he says, "I don't know where she is right now but I know where she'll be tomorrow."

"All right, lay it on me."

"I'm sending a link through now. Meet us there at ten."

Chapter 11

■ ■ ■

REESE

I'm ready to hunt that bitch down.

After paying the fees, having my gun approved for the field, collecting our rental equipment, and signing our life away in waivers, I managed to get Nicki away from the registration area while we wait for Lina. I don't know if Jared and Caroline are here yet, but I don't want to cross paths with either of them before I'm fully suited up.

"Good call on the paintball. I needed to de-stress after this week," Nicki says, stretching out her arms, her rental gun on the ground beside her feet. She's always loosening her muscles. In full-length black pants and a black turtleneck stretched over her strong frame, she doesn't really fit my idea of a social worker who helps troubled teens, but I'll bet she's better than most at it.

I went with my usual garb—camouflage pants and a matching long-sleeved shirt. It's loose and I definitely don't look appealing, but this is paintball. If you come here to look good, you're an idiot. And you leave with welts. "Where is Lina and this mystery guy of hers?" I mutter. "It's going to get hot out here if we wait too much longer." I'm not stepping off these grounds until I've unloaded at least one hopper on Caroline.

"Good question. Lina's never late," Nicki agrees. "And you're always late. I can't believe you were waiting on the doorstep for me when I pulled into your driveway."

"Just trying to be considerate." I decided not to ride my bike here today. Too conspicuous. I'd rather Caroline and Jared don't see me coming until it's too late. "And I guess I could use some de-stressing, too."

"Yeah, you've had a rough week, with the universe hating you and all," she says with sympathy in her eyes. I filled Nicki in on the car ride over about the whole Ben thing and about Jared and Caroline being in the city. Of my two best friends, Nicki is probably the easier to talk to. She asks questions while recognizing my unspoken feelings. She's also a better listener than Lina. Lina just tells you what she thinks, flat out, without tempering it with even a hint of grace.

Of course, no one knows that Caroline and Jared will be here today. That's just a bit too much honesty.

"Well, look who finally graced us with her presence!" Nicki exclaims, throwing her arms up in mock exasperation. I don't miss the strained smile and shifty-eyed glance toward me, though I don't understand why.

The second I turn around, I do.

"Mason?" I feel my face bunch up in a tight scowl. "What are you—"

It suddenly clicks.

"Oh my God!" I gasp out loud as my best friend steps forward to loop her arm through his, almost as if to keep him in place.

"Remember, I'm your friend and you love me," Lina states matter-of-factly. I simply stare as she announces, "Mason and I are dating."

What? What! I look from her to Mason—who's eyeing the paintball gun dangling in my fingers—and back to her. "Seriously? You're having *sex* with my stepbrother?" I can't help but cringe.

"I said we're dating."

I glare at Mason's beet-red face. All I see is a gangly kid with thick glasses, who loves *Jeopardy* and bitches at me about leaving gobs of toothpaste in the sink. If she's not sleeping with him, then he may still be a virgin. I hope she's not expecting great sex again for a long time.

Mason and Lina? But . . . But . . . "He wears old-man pajamas!" I cry out, as if Mason's two-piece striped, collared, button-down sleepwear—with pockets—explains everything.

Lina tucks her short blond bob behind one ear, her face calm and composed, as though she expected this reaction from me. "He's smart, cute, and nice. Don't be a bitch."

I'm fully aware that I *am* being a bitch, so I don't take offense. Plus, I'm still in shock. My best friend is dating my childhood nemesis? "But . . . how?"

Lina's arms fold over her chest. "I was going to tell you over dinner but you bailed on us, too busy working." Gray eyes dissect me as Lina lays that well-timed guilt trip on me.

"But . . . how?" I ask again.

"Remember when we came by your house to borrow some tools from Jack?"

I nod. It was the weekend Nicki and Lina moved down. They needed a hammer and a drill. I was busy studying for my final exam that following Monday, so I couldn't help.

"Mason offered to come by and help us."

"Does Mason even know how to use a drill?"

"Yes, Mason knows how to use a drill," Mason responds in an annoyed tone at the same time that Lina admits, "No."

His eyes flash to her as she shrugs. "You really don't, babe." As if to temper the blow to his ego, she leans in and kisses his cheek, leaving me gaping like a wide-mouthed bass. Nicki's too busy muffling her snorting laughter with her hand to say anything.

"Anyway . . . he spent the day *trying* to help us out"—Mason rolls his eyes at that—"and then I took him out to dinner as a thank you. After that, we started chatting over Facebook, and . . ."

"Fucking Facebook. The enabler of mutiny," I growl under my breath.

". . . he asked me out to the movies and dinner," Lina ends. "We didn't tell you right away because we wanted to make sure it'd be worth dealing with your inevitable fit, first."

"And?" I eye the two of them, the resignation clear in my voice because I already know the answer to that, given we're standing here right now.

"And you can go out there and shoot your best friend and stepbrother to your heart's content. After that, not a word. Got it?" Lina scolds.

Technically, I can't because they'll be on my team, but . . . I lift my gun in the air. "Fine. Can we go? Or are there any other surprises for me today?"

A set of strong arms ropes around my body, pinning mine to my chest as I'm lifted off the ground, a clean, sporty smell filling my nostrils. "So this is what you ditched me for?"

Chapter 12

. . .

BEN

"Good morning, sunshine!" I plaster on a wide smile as I drop Reese back down to the ground and watch her whip around, a mixture of surprise and irritation on her face.

"What are you doing here?"

I gesture down to my worn jeans and a crappy gray shirt. "Giving you a chance to get even with me for laughing at you."

Those caramel eyes flash, as if afraid that I'll elaborate. I step back a bit as she marches toward me, wondering if I should stop grinning like an idiot and protect myself against an imminent throat punch. "I mean, how did you know I'd be here?"

I jut my chin in Mason's direction. "After you bailed on me over text last night—really lame, by the way—I called Mason to kick your ass. He was over at your friend's place and told me what was going on. So . . ." I shrug and then offer her a smug smile. "Here I am. I figure we can head back to the office together after." Not waiting for her response—because I'll throw her over my shoulder and carry her stubborn little body to my car if I have to—I call out to Mason, "Is this the one you were givin' it to last night? If so," I nod once, "nicely done."

Mason's face bursts with color as he tries to keep the small, proud smile from stretching out across his lips. Good for him. The guy needs to get laid on a regular basis. And the girl—I recognize her as the non-Korean Korean friend of Reese's—is girl-next-door cute. "Hey! Long time no see!"

"You actually remember me?" The girl's tone is flat and thick with doubt.

"I don't forget a pretty face, darlin'."

"Cheesy" Reese mutters, skewering me with a strange look. "That's Lina and this is Nicki, since I'm sure you don't remember the names that go along with those *unforgettable* faces."

I open my mouth but falter as it clicks. *So . . . that's what jealousy looks like on Reese.* "Didn't you give me fake names?"

Reese's face twists up as the girl to her right, the one who looks like she could give me a good run for my money in an arm wrestle, bursts out in laughter. "That's right. We were Charlie's Angels that night."

Reese, on the other hand, isn't smiling. "Traitors. The lot of you!" She yanks her mask on, spins around, and marches toward the field entrance like she's on a mission.

And I watch her cute camouflaged ass the entire time, knowing that at least one of those paint bullets has my name on it.

■ ■ ■

"I haven't done this since I was, like, fifteen," I say as the five of us pick our path through the wooded terrain, my eyes peeled for our opponents. There are several teams playing at once today and we—the purple team, as picked by Reese—are hunting anyone with a thick red band on their arm.

How fitting.

We've shot four already, with no casualties on our side as of yet. "This place is great," Nicki purrs in a soft voice. "They could do a whole *Hunger Games* theme."

She's right, they could. It's like an arena out here—the forest is thick enough, and the ground cover high enough, to create the perfect hunting ground. They even have small outpost buildings scattered throughout. I wish I had known about this place sooner. I'll have to bring Nate and the guys here for a game. Maybe even Kacey.

"Too bad you're not allowed to climb the trees," I murmur with a head shake as I watch Reese wrap her arms around a tree branch and start pulling herself up. Handing my gun to Mason, I hook an arm around her small waist and yank her down just as she's about to throw her leg over it. "I have a feeling you're worse with following rules than I am."

She answers by spinning around to train that gun of hers on my chest. "I'm also not against shooting my own team members."

I chuckle, pushing it away. I know she's telling the truth. "You want to get kicked out of the game? Because there are refs everywhere here." The playing field is so big, they ride around on ATVs.

"I was merely trying to get a better—"

Her words are cut off by the clicking sound of a semiautomatic gun and bursts of paint splatters nearby.

"Take cover!" Mason's girlfriend shouts, oddly enough sounding like a soldier as she bolts, running for the small shack about twenty feet away. We're all tight on her heels, diving into it as the assault continues. Mason's howl just as he rounds the corner to protection tells us we have our first casualty. Lina spins him around to confirm the big blue splatter on the back of his tidy plaid shirt. "Yup, you're dead."

"That hurt," he complains.

I hear a fake cough muffling a "Sissy" coming from Reese as she peeks out the small window, followed by a soft punch in the shoulder from her friend Nicki.

"What do I do now?" Mason asks, ignoring his stepsister.

Someone outside answers for us. "Guy in the plaid shirt! We know you're hit! Don't be a cheater and try to wipe off the paint!" he yells.

"I'm not cheating!" Mason exclaims with indignation. "I don't cheat!"

"Yeah, whatever," comes the lazy reply. "Come out where we can see you with your hands up!"

"There's some real wackos around here," Nicki mutters, sticking the nose of her gun through the hole to shoot a few rounds out.

"I guess I'll wait for you guys at the front," Mason mutters, stripping off his purple band and heading out, his head hung a little. I think he was having fun. Plus, being the first one shot down in a group of girls probably hit his ego a little.

"Don't worry. I'll take care of the ladies for you," I stretch my arms out to reach around all three women as we watch Mason trudge down the path through the tiny window, toward the group, his purple band held out in surrender.

And that's when all of them let loose, paint pelting the skinny guy as he lifts his arms, trying to protect his chest from the sting of being that close.

"Those motherfuckers!" Lina screeches, elbowing me out of the way as she tears out of the hut with Nicki trailing her, guns out and firing ahead of them in a manic "banzai!" charge, yelling at the stop of their lungs while Reese and I watch from the safety of our hut.

When it's all done about twenty seconds later, all four male opponents and both Nicki and Lina are out of the game.

And Mason is covered in paint from head to toe.

"Poor fucker." I chuckle. "I guess she must really like him."

"No, that's Lina. It's inevitable that she goes kamikaze at some point. I'm surprised she lasted this long."

"Go win for us!" Nicki shouts with a wave. "We'll wait for you at the gate."

Reese sighs, shoving my arm off her shoulder. "Well, this isn't going to be a long game."

"We could always hide out in here for a while. Regroup." I smile, taking in her cute little camouflage outfit. The pants are tight around her ass, making it look all the more round and appealing.

Her mask shifts as she shakes her head. "Even though I can't see your face, I know you're checking me out."

I burst out in laughter and she responds by shoving me. "Shhh! We're *hunting!*" She leans forward to peer out the window, muttering more to herself, "You're too loud!"

"Fine. You go and hunt. I'll just be back here, admiring the goods." I pull my mask off and lift the hem of my shirt to wipe the sweat off my face.

"Not allowed to take your mask off while out here. I thought you were all about the *rules*," Reese mocks, pulling her own mask up to show her flushed cheeks, covered in a sheen of sweat, her hair in a damp, messy ponytail. Her eyes skate over my uncovered stomach for a second before landing on my face again, a strange expression touching her mouth.

I can't help myself. "Thinking about yesterday, aren't you?"

She rolls her eyes, but I don't miss the tiny smile that curls her lips. "No. Are you?"

"I haven't stopped." I'm not embarrassed to admit it. Fooling around with Reese was fun. Especially in front of that jackass she was stupid enough to marry. What is it with chicks going for the dark, moody, tattooed types? Because I can tell that's what he's like, just by the look of him. And even with the Stepford wife leeched onto his side, I caught the sharp glare he was shooting my way. I'm not surprised. I don't see how anyone can't miss kissing a girl like Reese, especially with the dime-a-dozen girl he hitched himself to.

Reese, well . . . she's all angry and fire-breathing bitchy until her lips find you, and then you're sure she must have a cocaine-laced tongue because you can't get enough of her sweet mouth.

I watch her face as she seems to ponder that for a moment, her chest rising and falling faster than it did only moments ago. I wouldn't be opposed to getting into Reese's pants right here, right now. "Fuck," I mutter, shifting on my feet.

"What?"

I sigh. "Nothing. I just hate wearing cups."

I feel the tip of her gun jab me in the groin, tapping against it. "Why'd you wear this? You afraid someone's going to go after your prized body part?"

I'm about to tell her that I'd like *her* to go after my prized body part but without the weapon, when a female giggle sounds outside. Quickly pulling our masks on, I hunch down to squeeze in next to her and look out the small window.

And struggle to stifle my laugh as we watch a couple climb the hill opposite us, the female in a pair of cut-off jean shorts and a shirt that's tied to the side. "Daisy Duke is playing paintball? What a fucking moron. Why didn't he make her wear more clothes? That's gonna hurt when she gets hit." The guy is turning this way and that, scouting the area for people.

"Yes, it is," Reese agrees, and I hear the wicked pleasure in her voice as they disappear into a hut. "Come on." Without waiting, she's darting out and around the corner, her gun aimed and ready.

"They're yellow!" I hiss, trying not to be too loud in case there are any reds nearby. She doesn't hear me, though. Or she doesn't want to. She keeps moving forward like a little ninja, silently leaping over bushes and avoiding branches that will crack. Picking up speed but not nearly as gracefully, I reach her seconds after she stops at the side of the hut. She holds a single finger up to her mask, to warn me.

I don't think there's any worry, though. From the sounds of it, they're preoccupied.

Doing exactly what I was thinking of doing only five minutes ago with Reese.

And by the way Reese is creeping around the corner, she's about to prove why I was smart to be worried.

Damn, I love this chick.

Leveling my own gun, I step in beside her as the soft, rhythmic thump against the wall inside picks up. It's obvious the guy is drilling Daisy Duke, and it's making my own discomfort all the worse. I can't help it. It's normal for a guy to get off hearing that kind of shit.

Reese seems to stall for a moment. I'd do anything to see the expression on her face right now, to know what's going through her head. She snaps out of it, though, and raises a hand to silently count down from five on her fingers.

And then we both leap into the doorway.

They were smart enough to keep their masks on at least.

The chick's shorts are on the ground, her bare legs wrapped around the guy's hips while he's plowing into her, his pants hanging below his ass. All in all, a lot of vulnerable flesh on display.

With a delayed battle cry, we open fire, pelting them from head to toe with paint. I focus more on the guy's back, but Reese holds no prisoners, unloading on his ass and her thighs as howls and shrieks of pain compete with the clicking of our guns.

My gun is out long before Reese's, and she doesn't look ready to let up. Finally, I grab her by the arm and pull her out. We run down the hill to screams of "You assholes!" carrying through the forest. I keep pulling her along until the valley and the hut are no longer in view and I can't run anymore because I'm laughing too damn hard.

Leaning back against a tree, I struggle to catch my breath. "I can't believe we just did that." We'll get kicked out of the game and possibly banned from this place if the couple reports us. Then again, they'd have to admit to what they were doing in there and, while there's no "no sex" rule in the handbook, I'm thinking it's frowned upon by the referees.

"It's their own damn fault!" she mutters, her breaths just as ragged as mine. "Did you see her? What if there were kids around? What a twat!"

Another bellow of laughter explodes out of me. "I haven't heard that word in forever. She has clearly offended you with her sense of adventure."

"That wasn't a sense of adventure. That was no sense at all," she growls between breaths. "What an idiot for coming dressed like that."

Between the midday heat, the mask, and the running, sweat is pouring off me. I'm dying to take my mask off but I'm not about to risk losing an eye. "Come on. Let's get going before a real opponent catches us."

She sighs. "I'm done with playing for today."

"What? Forget it! I'm not quitting until we find that flag or I've been shot." I'm competitive by nature. I also haven't had this much fun in a long time.

In answer, Reese points her gun at my crotch.

And fires.

■ ■ ■

With my arms folded across my chest, I watch Reese duck out of the changing room, her furtive eyes checking this way and that as she makes a beeline for my waiting car, tossing her bag of dirty clothes and gun into the trunk. Tucking a strand of freshly washed hair behind her ear, she cocks her head and looks at me somewhat sheepishly. "Will you survive?"

"Not sure. You'll need to take it for a test run," I smirk, pulling her into me, the smell of the soap from her shower catching my nose and proving that, yes, my dick is still able to at least stand.

She offers a small smile as she pulls away. "You should write to the manufacturers and complain."

"And tell them what, exactly? That their soft cups don't hold up well when a chick shoots you with a semiautomatic paintball gun at point-blank range?" The sting actually went away within a few minutes but, damn, did it hurt. It probably wouldn't have been so bad if I didn't already have a raging hard-on and a growing case of blue balls. Still, I've hammed it up for Reese's benefit, hoping I can guilt her into some hand action during the car ride back to the office.

She shrugs. "I don't know. Come up with something. You're the lawyer. Come on, let's go." She ducks into the passenger seat of my car before I can answer. Honestly, I thought I'd be forcing her into my car to come to Warner. But between the gun to the privates and her friends texting to say they've left ahead of us, she's not fighting me. In fact, she seems to be in a rush to get out of here.

"You okay?" I ask, climbing into the driver's side, ready to blast the air conditioning. Even with a quick shower in the changing room, I'm already sweating again in this heat. "What's wrong? Feeling guilty over ruining a magical moment for the happy couple?"

Her lips press together and she pauses. "No. I just thought it'd feel better than it did. It was . . ." She shakes her head. "Nothing. Let's go before I change my mind about work."

"Shit, we can't have that." I slide my key into the ignition and crank the engine. "I'm starving, though."

"That makes two of us."

"Good. We'll stop and get you some small children to eat on the way, you wicked woman." I'm about to throw the car into drive when I see a redheaded woman and a tall dark-haired guy walk across the parking lot toward us, taking slow, rigid steps. The woman's cut-off shorts are clean but I can't say the same for her legs, which are mottled with dry red paint. Welts run up the underside of her thighs.

"Wait a minute." I squint to get a better look at their faces. "Isn't that . . . ?"

"Drive!" Reese demands, pulling on her sunglasses and hunching over slightly.

As we pass by, Reese turns away at the same time that I get a good look at the big tattoo on the guy's shoulder that had been covered by long sleeves before. "You've got to be kidding me." I explode in laughter. "Did we just pull the ultimate 'fuck you' on your ex and his new wife?"

Reese doesn't answer, helping herself to my radio, tuning in to an alternative station. Chris Cornell's distinctive voice comes on over the speakers.

"Holy shit," I mutter with a chuckle. "Remind me *never* to piss you off." I let her have her moment of silence as I turn onto the highway, while the pieces start to click. It makes sense. Reese had to know they'd be here. And she had to have figured out who the idiot showing up dressed like that would be. Finally, I ask, "How'd you know?"

I don't think I'm going to get an answer from her. But then, with a heavy sigh, she admits, "Facebook. He messaged me last night. You were right. He was jealous of you. Then *she* posted something about coming here and, well . . . I couldn't help myself." A small, sheepish smile touches her lips as she ducks her head. "Do me a favor, though, and don't tell anyone."

I hazard, "I guess it probably hurt, seeing them like that, didn't it?" It must have. Here I was, thinking how much fun it was catching two people going at it, but for Reese, it wasn't just two people. It was someone she loved. By the way her mouth is twisting now, it's someone I'm pretty sure she's still hung up on.

After a long moment, she admits softly, "It's not the first time I've seen it, but, yeah, it still hurt." Though I really like her normal snarky side, I have to say that the forlorn side I'm seeing right now makes me want to pull over to hug her or kiss her or, hell . . . I'm seconds away from reaching across the console to hold her hand. That's when my Bluetooth starts ringing, cutting into the music. A giant "Mama" displays on the screen.

Shit.

Reese looks from me to the display to me. "Aren't you going to answer that?"

"I'll call her when we get to the office."

As quick as a viper snatching its food, Reese's hand snaps out and hits the green "Answer" button on my steering wheel.

I groan. "You really are a pain in my—"

"Hello?" My mama's lax voice sounds out clearly over the speakers.

"Hey, Mama." I shoot a look of exasperation to my passenger, whose dour mood has suddenly been replaced by a broad smile.

"Who were you just talking to?"

I take a deep breath. This is exactly why I didn't answer. The only girl Mama has ever met was Brittany Jo, a girl I dated in sophomore year for all of two weeks and got trapped into introducing after one of my football games. And the only reason I remember the girl's name is because Mama kept asking about her. For at least six months after I ended it by getting caught nailing her twin sister at a party.

Hell, I was drunk and they looked the exact same, except for their clothes, which I *probably* should have noticed. But her sister never said a damn word when I pulled her into the mudroom.

"Just a friend," I answer with hesitation.

"Hi, Mrs. Morris!" Reese chirps like an innocent church girl, batting her eyes playfully at me. "My name's Reese."

There's a pause for one, two, three seconds and then, "Why, hello dear."

Ah, fuck. I hear that inflection. That's my mama getting excited that some woman may have pinned her baby boy down. She's going to be searching out china patterns after we hang up, or whatever the hell it is moms do when they think they're getting a wedding. "Just a friend, Mama," I reiterate. "We were out at a paintball field with a bunch of other friends and now we're heading in to work after we grab a bite to eat." For good measure, I throw in, "She couldn't drive herself. Her motorcycle wasn't working properly." Maybe that'll turn Mama's little fantasy upside down.

"Oh, well you two should swing by first! I need you to take a look at the tractor anyway, Ben. It sounds funny and I don't want to call Bert out here unless I have to. You know how much he charges."

Swing by? I love my mama, but the grove isn't exactly down the street. That's part of its appeal. "Can't it wait until next Sunday? I have a ton of work to do."

"I suppose. Though I could have lunch ready for you when you get here . . ." Her voice is thick with disappointment.

"That's nice, Mama, but—"

Reese cuts me off with, "We'd love to come over, Mrs. Morris. We'll see you soon."

"Wonderful!"

Yeah, wonderful. I'm pretty sure I just heard wedding bells in her voice.

Dead Mau5 fills the car as the phone call ends. Reese controls herself for all of five seconds and then bursts out laughing. "You call her Mama? What are you, ten?"

"Her place is a hundred miles away. You're now stuck in the car with me for the next two hours."

Shifting in her seat, she closes her eyes. "Wake me up when we get there."

Chapter 13

. . .

REESE

"Not what I expected," I murmur as Ben's Jetta turns past the large "Bernard Morris Grove" sign and creeps along one of the longest driveways I've ever seen, lined with oak trees big enough to create a tunnel-like cover. With strands of Spanish moss hanging elegantly from their limbs, it looks like something out of a movie setting. One of those dreamy places that feels magical and you're sure has been doctored heavily by a stage crew.

"It looks like more than it is," he denies.

"It looks like a giant house on an orange grove," I retort as the sizeable white house with two levels of wraparound decks and stately pillars comes into view, windows flanked with black shutters staring down at us. The Confederate flag hangs limply from one corner, reminding me of a soldier, standing motionless as it awaits our approach.

"It *is* a giant house," he agrees. "My mama's great-grandparents, the Bernards, moved here from Louisiana and wanted to feel like they were back home, so they built a plantation house. Kind of out of place, but it was a cool house to grow up in. Needs a lot of work, though."

As we get closer, I see what he means. The exterior is in bad need of a paint job, shingles have begun to lift, and the front porch leans just slightly to the left. Still, it's beautiful in a historical, haunting way. And I'll bet it's brimming with all kinds of stories to tell—both joyful and heartrending.

Turning the ignition off, Ben half-turns in his seat to regard me with a rare serious expression.

"You're nervous about me meeting your mother, aren't you?" I knew the second he didn't answer his mother's call what was up. When he blows a mouthful of air out, I can't help it; I laugh. "Please don't tell me you have your mom convinced that you're a virginal disciple of Jesus."

"No, pretty sure that ship sailed when she caught me with the neighbor's daughter behind the barn," he answers with a wry smile, adding, "but please just don't give me any grief, MacKay." His eyes flicker over to the front door in time to see a small woman in a floral sundress and apron, identical to the photograph on Ben's desk but older, emerge.

I follow his lead and climb out of the car as a hound dog lets out one long bay before it waddles down the porch steps and toward Ben, its belly almost dragging on the ground.

"What are you feeding this dog, Mama? Hey, Quincy!" Ben crouches down to let the dog put its front paws up on his knee. He grabs both ears and scratches, mumbling something under his breath about a "good girl." With that greeting out of the way, the dog turns her attention on me, a little more cautious as I bend down to offer my hand. After taking a few sniffs and accepting a friendly pat, she turns and sways back toward the house and Ben's mother, who's watching me intently.

I wonder what this woman is going to think of me. I wonder why I suddenly care. I certainly didn't when I willingly walked into this trap.

I haven't done a lot of "meet the parents" scenarios. In fact, there was only one: with Jared's parents, just after we eloped. Considering their son hadn't had the heart to tell them that he had broken up with Caroline—the future daughter-in-law they would have handpicked for their only child—I'd say that meeting went exactly as expected. A catastrophic explosion.

As discreetly as possible, I reach up to finger-comb my hair, left to air dry after the speedy shower earlier. There's not much I can do about my jeans and T-shirt right now.

"Now who's nervous?" Ben throws over his shoulder with a smug smile as I watch him saunter toward his mother. He's in a blue and yellow Dolphins T-shirt and worn blue jeans, so I'm not exactly underdressed. The difference is, Ben still looks *good*.

"It's been weeks!" Ben's mom scolds, though there isn't an ounce of bitterness in her voice. He answers by scooping her tiny body up in his arms and spinning her around, much to her howls and laughter. It's hard to believe such a slight woman created something as big as this man. She can't be more than five feet tall. "Benjamin Morris! You put me down before I have another heart attack!"

His smile falls off at that comment, but he does as asked. She proceeds to ruffle her skirt gently before turning to regard me with eyes as blue and kind as Ben's. "And you must be Reese." A small hand shoots out and I take it immediately.

"You have a beautiful home, Mrs. Morris."

She waves her hand. "Oh, please! Call me Wilma, and this old house is all but falling apart. Sometimes I wish a bolt of lightning would burn it down because it needs so much work. Come on in. I have some sweet tea and sandwiches ready." She pats her son's stomach. "Benjamin's favorite."

He catches me pursing my lips together tightly to stop the burst of laughter from escaping. Flinging an arm over my shoulders, he asks, "What?"

"You are *such* a mama's boy!" I hiss, earning a giant grin.

Wilma steals a quick glance back and beams.

And it clicks. I know what Ben is nervous about. It's not about me teasing him in front of his "mama." It's about her getting the wrong idea about us.

Ben has made it pretty clear to the world that he has no intention of getting serious with anyone. Ever. And if he were anyone other than Ben, an arm over my shoulders might constitute misleading people into thinking we're dating. But it *is* Ben, and so I don't make the effort to push it off.

Plus, I have to admit, it makes me feel good.

Beyond the house, row upon row of trees stretch over the dips and rises of the property as far as the eye can see. We pass by a honey-colored barn to our left, obviously built much later than the house. Large doors sit closed at the front, flanked on either side by small windows. And in the darkness within, I'm almost positive I see a face peering out at me. But it's gone so fast I can't be sure.

"We can have lunch out on the sun porch," Wilma offers, leading us into the house. The interior is dated but in a quaint way, with worn wood floors and floral wallpaper—some of its seams starting to lift—stretching up to crown molding that trims the high ceilings.

"Ben tells me this land has been in your family for generations," I say as my fingers intentionally slide across the wood grain of a side table. Everywhere I look, I find a piece of rustic furniture. Each one is different, suggesting it's not mass-produced, and yet there's *something* about them that hints that they're part of a set.

"Over a hundred years," she confirms. "We've done a lot of living here."

I feel Ben's hand graze the small of my back as we step out into an all-white room of glass and wood. The wall-to-wall windows overlook the massive expanse of the family grove that I couldn't quite appreciate from the driveway. I can't help my eyes from bugging out at the beautiful oak table, laden with breads and meats and salads, partly because of my rumbling stomach, but mostly because of the amount. There's enough for ten people here. And I don't doubt that it's all 100 percent homemade and made especially for her son.

"Manners, Benjamin!" Wilma swats Ben's hand away from the sandwich platter. "Wait for Reese."

"She likes me just the way I am," he says through a smile, wrapping his arms around his mom's shoulders for another bear hug and planting a kiss on her forehead. It's cute.

And so completely foreign to me.

As we sit down to eat, I listen quietly to Wilma talk about the coming season—citing concerns over spreading disease and sub-ideal climate as well as the high costs of using the packaging company and having to cut back on staff—and how all the pipes in the house need replacing. All while I look for flaws in her. Deceptive flares, duplicitous statements, self-absorbed topics. Things that remind me of Annabelle. But I find none.

Ben's mom is genuinely nice and she very obviously loves her son.

Like any mother should love her child, I suppose.

By the time we're carrying the dirty dishes to the kitchen, my stomach is ready to explode, but I feel like an old resident of the Morris household.

"Reese, have you ever seen a grove before?" she asks, tucking one of her short chestnut curls behind her ear. The gray is just beginning to thread through.

"No, can't say that I have."

She pats Ben's back. "Why don't you take her out for a while?"

I'm expecting him to decline, insisting we have to get back. But he doesn't. He simply nods and throws an arm around my shoulders. I look up in time to catch the secretive smile touching his lips as we pass through the house, on our way to the foyer again.

"Where did all of this furniture come from?" I dare ask.

Wilma's blue eyes flash to Ben as she says, "They're beautiful pieces, aren't they?"

"Yes," I confirm, running my hand along the carved leg of a small desk.

"Ben's father made everything in here. He's a carpenter."

"Really?" Ben hasn't mentioned a word about his dad and, given no father figure has made an appearance as of yet, I was beginning to think he wasn't in the picture. Plus, Ben made that comment about helping his mom with her orange grove because she's all alone—while groveling for my help at the office.

But Wilma just used the present tense, so his father is obviously around. Otherwise why would she keep an entire house full of reminders? Poking Ben in the ribs, I ask, "Did you inherit your father's talent?"

"Nope. Can't say I did. Come on." He hooks his arm around my neck, pulling me into a gentle headlock, his shirt deceptively soft against my cheek. "Let's go, MacKay."

"Don't roughhouse her! She's not one of your brothers." Clasping his face between her hands, Wilma stretches onto her tiptoes and lays a kiss on his cheek. "Now go have fun. I'll pack all this extra food up for you to take home so you don't have to worry about cooking."

I stifle my snort. Ben doesn't worry about cooking. I've seen him walking past my office every day with a Subway bag in his hands. He may as well buy a franchise of the chain. That poor, unsuspecting woman . . . I watch her disappear down the hall and then can't help but whisper, "Does your mom have any idea what her sweet little Ben is *really* like?"

With an arrogant smirk, he leads me out the front door. "What do you mean?"

"That your pants are off more than they're on."

"Not lately." Eyes drive down the front of my body, stirring an unexpected flurry of nerves inside me, as he leads me toward the barn. "And that has nothing to do with whether I like to take my mama's cooking home with me."

"Fair enough." I start needling his ribs with my fingers until he loosens his grip on me. "So you have a brother?" Ben knows far too much about me and I don't know nearly enough about him, I'm realizing.

"Three. Jake, Rob, and Josh."

Four Morris boys. "And are they all like you?" I automatically picture four giant blond men sitting at that table, grins and obnoxious mouths determined to drive their mother nuts.

"Like me how?"

"Big, cocky, whoring mama's boys?"

He chuckles. "Well, we all look alike. I'm by far the best-looking, of course."

"Naturally." *Good lord, four men that look like Ben?*

"Rob's married, Josh is divorced. Both with kids. Jake's been with his girlfriend for a couple of years. They have a kid on the way."

"So you're the only one with commitment issues?"

He laughs. "I guess. I have an older sister, too. Elsie."

"Let me guess . . . you're the baby?" His grin answers me. *Makes sense.* "You milk that for all it's worth, don't you?"

"Can you blame me?" Deep divots form in Ben's cheeks.

"I guess not." As we pass the barn, I catch movement behind the glass window again. As if someone is watching. "Hey Ben, is there someone in there?"

"Probably my father." Ben weaves his hand through mine and pulls me around to the side of the barn.

"Does he not come out?" I can't help but think it's odd that his own father wouldn't have come out to greet him. Unless his mother is a Betty Crocker psycho who keeps her husband chained up in the barn like he's got an incurable disease. I'm sure I've seen a show like that before.

"Later tonight. He likes it in there." Ben yanks a blue tarp off an object hidden beneath and all concerns about Ben's peculiar dad disappear at the sight of thick-treaded tires and red-and-yellow roll bars.

"Yes, I'll marry you," I blurt out, heading straight for the driver's seat of the dune buggy.

"Whoa . . ." A thick arm ropes around my waist to hold me back, pulling me tight against him. "You think I'm going to just hand you the keys to this? It's fast."

"I'm sure it is!" I feel my eyes light up once again. While other little girls were waiting in line to spin in the teacups at the fair, I was the little brat crashing my go-cart around the track. I was never your typical girl. I don't know how many times I came home with grass stains on my clothes and mud in my hair.

"I don't know that I trust you. You're liable to take out half the grove and kill us."

"I'm a very responsible driver!"

"Is that what you told the cops when you got busted for drag racing?"

"It wasn't drag racing and no charges were *ever* laid!" I throw back.

"That's not what Mason said," he counters.

How Mason would . . . "Dammit!" Lina must have told him. *Change of plan.* I roll my body around and press myself against him.

A bark of laughter interrupts my very obvious attempts at seduction. "Oh, hell, I'm an idiot but I'm not falling for that." He spins me around and gives my ass a hard slap before he climbs into the driver's side of the dune buggy, moving fluidly for a man with such a large, tall frame. "Get in."

I do so but not without a grumble, mentally planning the steps of the distraction and siege.

"You'd better hold on. This thing is old and jumpy." He cranks the engine and a low, throaty rumble escapes as it comes to life, my entire core vibrating with the seat. It lurches as Ben throws it into first gear, chugging and jolting slightly before leaping forward through the tall grass.

Ben steers us down a sandy trail with a sea of trees and then shifts into second and then third gear, the rush of the acceleration exhilarating. It's too loud to talk and so I happily settle in as the trees whizz by and the sand kicks up a cloud dust behind us, the bumps along the path jarring my head this way and that. I don't care. We continue down past that path and to another one, and another, until I'm sure we're in an orange grove maze. I don't know how Ben knows where he's going.

We must be half a mile away from the house when Ben takes a sharp right turn that would have thrown me right into his chest if not for the seat belt cutting into my neck. He pulls over a crest and suddenly we're overlooking a sea of trees and other properties and, beyond that, far in the distance, blue water.

"Wow," escapes my mouth as I stare out at the mesmerizing view, no longer paying attention to the path Ben drives along, until he pulls up in a sandy spot next to a yellow farm truck, its tire flat and a giant rust hole eating into the side panel. Ben kills the engine and we climb out.

"Incredible, isn't it?" I hear him say, and I can feel his eyes on me as I just stand there, staring out at the view. Wandering over to the closest tree, he gently grasps at the small green sphere hanging from it. "You should see this place in spring, with all of these navel orange trees in bloom and the air filled with this flowery-honey smell. It's something else." Glancing over his shoulder, he must see my smirk because he quickly adds, "And don't make fun of me for saying that until you actually see it. And smell it."

"It does sound pretty," I admit, still a bit in awe that a place like this exists so close to my home. "You know a lot about citrus farming?"

Sliding his hands into his jeans casually, he turns and saunters back. "I grew up here and we helped my mama, so, yeah, I know enough." Kicking at the tufts of grass trying in vain to take root among the sand, he explains, "My granddaddy used to say this place is the perfect storm for growing. The soil, the sunshine, and warm nights, and being by the ocean—all of it together makes this the best citrus farming country."

Ben picks up a stick from nearby and slowly circles the old truck, slamming the wood against the metal and poking around the tires, watching the ground around it. "Mama's got eighty-six acres of trees; mostly grapefruit and navel oranges. Some tangerines. The season starts in October and runs through until May. There's no warehousing, no cold storage. The orders come in, we pick them, and then we send them to the packagers. Simple. I'm here most weekends during the season, helping. It cuts labor costs."

Of course he is. For whatever else he is, Ben is a very good son to Wilma and, while I may have teased him about being a mama's boy, seeing this side of him is endearing.

Tossing the stick to the side, he mutters more to himself, "Huh. Normally I get at least one rattler in here."

I shudder as Ben drops the tailgate. It lets out a loud creak in protest; I'm surprised it hasn't seized shut, as everything else about the truck is so old and decrepit. "This used to be my granddaddy's." He settles down on it and then holds his hands to beckon me forward. I relent, letting him grab me by the waist and lift me up next to him as if I weigh nothing at all. "Jake and I used to spend all day racing around out here, and then we'd sneak out of our rooms and hang out all night with friends, drinking under the stars. Those were the good ol' days." Ben leans back until he's lying in the truck bed with his legs dangling over the edge. He nestles his head within his arms, the move pulling his shirt up just enough to expose a strip of hard flesh above his belt line. I don't know when the hell Ben has time to work out, but he must still be doing it a lot. Maybe *I* should make more of an effort, given that he's acting like he's genuinely desperate to see me naked again.

But why am I thinking about impressing Ben? I'm so far from ready for another relationship and, when I *am* ready, it definitely won't be with someone like him. What I'd get from Ben would be exactly what I was looking for in Cancún.

Something easy. Fun. Harmless. With an end date and no expectations.

"Do you see your brothers and sister a lot?" I ask, trying to distract myself from those thoughts as I eye his torso, his shirt strained against its curves.

"Nah, which is crazy, considering how close we were growing up. There's only seven years between Josh and me. Jake and I are eleven months apart. He's out in Mississippi working in the casinos. I talk to him every once in a while but I haven't seen him in . . ." His brow bunches up in thought. "Three years now, I think?"

Is that normal? I have to think that it's not, especially after meeting Ben's mom. I'd think getting the family together would be a priority for her. "And the others?"

"Elsie moved out to San Diego for college and never came back. We talk on the phone once a month or so." I catch a hint of regret in his tone when he admits that. "Rob and Josh are both living in Chicago. I haven't seen them in years, but they send pictures of their kids."

"That's weird, isn't it? I mean," I look over my shoulder in the direction of the house, though I can't see it from where we are, "I'd think your mom would be big on family holidays together." I'm guessing Christmas with Wilma would be just like in the movies, the house smelling of gingerbread and decorated in mistletoe.

"Yeah, it used to be a big deal around here," he says with a sigh, and I feel a hand casually graze my back. "A lot of shit has gone down here, with my dad. No one comes around much anymore." I feel like Ben has more to say but he leaves it at that.

"Not even to see your mom?"

"She went to California a couple of years ago to see Elsie. And she went to Chicago for a weekend to see Rob this past Easter. She ended up having a minor heart attack while she was there. A fluke really, but it's a good thing it wasn't out here, all alone." Ben closes his eyes. "Everyone misses her, but not enough to come back here."

"Why? What happened?" I know I'm prying, but this is Ben. If he doesn't want to tell me, he'll find a way around it.

"Just . . . family drama. My dad's an asshole and he doesn't treat my mama well. He used to treat her *really* bad. You know, cheating on her and stuff. Now he's just an old, pathetic drunk who hates the world." Ben heaves a sigh. "I hate drama. I stay far away from it."

"Switzerland."

"Yup, you got it. Switzerland," he murmurs, seemingly peaceful with his eyes closed. But there's not a hint of a smile touching his lips and that's rare for Ben. It makes me think he may actually be sad. "What about you?" he asks. "Brothers? Sisters? Besides Mason, of course."

"Nope." Annabelle said she didn't want to ruin her body any more than she already had, having me.

"What's with you two, anyway? I can't tell if it's all an act or if you actually hate each other."

"It does seem like that sometimes, doesn't it?" I've often asked myself that question. "I know I drive him nuts with the way I don't hang my jacket up and how I leave coffee stains on the counter. I'm not sure if that's just him being a neat freak or what."

Ben chuckles. "Yeah, I love bugging the shit out of that guy. I go into his office and move all of his stuff around."

"You're the one doing that? He's been blaming me for it for the last two weeks!" I reach out and smack the width of his bare stomach, just above his belt line. I swear, I'd believe he was waiting for it because the hand that was touching my back hooks around my side and pulls me back until I'm lying down, my head resting in the crook of his arm. He chuckles softly. "Keep your hands to yourself or I'll tell my mama that you're trying to sully me."

"She won't believe you," I throw back, trying to squirm away.

When I realize Ben's not letting me go anywhere, I give in and nestle into the cushion of his chest. We lie in silence for a few long minutes as the sun beats down and the cicadas sing. I know a lot of people can't stand those things, but I kind of like the melody they create.

"What about when you two were kids? Did you get along then?"

"Oh, he *definitely* hated me then," I admit. "I remember the day we moved into Jack's house. I had only met him a handful of times and he seemed really quiet. Stupid me—I thought things would be different. It was going to be cool to have a brother . . ." I smile at the memory of nine-year-old Mason, a scrawny kid with glasses and really messy black hair. Funny, all that's changed is that he's a man instead of a kid. "Jack said Mason was just mad at him for 'replacing' his mom—she died of a brain aneurysm a few years before that—and that's why he was hiding in his room all the time." I shrug, a strange sadness enveloping me as I recall the day I realized that Mason would never be like one of those older brothers you see on television, who gives bear hugs and chases all the mean kids away. "One morning when I was about eight, I decided to put all three of his Siamese fighting fish in one tank. I didn't believe they'd actually *kill* each other. But when we came home from school and Mason went to his room, well . . . let's just say he was down to one pet."

"So you were one of *those* little kids." I feel Ben's head shake with disapproval but when I glance up, I see an amused smile.

Ducking back into his chest, I go on. "Mason was *so* mad at me that he went to school the next day and told Chase Butler, this loudmouth dickhead, that my daddy left me like a stray in a truck stop. Well, within ten seconds of walking into the cafeteria, Chase had the entire room chanting 'Stray MacKay.' I knew right away why. After that, I didn't have much love for Mason either." The nickname stuck all through middle school. Kids can be assholes.

"Huh, so that's what he was talking about . . ." Ben murmurs. "Is it true about your dad?"

I pause, picking my words carefully. This just isn't something I talk to with anyone and if Ben were to start teasing me about it . . . "Yeah, I guess. I mean, my dad did leave me in a diner, but I don't remember that day being scary or bad. I just remember taking a long ride in his truck, and chasing chickens and pigs around at some farm. And laughing a lot. The way Annabelle tells the story, though, it sounds like he was this awful man and I was in grave danger. Apparently they had a fight and he took off with me in his truck, saying he was leaving her and never bringing me back. So Annabelle called the police and reported me as kidnapped. My dad already had a record—some stupid bar fight that put a guy in the hospital—so adding a kidnapping charge was bad. I've always believed that's why he left me there." I add in a softer voice, more a confirmation to myself, "That's the only thing that makes sense." We fall into silence as I listen to Ben's strong heartbeat next to my ear, letting the afternoon sun bathe my skin, hoping that it'll scare away the gloom that always creeps in when I think about my father and how he just abandoned me, like I was a cat he didn't want anymore.

"Well, I think you have a pretty good thing going with Jack right now," Ben finally offers, his fingers trailing up and down my arm lightly.

I smile to myself. "Yeah, he's great." I always knew Jack was a good person, who without a doubt truly cared about me. I think that's why it hurt so damn much when he turned his back on me all those years ago. It's also how I knew that what Annabelle did must have hurt him terribly. It's why my relationship with her went even farther downhill after their divorce.

"And Mason's a good guy. I know he can come off as kind of weird, but he's someone you can count on. Maybe now that he's getting laid, he'll relax a bit."

I groan and then cringe. "I forgot about that until now. Thanks." I roll into Ben's chest, inhaling the scent of him—soap, laundry detergent, and a clean sweat from this heat—as I try to block the visual suddenly plaguing me. "Do you think he was a virgin before her?"

Ben chuckles. "No, I'm pretty sure he wasn't. I mean, I didn't pull up a chair and watch, but I think he got his dick wet at a party our first year."

That earns a second cringe. "Jesus, Ben! Does Wilma know you talk to girls with that mouth?"

"My mama would beat me senseless if she ever heard me talking like that to a girl," he admits soberly. "If you can believe it, I do filter myself."

"I *don't* believe it." If these are the kinds of things that come out of his dirty mouth, I shudder at what's hidden up there in that brain of his.

With a chuckle, Ben picks up a piece of my hair and begins twirling the ends in his fingertips. "So tell me a story about red paint."

The sudden change in topic startles me but I recover with a few seconds' pause. "It's an offensive color. Some would say satanic."

"Was the red paint yours?"

I sigh. "My, aren't we dragging all of my skeletons out on this fine, sunny day." I actually don't care if Ben thinks I'm crazy. Given that I just led him into a waylay to gun down my ex and his new wife, I've already done a pretty good job of painting a very unflattering picture of myself. Yet here we are. That tells me that either Ben's not the judgmental type or he's horny enough to screw crazy chicks. Possibly both.

"She moved into my apartment, Ben. She packed my things up in boxes and left them by the door for me." Ben's other hand finds its way to my belt to hook a finger in as he lies quietly, listening to me explain how I walked through each room of the apartment that day and found nothing but the smell of bleach and signs of *her*. Of them, *together*. Red decorative cushions were neatly laid on the couch, replacing my oversized, worn charcoal ones. On the walls, where my photos of rusty old trucks used to hang, were brilliantly hued pictures of Tuscan fields.

Each new item was a blade swiftly plunging into my chest. I no longer existed in Jared's life. Just *two weeks* after the devastating news. And it all looked so effortless. I remember clutching my stomach as I dared make my way back toward the bedroom, the scent of fresh paint catching my nose as I approached. I knew that it was the worst idea ever—that the outcome was guaranteed disaster that would cripple me. But I had to see it to know for sure. It was like walking head-on into an oncoming train. And when I pushed open the door . . .

The train ran right over me.

Everything about our bedroom felt different. Wrong. From the rearranged furniture to the red poppy–print sheets to the picture mocking me from above the iron headboard. The headboard that I had gripped as Jared lay beneath, staring up at me with heated green eyes *so many* times, while he told me he loved me.

I couldn't look away from that giant black-and-white picture of the two of them lying in bed, white sheets strategically covering their nudity as their limbs coiled around each other's bodies, even as it gutted me. I knew it predated our time together because my name was missing from his left shoulder.

The freshly painted crimson walls only served to magnify the intimacy of the photograph, to the point where they may as well have been lying in bed right there, in person. Gritting my teeth, I reached over and yanked the closet door open. Where my clothes used to dangle haphazardly, a new wardrobe hung neatly.

My teeth gnashed against each other as I threw open the top dresser drawer to find lace panties and bras mingling cozily with Jared's boxer briefs.

It was official. The bitch had *moved in*.

Tears streamed down my cheeks as I slammed the drawer shut, fighting the urge to scream. She should have had the decency to wait until I was gone! She should have had the decency not to touch my fucking stuff! As I lay curled up in the fetal position in Lina's apartment next door, crying over losing the love of my life, Caroline was playing Martha-thieving-Stewart, her snaky fingers defiling my belongings as she quickly packed me up. As she took over my life.

In that moment, as I eyed the clothes, the bed, all her pretty little "girly" things, the rage detonating inside of me had only one target. And it was a volatile type of rage that wasn't going to listen to reason or consider consequences.

All it wanted to do was dull my agonizing heartbreak, soothe my wounded pride.

And the can of red paint sitting in the corner, taunting me, was the perfect antidote.

There's a long pause after I divulge some of the finer details to Ben. Why I told him all of that, I don't know. But now that I have, I realize that it felt kind of good. A relief. He knows exactly who I am. What I'm capable of.

Ben's arm tightens slightly, bringing me closer to him, as he sighs. "You still love him?"

"I don't know. I think so," I answer truthfully. "And trust me, I know how stupid that is, so you don't have to remind me." The hollowness still swells in my chest every time I even think about Jared, every time I find myself checking to see if he has responded to my last message. I loved that dark-haired guy so much that even when things were good, it hurt. I loved him more than I thought ever possible and more than was probably healthy. I used to mock girls who couldn't stop themselves from clinging onto their man's limbs in public, who giggled and cooed and batted starry eyes.

But when I met Jared, I turned into one of them.

"Well, for what it's worth, I think he's an idiot."

"I'm not having sex with you."

"Oh, come on! No lies, no commitments. No fear of love. Just the best day of your life with a *nice* guy who happens to be drop-dead gorgeous."

I can't help the deep, throaty laugh that erupts from me. "You're such an arrogant pig."

"Fair enough. Can we at least fool around?" He lifts and curls his strong body, giving that appealing mouth access to my ear. "Because I know you want to."

I shiver as the depth of his voice courses through my limbs. My denial—a lie, I'm silently accepting—is on the tip of my tongue when my phone starts ringing. Ben falls back with a groan as I pull the phone out of my pocket, holding it up to read the caller ID, just to make sure. "What on earth is *she* doing calling me?"

"Annabelle Lecter?" Ben reads the screen.

"The woman eats male hearts. It's fitting." I hit "ignore" and tuck the phone back in my pocket. With my ear against Ben's chest, his loud boom of laughter is all the louder. I can't help but wonder what Annabelle would want. I left Jacksonville nine months ago and she hasn't made any effort to reach out to me before today. Not normal mother behavior. Not surprising Annabelle behavior.

"I take it you and her aren't best friends?" Ben asks lightly, his attempts at getting into my pants effectively stalled.

"I haven't talked to her since I moved to Miami and Jack made me call her to let her know."

"That's been, what . . ."

"It'll be a year in January."

He snorts. "How is that even possible? I talk to Mama every single day."

"That's because you have June Cleaver for a mom and I have Joan Crawford." There can be no doubt where I inherited my temper. More than one dish has been thrown across a room with Annabelle's anger. That's a side she guards well, though, not wanting the outside world to know she's anything but the refined socialite she portrays.

"Did you have a big fight?"

I sigh. "My entire life feels like one big fight with her. She wanted a debutante daughter and she got . . ." I gesture at myself.

"A daughter with piercings and sometimes purple hair who rides a motorcycle and can describe the back of a cop car in detail," he finishes for me.

"Annabelle wears Gucci and eats beef tartare. She goes to the opera and collects ice wine."

He nods slowly as if in understanding. "You must have been one hell of a rebellious teenager."

"We've been at odds long before my teenage years. Annabelle was never cut out to be a mother. All she cares about are appearances, money, and Annabelle." I close my eyes and sigh, wanting to get off the topic. "I feel so relaxed out here. This place is like a cross between *Forrest Gump* and *Anne of Green Gables*."

"I don't remember Tom Hanks picking oranges."

"No, I mean . . . just that house and the big ol' trees and the country air . . . Shut up. You know what I mean."

Ben's hand starts fiddling with my hair again. "Yeah. Right now it is. Soon, the orders start rolling through and then it gets busy. We get orders from all over the country. Since I had the website and online system updated a few years back, it's been busy." He sighs. "Between inspecting and sampling and picking . . . hell, even just going around to check the trees for disease or problems, it's getting to be too much. Especially for a fifty-one-year-old lady who's had a heart attack to manage on her own. I wish she'd just sell and divorce his pathetic ass."

"She won't?"

"No. This place is her life. She'd be buried here if it were allowed. And she's hung up on a bunch of words she said in church one day, so she lets him stay."

"I think those are called vows, Ben," I remind him dryly, rolling my head until my chin is resting on his chest so I can see his face.

"Call them what you want. They're a bunch of words that

trap people into thinking they have to be miserable for the rest of their lives."

Not everyone. "So I take it you won't be saying 'I do' anytime soon?" I ask lightly.

He closes his eyes again, a crooked smirk dimpling one cheek. "What do you think?"

"Have you even had a girlfriend, Ben?" Has he ever held someone in his arms all night, laughing and sharing his deepest secrets? Has he ever let someone cry on his shoulder or held her tight when life dealt him a shitty hand? Trusted her with everything, wanted to be someone she could trust? Has he ever watched the clock, waiting until he could see her again?

"Once, for two weeks, in high school."

No, probably not. "So you've really made an effort," I tease.

"Commitment just isn't for me." He says it so simply. Like, "Broccoli isn't for me."

"That's too bad, Ben. I think some foolish woman out there could maybe make you a blissful idiot one day."

He opens one eye to look down on me for a long moment, pondering something. "Yeah, but what if she's evil, like you? I wouldn't want to risk pissing her off and getting shot in the ass." He pinches my side as he says that, as if letting me know that he's only teasing.

"Funny." I know today's paintball incident isn't going to die quietly with Ben but right now, I don't want to be reminded about the few seconds before I opened fire, when I could hear them together, when I knew that Jared was inside her.

The dull ache in my chest is coming back. I need an effective diversion. "Speaking of evil . . ." I pull the key that I swiped from the dune buggy out of my pocket and wave it above his face. "It's going to be a long walk back for you when I leave you stranded out here."

"Are you fucking kidding me . . ." Laughing as he tries to grab it from me, I quickly shove it back into my pocket. "Really? Have you not figured me out yet?" As if to prove a point, Ben has me on my back in the truck bed, both of my arms easily pinned above my head by one of his in seconds. "Oh, wait. Just in case . . ." He shifts his body, forcing my thighs around his hips. "Wouldn't want you injuring the goods for a second time today. Not before you get full use of them."

"I would never stoop to that level," I exclaim with mock insult.

"Really?" His blond brow arches severely.

I offer a sweet smile. Truthfully, I was just getting my knee ready.

Feeling confident—I know because he's staring down at me with a grin that could charm the pants off half the women in the office, married or not—he reaches down with his free hand. I feel a tug as his fingers dig into my pocket and begin rooting around. I could try to buck him off me but, well, given my position, I honestly think he's hoping for that. And so I remain still as he takes his time, until he's got the old silver thing dangling off one finger in front of me.

"You can get off of me any time now, you know," I remind him.

With a sigh, he shifts his weight slightly as his free arm comes up to slide beneath my head, providing a cushion against the hard metal. "I could," he agrees, those brilliant blue eyes searching my eyes, my nose, my mouth, as if evaluating me.

And then he leans down and kisses me. No hesitation at all, as if there's no way I couldn't possibly want Ben Morris's tongue in my mouth, sliding its way around mine in a smooth, practiced dance. The problem is that in this moment, out here in the middle of nowhere, with reality so far away and the tranquillity of the grove, I do want it. Now I can see why Ben was so eager to give me a "tour" rather than head back to work.

He pulls away to peer down at me with a knowing smile.

"You do realize that normal friends and work colleagues don't do this sort of thing, right?"

"I like to bend the rules." He releases my wrists, freeing his to snake up the front of my shirt, lifting the material as he goes. The guy clearly has a goal in mind because his fingers have unfastened my bra without any stalling and pushed it away within seconds. "Oh, thank God," he says through a groan, his head dipping down to grasp onto the ring with his mouth.

As I reach up under that soft T-shirt of his to feel the tightness in his back, as I feel Ben's tongue coil around the ring and tickle me, I echo his words in my head. *Yes, thank God.*

He lifts his body ever so slightly, his hand reaching down to undo the top button and zipper of my jeans with a casual flick. "I never did take full inventory of your piercings."

When I make no indications of an answer, that wide grin takes over his face and I know what he's planning even before I feel the first tug on my jeans. They're too tight for him to squeeze a hand in. He wastes no time sliding off the tailgate to stand in front of me with intent written all over his face. Reaching down, he gets a good hold of my jeans and begins shimmying them down.

And that's when the sudden rumble of an engine and the squeak of brakes sounds.

"Who is it?" I ask as Ben's attention whips to his left. I can't ignore the disappointment flooding me, a dull ache in my lower belly forming.

His head tips back as he looks up to the sky. "Who do you think?" With a deep groan, his eyes rake over my exposed chest. He bends down for one last chaste kiss on my lips and then steps away, leaving me to button my pants and affix my bra and shirt just as a red pickup truck with a thick white stripe around the center pulls up.

Wilma hops out of the high cab quite easily for someone her

age. "Benjamin James Morris, did you bring this young lady out here in the hot sun without anything to drink?"

Scratching the back of his head lazily, he mutters, "I guess I did. Sorry."

I purse my lips tightly. Considering what Ben brought me out here in the hot sun to do, I think a cold drink was definitely not on his mind.

"It's like I didn't raise you at all, sometimes." Coming around the other side, she opens the passenger door and pulls a cooler off the bench. Ben's at her side in seconds, relieving her of the weight. "Mama, you know you shouldn't be lifting heavy things."

"Oh, hush. I'm not an invalid. One tiny heart attack isn't going to kill me." Ben's stern glare of disapproval only makes her smile wider at him. I can see where he got his impish charm from. But I can also feel the weight of his fear at Wilma's words. In just one afternoon, I can see how this woman might leave a sizeable hole in many people's lives when she's gone.

"I wasn't sure what you'd like, Reese, so there's some water, sweet tea, and Coke in there. I also packed a light snack. Some scones and homemade marmalade. Ben's favorite."

"Of course it is," I tease, reaching up to pinch Ben's cheek playfully as he sets the cooler down on the tailgate. "Thank you so much."

"How'd you know where to find us?" Ben asks as he fishes through the selection.

A knowing smirk curls Wilma's lips. "Because this is your favorite spot in the grove. Did you honestly think I didn't know it was you and Jake leaving beer cans out here?" She looks at me and shakes her head. "You know, Ben and his brother would sneak out here at night—thinking I had no idea—and then try to convince me that the grove workers were drinking on the job. Oh, but I wasn't *ever* allowed to confront or fire them without better evidence. My future football-player-slash-lawyer was so worried about potential lawsuits for doing that."

Ben has the decency to look sheepish as he sucks back a gulp of water. "So, is that why you came out here, Mama?"

She gives him a pointed look but then says, "I really need you to check out that tractor before you go."

"Sure," he offers, pulling his phone out to check the time, and heaves a sigh. "I didn't realize how late it was."

"Well, maybe you should just stay for dinner." I hear the hopefulness in her voice. She really likes having her son here. I'm betting she'd love to have her other children here, too.

"Yeah, I'm sorry, Mama. But I'm just learning the ropes at work. I've already lost a lot of time today."

By the tone of his voice and his sincere look, I can tell he's disappointed. I guess I didn't really help with that, given the change in plans I forced this morning, all in the name of revenge. "We'd love to stay," I interrupt, elbowing Ben gently in the ribs. "I'm already stuck with you all week. I guess they'll be long days."

He peers down at me for a moment, an unreadable look on his face.

And then he winks.

Chapter 14

■ ■ ■

BEN

"I'll remind you of this the next time you mock me for taking her cooking home." I give Reese's ass a playful slap as she passes me on the porch, her arms laden with leftovers.

"I didn't. I mocked you for being a mama's boy, and that still stands," she clarifies, sticking her tongue out at me.

Since my bold move earlier today, out in the grove, I've been itching to get my hands on her again. I'm seconds from chasing her down the steps when my mama appears with a box of her homemade jams and preserves. "These are for Reese," she clarifies, shoving it into my chest. "Carry them for her, darling."

"There's enough for me, right?" I ask, counting out eight jars.

I get a smack upside the head for that—I don't know how Mama, at five-foot-one, always manages to reach me, at six-foot-three, when she needs to do that.

With her arms free, she meets Reese at the bottom of the porch. "Don't you be a stranger now, you here? We'd love to see you here again." Pushing a strand of fallen hair off Reese's face, she grasps the girl's shoulders and leans in to lay a kiss on her cheek.

I've only ever seen Reese unnerved twice—the day we ran into each other in her office and yesterday, running into her ex.

Now, though, she's peering up at me with wide, questioning eyes, looking as stiff as a tree. That doesn't dissuade my mama, who rubs her back as she adds, "And the 'we' includes Ben."

Oh, hell. Why'd she have to go and say that? It's true, but, still.

Caramel eyes flash toward me, a sudden wicked gleam in them. "Only if Ben lets me drive that dune buggy out next time."

"Oh, Ben. You didn't let her drive?" Mama scolds, a stern furrow in her brow.

Of course, Reese hams it up, her bottom lip pouting out just enough to look sad without seeming pathetic. "I begged, but he said something about women not belonging behind the wheel."

My mouth drops as Reese scampers away with a howl of laughter, just as I get a second—gentle—smack upside the head. "I think you've met your match," Mama murmurs, adding, "I like her."

"That's because she humored you by going through my baby album."

"And I'll be sure to dig up your awkward years for next time," she retorts, beaming.

I shouldn't let this go on. "She's just a friend, Mama," I remind her.

"Yes, I heard you before, son." Her voice is light and airy. Dismissive.

"I'm serious. Don't go booking any ceremonies with your pastor. Reese is the stepdaughter of my boss and if I get caught with her as anything more than just friends, my ass is gone from Warner. You don't want me getting fired, do you? I'll end up settling fishing disputes in Alaska." I pull her frail body toward me, remembering a lifetime of car rides to football practice before the sun was up, when she was struggling to balance running this place and five kids in their teenage years. The woman has given me so much. "*Then* who's gonna come out here and take care of you?" Sure as hell none of my brothers. They've all but washed their hands of this situation.

"You don't worry about me. I'd rather see you happy."

"I *am* happy."

"With a wife," she clarifies sternly.

"Well, I can guarantee Reese isn't looking to become a wife again anytime soon."

"Again?" Mama repeats, her brow arched.

"Yeah." I give her a knowing look as I add, "Until her husband cheated on her."

Mama makes a *tsk*ing sound. A pause, and then she murmurs wryly, "You didn't seem too worried about losing your job out in the grove earlier today."

I open my mouth but she hushes me with, "Oh, Benjamin. I've watched you chasing girls since you were six years old, so don't pretend otherwise. I can only imagine what you've been up to all these years, working in that club. This one's different, though, isn't she?"

"No." The bells. The fucking church bells are ringing in her head. I just know it.

"I'm your mama, Ben. I know when you're lying." She pauses. "You haven't been this relaxed at home in years."

I can do nothing but sigh. She's right, to be honest. Usually when I turn into this driveway, all I can think about is how lonely the place is, how much fun I *used* to have here. But today, I got to see it all new again through Reese's eyes, which lit up as she took it in.

I glance over to see her ass sticking out from the backseat as she loads the food in and I chuckle, a flash of Cancún hitting me. "Think whatever you want, Mama, but don't get your hopes up."

"I don't know why you have to be so thick-headed about settling down."

"You know exactly why," I remind her softly, leaning down to kiss her forehead. "See you next weekend." I'm halfway toward the car when I remember why she called me. "That tractor needs a good tune-up is all. Don't let Bert sell you on anything more." That tractor is as old as I am. Years of watching Granddaddy and then Josh working on it has taught me the basics.

"Okay. Thanks, son."

"No problem." Mama shouldn't have to deal with any of this. That sorry hump of flesh hiding out in that old barn should be man enough to do it. Unfortunately, he proved what kind of person he is years ago.

Reaching Reese, I slide the box into the backseat.

"She could sell this stuff," Reese murmurs, lifting out one of the jars. "She could have her own little shop, like in a farmers' market or something."

"Yeah, she could," I agree. "A lot of groves have markets on their property nowadays. She talked about doing that but, again, it's just more work and she's all alone."

Reese ponders that, a crooked curl of her lips. "Too bad. That barn would be a great place for it." She points out the old building.

I fight against the shudder that threatens. It happens every time I think about stepping in there again. "It's full of saws and shit. My dad's woodworking tools."

She nods slowly and I hear the unspoken question. *Why didn't he come eat with us? Why hasn't he come out to say hello?* I already told her more than I usually tell people.

"We should get going." Waving a hand at the backseat, I add, "And we'll pretend like you're getting all of this. Maybe I'll let you have one jar if you're *really* nice to me on the ride home." My eyes graze over her body. I can't even think about the afternoon in the grove. It's torture. In fact, most of this day has been torture. It's also been a ton of fun.

An impish grin passes across her face. "Wilma! Ben says he's not sharing if I don't—"

I hug her from behind, pulling her tight against me as I muffle her yells with my hand. "You brat!" I'm rewarded with a wet tongue against my palm. I start laughing. "After Cancún, you think a bit of spit on my hand is going to gross me out?" Sharp teeth digging into the meaty part of my forefinger a moment later has me jumping back and checking for blood, a curse trying to push its way through my gritted teeth.

"He'll do no such thing, honey. And if he does, you call me right away. You've got the number now," Mama calls back from the porch.

What? They're swapping phone numbers? Ah, shit. I'm about to ask when the hell my mother gave Reese her number when the sound of doors rolling on casters fills my ears. The hairs on the nape of my neck instantly spike. I turn just in time to see my father stumble out from inside the barn, his only hand wrapped around a bottle of Wild Turkey, the dank darkness of his workshop a fitting backdrop beyond. The remains of his other arm hangs there, the stump that begins just above his elbow proudly displayed in an old, navy-blue T-shirt.

He normally goes out of his way to keep it covered with a long sleeve, even in the hottest of Florida days, so I know this is intentional. A reminder, for me.

"Joshua, come say hello to Reese," Mama calls out. I hope Reese can't hear the strain in her voice. Mama's worried that we'll start fighting, but there's no need. I have nothing left in me for this man. No hatred. Certainly no love. All of that was lost long ago. I'm over him.

Joshua Morris Senior takes slow, steady steps forward and gives Reese a nod, his eyes drifting over her and then shifting to me again.

"Hi, Mr. Morris. I'm a co-worker of Ben's," Reese explains. By her voice she sounds at ease, but by her shrewd eyes, narrowing as she regards him, I know she's anything but. I understand why. I may look like my dad but the hard, cold glare in his eyes separates us completely. Almost hesitantly, she adds, "Jack Warner is my stepfather."

A slow, wicked smile creeps over my dad's face. "Earning your way to the top the hard way, Ben?" he slurs.

"Joshua!" My mother's sharp, surprised cry pulls his attention away from us.

"My dishes are in the barn, Wilma," he mutters almost incoherently, hanging his head as he turns and picks his path up to the house, staggering all the way up the stairs to disappear inside.

My mama's face is a mask of sorrow and embarrassment. "I'm so sorry, Reese. Ben and Joshua just . . . He . . . he must have had a bad day." Mama stumbles over a suitable apology, though nothing about that explanation would make sense to anyone with half a brain. I can't keep the snort from escaping. Yeah. Real bad day, staring at his tools and nursing a bottle of whiskey all while hating the world and this "shitty life" that was handed to him. Mama waves us off and follows him inside, but not without first mouthing, "I love you," my way.

It's not until we're both seated in my Jetta and I've cranked the engine that Reese speaks up. "So, your father's charming."

I wondered how she'd respond to that display. "I warned you, didn't I?"

She seems to ponder that for a moment. "Annabelle's usually four gin martinis in by dinnertime. But she doesn't have a 'problem,'" she mock-clarifies, making air quotes with her fingers. After a pause, "How'd he lose his arm?"

"Accident in his wood shop about nine years ago." I really don't want to get into this with Reese. She's got her own family issues and if I throw mine into the mix, we'll become all about feelings instead of fun.

She lets out a low whistle. "A carpenter losing his arm? That's a raw deal."

"Yeah." I throw my car into first gear and have us heading down the driveway, the oaks I used to climb as a child—when I was already completely disillusioned about my parents' marriage—providing us with cover along the way. "He definitely took it hard."

■ ■ ■

"I can't believe you're letting me take it all without even a blow job." Reese's eyes brighten as she surveys the contents once again, this time standing on her front porch.

"How about we don't joke about shit like that with Jack in the house, okay?" His Escalade is in the driveway, so I know he's home. That's the last thing I need him to hear. Plus Reese just saying the words "blow job" is killing me right now. "And consider it fair trade for all the hours you're going to be putting in with me this week."

"Do you know who loves raspberry jam?" One eyebrow arches expectantly, holding up a red jar. "Mason."

I chuckle, already seeing where her evil little mind is moving. "Let me guess . . ."

"Maybe I'll eat it right out of the jar in front of him. With a spoon." She grins viciously, and I have to stifle my loud laughter.

"He's giving it to your best friend now, so maybe you two should try to get along."

She cringes. "Right, I forgot about that. Thanks for reminding me . . . again."

Wary of standing here any longer, I back up a few steps. "I'd better get out of here before Jack fires me." If I don't, I'm liable to do something stupid. Like kiss her, because that's all I've been thinking about doing the entire ride home. Jeez, I need to get laid. It's been weeks. That's a new record for me.

"Not with this, he won't." Reese waves a tinfoil package of meatloaf leftovers in my face. "In fact, he may even sell me to you if he thinks it'll get him more of Wilma's home cooking because unless Mason's cooking, the only thing that gets used around here is the microwave."

"Mason cooks for you guys?"

She rolls her eyes. "Sometimes. Tofu and seaweed and . . ." Her face scrunches up with displeasure. "I don't eat it." Reaching behind her to grab the door handle, she stalls a bit and then offers, "Thanks for coming with me to shoot my ex and his wife today."

"Anytime."

"I had fun today." And then she frowns as if she's surprised by that realization.

"It *was* fun," I admit with a smile. "I can't remember the last time I spent an entire day with a woman without getting laid. Hell, even with sex, I don't think I've ever spent an entire day with a woman."

She shakes her head at me but there's a smile at the end of it. "Where are you going now?"

"To a cold shower," I admit, taking several reluctant steps backward, away from her. I've never been so excited to jerk off in my life. "See you tomorrow morning?"

With a wink and a fake lusty voice she offers, "Think of me," before cracking the door and stepping through.

And . . . I'm rock hard again.

Like I wasn't already going to be thinking about her.

Chapter 15

...

REESE

"I come bearing homemade preserves from the Indian River grove district." I drop the box down on the counter in front of Jack.

Newspaper in one hand, chopsticks in the other, he first glances at the crate and then up over his bifocals at me. "You paid for those, right?"

"Paid?" I pause for effect and then wink. "They were a gift. There's some homemade cooking here, too."

That piques his interest. Jack's a lot of things, but a good cook is not one of them. He frees a hand to reach in and pull out a jar. "What were you doing in the Indian River grove district today?" His brow furrows as he reads the label, adding, "At the Bernard *Morris* Grove." By the suspicious look on his face, he's already made the connection.

"Oh, you know . . . just helping out a friend." I leave it at that, reaching for the chocolate milk jug in the fridge, feeling his inquisitive eyes boring into my back. "Are Mason and Lina here?"

With a sigh, he lets the question that I know is on the tip of his tongue go and answers mine. "They went out to dinner and a movie. They seem to get along well. She even took him shopping today for some new clothes and things."

"Don't get ahead of yourself. Lina will discover how weird your son is soon enough and run for the hills."

He chuckles. "Well, she's best friends with *you*, so she must be *extremely* tolerant." Pausing to watch me fill a glass—I drink out of the jug only when Mason's around nowadays—he finally asks, "Have you spoken to your mother in a while?"

"No. Why?"

He pulls his glasses off. "She called the office this afternoon, looking for you. Asked that you call her back as soon as you got home." He watches me carefully. "It sounded important."

"Huh." First my cell phone, now Jack? If this were a typical woman, there'd be cause for concern. But what is important in the world of Annabelle usually doesn't translate to important. Though I have to admit that I'm intrigued.

"Yes . . . 'huh.' My thoughts exactly." His mouth twists with distaste as he asks, "Please do call her back, sooner rather than later. I'd prefer not to get daily phone calls from my ex-wife." Once Annabelle gets something in her head, she's like a dog on a bone.

That's why I immediately pull my phone out. "Well, let's just see what Mommy Dearest wants, shall we?"

Her deceptively soft voice—still seductive at forty—fills my ear on the second ring. "Reese?"

"Yes."

"Didn't you have your phone with you today?"

"I did."

A pause. "So you screened me."

"Nice to hear from you, too. It's been a while. I just got home and Jack told me you called him."

"I'm surprised he gave you the message."

A sharp pain shoots up my jaw and I realize that I'm gnashing my teeth. That's always been a problem for me around Annabelle. At one time, I even wore a mouth guard at night because I was grinding my teeth while I slept. It wasn't until I moved out that the constant throb abated. She's probably into the martinis tonight. It's sometimes hard to tell because she holds her alcohol so well. "What do you need?" That's what this is about—let's be honest.

She huffs a sigh. "Ian and I are holding a charity ball in November and we think it would look best if our *entire* family is in attendance." So this is a political thing. I guess she's found someone perfectly suited to her, as concerned about his appearance as she is about hers. "I'll send a suitable dress for you to wear. Have you gained any weight? And I hope your hair isn't still that hideous color. You'll need to have that fixed, if it is."

I roll my eyes but don't respond.

"I have the perfect escort for you. He's a—"

"No." We've been down this road before. When I was sixteen, she made me go to a stuffy country-club Christmas party with one of Barry's law firm partners' sons. The guy was a twenty-four-year-old med student with aspirations of becoming a gynecologist. Call me sexist—I don't really care—but in this day and age of equal rights and women becoming doctors, I wonder about men who choose to poke around in vaginas all day long as a career. Naturally, I spent the entire meal interrogating him on his intentions and his motivations.

Much to Annabelle's horror.

"Well, I can hardly trust you to bring a suitable man with you. Look what you married."

"I'm not going, Annabelle."

"What do you mean you're not going?" That slight, distinctive whine escapes now. She has definitely been drinking.

I've never said no to Annabelle, as much as I've always wanted to. Sure, I've put up a fuss, I've made myself out to be the spoiled little rich brat, I've usually made great strides to damage our relationship further by the end of the night, but I've never just given her a flat-out no. I'm not sure if I ever believed it was an option.

And now that I have said no, she has no idea how to handle

it. "That's impossible. There will be publicity behind this and eyes on us and on me, on our family values."

Annabelle and family values? There's an oxymoron.

"I'm sure you'll do just fine without me there."

"After all that I've done for you—"

"I'll think about it and let you know." There's no way in hell I'm going, but I've picked a bad time to argue with her. The woman is the master at painting herself the wounded war hero. When she's drunk, it's tenfold. I can't deal with it right now. I live four hours away from her anyway. *Good luck, Annabelle.* "I've gotta go."

"Fine." The phone clicks, leaving me staring at my phone in bewilderment.

"Anything important?" Jack asks, feigning disinterest.

"Yes. Earth-shattering. Annabelle's having a party and she wants me there to make her look like the respectable, loving mother."

"You don't have to do anything that you don't want to do, Reesie."

I smile. "I know. Thanks, Jack. I'm tired. Going to call it a night." I collect the two jars of raspberry jam from the box. "If you see Jiminy Cricket tonight, tell him I have something he wants and am open to negotiations beginning in the a.m."

Jack watches me pass, shaking his head. "Weren't you two going to start acting like adults?"

"Soon."

■ ■ ■

Lying in bed, I find myself staring up at the ceiling for a good hour, trying to rid myself of the ache that comes with thinking about Jared and what I saw in the paintball hut. But there was a part of today—a few hours, out in the grove with Ben—when I felt steady, like I'd stepped off of this emotional roller coaster I've been riding. There's magic in the air up there, in the walls of that big old house. I can feel it. The kind of magic that has protected generations of life from its precious beginning until its fragile end; has watched love blossom and then die; has listened to the sobs of a broken heart and the eventual laughter again. And much like the family within it, though slightly run-down, it still stands proud, welcoming new people into its life.

Between the silent strength and comfort of the house and the expanse of the grove, I found myself able to take deep, lung-filling inhales of fresh air, after months of only shallow draws of something stale and altogether unsatisfying.

Or maybe it wasn't the magic or the fresh air at all. Maybe it was the company.

On impulse, I grab my phone and scan through my speed dial.

"You missed me that much already?" a very groggy Ben answers.

I feel my mouth pull into a smile of its own accord. "How was your shower?"

He heaves a sigh. "Quick and productive. I was almost asleep." I'm immediately hit with an image of him stretched out in his bed. Naked. This isn't good. Those kinds of fantasies were always reserved for one guy and one guy only. "What's up?"

"Nothing. Just . . ." I hesitate. "Thanks for today."

"You already said that." There's a smile in his voice.

"Right, I did." He's going to think I'm an idiot.

A slightly awkward pause hangs over our conversation and then Ben asks, "What are you wearing?"

I roll my eyes. It's such a cheesy line, but it makes me want to laugh because Ben is saying it. "Nothing at all. Good night." I click "end" before he has a chance to respond.

■ ■ ■

A giant Starbucks coffee—still hot—and an orange await me on my desk on Monday morning with a note:

Black tar for a black heart.

I smile.

I'm still smiling as a knock on my door has me turning.

And staring, wide-eyed.

It's Mason. But not Mason. Because Mason is a geeky buttoned-up, skinny-tie-wearing, thick-glasses, boring-hair kind of guy. The guy in front of me has transformed into something one may call, at minimum, cute. His unruly curls are tamed and styled and the trendy new collared shirt and pants make him look not quite so wiry. And those glasses are gone, revealing large olive-green eyes. I've never seen him without his big, thick glasses.

"How was the rest of your day? Besides the alien abduction, of course," I ask, savoring the rich, dark flavor of my coffee as I eye him suspiciously.

Mason's cheeks redden. "It was fine. Can I talk to you for a second?"

Mason has always been only too happy to abide by my "stay the hell away from me in the morning" rule. "This must be important. Take a seat. Tell me what you've done with my *loving* stepbrother."

He pushes the door shut and strolls over, inspecting the chair before sitting in it, folding his hands in his lap nervously. His eyes roam my desk. "You must have half the firm's caseload sitting on your desk."

"That's what I get for being smart and efficient. Out with it. Between you and Ben, everyone's going to start thinking my mornings are open season." I've already seen the law bot pass by twice, her head bobbing like a pigeon this way and that, trying to get a good angle on which case file I might be working on.

"Jack asked me what was going on between you and Ben."

Unease twists my stomach. If Mason ever wanted to get even with me, now would be the time. "What'd you say?"

He shrugs. "I told him that you guys were just friends."

"Huh. Good."

"I'm assuming that's a lie?"

"No, we are *just* friends." Friends that may fool around a bit, but . . . Jack didn't ask for specifics.

The small frown tells me he doesn't believe me. "Okay, good, because Ben's not the kind of guy you want to get hung up on. I like him. I mean, he's a good friend, but he's not one to commit and I wouldn't want anyone getting hurt."

"Anyone . . . meaning me?" Does Mason actually care?

Mason squirms in his seat, his hands automatically reaching for his glasses, which aren't there. "I know you've had it rough with all . . . that."

As awkward as he is, I have to admit, this new alien-abducted version of Mason is kind of nice. I nod once but keep my mouth shut for fear of saying something to ruin the *Twilight Zone* moment.

"So . . ." He pauses, strumming his fingers on the chair arm.

I should have known he was being nice to me for a reason. "What do you want, Mason?"

Clearing his throat, he finally gets to the point. "Hey, what does Lina really like to do? You know, to have fun."

"Why don't you just ask her? I mean, you've been together for, what, almost *three months*?"

He shrugs. "Because I want to surprise her. So . . . Help me out here."

"You could go to Vegas and get married. That'd be a surprise."

He groans with annoyance, but then I see a flash of something else as his eyes settle on me once again. Sadness, pity—I'm not sure. I purse my lips. And decide that if Lina is somehow happy with him, then, well, I need to start being a better friend about this. "She loves planes. Take her to that airplane museum."

He nods slowly. "Cool." A pause, and then his eyes narrow. "Hey, you're not lying to me, right? Because if I find out that the sight of planes causes her spontaneous seizures, that won't be funny."

I snort. "No, if I were screwing with you, I'd tell you to take her to a butterfly museum."

His brow puckers up. "Butterflies? I thought everyone liked butterflies."

"Not Lina. Their little bodies freak her out."

"Oh." He snorts. "Okay, thanks." He moves to stand but stalls, clearing his throat. "For what it's worth, I'm sorry for calling you a demon spawn when Jack and your mom split up."

It clicks. Lina has got to him. That's what this is all about. It must be. Standing, he makes his way to the door. "Oh, and that red substance you used to write 'Redrum' on my computer screen is . . . ?"

"Raspberry jam."

"Right." A slow, thoughtful smile stretches across his face. "I love raspberry jam."

"I know." On impulse, I reach into my drawer and pull out a jar. Tossing it to him, I watch as he fumbles once, twice, three times, just barely securing it in his non-athletic grasp before it smashes against the ground.

With a sheepish grin, he holds it up with a crooked, "Hey, I actually caught it!" smile.

"Oh, and Ben's the one moving your stuff around in your office. It's not me."

He rolls his eyes, a very non-Mason thing to do. "Thanks."

The second he steps out of my office, I dial Lina's number. "Are you and Mason plotting to kill me or are you just that good in bed?"

"The latter, though if you don't start being nice to him, I will give him enough ammunition to take you down permanently," comes her deadpan response without a moment's hesitation, as if she were ready for my call.

"That's highly prejudicial."

"It goes both ways. I told him that I'm not going to be the

buffer between you two, so you need to start acting like normal siblings."

"Says the only child." A knock on the glass distracts me. Ben standing at the window, pointing at the red golf shirt he's wearing, that appealing broad smile on his face. I grab the orange and toss it at the glass where his head is. Mouthing, "Good aim," he winks and strolls away, that smile so infuriating and yet sparking within me the need to giggle.

I'm still giggling to myself when Natasha pokes her head in.

■ ■ ■

Are you free for lunch today?

I stare at my phone to see if I've read Jared's message correctly. *Shit!* What do I do? Reaching for my desk phone to call Lina a second time this morning, I hang up immediately. There's no point calling her or Nicki. Or anyone. Because I know exactly what the right answer is.

Tap, tap, tap . . . the pen in my hand flicks back and forth against the stack of folders as I toil over this. I have so much to do for Ben, I really should work through my lunch break . . .

Café. Noon?

His responding "yes" comes within seconds.

■ ■ ■

"You should try the key lime," the brown-haired waitress suggests, placing a plate of chocolate pecan pie in front of me. I swear, the way they all push it around here, you'd think they were trading key lime stock. I offer her a tight smile and ask her to bring my check, my eyes fixated on the street entrance. Jared has always been notoriously late but half an hour is ridiculous, especially without at least a message.

I'm beginning to think he ditched me when I hear a familiar deep voice say, "Still not willing to try something new?"

I'm instantly pulled from my silent lamenting and straight into that special place where heaven and hell cross paths, where mint-green irises make my heart skip one, two, three beats before it kicks into high gear, despite my best efforts to feel nothing at all. "I stick with what I know."

He smiles in response. "I'm sorry I'm late."

I hold my breath as I watch him pull the empty chair out to sit. "No problem. I've got to get back to work soon, though." I was already planning on using work as an excuse for a quick exit, should I need it. Facing him now, I know that I probably will. That pain is an angry bubble swelling once again, only it's mixed with confusion and fear and . . . yes, anticipation.

He flinches as he adjusts himself in his seat. "I was at this awesome paintball field north of the city yesterday and took a close-range shot to the ass."

More like thirty shots, if you want to be specific. I purse my lips to keep my vindictive smile from outing me.

"You should go there sometime. I think you'd like it."

"I'll look into that," I manage to get out with a wobble. The only thing keeping me from howling with laughter right now is replaying the visual I have in my head of the moments before we actually attacked, when I was ready to turn and run, listening to *that.* Thank God for my mask, or Ben would have seen my tears.

There's a long pause as Jared takes in the other tables, his hands softly strumming against the surface. That's a nervous gesture of his. "This is kind of awkward, isn't it?" he finally admits with a lazy chuckle. Another sign of being nervous.

"Not as awkward as the last time." My eyes inadvertently dart to his arm, to the large reaper tattoo peeking out from beneath his shirt.

Seeing where my focus lands, Jared rubs over it, offering sheepishly, "I'm sorry that you found out like that."

I sigh, wondering if he's referring to the tattoo or the cheating. Or both.

His eyes roam my hair. "You look *really* good, Reese. Not that you didn't before. You just look more . . . grown up now. More responsible."

I feel my cheeks flush as I study the plate in front of me, my appetite nonexistent. "It's a little too boring for my taste."

"You will *never* be boring." A quick dart of my eyes catches that gleam in his. Is he flirting with me? Regarding me with that gorgeous face of his that I can't believe I had license to kiss at all times, he finally sighs. "I fucked up with us, Reese, and I'm so sorry."

A tinny taste fills my mouth as I bite down on my tongue to keep myself from talking, because I know I'll get emotional and probably say something defensive. I need to remain calm.

"I've loved Caroline since we were six years old. When she broke up with me out of the blue, I was crushed. Then you appear out of nowhere a week later, *completely* opposite of her."

"I definitely am that," I mutter dryly.

That cute smirk only increases the appeal of his face. "You sure are." It falls quickly. "I was on the rebound. I wanted so bad to be over her, to not think about her, to move on, that I rushed things with you and me. And before I knew it, we were married. Then, about a month after Vegas, Caroline phoned me, crying. I hadn't talked to her since the breakup, so she had no idea. I guess my parents phoned her parents after we went to meet them, and they told her."

I roll my eyes at the memory of that disastrous day. I swear, his mother was silently putting a hex on me from across the dinner table.

"Anyway, she called me, crying, telling me how she had truly meant she just needed some time and space but always thought we'd get back together. We agreed to meet up for dinner one night and . . ." He shrugs. "Things happened and I didn't know how to stop them. So many old feelings flooded back and they confused me. And then you caught us that day in the shower and . . ."

I squeeze my eyes tight against the memory, of hearing him coming as I walked in. That's why they hadn't heard me in the first place. But there's something more important here. "You were already cheating on me *a month* after we got married?" I can barely hear my own voice—it's barely audible—as the truth starts revealing itself. How can I even call what we had a marriage? It was a total sham.

"No! After that first night, I told her I couldn't see her again and I didn't for a month. But then she was at my parents' anniversary party." The one I refused to attend.

If I had gone, would we still be sitting across the table right now, talking about our failed marriage?

He drops his gaze to his hands. "She's always been so sweet and caring, and . . ." I clear my throat to stifle the bitter laugh. She has him fooled. ". . . she fits with my family well and . . ." Yes, his family, who was crushed when he brought me home. ". . . she'll make a good mother one day." He sounds like he's spewing out his parents' propaganda, but the more he goes on, the more desolate I become. If that's what he wanted in a wife, then we never had a hope in hell. Sweet . . . caring . . . fits in . . . future good mother . . . None of those labels fit me, regardless of whether they're real or fraudulent on her.

It feels like he's the one with a paintball gun aimed at point-blank range at my heart, firing mercilessly. I didn't come here to listen to this. I make a move to push my chair back when I hear, "But I miss you, Reese."

My mouth drops open, the conflicting end to that "Ode to Caroline" startling.

Eyes thick with emotion blaze into me. "We were pretty fucking great together, weren't we?"

And then he reaches out to grab my hand.

The still vivid memory of them together yesterday wraps its

fist around my guts and squeezes, reminding me not to let myself drift into the nostalgic, not to let myself get caught up in his words now. I want to be screaming at him, agreeing, "Yes! We *were* fucking awesome together and you ruined it!" I should be stabbing his hand with my fork. But instead I let myself accept the physical contact for just a moment longer, until I manage to lose my gaping jaw, and then I pull my hand out from beneath his and use the fork to jab at my pie. It's untouched, but at least they can't serve it to anyone else with holes all through it.

He waits in silence as I take three long, deep, calming breaths. "Does she know you're here with me right now?" I do a cursory glance around the patio, looking for the little ginger-haired husband-stealing bitch hiding behind a plant.

A frown zags across his forehead. "What? You think she's watching from somewhere?"

"No, only a crazy person would do *that*."

He pauses, a smirk curling his lips. "No, she doesn't know. She's not even talking to me right now."

"Oh yeah? Had a big fight?" My conscience starts to laugh—a wicked, triumphant cackle inside my head.

"Yeah. Over something stupid that happened at paintball," he murmurs absently, cocking his head. "Don't look so happy about it, okay?"

"I'll try my best," I offer, deadpan.

He folds his hands into one another. "We've been fighting a lot, actually. I've known her for eighteen years and yet the second I said those vows, it's like she changed into an entirely new woman and she's trying to change me with her." He works his mouth for a moment, watching me carefully. "You weren't like that, though, were you?"

That's because we only knew each other for six weeks before we got married. And no, I wasn't. I accepted him as he was. I hold his gaze—a heated look that I've seen plenty before, though never while sitting in a public place—but I say nothing to that.

"So this lawyer you're seeing, how long has that been going on for?"

"A few months," I lie.

He nods slowly, reaching out to curl his hands around my empty mug, pushing it back and forth slowly. "I was thinking we could all go out to dinner or something, sometime."

Now my bitter laugh does escape. I know Jared can be kind of dense sometimes—letting me walk into the apartment to collect my things that day is a good example of how he sometimes doesn't think through his ideas—but this? Chewing food . . . carrying on a conversation . . . not slitting Caroline's throat with a steak knife . . . all things that sound impossible.

Green eyes flicker to my face, assessing me. "Too weird?"

"Just a little."

He shrugs. "Okay, well . . . maybe drinks or something more casual at first. Even just the two of us. I really want to be friends, Reese. At least."

At least? What the hell else could we be? He's married! Is he actually doing what I think he's doing? Flip-flopping back and forth between Caroline and me like a beached fish? Like he wants to have his cake and eat it, too? If I were an outsider watching in, I would be pointing and laughing at the lot of us right now and especially at the idiot blond, for even sitting here and speaking to this douchebag. If I were an outsider and not the idiot blond who not so long ago hopelessly loved said douchebag, who was left broken-hearted and humiliated in a ditch.

"I'll have to think about it," I say, standing. He follows suit, and we're left facing each other in this uncomfortable stance. Do we just walk away? Do we hug? Do I punch him in the junk so maybe he starts using that dense mass of gray matter filling his skull, for once?

"You got a new number, right?" He pulls his cell out of his pocket and starts scrolling through it.

I hesitate. "Yeah, Miami local."

Frowning, he mutters, "Weird. I had your contact info in here. I don't know where it went." I think I have a pretty good idea. *To deleted heaven, care of your sweet new wife.* "Here. I'll put it in again. Okay, shoot."

I pause.

Do I do this?

Do I give him my number?

I give him my number.

"Great. Well . . ." He frowns and then, stepping forward, envelops my stiff body in a hug that I don't reciprocate. "See you soon. I hope." His lips brush against my cheek as he pulls back. I watch him stroll away, whistling happily.

And I release a lung's worth of air.

I don't know how I feel about all of this. Jared's not happy with Caroline. In the nasty swirl of hurt that has encased me for months, there's no mistaking the sweet feeling of that knowledge. Now he's come right out and told me that he misses me. He's showing me that he still has feelings for me. If I ever wanted Jared . . .

To hurt.

To suffer.

To love me again.

This could be the perfect opportunity.

But first, I would need Switzerland to play along.

Chapter 16

■ ■ ■

BEN

"Well, look at you, big-shot lawyer."

Fuck . . . Just the sound of that smooth voice has blood rushing to my cock. It's nothing I can control. Mercy has always had that effect on me. It's only gotten worse since my farewell party at Penny's. Cain's "no screwing the strippers" rule got publicly launched out the window by her *and* Hannah that night. At the same time. I didn't even suggest it, but I sure as hell wasn't going to pass up the chance.

But the look on Mason's face now as he turns around to find the platinum-blond stripper in my office is *almost* as entertaining. His face goes from pale to beet red in an instant as the poor guy's eyes bobble around uncontrollably—from her face to her tits to her face to the wall and back to her tits before he turns around to stare at me with pleading eyes.

"This is my good friend Mason. Mason, this is Mercy."

She reaches out with a giggle. After a somewhat awkward-looking handshake, he mumbles something about photocopies and then bolts from my office.

I stand and round my desk to scoop the tiny blond stripper into a big hug, the smell of her flowery perfume—almost too strong—attacking my nose. "Hey, babe." I've never had any interest in her as more than a friend, with a few occasional benefits that we kept very discreet and far from Penny's. I do respect Cain and his rules . . . to a degree. And, if I thought she'd ever want more from me, I never would have let it happen.

But I'm starting to worry that something has changed.

I'm getting texts from Mercy almost daily now, asking me to come visit her at the club.

Her big blue eyes appraise my office, the endless stack of paperwork. And me, her gaze drifting over my chest as her fingers toy with my shirt collar. "You look all grown up." She's wearing more than I'm used to seeing her in but there's really no hiding what she does for a living in that short, tight dress. Her enhanced curves, her face, the way she carries herself . . . it all screams, "I get naked for money."

And, by the multitude of glances into my office, everyone in the building can hear those screams. Based on what Mason told me of Jack's worries about my past workplace transgressions, bringing this into the office probably won't look good on me. Still, I can't kick her out. I can only hope she leaves soon.

"I'm trying to be, anyway. What are you doing here?"

A cute little giggle escapes. "I was in the neighborhood and thought I'd stop by. Penny's just isn't the same without you." A delicate hand runs across my chest and then descends quickly, nails dragging along my stomach until her fingers find my belt. Mercy has always been a tease like that. She likes knowing that she can get an instant reaction out of me.

"Come here." I use the excuse of pushing my door shut to step away before her hand drifts even farther down. Leading her to the spare chair, I then dive into mine, letting the desk act as a barrier between the two of us.

"I thought you were coming to visit me at Penny's on the weekend," she says with a small pout.

"I was stuck here all weekend." Honestly, between work and

Reese, I didn't even think about Penny's. I was exhausted on Saturday night. I can't believe I haven't stepped foot in the club in over three weeks. It's a record for me.

"It's not fun over there right now." Her smile falters. "I don't know what happened, Ben. Charlie disappeared, China got fired . . ." Her face pinches up. "I've never seen Cain so miserable."

"Yeah, I don't really know what's going on either." That's a lie. I know more than most, seeing as one of my best friends and the head bouncer at Penny's, Nate, called me last week to fill me in. It seems that Cain, my good friend and the owner of Penny's, fell in love with a stripper who has more secrets than he was able to dig up through his clandestine methods that I'm not supposed to know about. She took off in the night and now he's a wreck. I've never seen Cain anything but cool and composed.

With a sigh, Mercy uncrosses and crosses her long bare legs, distracting me completely with a momentary glimpse of black lace panties. At least she wore them today. That's never a guarantee. Fuck, it's also been over three weeks since I got laid. That's another unnaturally long span of time for me. And now I'm sitting across from a girl who actually enjoys giving private lap dances. I don't know how the hell an Amish community produced the likes of her. Clearly, I need to go visit one of those places to see if she's just a freak occurrence.

After another ten minutes of polite conversation, Mercy abruptly stands. "Well, I should let you get back to work. I just wanted to see you in your office." She bends down and lays a semi-inappropriate kiss right on my lips. "Dinner later?"

Is dinner code for sex? We've never gone out for meals. With a long, drawn-out sigh and a visual dip down her low-cut dress, I say, "Yeah, I'll see if I can get out early tonight." I can't help it. Mercy offers no frustrations.

It isn't until she steps away that I notice Reese standing in my doorway, holding at least a dozen yellow folders tight to her chest, a sardonic expression on her face as she eyes my company.

Turning toward the door, Mercy offers Reese a stiff smile—Mercy may be sweet but she's no idiot; she can read the edge of judgment in Reese's sharp gaze—and then strolls out, humming softly.

Reese saunters into my office to unceremoniously drop the folders on my lap. I'm pretty sure she was aiming to crush my dick with them. "So are you dating that Twinkie? Because after bringing me home to meet your mother, I was so sure you were in love with me." She sounds so disinterested that I know I don't have to worry about her actually believing that.

I bite my tongue as I decide how to respond. Answering Reese is sometimes tricky. I actually care if I come off sounding like a moron, and I don't normally care about that. I finally settle on, "You're safe, I promise." I remove the files from my lap and drop them onto my desk. "So what'd you find?"

"I've posted some notes of things you'll want to follow up on and some cases for precedence-setting when the law bot takes this to court. I've also solved the Kensington case for you. You're welcome."

I can't help my eyes from drifting over her frame. Having Mercy in here only magnifies how naturally attractive Reese is. How *real*. No silicone. A solid body, without being too over-the-top. I'd kill to see this girl naked again. If my mama hadn't shown up when she did, I would have had her stretched out in the back of that truck in another thirty seconds.

She pulls out a sheet of paper from the top folder, slapping it onto my desk. "The good doctor's out. See?" Her long, slender finger jabs at the paper. "The wife's company donated a hundred thousand dollars to his private clinic's fundraiser six months ago."

Pulling my attention back to the case, I scan the tax receipt. "Shit. You're right." It's definitely enough to discredit the expert witness who's trying to paint our client as a psychologically abusive father to gain his ex-wife sole custody of their three-year-old girl and all the child support that goes along with it. "Without this jerk's testimony, this custody battle is dead."

"Okay, Erin Brockovich, where the hell did you find this?"

She shrugs. "Wasn't that hard."

Natasha was stumped. I was stumped. We thought we'd be searching for something to win this case right up until we lost it. I look up at Reese's smug smile again. I'm seriously thinking about taking her into that corner conference room across the hall to thank her the way I'd *really* like to. The one with blinds and a lock. Jack's out of town at a conference. Other than Natasha, no one would be looking to interrupt us "working."

Dammit, thinking like this is not helping the current predicament I'm trying to hide under my desk.

I throw my pen down and lean back in my chair. "You're awesome. You know that, right?"

"I prefer spectacular." She pushes a lock of hair behind her ear, her face scrunching up with apology. "Look, I know I promised I'd stay late, but today's been weird and I'm not feeling great. I'm going to grab a nap at home and work some more later."

She *is* kind of pale, now that I think of it. "Yeah, I guess."

"So, is there anything else you absolutely need me to do for you before I go?" Her eyes drift to my lap as she adds dryly, "Besides the problem that the Twinkie will be fixing later." There's a biting edge in her tone.

"Jealous?" Just the possibility has me smiling like an ass. I hook my hands together behind my head and admit, "Because I'd much rather have *your* help with that." And I honestly would.

Reese's lips twist in thought as she slowly appraises my body with that raptor gaze. She's normally so much more covert when she's ogling me, preferring to do it when she thinks I'm not paying attention. Her voice drops a few octaves as an "Okay" slides from those thin lips. "Conference room?"

"What?" My eyebrows shoot up. *Shit*. I wasn't expecting that. My wide eyes scan the office for anyone who might be watching or listening in, seeing as the door isn't even closed. Is she serious? I can't tell! All I do know is that I'm sure going to be in a lot of fucking pain if she doesn't follow through.

A wicked cackle erupts from her. "Mrs. Cooke!" she hollers as Jack's assistant passes by my door.

Mrs. Cooke retraces her steps and pokes her head in, out of breath and wiping her sweaty forehead with a tissue. "What's the matter, dear?"

"Ben was just telling me how he ate all of your muffins over the weekend and wonders how you make them so peachy."

The kind woman's eyes light up as they settle on me. "Oh, you sweet boy. I'll give you the recipe, for your mama. Do you have a pen and paper handy?" Her hands flutter about as she starts giggling—a funny Betty Rubble sound. She waddles into my office and squeezes herself into my spare chair—and I mean squeezes—as I shoot a look Reese's way.

"Was I helpful?" Reese asks sweetly.

I can't help but smile. "Yes, you were." *Like a bucket of ice.*

"Good. Maybe you won't need any Twinkies after all." She struts out.

■ ■ ■

I'm sinking into total oblivion when the knock sounds on my door.

"Yeah?" I call out groggily, cracking an eye to see the glowing red numbers on my digital clock staring back at me. Two a.m. I'm fucking exhausted.

The door creaks open and a sliver of the hallway light behind shines down to reveal platinum-blond hair and a sparkly tight blue dress. "Hey," Mercy offers, leaning back to close the door with her ass. "Travis let me in."

I roll onto my back and murmur, "That was nice of him." I've shared a house with five guys for almost six years. Someone's always home and they've never *not* let Mercy in. I should probably set some new ground rules, given the situation.

Sauntering forward in that way she has—slow and graceful, like a cat—she reaches the side of the bed. I've started sleeping with the curtains open, finding the morning light helps me adjust to my new sleeping pattern. Now, it casts enough street light that I can just barely make out her figure. "You said you'd call."

"I got caught up with work." I actually forgot all about Mercy. After getting detailed instructions on Mrs. Cooke's peach muffins—which I'm actually gonna give to my mama—I spent hours churning through all the files Reese gave me. Mercy's gaze skates down along my exposed chest and stomach, her brow arching slightly as her attention drifts farther down to where I'm already pitching a tent under my sheets. I can't help it. Reaching up, her fingertips do this little curling motion around the straps of her dress and then, giving them a slight tug, she pushes the material down until her dress hits my floor in a shimmering heap. Working six days a week at Penny's, I've seen Mercy naked so many times that I could almost map out all her freckles in the dark.

"I thought maybe . . ." she says as she gingerly pulls my sheet down and climbs into my bed, sliding a leg over my body to straddle my thighs, ". . . I could stay here for the night and," she leans over, her arms resting on either side of my pillow, her fake double-Ds pressing against my chest, "get my fill of Ben. Is that okay?"

I can't help but chuckle. Mercy has a way with words. She never comes right out and says anything dirty, but the implication is thick. My brain conveniently skips over the "stay for the night" part and goes straight to the part where she's shimmying down my body, until her long hair grazes my stomach and the heat of her mouth wraps around me.

And then, with a deep groan, my brain just shuts down altogether.

■ ■ ■

"Are you okay?" I hear Mason ask from the doorway.

"I'm going to get my ass kicked and I probably deserve it," I
mutter, staring at my phone.

> Do you want to go to Storm and Dan's together this
> weekend?

I knew I shouldn't have let that happen. But what do you do
when a gorgeous stripper shows up in your bedroom in the middle of the night? No guy would say no to that. I don't care who
you are. And if you tell me you'd say no? You're fucking lying or
you're gay.

She had never slept over before, though. I was up and out
before she woke this morning, so at least there wasn't an awkward
goodbye. And now she's texting me about going to a *wedding*
together? Yeah, it's Storm and Dan, but . . . still. I don't like the
way my gut feels about this. It's telling me that Mercy is *definitely*
wanting more. Telling her I just want to be friends isn't going
to work. She'll bob her pretty head and say, "I know, Ben," and
then she'll grab my cock. Short of me bringing someone else as a
date, I'll end up with my pants around my ankles in a bathroom
by cocktails.

Shit. That means I need to bring a date! But who? Who is
there to bring? I can't bring anyone that I've screwed around
with in the past—that'll just get me into the same boat as the
one I'm in with Mercy. I mean, it's a wedding. Chicks get weird
at weddings. They trample each other to catch flying flowers. I
need someone who's not looking for *anything* from me. I need . . .

"Where's your sister today?" I ask Mason suddenly. I've been
eyeing Reese's office all morning and there's been no sign of life.

She promised she'd be here to help me. Plus, as much as I hate to admit it, not getting my morning dose of Reese is noticeable. It's like I'm in withdrawal.

"Stepsister," he corrects. "And she's at home, sick."

"Seriously?" *Shit.* She did say she was leaving early yesterday to catch some sleep.

He nods. "And she took a bunch of files with her, including one of mine accidentally. I'm heading over there now to go pick it up." Adding under his breath, "Into that infested house."

That's right. Mason tends to avoid sick people like they're all potential carriers of the bubonic plague. "I'll go. I'm not a sissy," I quickly throw out.

"Ben. Trust me, you don't want—"

"It's fine. Besides, she likes me more."

Some thought passes through those green eyes of his and then I think I catch a flicker of a smile. It's too fast to confirm, though. Fishing his keys out of his pocket, he tosses them onto my desk. "Here—she probably won't answer the door." He scribbles down the address. "I need the files back by noon today. Can you pick her up some cold medication? I promised Jack I would."

"What does she want?"

He shrugs. "Tylenol? Nyquil? Valium?"

"All right." I collect the keys and the address. And wait for it. And wait for it.

Finally, I give up. "Dude, aren't you going to warn me not to try anything on your sister?"

"Stepsister!" he corrects sharply, but then that little hint of a smile is back. "And no. I'm not too worried about that." Mason takes off, throwing over his shoulder, "By twelve. I need the file by twelve."

Well, that gives me almost two hours to figure out how I'm going to convince Reese to come to a wedding with me.

Chapter 17

. . .

REESE

"How are there no drugs in this damn house!"

"You know all that stuff does is suppress your immune system," Lina's voice blasts over the speakerphone in my room. "This is why I tell you to take ginseng every day."

"You and Jiminy Cricket both," I mutter, staring at the wall across from me, my head propped up by three pillows until I'm almost sitting. Because I can't breathe otherwise. I've already raided Mason's bathroom vanity. It's brimming with vitamins and supplements, but there's nothing of any real value. Jack's not much help to me either right now, given that he believes a shot of vodka a day keeps all illnesses at bay. The only thing I found of any use was a small tub of Vicks, with which I've already coated my chest, my back, even my upper lip.

"And does Jiminy Cricket get sick? Because *I* don't get sick."

"I'm convinced that neither of you are quite human. That's probably why you've found each other," I mutter, my ratty but comforting gray robe wrapped around me in a cocoon not warding off the chill running through my body. I thought it was simply lack of sleep with all the Jared stuff on my mind. I left work, planning to take a nap and catch up in the evening. I may as well have just left all those file folders at work, because I passed out the second my head hit my pillow and didn't wake up for thirteen hours. Now I can't stop shivering and my head is about to explode from the sinus pressure. All I want to do is self-medicate but, short of some pills that expired ten years ago—which I'm seriously considering taking—the house is empty of all worthy narcotics.

"I saw some ginger in Mason's drawer. Should I take that?" Yes, Mason has his own drawer in the refrigerator. And yes, he'll have a mild coronary when he discovers I've rifled through it.

Lina's loud sigh of exasperation answers before her words do. "Ginger must be taken *before* you get sick. You know, if you're going to take anything raw, take garlic."

"Is that another one of your weird Korean things?"

"No, it's a weird naturopathic thing." With her flat tone, Lina comes off as patronizing at times, especially to those who don't know her. "I usually cover a piece of bread in it to make it more palatable."

"There's no bread in this house except for Mason's rice bread, and it makes me gag," I grumble.

I swear I can hear the eye roll crackle over the speaker. "I forgot how irritating you get when you're sick."

"Can't you just bring me something?"

"Not for a few hours. I have client meetings all day. Have you tried Nicki?"

"She's an hour outside of the city today."

"Jack? Mason?"

"Jack's in court, and Mason? Really? He won't come in here without a hazmat suit. Don't be surprised if you have another roommate for the week." I release a series of guttural moans and groans to amplify my misery. When I've finally shut up—I'm starting to annoy even myself—Lina says, "So, there's this guy at work that I think you'd like."

"Oh my God, Lina. Now is *not* the right time."

She goes on, ignoring me completely. She and Nicki are

champions at that. "I was thinking we could go on a double date this Saturday. You and him, me and Mason."

"No."

"Because of Ben, right? You guys are dating?"

I sigh. "No. There is nothing going on between Ben and me." Nothing real. Although, the idea of him playing my fake boyfriend does have an appeal.

"Really. Nothing at all?" Her words are thick with doubt.

"Nothing, Lina. I'm still a bitter old hag and Ben would bust out some serious Houdini moves if he even heard the word 'date.' Plus, he's not my type! You know that." Lina has seen the kind of guys I'm attracted to. Broody guys on bikes, with tats; lean, dark, and shaggy-haired. Stick a big, blond, grinning ex–football player who knows about oranges into the lineup and all I hear is Big Bird singing, "One of these things is not like the others."

"I know, but, come on. You don't find him the least bit attractive? Because I think he is. Nicki thinks he is. Even Mason admitted he'd totally be into him, if he were gay."

Because picturing Mason with Lina wasn't bad enough . . . Keeping my eyes open is a struggle and so I don't bother. Maybe I'll talk myself into unconsciousness. "Yeah, he's attractive." I add begrudgingly, "He's freaking hot, actually. And he's an amazing kisser. And he knows it. He's a bit of a jackass, but nothing a piece of duct tape can't fix."

"And? Has he disturbed those cobwebs that he's *not allowed* to disturb?" Obviously Mason has told Lina about the no-dating policy, so I'm not sure what answer she wants to hear.

"We fooled around a bit, but otherwise, Charlotte's web is still safe and secure." I'd be lying if I said things didn't feel different after this past weekend. Seeing him with that stripper yesterday bugged me. It's not because I have some deep feminist reaction to seeing a woman who sells her body. I was more interested in how many times he has slept with her, if he's still sleeping with her, and how I can get him to *stop* sleeping with her.

"Well, don't do anything to get yourself or him fired. Mason's really worried about that. He likes Ben, but he knows him pretty well."

"Jack would never fire me."

"Reese . . ."

"I'm not going to get Ben fired," I mutter with annoyance, adding, "but thank you for thinking so highly of your best friend."

"I'm serious. I don't want you getting all bitter if something doesn't work out."

"You're safe. I'm all bittered out. Plus, are you kidding me? I don't want a relationship with Ben! He's like a bad rash that won't go away half the time."

"Okay, good. Well, you know, Nicki's sister is doing those passion parties now. You should order something through her."

I sigh. "My best friend is suggesting I resort to a vibrator at twenty-one? You've completely given up on me. That's wonderful."

"I'll second that idea," a familiar male voice suddenly teases, inches away. My eyes flash open to find big blue irises and an enormous grin hovering over me. So I do what any normal young woman half passed out with the flu would do when she's surprised by a guy in her bedroom. I let out a yelp as my hand flies out to connect with his nose.

"Jesus, Reese!" Ben jumps back, one hand going up to protect against further attack while the other cups his face.

"Shit," I mutter as I see a small trickle of blood run out one nostril.

He looks down at his blood-coated finger in shock. "You think?"

"Reese?" comes Lina's wary voice.

"Oh, she's fine. The freaking-hot lawyer that she wants to duct tape isn't," Ben mutters.

Fantastic. He heard *all* of that. My cheeks burn. I grab a tissue from the box on my nightstand and shove it into his hand, unable to keep the bite from my tone as I ask, "What are you *doing* sneaking up on me in my bedroom?"

Dabbing at his nostril, he mutters, "I came to get a file for Mason." Checking the tissue for the growing stain of blood, he adds, "Why are you so violent?"

I roll my eyes. "Did you happen to bring me cold medicine? Mason knows I was looking for some."

"Is that your way of apologizing?"

"You want me to apologize to you for breaking into my house, sneaking into my bedroom, and scaring the shit out of me?"

He holds up Mason's keys.

"Semantics," I mutter, flopping back into my stack of pillows, the small fright having drained me of every last bit of energy.

Lina's throat-clearing reminds me that she's still on the phone. "Gotta go to my meeting. I'll call you later. Have fun, Ben. She's even more pleasant when she's sick." The phone clicks over the speakerphone as I watch Ben wriggle his nose.

A twinge of guilt stirs. "Is it broken?"

"Nah, I think I'll be okay." After a pause, "Mason said you have the flu?"

I close my eyes. "I don't know. It could be the Ebola virus. Or the black plague. Too soon to tell. I'm sure it's highly contagious, though."

When I hazard a look at Ben again, I find his gaze drifting over my frame and I know what he sees—uncombed hair, a blotchy face, bloodshot eyes, baggy gray track pants, and my shabby, oversized Depeche Mode T-shirt that reaches mid-thigh. Jared's shirt that I stole during my red-paint incident. Ben dips his head and smiles secretly.

"What?" I snap, fully aware of how unappealing I am at this moment and highly annoyed with my stepbrother for sending our hot, obnoxious co-worker here to witness this. "Ready for me now?" I ask snidely, pulling my covers up and over my body.

Chuckling, he tosses the tissue in the trash can. "Let me get that file from you so you can go back to talking about vibrators and cobwebs."

My cheeks heat up again, silently cursing Mason. "Pass me those files over there." I wave a lazy hand at the floor and watch as he reaches down, quietly admiring how well his pants really do fit him.

I feel Ben's eyes on me as I search through the stack. Finding the one my stepbrother wants, I slap a Post-it note onto the first page and scrawl, "I spy with my little eye something of yours that I just licked. Guess what?" *Payback's a bitch, Mason. I thought you'd have already learned that.*

Ben chuckles softly. "I'm not sure I like that evil grin."

"Don't worry. You're not my target." I close the folder and toss it onto the floor at Ben's feet. Scowling, I pull the covers over my head. This only makes it harder to breathe but I'm much like a wounded animal when I'm sick, looking for a quiet corner to hole up in and die. Something that Mason was well aware of when he sent Ben over here. I'm going to ring my stepbrother's scrawny neck when I see him next. "Make sure you lock the front door."

I hear Ben's feet pad across the floor. Hazarding a peek a moment later, I find him wandering through my room, his finger running along the frame of my old blue Yamaha electric guitar. "Huh, you weren't lying about this," he murmurs.

I've had it since I was fifteen, when I lifted a hundred bucks from Annabelle's purse and headed straight for a pawnshop. I was smart about the whole thing. I waited until she stumbled through the door after a night out at the Fair Oakes country club, knowing she'd just assume that she'd bought an outrageously expensive bottle of wine that night. This kid named Len sat with me in the bleachers of a nearby public school every afternoon and taught me how to play. I was a natural, playing by ear and strumming Led Zeppelin within a year.

The smile comes unbidden as I recall Ben's comment in Cancún. "Yes, I'm fully aware of how hot that makes me."

"Fuck, yeah," Ben mutters, adding with a smile in his tone, "Maybe not right now, though."

"Shut up."

His eyes invade the rest of my belongings, skating over the vintage trucks and albums on my wall, the giant beanbag chair I love to sit in while plucking notes absently, the little toy Harley on the bookshelf, a closet filled with clothes dangling haphazardly from hangers. Everything that represents me; everything that helped make the spare room at Jack's feel like home; everything that I briefly considered torching after Caroline's hands had been all over it. "You're an odd one, Miss MacKay. I'm still trying to figure you out. Harleys and rusty old trucks and Depeche Mode." He pauses. "You like gray, don't you?"

"My favorite color." I watch with wariness as Ben approaches me, turns, and then lies down on my bed beside me, the mattress sinking and creaking with his weight. A weird half-groan, half-growl escapes my throat as he weasels a hand under my back. "Come here. And don't hit me." Despite my grumbles and protests, I'm scooped up and resting against his hard chest within seconds.

"Don't complain when you get sick," I warn with a scowl, closing my eyes and fighting the urge to sigh as deft fingers begin smoothing through my hair. If this is Ben's idea of foreplay . . . I'll take it. Even with my sinuses being clogged, I'm still able to distinguish that clean, sporty-smelling cologne of his. It reminds me of the weekend. It also reminds me that I have a rather unattractive Vicks mustache that he hasn't teased me about . . . yet.

"Listen." He clears his throat loudly. "I have a favor to ask you and, seeing as you went and got yourself sick to avoid working with me all week . . ." Though he can't see it, I roll my eyes. "Remember how I helped you out with your ex-husband?"

"By licking my tonsils, yes—I recall something about that."

"And then by tricking me into becoming your accomplice. Don't forget that. Well, I have this *thing* on Saturday and I could use your help."

"This *thing*?"

"Yeah, kind of like a party. At a friend of mine's house. I need to look unavailable."

It clicks. "Switzerland wants to go rogue?"

"Basically."

Huh. Is the universe cooperating with me for once? This could actually work out in my favor. If he's truly desperate . . . "I don't know," I begin to say, feigning wariness in my voice.

"Oh, come on, Reese! I helped you out. Please?" I smother my smile by leaning into his chest. I like it when Ben begs. "I just need you to run some interference."

Great. Football lingo. "Why me?"

"Because you won't get the wrong idea."

"Yeah, no worries there. I know exactly what you're about," I mutter. "I'll probably be dead by Saturday, though."

"What if I were to get you something to keep you alive?"

"Tell me more."

Leaning forward to roll me off his body, Ben eases himself out of my bed. I was just getting used to the feel of him. The sudden absence is oddly discomforting. "Where are you going?" I ask as I watch him step out of my room. A second later he's back beside my bed, holding up a white CVS bag and a Styrofoam bowl. "Half a pharmacy and chicken noodle soup in exchange for one fake date."

My hand shoots out but it's not fast enough, Ben moving the bag just out of reach, letting it dangle there. "Deal?"

"You don't fight fair."

"Probably more fair than you."

This is my chance. "Half a pharmacy *and* fake boyfriend duties for a night in exchange for one fake date to this *thing*."

His smile drops. "What? Fake boyfriend? Why?"

"The why doesn't matter. All that matters is the when, and I'll let you know."

His nostrils flare as he inhales deeply. "You're up to something, aren't you?" I stay quiet, watching him as he ponders the deal, his eyes resting on my mouth. "Full-service fake boyfriend?"

"Highly unlikely." Then again, my track record with this guy may beg to differ.

He gives me a "we'll see about that" kind of smile but it drops off with a quirk of his brow. "Any risk of me getting fired for this?"

"It'll be our little secret." I make a crossing motion over my chest.

He sets the soup down on my nightstand and tosses the bag at me. "I'll pick you up at five on Saturday. Wear a dress. A red one."

That earns my eye roll. Ben really seems to love ongoing jokes.

Hesitating for a moment, he leans in to place a kiss on the top of my head. "Get better, and call me if you need anything else."

I watch him head toward the door with a mixture of discontent and delight. "Give Mason a hug, and then tell him that you're pretty sure my body rash is highly contagious."

Ben's loud bark of laughter echoes through the hall as I reach in to inspect the contents of the bag. He must have bought every brand of cough and cold medicine on the shelf.

And condoms.

With happy-face packaging.

I can't help it. Despite how shitty I feel, I start giggling uncontrollably.

Chapter 18

...

BEN

I'm not used to quiet Reese. Right now, sitting in the passenger seat of my Jetta, peering at me from above slanted sunglasses as the early evening sunset beats through my windshield, I'd think someone has cut out her tongue.

Of course, that doesn't stop my eyes from drifting over her body—again—to take in her white dress. I don't know styles besides "short and tight," but whatever the hell Reese is wearing, I like it. The top makes her tits look bigger than normal and, while I can't see her ass with all that fabric on the bottom, I sure as hell remember exactly what's there. All in all, for a guy with a healthy imagination, I can't keep my attention off her.

Not just because she's stunning. Because I *missed* seeing her. I haven't seen her since I went by her house four days ago, she was *that* sick. I'm just so happy she made it. I didn't think she would.

A throat clearing and an arched brow tells me she's had enough of my ogling. "You must be hot in that."

"Yeah," I mutter, climbing out of my car and into the late-day heat, reminding myself for the tenth time that I *have* to keep the tie on until after the ceremony.

"Sorry, no red in my closet," she explains with a little smirk as she steps out and onto the driveway, holding her dress out.

"Nothing at all?"

She shrugs and begins walking ahead, giving me a fine view of those legs. I'm still wondering if that nipple ring is the only thing hidden under there. "Nothing you'll be privy to," she throws over her shoulder.

"Huh. I thought the freaking-hot lawyer had a shot." I almost drew blood that day, biting down on my tongue to stop from laughing out loud when I overheard her talking to her friend on the phone. And then they started going on about vibrators and . . . damn! I've been with a few chicks who like to pull their toys out of the drawer when I'm over. Those nights have always been memorable.

The look Reese shoots me over her shoulder, her cheeks bursting with color, makes me raise my hand in surrender. I've learned enough to know that Reese may act tough but she does not like being embarrassed. The last thing I want to do is piss the little commando off.

"What kind of party did you say this was again?" Reese asks, studying two of Penny's strippers walking up the path ahead of us, both in skin-tight dresses that would get a mannequin off.

No way was I going to tell her the truth. She'd never agree to come. "The kind of party that you have fun at." I smoothly loop an arm through hers and begin leading her around the side of the Miami mansion that overlooks the beach. God knows she may still run. But for now, she slowly matches my steps along the path. "So I'm clear, am I just a casual date or the new girlfriend?"

"Casual date. No one who knows me would believe other-wise." I shoot my winning smile at her as I add, "A highly amorous one, of course. I wouldn't have brought you otherwise."

I catch her tiny eye roll as we round the corner. And then her feet stall like a skittish cat facing a bath as all the white folding chairs and the archway come into view.

"You brought me to a fucking *wedding*?" she hisses and I instinctively flex my arm around hers.

"Don't swear; it's bad luck."

By the way her fingernails are digging into my forearm, I'm starting to regret going with the element of surprise. "I'm in *white*, Ben!"

"And you look damn fine," I assure her, but her eyes are closed and her head's already shaking in that "God, you're such an idiot" way.

"You can't wear white to a wedding! I'll look like I'm trying to compete with the bride."

"Oh, fuck. Don't worry about that. You can't compete with her." *Shit.* I heave a sigh. "I mean . . ." Even *I* know I've just stuck both feet into my mouth, and the flat glare I get confirms it. "That came out wrong. You know what I mean. Come on." I give her a tug forward. "Let's get a drink. They'll have the good stuff out." Knowing Storm, the bar will be stocked with only the best for their guests.

"Please tell me you know these people, Ben. And that they know I'm coming? Because I'm feeling like an offensive wedding crasher right now."

"Relax. Storm and Dan are two of my closest friends. And, yes, they know you're coming." When I phoned last night to tell Storm that I was bringing a date, she of course grilled me a bit and scolded me for waiting until the eleventh hour but then giggled, saying she couldn't wait to meet her. She's great like that.

Reese's perfectly shaped eyebrow spikes. "Her name is *Storm*?"

I expected that. "Old stage name, yeah. The pregnant woman whose pie you destroyed last week? She's the one getting married today." Greeting the bartender, I order two shots of tequila and a bottle of Corona.

"No tequila," Reese argues with a furious headshake.

"Oh, come on. You'll need it to deal with me." This act will work better if I can remove that rod from Reese's spine.

"Why? Are *we* getting married, too?" I love how she cracks jokes to downplay her irritation. Especially ridiculous ones like that.

"Babe, the only way a wedding ring is landing on this finger of mine is if I'm in a coffin."

"You may be in one by the end of tonight," she mutters more to herself, and then tells the waiting bartender, "I'll have a Jim Beam, neat. Thanks."

"Jeez. Guitar playing . . . Harley riding . . . bourbon . . . Do you even like men?" I tease as the guy pours and hands her the drink.

"Not right now," she throws back in a dry tone as she takes a healthy sip. At least she hasn't pulled away from me yet. That's good. It gives Mercy—who I see in my peripherals, standing with her partner in crime, Hannah—less room to attach herself. Not that it would necessarily deter her.

"Isn't that the Twinkie in the blue?" Reese's brow pulls together as she assesses the stripper's extremely short blue dress.

"Yeah. You want another introduction?" Leaning in close to her ear—she smells like strawberries and cream again today—I whisper, "The one on the left may be more your type, though." The words are barely out of my mouth when Reese's bony elbow collides with my ribs.

I watch her observing them, her eyes narrowing slightly, her fingers smoothing her skirt out, tugging it this way and that. She's normally so hard-edged that her sudden self-consciousness is a nice, humanizing change. "Do you actually like all that silicone?" she finally asks.

"It has its merits," I admit but add, "Girls like that get boring quick, though. And I prefer your tits. Though I think I need a refresher on them." I'm not lying, either. About either assertion.

"Another Hallmark sentiment." Her caramel eyes shift up to stare at me, as if weighing my words for their truth and deciding what kind of smart-ass remark she should fling at me. As her lips part, I'm tempted to test this fake date out and shut her up with a kiss—that I damn well know she'll enjoy—but before I get the chance, a familiar hand slams down on my shoulder.

"I thought you were dead in a ditch somewhere," Nate's deep voice rumbles.

It's always fun to watch a new person take in Nate's size for the first time. Reese does not disappoint, her eyes widening as they scan the head of security at Penny's. I don't blame her. The guy is almost three hundred pounds of solid muscle. It was Nate who sat me down in a hard plastic chair and hammered me with question after question before even letting me meet Cain for a job. The sheer size of him—bigger than any left tackle I ever played with during college ball—kept my mouth shut beyond simple "yes" and "no" answers.

I clasp hands with him. "I know, man. This day gig is killing me right now. Steep learning curve." I'm used to seeing him every night, but aside from a quick phone call and a few texts, I haven't talked to him in weeks. One of a few downfalls to growing up and moving on. "Nate, this is Reese." I pull her tight to me again. "She's my date."

"Date?" He chuckles. "I guess you don't know Ben very well yet."

She doesn't miss a beat. "He lied and used medicinal narcotics to bribe me into coming here, so I think I have him pretty well pegged."

Nate's head falls back as a deep bellow of laughter escapes him, earning more than a few curious looks. "Where'd you two meet?"

Tilting her head slightly to the side as she eyes me, I see the devilish smile curling her lips. "I work at Warner."

"Lawyer?"

"Yes. Soon to be partner. In fact, I'm training him." It should probably bother me that she's openly lying to one of my best friends, but I'm actually amused. She's convincing, too.

Another big grin from Nate. It seems that Nate's got a lot of big grins for Reese. "And how's our boy doing?"

"To be honest, he's a little *slow*. I'm not sure he'll make it."

Well, it's good to see she's gotten over her initial discomfort.

Another roar of laughter from Nate has me holding my hands up in surrender as a flash of red whizzing past catches my eye. "All right, you two. You have all night. Don't tire yourselves out early at my expense. Kacey!" I holler, waving at the feisty siren, the only woman I've ever considered committing to. If she wasn't already practically married to Trent, that is.

"What?" she snaps as she rushes over. But she quickly tempers that with a kiss on my cheek before grabbing my beer from my hand and taking a long swig of it.

"You look hot."

That gorgeous face of hers splits into a wide smile. I still can't get enough of those; they were so few and fake when I first met her. "Now's not the time to hit on me. I've got to get back to the bride. Wait until later, when Trent's around and can kick the shit out of you, okay?"

I chuckle as she hands me my beer, remembering the night a few years back that Trent and I got loaded and I, like the complete jackass that I am, mentioned what happened between Kacey and me in the women's locker room at the gym, way back when. I only meant it as a compliment for what he's got.

Trent's got a solid right hook when he's pissed.

Turning to level Reese with those crystal-blue eyes, Kacey wastes no time asking, "Who's this?"

"Reese. Wedding hostage." Reese's deceptively delicate hand juts out.

"And your new best friend," I add. "You both like to break my balls, so I figure you'll get along well." With her sharp wit and temper, Reese actually reminds me *a lot* of Kacey, so I think they'll either be fast friends or tear each other's hair out in a catfight. Either would be entertaining to witness.

Kacey's face lights up. "Sounds about right. I've got tons of unflattering pictures to make you reconsider being here with him. We'll bond over Ben's misery later."

"Perfect." I knew that night was going to come back to bite me in the ass.

With lightning-fast reflexes—Kacey used to spend hours at the gym kickboxing—she reaches up and pinches my nipple through my shirt before stalking away, that evil cackle of hers filling the air.

"I swear, between the two of you, I'm going to be in the hospital soon," I mutter, rubbing my chest.

From somewhere behind us, the violinist begins playing music, signaling the need to sit. Nate leans in, out of Reese's earshot, and murmurs, "Sounds like Mercy was really looking forward to seeing you today."

"Fuck," I mutter, shaking my head and then heaving a sigh. "She knows me better than to expect something."

Nate's severe glare—the whites of his big eyes a stark contrast to his ebony skin—lets me know that excuse isn't going to fly. "Well, it's looking like she doesn't, so you better straighten that shit out. Just because you're not working for Cain anymore doesn't mean I won't beat your ass."

He's not kidding, either. Both Nate and Cain take a special interest in making sure people don't take advantage of the dancers at Penny's. Best friend or not, good intentions or not, I'm going to end up with two black eyes over this, even if *I* wasn't the one showing up in anyone's bedroom.

"Got it, man. Trust me, that's over."

I hear a "dumbass" slip out as Nate walks away, followed by that low chuckle of his.

"Your friend looks like he wants to kill you," Reese, ever

observant, says as we make our way to find a seat. I'm catching a lot of nods and smiles thrown my way from familiar faces. Pretty much the entire staff of Penny's—anyone who knows Storm, anyway—is here.

"That's why you're here. To make sure he doesn't." She lets me entwine my fingers through her hand as I lead her toward the back right corner and into two available seats, as far away from Mercy as possible. "Remember that girl who came by my office?"

"The Twinkie?"

"Mercy, yeah. I need to keep things platonic between us and you are going to help me do that. But you can't be mean to her, okay?"

"*Moi?*" Reese says with mock innocence, her free hand clutching her chest as she scans the crowd, quickly settling on the back of Mercy's head.

"I'm serious, Reese. She's a friend, but I think she may have gotten the wrong idea."

Reese's glare is full of suspicion as she asks dryly, "And why would she get the wrong idea, Ben?"

I give her a knowing look. "Kind of hard to say no to her when she's throwing herself at me."

Shaking her head, she mutters, "You don't even try to hide what you are, do you?"

All I've got to answer that with is a shrug.

"I guess you did kind of save the day for me with my ex last week," she says with a sigh, though clearly unimpressed.

"And you didn't exactly hate it, did you," I remind her with a smile. And she didn't hate the afternoon at my mama's, either.

"God, you are so damn cocky." The tiniest smile softens her tone. With a heavy sigh, she reaches up to lay a hand on my cheek. She pulls my face closer, until I feel her hot breath against my ear. Her lip grazes my lobe as she asks in a low voice, "Is this amorous enough?"

"Uh . . ." I clear my throat as shivers run down my back. "Yeah, that'll work." To give me a raging hard-on before the bride even walks down the aisle. If the incident with Mrs. Cooke the other day tells me anything, it's that I'm gonna regret asking Reese to do this by the end of the night. This girl enjoys torturing me.

Reaching up to finger a strand of hair at the nape of my neck, her mouth still against my ear, she laughs softly. "What would your mama say about all this?"

I curl my arm around her shoulders as Dan and Trent take their spots under the arch in tuxes. "She taught me to be nice to girls. She didn't specify exactly how." I think my mama has a pretty good idea how I do that.

Pulling away, Reese regards me with an unreadable expression.

I shrug. "What?"

"You're a special breed, Benjamin Morris," she finally answers, though that tells me nothing about what she's really thinking.

But when I take a gamble and draw her close to lay a quick kiss on her lips, she doesn't pull away. Or punch my junk. "The Twinkie's not watching," she confirms wryly, without even glancing to check.

"Really? How about now?" I don't wait before I steal another kiss. Another one she doesn't refuse.

Her eyes do narrow slightly, though, as I pull away.

She's definitely gonna make me pay for this by the end of tonight.

Chapter 19

. . .

REESE

"I like your friends!" I holler, my shoes dangling from my finger-tips as my naked toes relish the cool, wet sand along the beach.

"More than you like me?"

"Yeah, but that's not hard." I turn and begin walking back-ward as I absorb Ben's responding grin, perfectly visible in the light of the full moon. Maybe it's the Jim Beam, but I'm finding it even more charming than usual tonight. In fact, the entire package—whore and all—has had me checking my hair in the mirror and sending little shocks of electricity through me the entire evening. Even with his shirt hanging out of his pants and his tie long since removed, the big jock looks sharp in a suit. I'm kind of glad he doesn't wear one around the office all the time. It would be distracting.

"Is that so? Is that why you've been all over me tonight?" he asks, his brow raised as if he knows some little secret.

I can't contain the bark of laughter. "What? You gave me a task and I like to overachieve." It's funny, when we first stepped around the corner and into a wedding scene, the only thing that stopped me from wrapping my hands around his neck and chok-ing him was knowing my hands wouldn't cover even half the span needed to succeed. But I quickly adapted to the situation and met a few of his friends—who I can tell I'd actually like.

Especially that redhead, Kacey, the maid of honor. She's got a wicked sense of humor. She kept her promise, spending a good fifteen minutes scrolling through her phone to show me "the best of the best" from Ben's farewell party. Which turned out to be the "worst of the worst." There were a few she wouldn't show me, though, and I'm thinking they involved the strippers. I guess she assumes that, as Ben's date, seeing pictures of Ben getting molested by other women would bother me. When I accidentally caught the one of the Twinkie straddling his lap and my stomach twisted uncomfortably, I thought I might agree with her.

When Ben leaned down and laid that first kiss on me right before the ceremony, I could have refused. I could have pushed him back and said no. But I didn't. I went along. It was an unpredictably easy decision to make, especially after catching Mercy's furtive and frequent glances over at him. I knew that if I strayed more than a foot away, I'd turn around to find her hanging off of him, trying to entice him with her bedazzled vagina or whatever it is the stripper has that lures in a guy like Ben.

So I hung off him instead.

And let him steal kisses.

They felt more like borderline inappropriate tests than anything, partly because he knew he could get under my skin with them but also because he knows that, though I'll never admit it, I'm secretly enjoying them as much as he is.

"Do you think it worked?"

"My pants are still on, so hell yeah. Saves me from an awkward situation for tonight."

"*Just* for tonight?" I sigh with exasperation.

Taking five quick steps forward, he's suddenly scooping me into his arms. I cringe at the squeal that escapes me as I find myself whirling through the air as if I weigh nothing. The shock only continues as Ben sets a perfectly timed kiss on my mouth as my toes touch the sand.

I manage to break away from his lips, but not his arms. "You know she doesn't have bionic vision, right?"

"No, that's not one of her talents," he agrees.

"Jackass" escapes before I can stop myself.

He offers me only a crooked smile. "What? I can't help it. This is fun. You're having fun, right?"

"Yes," I admit reluctantly, gazing up at the lines of his square jaw as my hands settle on his biceps. I really wish he weren't so attractive. But then I wouldn't have agreed to this, so . . .

"Still friends?"

"I suppose."

"And you're not going to try to marry me because I kissed you a few times, are you?"

"A *few* times?" I know my eyebrows are crawling halfway up my forehead. "You're like a dirty little neighborhood boy who runs around, kissing the girls and making them cry."

"Only one girl today," he corrects me as he leans in and steals yet another kiss—at least the twentieth tonight. "And I don't see you crying."

I don't know what it is about Ben. He's as obnoxious as they come, but a small part of me, as idiotic as it is, is flattered that he finds me attractive, especially given that he could be with a stripper right now who I have to admit is drop-dead beautiful, silicone and all. One of those girls who makes you wonder if you should switch teams for a night to see what all the fuss is about.

Then again, it doesn't sound like there's much of a pursuit there. That could be the problem.

"Well, seeing as I'm seeking revenge on my ex-husband, I don't think I have time in my schedule for a second unhealthy relationship. But thank you for being concerned."

His loud laughter carries over the empty beach. "Good. I don't need any more women obsessing over me."

That earns a snort from me but his words provoke a new thought. "So when did you sample the Twinkie last?"

Furrowing his brow as if in deep thought, he offers, "What was it: Monday? Or Tuesday? I don't know. All these days are starting to blend together."

"While the love of your life was on her deathbed fighting the flesh-eating disease and certain death?" I exclaim dramatically. I'm actually shocked he answered that so openly. That's something a normal guy would outright lie about. I'm even more shocked that he slept with her only *days* ago, just after fooling around with me at his mother's. I mean, I knew he had slept with her because, let's face it, it's Ben. But I was thinking this was something from the past. "You know you're a dick, right?" I say as an unanticipated sourness stirs in my stomach.

He shrugs. "It wasn't my fault."

I almost stumble over my feet. "Did you *actually* just say that to me?"

"What?" Serious blue eyes stare back at me. "I was half asleep in my room and she just showed up and took her clothes off. Then she climbed on me and gave me a blow—"

"All right!" I cut him off, smacking his chest, my irritation spiking.

"Hey, you asked and I'm big on the truth, so . . ."

"Good, I'm glad you've retained at least one of your Boy Scout values. But we really need to work on filtering the unnecessary details."

He scratches the back of his head, a sheepish smile on his lips. "What was I supposed to do?"

"Well, *obviously* you were supposed to sleep with her," I agree with mock seriousness, breaking free of his grasp to reach down and grab the bottle of Jim Beam that he snagged from the bar earlier and dropped in the sand before scooping me up. Given I'm a last-minute guest at a pregnant girl's wedding—and I showed up in a white dress—I've been good tonight, welcoming a nice, light buzz and nothing more. But now, taking a long swig, I accept that this enlightening little "romantic" walk with my slutty fake date will probably change that.

"Why are you turning all moody?"

"Gee, I don't know. Because I look like the moron who's all kissy-face with her date, oblivious that he's a whore and has probably slept with every woman here? Because being the blind wife who's oblivious to her husband cheating on her for *months* wasn't enough for me?" I bite my tongue before any more deep inner thoughts tumble out of my mouth unbidden, but it's too late. The damage is already done.

I can tell by the sad puppy-dog eyes Ben's settling on me.

"Let's go back to the reception," I grumble, stepping around him. He's having none of that, though. Roping his arms around my waist, he drops down to press his forehead against mine in a very friendly yet intimate way. In a way I didn't think Ben capable of acting. The proximity to him is both comforting and heady.

"She's the only one here that I've been with. Well," he cringes slightly, "Hannah, too, but just the one night and for like a minute. She was more into Mercy that night." *Oh my God!* "And I'm sorry. I didn't think about that when I asked you to do this."

Digesting that rather graphic detail that I didn't need for a long moment, I finally heave a sigh. "I guess my pride is just having a hard time getting over that mess."

With a devilish gleam in Ben's eyes, he dives down—yet again—for another kiss. Only this time he doesn't pull away quickly, instead coaxing my mouth open. In no time, my head is cradled in his hand, his tongue is tangled with mine, and I'm not refusing him. He really is good at this.

And this is so easy. And straightforward and painless, because we both know it's completely physical and neither of us is looking for more. And, oddly enough, I feel like we're friends. Ben's kind of like a kid I used to play with in the sandbox who's seen me through my embarrassing gangly years and makes me laugh.

Who is now making his intentions known by pressing them up against my thigh.

He suddenly pulls away. "Are you actually jealous of Mercy?" There's a pause, and then his eyes are twinkling as he lets go of me and starts unfastening his shirt buttons, the beginning of that solid upper body revealing itself. I'm not quite sure what he's doing until the shirt hangs open and his hands reach for his belt, the dimples on his cheeks set deeply. "Because there's no need. I'm more than willing to—"

"No!"

His hands pause, a knowing smirk stretching his lips. "You sure?"

"No?"

Ben's head cocks to the side in surprise that matches mine. We're left standing there, staring at each other as the water laps up on the shore, me wondering what that hesitation was. I'm sure he is, too. Then I see his eyes start taking on that heated look, like he just realized that he's about to get laid.

So I turn and bolt.

"Where are you going?" he hollers.

The lights from his friends' wedding shine bright up ahead. With a glance over my shoulder, I see him jogging toward me, seemingly unperturbed. He's definitely not trying too hard. I'm not that fast a runner, though, so he'll probably catch me before I reach the house.

Fuck. And then what?

Vagina exorcism attempt number two, right here? Contrary to what people say, rolling around naked in gritty sand is neither romantic nor comfortable.

Houses line my left—all expansive buildings with big, beautiful windows and landscaped backyards lit up. All except the one . . . two . . . I visually count . . . the fifth one down from Storm and Dan's. A few property lights on the side and front of this house are on, but the back lights are off and inside, it's completely dark.

And it hits me. An idea out of nowhere, of the mischievous variety that I seem to find impossible to ignore. Especially when I've been drinking.

Running up to the property line, I hop over the low hedge, my bare feet silent against the soft grass beneath.

"Reese?" Ben's sharp whisper cuts through the quiet night.

"Yeah?"

A moment later, a bit closer, "Jesus. Please tell me you're not about to rob someone."

I turn around to see him standing just outside the property, a rare look of panic marring his carefree mask. "I'm not a criminal!"

"What are you doing, then?"

Reaching back, I unfasten my zipper and let my dress hit the pavement, revealing the secret I had hidden beneath the thick white material.

A "Jesus" escapes Ben's lips in a hiss as his eyes graze over the matching red underwear set. I actually used to love the color, and this particular set was one of Jared's favorites. I remember staring at it in my trash can for two hours before saving it, way back when I first moved to Miami. The bra really does do wonders for me.

"You know, there's an ocean out there that no one owns."

"It's too cold." I fight a sudden rash of nerves as I unfasten my bra next. "Have you never snuck into a person's pool before?"

Covering his mouth with his hand as his eyes remain glued on my now bare chest, he mutters, "Not at a random multimillion-dollar Miami home."

"A random multimillion-dollar Miami home with no security and no signs strictly forbidding it. In my opinion, they're asking for it." Taking a deep, calming breath, I shimmy out of my panties, Ben's eyes unpeeling themselves from my chest to shoot downward. "I knew you were a wuss." The glass surface of the pool barely ripples as I slide soundlessly into the water.

He purses his lips for a moment as if deciding his next move. "I'm not a wuss. I just don't feel like getting arrested tonight."

"Wow. This feels *so* good against my skin," I taunt in an intentionally seductive tone, trying to keep my splashes to a minimum as I sail across the span of the deep end.

"Fuck," I hear from the shadows behind me. *And three . . . two . . .* There's a rustling of branches as Ben climbs over the hedge, tossing off his shirt. "Dammit, Reese. Mason was right. You *are* trouble." I ignore the comment and watch in silent appreciation of his physique as his shoes and socks come off next, followed by his pants and boxers.

Okay. I'll admit it. Ben has something to brag about. I'll also admit that I'm probably about to do something really stupid with him. And that little switch inside that's supposed to kick in and make me care—I think it's called morals or a conscience, or . . . I'm not really sure—well, it hasn't done anything but sit back and enjoy the show so far.

Ben slips into the pool on the other side much more quietly than I would expect someone of his size to sound. And when he begins wading over to me with intense purpose on his face, those dead butterfly corpses lying in my stomach—the ones Jared smashed long ago—begin fluttering like mad again.

Ben makes me feel good. He makes me feel important.

Maybe I *do* want this to happen.

But I'm not about to make it *that* easy for him. With a small, giddy giggle, I push off the side and skim across the water until I'm on the opposite end. I manage this two more times but, with Ben's huge arm span and strength, I soon find myself in a game of cat and mouse that has me caged against a wall with my predator's hot breath warming my cheek and his broad chest pressed against mine, holding me in place. We're standing on the slope down to the deep end, the water leveling just above my collarbone. "I feel like a fucking sixteen-year-old kid right now. Thanks."

"I liked being sixteen, so you're welcome." I'm having a hard time steadying my voice. I'm not sure if it's due to the thrill or nervousness.

Ben snorts, one hand sweeping my hair off my shoulders. "Why? Because you could only be tried as a minor?"

"None of those charges ever stuck." Damn, was I ever a pain in the ass to Barry. *And* Jack. I should probably apologize to both for the premature graying I must have caused.

Resting an arm on the edge of the pool, Ben brushes a rivulet of water off my cheek with a fingertip. "If we get caught tonight, I'm the one who stands to lose. Do you even care?"

"Oh, relax! It's only a second-degree misdemeanor and there are no trespassing warnings. We can plead a misunderstanding and get off completely free. Unless you have a weapon, and then it's a third-degree felony. How do you not know this off the top of your head?"

"How do *you* know all of this off the top of your head?"

I let him see my exaggerated eye roll and then reveal my little secret. "The owners are *at* the wedding. You remember that guy that looks like an older version of The Situation?"

I watch him as he picks through his memory. He totally has no clue. "And the woman with giant duck lips and a big head of blond curls?"

One dimple appears as Ben gives me a crooked smile. "Yeah, I saw her."

Of course he did. "Seriously? This is their house?"

"Yeah. And the twin boys hovering over the dessert table are theirs."

Ben pauses. "Well, what if they come home right now? And what about silent security alarms? Have you never heard of those?"

"Trust me. Between the wife and kids asking about the late-night buffet and the husband chatting up every stripper there, they won't be home anytime soon. And . . ." I let my finger graze over the solid curve of Ben's shoulder and slide down to his chest to toy with his nipple, ". . . I heard the wife bitching to him about staying relatively sober because the security company is coming at nine a.m. to fix the security system around the pool." I give him a smug smile. "Because it's *not* working."

Realization sweeps over his face. "Huh . . . So there's no real risk of getting caught for this, is that what you're telling me?"

"Basically."

His chest rises and falls with relief and then he presses farther into me, his nose skimming my cheek playfully. "Well, this changes things."

"So . . . the water's really warm, right? Better than the cold ocean?" I tease.

He chuckles, his naturally loud voice crackling with the strain of trying to keep quiet. "Yes, otherwise *we'd* have a *real* problem here." And by the feel of Ben against my stomach, we certainly don't now. The next thing I know, Ben's hands are diving under the water to wrap around the backs of my thighs. Lifting me, he guides my legs around his hips and then steps in to secure our position against the pool wall. With a free hand, he reaches up to grasp the nipple piercing, sending a current of excitement through me. "Have I already told you how glad I am that you kept this in? You're not allowed to take it out."

"Jack doesn't know about it, so I figured it's okay."

Ben's head falls into the crook of my neck with a grunt. "Can we not talk about the guy who will fire my ass if he ever finds out about this?"

"Deal," I agree as a hand curls behind my neck and his lips find my collarbone. I lay my head back against the edge of the pool, my breathing now coming in short, ragged drags. It's been so long since I felt like this.

"While we're talking about hidden piercings . . ." As if afraid to lose the opportunity again, Ben wastes no time sliding a hand down my chest, my stomach, and down farther. A tiny gasp escapes me as he begins searching me inside and out.

Another way in which Ben appears to be supremely skilled.

"Are you disappointed? I chickened out," I admit, struggling to sound unaffected.

The hand that nestles my neck forces my head up to face a set of sparkling blue eyes. "Nothing here is a disappointment, Reese." Wedging his free hand between the small of my back and the pool wall, he crushes me with his body and a mind-numbing kiss that ends all thought processes.

Except one. "Did you bring a condom?" I whisper against him, wondering how well they work in pools and knowing that he needs to get something on himself very soon.

He chuckles as I feel his arousal jump to attention against me. "Do you think I go *anywhere* without a—"

His words are cut off as a blinding floodlight suddenly shines down on us from the house. We turn in unison to find an old lady standing by the sliding glass door, her frail little body clad in a pink robe, her hair set in curlers, bifocals sitting on her nose, and a rifle pointed at us.

"Ah, shit," Ben mutters. "I take it Granny wasn't invited to the wedding?"

"Stay still!" she yells in a reedy voice, squinting at us. Her hands are trembling. From fear, or anger, or old age, I'm not sure. But I'll admit that I'm more than a little concerned that one of us is going to end up with an accidental gunshot wound because of it.

"Just let us get dressed and we'll be gone in a minute," Ben offers, but she's apparently having none of that, her head already shaking from side to side.

"Why you young folk think it's okay to fornicate in the pool my grandkids swim in . . ." She works her bottom lip as though maybe her teeth aren't firmly in place. "The police are on their way!"

Ben's forehead falls against mine with a quiet curse.

Chapter 20

■ ■ ■

BEN

"Can I grab a ride back with you?" Dan asks the officers as they turn to leave. One of them offers me a lazy salute and a smirk as he passes by. I recognize him as a customer from Penny's. Not that that connection was enough to keep us from getting into trouble tonight.

I called Dan and asked him to intercept the cops in case Reese was wrong and they could find a reason to haul our asses down to the station. I'm pretty sure Reese is right and they can't charge us with trespassing. I'm not 100 percent sure about the indecency charges and I'd rather not have to figure that out while in handcuffs.

I think I know how Reese has avoided a criminal record up until this point: she's a compelling liar. When Granny announced that the cops were coming and Reese saw the look on my face, she immediately turned the tear tap on, swearing that Sara—how Reese remembered the woman's name is beyond me, unless this entire stunt was premeditated, which, given Reese's reputation, could very well be—told us we could come over for a late-night swim. The old woman was sceptical, but she at least allowed me to dig my phone out of my pants pocket to call Dan.

All of this while still in the pool because she wouldn't let us get out. She said she didn't trust us not to run. I'm sure that's mostly true, but I damn well know that with the light shining down on us the way it was, glasses or not, the old coot was getting a good eyeful.

If I had known she was pointing an eleven-year-old's BB gun at us, I would have pulled Reese out and run.

Dan arrived just minutes after the cops, driving the blitzed homeowners and their kids home. Apparently Sara bowled out of the car and stumbled inside to pass out on the couch, so she couldn't corroborate Reese's story. Jim, the husband, was thankfully a little more lucid. He quickly brought towels out for us and sent his mother inside with the boys, swearing up and down that his wife did in fact invite us to use their pool. I think everyone standing around that backyard knew that was a fat lie, but no one, including the cops, wanted to deal with this tonight. Seeing as we hadn't hurt anyone, and our "public nudity" was on private property at night and hadn't offended anyone besides Granny, the cops were happy to leave with a warning.

All because I can't think with the right head when there's a naked girl around.

"Can I please go back to my bride now?" Dan asks me, irritated.

"I'm sorry, man," I mutter, buttoning up my shirt. Fuck, am I going to get the gears about this one later!

"Thank you, Dan," says an already dressed and very sheepish-sounding Reese.

Dan exhales and then softens. "Don't worry about it." Running a hand through his blond brush cut, he adds in a very cop-like tone, "But let this be a lesson to you, young lady. This is the kind of stuff that happens when you hang around with a guy like Ben."

Stealing a glance Reese's way, I see her lips pressed together tightly, like she's fighting the urge to laugh. She merely nods in silent agreement.

And all I can do is shake my head at her.

■ ■ ■

Jack saw you drop me off this morning.

Reese's text couldn't have come at a better time. Or worse.

"Ben! A moment?" Jack calls out as I speed past the open door, hoping to go unnoticed.

"Shit," I mutter under my breath. With a low exhale, I slide my phone into my pocket and turn around to make my way into Jack's spacious office. I hoped it would be empty in here, on a Sunday afternoon. I should have known better.

Jack gestures to the chair across from him. "Take a seat, please." He looks as rough as I feel, the dark circles under his eyes more pronounced than usual. The guy's in his mid-fifties and he works longer hours than anyone else here. Not what I want to be known for when I hit that decade of my life. Very casually he asks, "How was your night?"

I sigh before I can stop myself, as the tightness of regret sets into my chest. Reese could have shared a little more on what exactly she told Jack. Now I'm bound to get caught in a lie. I mean, other than *almost* nailing his stepdaughter in the pool and *almost* getting into trouble with the police, nothing happened. When we got back to the reception, Dan had already highlighted "another night of Ben's idiocy" to everyone. They wasted no time laying into me. The only plus to that was that Mercy heard about it and I guess figured that if I was giving it to anyone, Reese would be the lucky receiver.

We hung out in the den with the usual gang for a while after the crowd died down, intent on heading home once the few beers I drank worked their way out of my system. We would have left had we both not passed out for a few hours on the couch, Reese curled up against my side, her cheek on my chest. It was sweet. If Nate and Ginger weren't asleep on the other side of the sectional, I might have awakened Reese to pick up where Granny had interrupted.

So, all in all, it was a relatively innocent night for me. I feel like no matter what I say now, though, I'm still gonna look like a little boy caught with his hand in the cookie jar. So I settle on, "Good."

Jack's chair bops back and forth as he shifts his body. And then he starts to chuckle. "Sometimes I forget what it was like to be your age."

I choose to keep my mouth shut and see where this conversation takes us. Hopefully it's not to a pink slip.

"I remember the day Reese's mother, Annabelle, strolled into my office, looking for a divorce from her first husband. I was taken by her right away. A mesmerizingly beautiful woman. When she started flirting with me, I was dumbstruck. A woman who looked like that, interested in *this*?" He gestures at himself. "But she seemed to be and we married a year later." A derisive snort escapes Jack as he stands and starts pacing, absently spinning a globe as he passes. "Obviously things didn't work out for us. I came back from a business trip early and swung by here to collect some paperwork, only to find my partner with her." He nods toward the impressive desk in front of me. "On *there*."

Sitting up straighter, I find myself looking at the desk under a whole new light. "And you still use it?"

"Five generations of Warners have sat at this desk," he mutters, walking over to rap his knuckles against the smooth, polished mahogany wood as if to make a point. "I wasn't going to let that she-devil ruin that. She ruined almost everything else." He exhales heavily, as if just talking about it tires him out. "We divorced immediately after that. Barry had helped me double the size of the Warner clientele list since joining, and I had to put everything up as collateral to buy out his share." He shakes his head. "My father warned me not to take on an equity partner, even if Barry and I had been best friends since we were two. I should have listened."

Sitting back down, he continues. "As painful as that whole experience was, the only thing I regret was letting Annabelle cut Reese out of my life when the girl was twelve. My first wife and I always wanted a daughter but after Mason, she kept miscarrying. Then she died. I had all but given up until Reese came along. I've known that girl since she was six years old. I thought of her often, but . . ." He shakes his head. "I lost a lot in the divorce, but the biggest thing by far was losing touch with that girl."

This is the kind of shit I don't ever want to deal with. When you avoid making commitments involving signatures and precious metal and mixed DNA, there's no collateral damage.

But why is Jack telling me all of this? Is this the part where he tells me that I'm getting canned for trying to defile the stepdaughter he finally reconnected with and loves so much; where three years of law school goes down the toilet because I let my dick do all my thinking for me?

"You're probably wondering why I'm telling you all of this."

I answer with a shrug that says "kind of," and a simultaneous stomach clench.

He starts chuckling lightly. "I'm not going to pretend that Reese is a sweet little girl. She was a holy terror when she was six and she's still wild, though she seems to have settled down quite a bit since I brought her down from Jacksonville."

Not that much, based on last night's pool incident. "She does love red paint," I dare to bring up.

His chuckle deepens. "You should have seen her, splattered head to toe like some scene out of *Dexter*, sitting in the police station interrogation room. I'm glad she called me when she did, even if it was to bail her out. Surprised, actually. I called Barry on the way up to Jacksonville because I couldn't believe Annabelle hadn't forced him to help keep her reputation from getting smeared by a daughter with a criminal record. That's when I found out that they divorced two years ago. We had a good talk." Jack's eyes drift off out the window, as if catching up with the past. "Anyway, I saw my trip to Jacksonville as my chance to make amends." A frown zigzags across his forehead. "Reese is shrewd. So is her mother. She can also be quite selfish and spiteful. Again, like Annabelle. She's passionate, and that gets her into trouble more often than not. I've spent a lot of time talking to her about accountability and control and consequences, while trying to treat her like a responsible adult. Hence the Harley." There's a pause. "Her dad rode a bike; did she tell you that?"

I shake my head.

"She always talked about getting one, just like him. Even as young as six."

Huh . . . The mystery that is Reese is starting to unfold. "Daddy's little girl?"

Jack snorts. "Through and through. It sounds like she spent *a lot* of time with him before he left her. Broke that little girl's heart when he did." He heaves a sigh. "She was still asking where Daddy was every night a year later, when they moved in with me. When he'd come back. Why he didn't come back for her. That broke *my* heart."

"Yeah, she mentioned something about him the other day."

Jack turns to regard me with an arched brow for a long moment. "Really? She doesn't normally."

"What ever happened to him?"

Jack shrugs. "He dumped her in a diner and took off. As far as I know, he never tried to get in contact with Annabelle again, but she was pretty tight-lipped about anything to do with her first marriage." He pauses for a moment. "Whatever happened, I don't think Annabelle ever recovered from it, and it has made her a bitter woman. When I heard what happened to Reese, warning bells went off inside my head. I don't want her to end up like her mother, breaking some poor shmuck's heart because some idiot first broke hers. That's how people get into trouble."

"She sure does like trouble," I agree softly.

Twisting his mouth, he adds, "And I don't doubt that you were no match for whatever she was up to last night that made you dare drop her off on my doorstep at six in the morning."

The sudden change in topic startles me. It brings with it the memory of Reese's svelte, naked silhouette and I have to duck my head, for fear of Jack reading the vulgar thoughts coursing through my mind.

"Look. You know my policy here on interoffice relationships. I have them in place for a good reason. I've lost more than one good employee due to emotional messes. I told you all of this to help you understand that Reese is a passionate, emotional young woman who's finally on the right track. I won't let her fall apart because of a soured romance with one of my lawyers."

"I'm not looking for a relationship," I promise him, hands held up in surrender.

That earns me a stern glare. "Well, I can guarantee you that I don't approve of what *else* you may be looking for, Ben. I can only imagine the kind of workplace experiences you've become accustomed to, given your previous employment."

I open my mouth to deny his assumptions, to explain that Cain would have fired my ass and crippled me had he heard I screwed around with his dancers while working there, but Jack puts his hand up to silence me. "Your position at Warner is safe. For now. Reese says you two are just friends and I have no reason to believe otherwise. Yet."

"Yes, sir."

"And Mason has even corroborated it. We both know how much of a stickler he is on following the rules."

"Yup. He sure is." The guy's like a programmed robot. He gets all flustered when he has to function outside of them.

Giving the stubble on his cheek a rub, Jack muses, "I liken Reese to a wild horse that's become accustomed to humans. She'll tolerate you, she may even come close to you, she'll certainly bewitch you, but you never know exactly what she's going to do next. She has trust issues that run deep."

"She trusted a guy enough to marry him," I remind him.

"After six weeks . . . and look where that got the crazy girl," he mutters. "That wasn't about trust. That was about needing to feel loved. About someone choosing *her*, making *her* come first. Everyone who was supposed to make her the priority had failed, leaving her lying on the ground to figure out how to pick herself back up. Her father, Annabelle, me . . . and then that joker she married."

I wonder if Jack knows that said joker is now living in Miami and Reese is on a mission for revenge. Based on the fake boyfriend deal she cornered me into, I don't think she's gotten enough payback. Whatever else she has planned, I'm pretty sure I don't want to know.

"The poor girl has felt rejection over and over again." Taking a seat once again, Jack steeples his fingers in front of his face and says in a calm, cautionary tone, "If anything were to happen between the two of you and then fall apart, I will choose her. I don't care how good of a lawyer or friend to Mason you are. She will be my priority. Am I clear?"

"Got it." He'll fire my ass if I hurt her in any way, shape, or form. Luckily, she seems to be interested in me for only one thing and it's the kind of thing I can readily give her.

With a slight nod, he leans back in his chair. "I'd like this little conversation to stay between the two of us, if you don't mind. Reese doesn't take well to being told she can't do something and I don't want to give her a reason to feel she needs to start rebelling against me."

"It won't ever come up."

"Good. Now get out of here."

With a quick salute, I jump up, gladly accepting my get-out-of-jail-free card.

Chapter 21

...

REESE

He doesn't notice me leaning against the frame of his door, he's so intent on a file folder spread out on his desk. And so I simply stand there and watch him for a moment. Ben may not take two steps without having that charming little smirk on his lips, but when he's concentrating on something, his brow is usually furrowed and his mouth is ever so slightly downturned. It's another very handsome side to him. I almost don't want to interrupt him.

"I finished these for you."

Blue eyes shoot up to take me in, flickering downward over my body before returning to my face, as if it's impossible not to check all of me out. For Ben, I think it may be. Then again, now that I've gotten a good glimpse of everything beneath his clothes, I've been taking *every* opportunity to check him out as he passes by my office, too. It usually ends with my heart rate quickening and me losing focus. Ben has become incredibly damaging to my concentration.

Setting his pen down, he leans back and heaves a sigh. "Hey, Reese." The smirk is there, but there's an edge of something to go with it. The same something that's been lingering every time I've crossed paths with him this week. I think it's wariness.

If I had to guess, Jack said something to him about dropping me off on Sunday morning. When I texted Ben about it, though, he denied that any conversation had ever taken place. And then he asked me what I was wearing.

Walking in, I place the folder on his desk. "Pages are all marked. I've also prepared the additional paperwork for your client to sign."

"You've been busy." The words that would normally be flirtatious from Ben seem almost clipped now. I want playful Ben back. I also think I want him to kiss me again. "Tired?"

"Yeah. This work just never ends."

I slink into his spare chair and put my feet up on his desk. "How can I help?"

I don't miss his quick glance out toward the left, where Jack's office is. He leans forward and lowers his voice to a low crackle just above a whisper, because I don't think Ben is capable of whispering. "Look, I've seen you completely naked twice now. Having you in here is giving me a raging hard-on that I won't be able to hide if I get called into a meeting, which is about to happen. You need to get your cute ass out of here now so I can focus."

I let my legs slide off and drop to the floor noisily. "Suit yourself." A strange mixture of excitement and disappointment sweeps through me with his words.

Jack totally threatened him.

It's my own fault. I should have had Ben drop me off down the street. Jack is always up that early and I knew there was a chance that he'd be on his treadmill, the one in the room above the garage that overlooks the driveway.

Standing, I head toward the door. As my hand grasps the doorknob, Ben's heavy sigh fills the air. "Look, I just can't risk losing my job over this."

I pause to look over at him. "Over what? We're just friends, right?"

The pen in his hand flicks back and forth as he regards me for a moment. And then he smiles. "Yup, just friends."

I hold up a finger. "But don't forget, fake boyfriend, we still have a deal." I haven't talked to Jared since that day at the café, more than a week ago. I hear that little voice screaming inside my head, the words "let him go" on repeat, but a part of me—the part that makes me open up Facebook and type in his name as soon as I wake up in the morning—isn't ready yet. I just can't figure out exactly why. Is it for the sake of pride? The promise of retribution? Or is it because I know all is not well in Caroline's stolen paradise? Because I want *my* paradise back?

"Yeah . . ." That one word draws out of Ben's mouth with another glance toward Jack's office as he shakes his head, a strange frown marring his face. "Just don't get your fake boyfriend fired."

■ ■ ■

"Here." I set one of Mrs. Cooke's muffins down on his desk, my stomach doing a small flip at the sight of Ben's arms, looking all the more defined in a fitted silvery-blue golf shirt. I think blue is my favorite color on him. It makes his eyes pop. "They're going fast."

Ben looks up from his desk, glancing at my offering, and then up at me. "That's because I've already eaten three this morning." Reaching out to wrap a giant hand around it, he says with a wry smile, "But thanks. I'll gladly take this one, too."

"You're going to grow a belly like Jack if you don't slow down on those."

Taking a bite, he watches me with curious eyes while he chews and swallows. "Will you still love me when I don't look like this?"

"Absolutely not." I turn to walk out, his snicker making me smile.

But then his words catch me at his doorway. "You know, you're acting awfully nice to me. It's out of character. People are starting to notice. They think Rancor is developing a little crush."

I look over my shoulder in time to catch his wink. "We wouldn't want that, now, would we?"

I can't tell if he's just teasing me or if people are actually saying that and noticing a difference in me. But I do know that we definitely don't want that kind of rumor floating around. "You know better, though, right?" It almost comes out as a warning.

Grinning broadly, he holds the muffin up and says, "No worries here, Reese. Thanks for this."

I didn't realize I was holding my breath but I guess I was, because I release it in a heavy sigh. Just to be on the safe side, I add in a calm but loud—loud enough for half the office to hear— voice, "I hope you choke on that and die. Have a nice day!"

Reese MacKay does not "crush" on anyone.

Ben's laughter trails me past a dozen nosy clerks and admins, all the way into my own office.

■ ■ ■

Life at work has taken a turn down Dreadfully Boring Street. It's not that I ever particularly enjoyed it, but the last few weeks had felt different. More lively. Now, my office feels empty and dull. Not for the lack of file folders or coffee cups, though.

It's because a certain six-foot-three-inch blond guy ensures he's never in a room alone with me anymore. I'm still focused 100 percent on Natasha's and his cases, but he has started going to the other paralegals—who aren't half as quick or efficient as I am—for answers.

For a while there, I was worried he might believe these "rumors" that I have a thing for him and was intentionally avoiding me because he doesn't want to lead me on. But I catch those blue eyes on me *all the time*. He's not embarrassed about it, either. I know because he winks at me every time our eyes connect.

I can't even corner him in his office, because he's in meetings with Natasha *all* the time.

And now I'm starting to get paranoid that there's something

going on between him and the law bot, even though she's engaged and I'm pretty sure she'd never agree to casual sex. She's probably as militant in bed as she is with everything else, something I doubt Ben would be into.

I *hope* he wouldn't be into.

Unless she's one of those people who tie their men up and whip them. Ben *might* be into that.

I hate this.

I don't even *want* anything with Ben besides what we already have. I just don't want him to have that with anyone else.

So now I find myself looking for every excuse possible to stop by Ben's office. That's why I'm standing in line, buying a cup of this dreadful coffee—a joke, really—and some scones.

"I've seen you here before. I can't believe I didn't realize who you were."

People say that southern drawls are beautiful and relaxing. At nine a.m. and coming from its source, I would describe it more like nails-on-a-chalkboard grating.

I glance over my shoulder to catch Caroline's sour expression and wonder why she's here so late. The four times I waited on that park bench outside for her, the girl walked in at eight thirty, like clockwork. Though, by the sharp look in her eyes, I'm starting to think that she may have been doing the waiting today. "Sorry, can't say I ever noticed *you*." I pay for my purchase and step away from the counter. "Have a *great* day!" I offer in the most annoying, chirpy voice I can manage as I pass by her and head out the door.

A vice-like grip latches onto my arm. "You don't think I know what you're doing?" Caroline hisses.

I glance down at her hand and she releases it quickly as if suddenly spotting lesions. "Was that a trick question? Because I'm heading to work. It's not exactly surreptitious."

She stabs me with an icy glare. "There are an awful lot of coincidences at play here, wouldn't you agree?"

"Aside from us having the same taste in men and cafés, I'm

not seeing it." She's standing so close to me that I can smell her breath. It smells like watermelon. The simulated-flavor gum kind. I *hate* watermelon. Figures.

Her eyes narrow. "How did your number end up in Jared's phone again?"

I struggle to hide my surprise. Jared has a thing about his phone and keeping people out of it. Or maybe it was just keeping *me* out of it, because he was texting his ex.

Her next words answer my confusion. "That's the thing about knowing someone since you were six years old. They're pretty predictable. Even with their passwords."

"What's wrong, you don't trust him?" I doubt Jared would be happy having his jealous wife snooping through his things, and she's jealous all right. I feel the spike of joy deep inside.

"You will *never* get him back," she says slowly and evenly, with the kind of confidence that can't be faked. "Jared has been in love with me all his life. He was so crushed when we broke up that he would have taken anything. Why else do you think he'd marry a motorcycle-riding psycho like you? You were a mistake that he regrets every day. He's *mine* and he always will be."

Emotion erupts inside me—a hazardous mixture of anger and humiliation and hurt that burns at the rims of my eyes and makes me want to dump this scalding coffee over her head. Not for one second have I forgotten the look on her face when I pulled open the shower curtain that day. I swear, I think she was waiting for that moment because she quickly locked eyes with me, a triumphant gleam shining through.

And now she's throwing down the gloves in the middle of a café, surrounded by baked goods and strangers. I catch a slight tremble in her hand and I have to believe she may be a little bit afraid of me. Seeing as I left a pair of scissors jabbed through her eyes in that picture of her and Jared, she should be. She should probably be afraid that I'm going to hit her right here, in the middle of this crowd. Maybe she's hoping that's exactly what I'll do. That's exactly what I *want* to do. She knows I have a temper. She could press charges against me and be rid of me. There'd be plenty of witnesses here.

Clever girl.

"Why are you so worried that he has my phone number then?" I ask in a forced calm voice, feeling the scone in my hand crumble within my tight grasp.

"I'm not," she sputters out, seemingly caught off guard. "You just need to know that I know and I'm laughing at you. All of my friends are laughing at you. You are *pathetic*."

Yeah, she's definitely provoking me.

I bite my tongue against the irresistible urge to ask how her legs are after Sunday. No use giving her something worthy of a restraining order. "Well, it's nice to see that Jared's moving on from one crazy to another. Have a great day," I exclaim with forced exuberance as I turn my back to her and walk away, my teeth gritted tightly.

I pull out my phone and hit number two on my speed dial.

"Reese? Are you okay?" Jack asks right away.

I frown, scanning the cars and pedestrians on the street. "Yeah . . ."

A deep exhale carries through the receiver. "Okay, good. I just thought . . . because you're calling me," he says with a chuckle. "You're usually holed up in your office, hating everyone for another hour or two."

"Oh, yeah. I'm fine."

"So, what's up?"

"You mentioned a little party for Ben and Mason?" It was official last week. Ben and Mason got their bar exam results and both passed. They're now associate lawyers.

"I did. Why?"

The wheels of my devious brain are picking up speed. "I'm going to plan something for this Friday."

"Well, Mrs. Cooke has already—"

I cut him off. "No, Jack. We're not doing this in a church base-ment. I'll find something good." A casual bar, a relaxed situation. Neutral ground. Somewhere I can come and go as if I don't give a shit.

And remind my ex-husband how much he misses me.

As soon as I'm off the phone with Jack, I message Jared.

I'll be at The Grill on Friday night around eight, with friends. Casual.

After a moment, I add:

You may want to change your phone password. According to your lovely wife who I just ran into, you're very predictable.

Chapter 22

. . .

BEN

T.G.I.F.

Every day seems to blend into the next around here. I guess I pushed my office door shut a little too hard because it slams, causing at least a dozen heads to pop up from cubicles like in that carnival groundhog game. I wave a lazy apology as I toss another folder down.

Damn, what I'd do to have Reese attached to me all hours of the day and night! I like working with her. No, I fucking *love* working with her. Just having her around somehow makes everything more entertaining.

That's why I've had to all but avoid her this week. And it sucks.

Jack is right: the girl just has a bewitching way about her. Idiots like me are doomed.

As I round my desk, I find a red gift bag sitting in my chair with bits of white tissue paper sticking out. After weeks of hiding in rooms and doing Natasha's bidding, bar exam results were posted this week. Mason and I passed. I'm finally a real lawyer. I'm guessing this is some sort of congratulatory thing.

I rifle through it with curiosity to discover a folded note:

Congrats on becoming an official law bot.

In case the nickname didn't give it away, I know by the messy chicken scratch that it's from Reese. The woman has worse handwriting than any doctor I've ever met. I think it's because she's always rushing. Digging down farther, I pull out a bright red T-shirt that says: "I got puked on in Cancún and all I have to show for it is this ugly red shirt."

I'm sure the entire floor can hear my bellow of laughter.

Damn, I love her sense of humor.

And I'm really disappointed when I find no one but the Rancor cutout in her office, her computer shut down already. I guess it's not a big deal. I can thank her at the little after-work party they're throwing for Mason and me tonight.

Still, I don't even want to wait that long.

■ ■ ■

"Good pick," I yell over the live band as my eyes roam the crowd at The Grill, resting on a couple of brunettes who have already noticed me and, by the small waves and winks, are not shy about making me aware of it.

"Reese arranged it all," Mason admits with no small surprise in his tone, clanking his draft against mine. "Cheers. To being a real lawyer."

"Where is the little minx, anyway?" The entire attorney staff, including Jack, are here tonight to celebrate. They have an area cordoned off for us, set with platters of food and a few tables. I've been doing the rounds for the last three hours, watching the clock and the door way too much.

"With Lina and Nicki. Lina just texted me to say they'd be here soon."

"How's that going? Is she the reason behind this whole 'Can't Buy Me Love' look you've got going on?" Mason has never been known for his keen fashion sense, but now he's got new clothes and he's styling his hair differently. He's even wearing contacts. We used to ride his ass about those thick, dorky glasses he wore, but he refused to change them.

His cheeks brighten as he shrugs. "I felt like trying something new and she helped me."

Getting laid certainly is doing wonders for this guy. "And things are good between you two?"

A sheepish grin passes over his face. "It's good. It's . . ." The smile fades as his head nods up and down. He finishes with, "It's complicated."

"Oh hell, you're not fucking *in love* with her, are you?"

"No! I mean, I like her. *A lot*. But . . ." His voice trails off as he stares at his beer.

"But what? And I don't do relationship talk, so this had better not be deep," I warn him.

"She's Reese's best friend, so . . ." He hesitates, as if he's reluctant to admit the rest. "I'm waiting to find something majorly wrong with her."

He doesn't look too pleased when I burst out laughing at him. "I thought you and Reese were sorting your shit out." I've seen them talking more in the office. Reese even offered to help him proof some legal letters going out to clients the other day.

"I think we are," he concedes with a shrug. "Slowly."

"Well, from what Jack says, Reese is not leaving your lives again. Ever. And my money's on her if you two go to war, just so you know."

He shrugs and takes another big gulp of his drink. And I smile to myself. Mason's a lightweight. He'll be giggling like a little girl by the time he reaches the bottom of that. Speaking of drunk, I need to slow down on these or I'm liable to do something stupid and unprofessional and, well . . . me. Probably not the right place or time for that. Later, at my house, where the guys are throwing a little party for me, is fair game.

"What's going on between you and Reese?" Mason asks suddenly.

"I already told you. Nothing."

"Ben." He leans forward and drops his voice. "I don't want to see you get fired." The skin between his eyes pinches together. "I know I don't really fit in with the rest of the guys, but you've always made me feel like one of the group. You've always been a good friend to me. I'm just trying to look out for you."

It's funny that Mason is saying this to me now. When I started law school, I felt like *I* didn't fit in. Going from my undergrad, where I was still seen as the star quarterback even after I wasn't playing anymore, to a nobody who lacked the scholarly vibes and refinement that everyone else seemed to have, was tough. I mean, I had the GPA, the LSAT scores, the letters of recommendation and all that, but for a while there, I thought I'd made a big mistake applying to law school.

I drop a heavy hand on his shoulder as a platinum-blond head catches my attention behind Mason. "Don't worry. I'm not getting fired." I watch the crowd shift as Mercy and Hannah make their way toward me, every guy's head turning to trail them. "Damn," I mutter. It's impossible to see those two together without thinking about my farewell party. This is going to be a long-ass night. I really hope Reese shows up soon.

"Are those the two?" Mason's index finger pushes against the bridge of his nose—where his glasses would be if he was still wearing them—as he stares wide-eyed at them.

"Yup," I grin. Giving Mason the details of that night was almost as fun as experiencing it. The guy hung onto my every word as if I'd been revealing the secret to the Holy Grail.

"Ben!" I barely get my glass down before Mercy is on me, her arms wrapped around my neck tightly, laying a kiss right smack on my mouth. "Congratulations!" I know she's genuinely happy for me and, hell, I can't push her away. That would be mean.

Still, I gesture forward, trying to peel her off me politely. "You remember my good friend, Mason."

"I do." Her eyes light up as she steps past me. I watch with a grin, knowing what's coming. The appropriate thing would be to shake his hand and say hello. Given Mercy has already met him once, though, she leans into him and lays a slow kiss on his cheek, setting his face on fire instantly.

"Hey, Ben, it's okay that we're here, right?" Hannah's voice purrs next to me. She's so much more reserved than Mercy is. "I tried to dress down so I'm not so *obvious* around your lawyer friends. Do you think they know?"

That earns a loud bark of laughter before I can help it. Hannah's another girl who could come in here wearing a potato sack and people would still have a good idea what industry she works in. Unlike Mercy, though, she's self-conscious about what she does and can't wait to finish nursing school. Those will be some lucky patients.

I throw my arm around her and pull her into a friendly side hug. "Not a clue. You're good."

"Okay. We just wanted to say congratulations and we miss you." She leans in to give me a respectable kiss on the cheek. I know for a fact that that night meant nothing more than friends getting railed on shots of everything and having a good time to her. She's been in love with the head bartender at Penny's, Ginger, for years. "Grab yourself a drink," I suggest with a smirk, nudging her forward as I scan the crowd for Reese.

I'm swarmed with envious looks from every male attorney at Warner. I predict all kinds of phone calls and invitations come Monday. I'm used to it. Kent and the guys are always begging me to get the Penny's girls over for a private show at our house.

Tonight, I obliged them.

Unlike the smooth shifting for the two strippers, the crowd parts like the Red Sea as Nate's looming frame makes its way toward me to clasp hands. "Ginger couldn't make it, but she wanted me to give you a big wet one from her."

"Tell her to stop trying to turn us, man."

His face splits into a grin. "I can only stay for a few. I'm run-ning Penny's tonight, even though it seems like half the dancers are going to some house party for this jackass I know later on."

His ribbing makes me chuckle. "Where's Cain?"

"Out of state." My frown gets nothing more. Nate's as loyal as they come and whatever Cain's doing, he doesn't want anyone knowing about. I hope it has something to do with Charlie. Something good. That guy deserves to be happy.

With that, Nate wanders off to the other side of the bar where someone he knows sits, revealing a much smaller man hidden behind him. "That's a good friend to have in your corner," Jack murmurs, his eyes trailing Nate for a moment before shifting to Mercy and Hannah, who are flanking Mason, Hannah flutter-ing her lashes and Mercy toying with his collar.

"So are those two, if you were to ask your son right now," I joke.

"Yes," Jack smirks through a sip of his beer. "It would be nice to see him work a little less and enjoy life a little more." He hesi-tates. "I'm not sure about *that* much, though."

"Baby steps for Mason," I agree with a chuckle.

Glancing around, he asks, "Have you seen that wayward stepdaughter of mine? She arranged this entire night and now she's not here."

Good question. Part of me wants her attached to my side to fend off Mercy's advances. The other part wants her roped off on the other side of the bar so I don't get myself into trouble with Jack. I'm beginning to think it's only a matter of time.

"Spoke too soon!" Jack exclaims, his face instantly lighting up.

I can't help but notice that my stomach jumps as he says that. It does a full flip as I turn to see a blond in the doorway wearing a sexy red dress and a dangerous smile.

"Oh, fuck . . ." I mutter under my breath.

She's definitely up to something.

Chapter 23

■ ■ ■

REESE

"So I forgot to mention something to you guys," I shout to Lina and Nicki as we push our way through the crowd. The Grill is usually busy on Friday evenings. Located right on the beach, it's kind of like a tiki sports bar, with a faux grass-hut roof, open walls, and lots of flat screens. Tonight, the place is crawling with Warner staff.

Too many. And they haven't left yet. I said the work party was from five until seven—cocktail hour. At eight, they're still lingering.

"You got married again," Lina answers deadpan, as if she's been expecting that announcement.

"Not exactly," I mutter under my breath. They're going to flip their lids.

I may flip my lid.

"Where are these lawyers you speak of?" Nicki says, looking as striking as always, this time in a purple corset dress. "And do you think they'll believe me when I tell them that I'm a lawyer?"

"They're up ahead. Just say the word 'deposition' really slow while you bat your lashes and they'll believe anything. But I need to tell you guys—"

"Wow! Look at your hair!" Fingers reach uninvited to the nape of my neck, to the layer of black cherry that I had done after work at the salon. The all-blond was boring me to tears and I figured this was still semi-respectable by office standards. "Looking *très chic*. I love it!" Natasha cries, all hand-flappy, which tells me that she's most probably drunk. Without stopping to actually hear my answer, she continues, "Who're your friends?" She sticks a hand out. Lina's perfectly shaped left brow arches as she accepts it.

"Lina, Law bot. Law bot, Lina."

Natasha's heard me call her that so many times, I don't think it even fazes her anymore. She's too busy gawking at Nicki's sleeve of ink, anyway. "Did that hurt?" She reaches out to begin pawing at Nicki's arm.

"You get used to it," Nicki offers politely, but her lips are pressed in a tight smile. She hates being touched like that. Giving them wide-eyed looks, I mouth, "Let's go."

"So, where was I . . ." I can see Ben's blond head towering over the others, standing next to Jack. He's smiling at me, though it's slightly strained. But his eyes are still raking over my chest and flashing with approval at the strapless red number I bought today. It's fitted and short, but the skirt flows out like a bell to show my legs off nicely. Slightly formal for the night—especially paired with heels—but with my loose hair and lack of jewelry, I think I can pull off the look. I'll just channel my inner femme fatale like Nicki does.

I do a cursory scan of heads as I close the distance. Jared texted back to say he'd be here, but I don't see him yet.

Jack turns to find me standing behind him. "Hello, Reesie." He wraps an arm around my shoulders and kisses my cheek. I instinctively lean into his affections with a smile, feeling like his little girl again. Then his gaze flickers over my hair and he frowns. "Something's different."

Jack's a true guy's guy. Flipping up a few strands of my new hair, I offer with a sheepish smile, "At least it's not my entire head."

"Hmm . . . yes." After a moment, "It looks good. Not too wild." Glancing over my shoulder at my friends, he smiles and offers, "Nice to see you ladies again. How's the new condo and the jobs?"

"Condo is good. Job not so much." Lina doesn't waste words. If she can say something in seven words, she says it in seven words. Some would take her as bitchy or abrupt.

I think she's charming.

"Well, half ain't bad. Get that license and you can come work for me, okay?" I'm pretty sure he's not kidding about that, either, which is great because I'd love to work with Lina.

"I'm heading out, Reese, but thank you for setting this up." He leans in to add in a low tone, "You're right. Better than Mrs. Cooke's church basement."

I shrug. "It's the least I could do for my loving stepbrother."

"Right. Try not to torment him too much tonight."

"That's what *she's* here for." I jab my thumb in Lina's direction.

Shaking his head, Jack walks away, leaving me to face Ben, who quickly reaches out and throws an arm over both Lina and Nicki. "Good to see you two again. Thanks for coming to my party."

A small part of me spikes with jealousy, wondering if Ben would have tried for one of them had I not been there. There are definite drawbacks to being friends with a male slut who you occasionally mess around with, like that little voice in the back of your head that tells you he'll probably sleep with your friends, too.

"I'm here for *him*," Lina corrects a little too sharply, her gray gaze on Mason, who's standing next to Ben—and, more importantly, to the Twinkie and her friend hanging off him.

"Hi." Mason wastes no time breaking free of his fawning fans to shift next to Lina, his tone dropping an octave, sounding oddly softer and less robotic. "You made it all right?" He leans in to kiss her cheek.

I don't know if I'll ever get used to them together.

I'm still watching them as Ben grabs my attention, yanking on a dark purple tip of hair. "I like it. And I *really* like the red dress." Pulling me into his chest—to an innocent bystander, it could *probably* pass as a congratulatory hug—he murmurs, "What are you up to?"

"Whatever do you mean?" I ask in mock innocence, the comfort of his arms conflicting with the tension running through my spine, knowing Jared's going to be here.

I feel the vibration from his chuckle through my entire body. "I know it's something bad. I'm just not sure if *I* need to be careful or if you have another victim in mind."

I reach up and give his nose a gentle flick as I step away, realizing I'm slightly reluctant to do so. If I weren't on a different mission tonight, I might not want to at all. Ben feels really good.

His face softens as he gazes down at me from his impressive height. "Thank you for arranging this night for me."

"And Mason," I remind him.

There's that playful smile of his. "Who's kidding who? You did this all for me."

"Are you going to get all emotional about it?"

"No . . ." A wistful smile touches his lips. "But I wish I could kiss you for being so uncharacteristically nice."

A tiny knot of guilt is forming in my stomach. But then I remind myself that this is Ben. He doesn't really care why I did it. "Well, then this could work out in your favor. I may be calling in my fake-boyfriend card tonight."

His head tips back. "Ah, shit, Reese. You can't do that to me tonight!"

"I'm doing it. You promised."

"And you promised you wouldn't get my ass fired." He looks around as if to make a point. "Half of the firm is here! Including Jack!"

"Relax. Jack is leaving."

"Yeah, well, so am I." I watch him suck back a big gulp of his beer, a spark of panic igniting in me. *Ben, leaving?* "My buddies are having a little party for me back at my house. You and your friends are more than welcome to come—just keep it to yourselves. I don't want a bunch of lawyers there."

Relief immediately pours over me and I realize how much I really want to hang out with Ben tonight, Jared or not. "What about Mason?"

Ben lets out a derisive snort. "I'm not worried about Mace. He knows exactly what I'm about." His eyes drop to settle on my mouth.

"I didn't order the full-service fake boyfriend model," I remind him with a hard poke to his stomach, though I feel my heart speeding up its rhythm. Ben doesn't even flinch, the thick layer of muscle protecting him.

"That doesn't mean you're not gonna get it." He winks, adding somberly, "Just not here."

"Well . . ." I feel my teeth slide against each other in thought and catch Twinkie's casual glance over her shoulder as she pretends not to watch us. "Can you at least not make out with anyone else while you're here? Or I'll look like the idiot getting cheated on a second time." I tack on a soft "Please?" at the end for good measure.

"I was hoping to use Mason as a distraction for Mercy, but your friend here kind of fucked that all up for me." After a pause, he murmurs, "Hold on," and pinches my ribs gently. My eyes trail him as he cuts through the crowd to talk to two attorneys from Litigation who can't stop looking over our way. I'm guessing they're focused on the two strippers, because their faces light up when they follow Ben over.

"Uh, Reese?" I hear Nicki call out, a shot of tequila resting against her lips as her eyes stay focused on something across the room. "That thing you forgot to mention?"

I don't even need to look to know what she's talking about. Casually flipping my hair, I glance over my shoulder to find Jared and Caroline sitting at a table with a group of people, Jared's foot tapping to the beat of the cover band playing onstage.

When I turn back to take in my friends' faces, missing the panic they'd expect in mine if this were an accident, matching scowls form. "What have you done now, Reese?" Nicki says with a sigh, a millisecond before Lina asks, "Did you know that they'd be here?" There's that hard tone in her voice she has when she's entirely unimpressed with me. Mason just looks bewildered.

"I may have had an inkling," I admit.

"Who's here?" Mason asks, but no one answers him.

Lina slowly rolls on her feet to face the bar. "And *how* exactly did you know?"

"Long story, and you don't really want to be an accomplice to this, do you? Just follow my lead, okay?"

She sighs. "I always do. Even when you're being a bad, bad person. Are you being a bad person tonight, Reese?"

I pat the top of her head, ignoring her question. "Good, supportive friend."

"What about Ben?" Nicki asks.

"What about me?" his deep voice behind me, surprises me enough to jump. I feel the heat of his hand as he settles it on my back. Dipping down to reach my ear, he offers quietly, "Problem solved. Those litigation boys are in heaven."

I reach back to pat his firm chest, angling my head to see him, "Good fake boyfriend."

A grimace crawls over his face for a second before it smooths into a smile and his hand disappears from my back. "Fifteen minutes," he reminds me softly.

From my peripherals, I can see that Jared has caught sight of me and is watching me now. I don't turn, though. I don't want it to look like I'm looking for him. Or that I really care one way or another that he's here. "Okay, there's something I have to do first. Can you please order me a drink?"

"Where are you going?"

I glance over at the band as the singer announces a short break. "To talk to them." When I called up The Grill to make reservations and found out that they have a live band on Friday nights, I knew beyond a doubt that this night would be brilliant.

Ben grins. "You going to request a song for me?"

I lean in dangerously close—maybe I shouldn't be doing this with Jack possibly still floating around and surrounded by the Warner lawyers, but I feel Jared's eyes on me and the idea of this bothering him spurs me on—and whisper, "How about I do one better for you?"

Ben's jaw grows taut as he takes a small, rigid step back, casually checking heads.

With a grin, I practically skip over to the stage in my flirty red dress—when one is possessed by the devil, one must truly embrace the part. I zero in on the singer. He's the one I have to charm.

And that's how I end up slinging a guitar over my shoulder five minutes later. I wish I could have brought my own. It's old and crappy, but I know all its little tricks and secrets. This one will have to do.

Tapping the microphone, I clear my voice. The stage lights aren't quite strong enough to hide the crowd beyond and so I see the sea of heads turn my way. I'm only slightly nervous. I was never one to get anxious in front of crowds. Perhaps if I was, I wouldn't have done half the stupid things I did. Now, at least, I'm actually doing something that I'm good at, something I haven't done since Jared and I were together.

"It's been a while since I've been up on a stage." That's all I say, and then I signal the band with a raised hand. Every single employee from Warner is staring slack-jawed at me as the band kicks off the opening notes to "Call Me" by Serena Ryder. Except for Ben, of course. He's just standing there with his arms folded over his chest. Watching curiously.

And then I start to sing.

Breathing slowly, carrying the notes from the depths of my diaphragm, letting them sail out of my mouth, I sing as my fingers slide and curl and press each chord. It's a deep, gritty song and it suits my low vocal voice perfectly. Just being up here again, letting my own emotions pour out through someone else's words in a way that lets me speak my mind without judgment, sends a thrill through my body. I've always loved to sing, even when I was little and couldn't carry a tune. That was one thing Annabelle did for me—put me in singing lessons. She did it because all the other socialite wives had their daughters in choir. But I had no interest in singing in a choir. I joined a band instead. We were pretty good, but we didn't last long. The drummer and the bassist—brothers— argued too much.

The first night I got up and sang in a dingy Jacksonville bar for Jared was, according to him, the night he knew he wanted to marry me. He said my throaty lilt sent shivers down his spine and through his limbs, not stopping until they wrapped around his heart. Jared has a way with words.

And even now I see that odd, secretive smile touching his lips, his attention glued to me.

A look that Caroline studies intently and, by the way her nostrils are flaring, does not like in the least.

Inside me, bright, glorious, satisfying fireworks are exploding.

Dead silence hangs in the air for two seconds after the last note of the song plays and then a roar of applause explodes. I can't help but beam. I let my eyes skate over Jared for only a millisecond, enough to see that familiar glow, and then I focus on Ben as he makes his way over to scoop me off the stage with a set of strong hands around my waist.

Good fake boyfriend.

"Why do you want me fired so bad?" Ben asks, his voice crackling as he leans into me. Not too close, but surely close enough to be inappropriate for Jack's romance barometer. I hope he left before I took the stage.

"I think you're going to do that all by yourself." I take a step back, just in case he didn't. I truly don't want Ben to become a casualty of war and, if Jack's still here and he sees this . . . "Where's my drink?"

"Lina has it," he murmurs, his chest rising as his eyes fall to my cleavage. "And you'd better guzzle, because *we're* leaving right now."

Oh boy. Ben obviously has plans for me. Tonight. That's probably a good thing. It helps with this plan of mine: In. Impress. Out. I don't want to linger too long and be forced to face the two of them together. Leaving on a high note gives me the upper hand here. "I'll be there in a second, okay?" I pull the guitar strap over my head and hand it back to the guitar player, who offers me a nod of praise before jumping back onstage. With a gentle jab rub against Ben's arm, I head to the ladies' room, feeling his eyes scorch my back the entire way. Or maybe they were Jared's eyes.

Or both.

But the second I step out of the stall, I find a very different set of eyes scorching me. Ones full of hatred. And fear. They're attached to the ginger-headed bitch waiting by the sink, her hands planted on her hips.

"What are you doing here?" she snaps.

So predictable. I turn on the tap. "Right now, I'm washing my hands. Do you want to know what I just did in there?" I jam a thumb over my shoulder to point at the toilet. "Because that'd be a bit weird." If roles were reversed, I'd have punched her by now.

"I warned you!" She sticks her French-manicured fingernail in my face, so close to my nose that I fight the urge to swat it away. "Stay away from him!"

I give her my best confused look. "I'm here for a work party."

"Really?" A haughty smile creeps over her lips. "So you haven't been sending messages to Jared? Because somehow he found out that I knew his password."

"And how'd that work out for you?"

The visible clenching of her teeth tells me not very well. "You asked him to come."

"No. He said he wanted to go out for drinks and I told him I'd be here tonight," I say slowly, and then switch my tone to something more patronizing. "I think you should be more concerned with why Jared wants to meet up with his ex-wife in the first place. Why he's going out of his way to be *friends* with me."

Her brow pulls together. I can see the wheels of suspicion begin churning, the once supremely confident Caroline suffering from the affliction of doubt. *Is Jared cheating on her? Would he?* My work for tonight could be done. I could just leave her with that.

But, of course, I don't, because the burn from their treachery has left emotionally crippling scars inside. "I wonder what it'll feel like when *you* catch him with another woman."

"He wouldn't do that to *me*."

I stare hard at her, looking for the truth behind that. I can't tell if she actually believes it. If she believes she is that important to him. "No?" I plaster on my own wicked smile, and I know it's a winning one because her face pales. And then, because this woman still hasn't shown an ounce of shame for what she did to me, hasn't attempted to say "I'm sorry," I go straight for her jugular by hissing, "I'll be sure to let you know what I think of your shower."

Her eyes flash with rage. "You whore!"

I'm guessing Lina and Nicki saw her follow me in and had their heads pressed against the door because the second Caroline shrieks, the two of them plowed through it, followed closely by Ben and Mason and a couple of curious women on their way to the bathroom. It's perfect timing, really. I was just standing there, my arms folded across my chest, when Caroline flew at me, claws out.

I let her get one scratch across my collarbone in and a few solid fingerprints over my throat before I shove her away.

Nicki intercepts any further attack by firmly holding Caroline's arms to her sides. I've seen her put people in headlocks before, so this is rather gentle. I doubt it's necessary, though. By Caroline's splotchy red face and the way she's smoothing out her dress, she's embarrassed. "I'm filing a restraining order against you."

I dab a tissue that Lina provided against the scratch along my neck. It comes back with a few spots of blood. "Good luck with that. I haven't done anything wrong. If you'll recall, I moved *away* from you. *I* have never approached either of you." Well, that is technically a lie, but she doesn't know about the paintball. "*I* did not get your new phone number. *I* did not message Jared first. And *I* certainly did not just physically attack you. In front of witnesses. I'm just here, celebrating with my co-workers. And my boyfriend," I add, gesturing to Ben, who shoots an exasperated look my way while Mason has one of his own for his friend. "Maybe I should be filing a restraining order against *you*? What do you think?" Just to be a complete ass, I ask Lina. "What do *you* think?"

"I think the court would be on your side, but I'm no lawyer." Turning slightly, Lina muses, "What do you think, lawyers? Would Reese have a case here?"

Mason pushes a hand through his hair for the tenth time. I wonder what's stressing him out more—being in a women's bathroom or having no clue what the hell is going on and who Caroline is. Clearing his throat, he manages to get out, "I believe Reese would have a very strong case. In fact, we should call the police and file assault charges right now."

I don't believe it. Jiminy Cricket is actually defending me. Sure, it probably has more to do with him wanting to please my best friend, but . . .

I'm going to buy him a club-sized pack of Lysol wipes as a thank you.

"Caroline?" We all turn to find Jared stepping into the women's washroom with who I presume is the manager behind him. I make sure any trace of a smile is wiped clean off my face as I clutch my throat a little more obviously. Not that Jared is necessarily going to buy the wounded act coming from me, but . . . "What's going on in here?" He looks from her to me, to the paper towel across my neck, and back to her with surprise. "Tell me you didn't just attack Reese in the bathroom."

Caroline's face turns an even darker, more unflattering shade of red. I think the sweet little Georgia peach has been caught with her prissy drawers down, exposing the very unladylike underside that she prefers to hide.

"I'm not going to press charges. I just want to go back to celebrating Ben's night with him." Looping arms with Ben, who's still watching me with an odd look on his face, I walk out of the bathroom and down the hall with my head held high, the others trailing.

"We'll catch up to you guys in a minute," Ben calls out, pulling me back and into a small alcove near a service entrance, off from the main room and away from spectators.

"Sure. Maybe Lina can fill me in while we wait," Mason mutters, shooting me a glare as they continue on.

Ben lifts my chin with his finger to inspect the scratch. "It's not too bad."

"Unless she's rabid."

That earns a small smile. "She *was* practically foaming at the mouth. I'm surprised you didn't hit her back. Then again, I figure that all went down exactly like you wanted it to, didn't it, Miss Devious?" The smile falls slightly as he asks a little bit more softly, "Was *all* of this for *him*?" I hear the question behind it. *Was any of tonight for me?*

Shit. Maybe I was wrong. Maybe Ben does actually care.

Ben's eyes drift to my mouth, reminding me of last weekend, making me feel as though I've somehow just betrayed him. Even though I *haven't*, because we're just friends, something both of us were adamant about. *Are* adamant about. Still, I'm starting to feel a little bit guilty.

"Hey, Reese, are you okay?" I guess we're not as well hidden as we think, because Jared has easily found us.

"She's fine. Take your crazy wife and get out of here," Ben answers for me, his hands tightening around my waist as if to hold me in place.

Jared's gaze hardens as he stares at Ben. I've seen Jared turn into a hothead before, ready to pick a fight.

"Don't even think about it, man," Ben murmurs in warning. "Just turn around and take that welted ass of yours home."

He did not just say that.

Jared's light green eyes narrow as if processing, darting from me to Ben and back to me. And . . . there it is. The recognition. *Oh my God.* My stomach just dropped to the worn wood floors. I'm going to kill Ben.

Jared opens his mouth to say something, but a sobbing Caroline comes out of the ladies' room and, from the looks of it, she's being escorted out of the restaurant by the manager. With a small head shake, Jared turns and follows her, his jaw set with annoyance.

Ben pulls me around the other side of the alcove, until we're practically in the kitchen.

"I can't believe you just outed me like that! Now *he's* going to file a restraining order!"

"No he's not. And no judge will grant it, anyway," Ben states, shaking his head. "Please tell me you don't actually want that asshole back?"

"No." *Maybe.* "I want to hurt him," I admit openly. It's the truth, and when I say it out loud, I can't help but accept that Lina is right: I am a bad, bad person. I also can't help but think that maybe this is too much drama for Ben. Maybe he's going to throw his hands up right now and hightail it out of here.

And something about the idea of that pricks at my stomach.

Ben nods slowly as if he somehow understands, as if he gets me. That doesn't mean I can't see the disappointment in his light blue eyes, dousing my moment of malicious glory. "You know you're only going to hurt yourself in the end, right?"

"It's a risk, yes."

"Well then why bother? You could be spending all that effort impressing *me*."

That earns a raised brow. "To what end?"

"To a king-sized bed with Buzz Lightyear sheets," he answers matter-of-factly.

The snort escapes unbidden. Well, at least he's consistent. Folding my arms over my chest, I challenge, "You do not have Buzz Lightyear sheets."

He shrugs, his eyes dipping down the top of my dress. "Only one way to find out."

Checking behind him, likely to ensure we have no spectators, he turns back to stare at me for a long moment, his eyes searching my features. I'm still a little high on revenge fumes, but I'm pretty sure the sudden quickening beat of my heart has more to do with flashbacks of being in the pool with Ben than to anything related to Jared.

"I need to get out of here before I get into trouble." There's a slight pause, and then a sly smile makes those dimples all the more prominent. "And you have to make up for lying to me."

■ ■ ■

"You live in a frat house," I state, taking in the sizeable brown brick house in an older part of Miami.

Ben's friend Nate's deep chuckle fills the interior of the Navigator as Ben explains, "It's not a frat house. It's just a big house where six guys who went to college together live."

"You sure about that?" I climb out of the SUV to hear shouts from the porch. A group of guys chug their beers to a chorus of something that sounds like an Irish drinking song. "Because I don't think your roommates know yet."

Slapping the hood and thanking his friend for the ride, Ben

ropes his arm around my shoulders just as Mason's Subaru pulls up behind us. "Didn't even want to be separated from me for a car ride, did you?" he says with a smirk.

"Have you ever ridden anywhere with Mason?" I had to once, for a total of twenty minutes, to get a ride to campus when the Audi was in for a tune-up and it was raining too hard to ride my bike. When Ben shakes his head, I explain, "He signals half a mile away from his turns."

"And I'll bet you pointed that out to him."

"It's a public safety risk!"

"Hey, Mace! How's that signal indicator working?" Ben shouts, looking over my shoulder.

I turn in time to see Mason throw an annoyed glare my way. And then he stumbles over a crack in the sidewalk and drops his keys.

"It's a good thing that guy is so smart," Ben murmurs with a smirk as he leads me forward, away from my two best friends, who have been wearing those same scowls since the bar. That's the other reason I avoided the car ride—I don't want to deal with an intervention right now.

We climb the stairs to the porch, Ben's arm around me the way I'd imagine a boyfriend's would be, giving lazy high-fives to a few of the guys standing there.

"Why are you still living like a frat guy?" I ask as he pushes the door open.

I get my answer immediately.

"Because it's not a frat house; it's a brothel," I correct as I take in the crowd of people milling about. Some are just lounging on couches with beers in hand and college-aged girls perched on their laps while they giggle and shout over the baseball game on the television. But others are circling a small group of scantily clad and disproportionately figured women, pretending to be interested by what they're saying, all while their pants are stretched over their crotches with hopes of what tonight may bring. "Why am I not surprised?" I shout over the shitty house music, courtesy of a guy and his mixing table in the corner.

Ben's shaking his head in denial but he's smiling. "These girls aren't like that." My doubtful stare has him elaborating, "They're Penny's girls. They just dance."

"Really? And the Twinkie? Does she just dance for you?" Why is it that she's really annoying me tonight?

People start noticing Ben and a loud roar of approval and clapping erupts.

He chuckles, pulling me in farther. "Do you remember Travis? From Cancún?" Ben asks as we come face-to-face with a tall, shaggy-haired, decent-looking guy.

The guy sticks his hand out. I'll bet the confused look on his face matches mine. At least I wasn't the only shit-faced one down there that night. "Did we meet?"

I point to my head. "Used to be all purple, if that helps."

His eyes widen. "No way!" He turns to look at Ben. "You finally found her?"

What? "Ben was looking for me?"

"She works with me," Ben explains to his friend, tightening his arm around my neck until my cheek is pressed up against his chest.

"Man, I can't tell you how pissed he was when you didn't leave your number," he tells me with a laugh. "He kept going on and on about you."

Oh, this is getting better and better. "Seriously?" I manage to twist my head until I'm looking directly up at Ben's square jaw. "Were you pining over me all this time, Ben?" I know he doesn't pine, so this guy is clearly teasing him, but it's still funny to see Ben getting instead of giving for once.

Ben shakes his head, but he's laughing when he calls his friend a liar. Leaning down to press his mouth against my ear, he murmurs, "No, I just really wanted a new shirt."

I roll my eyes and try to pull away from Ben. It's futile. I'm trapped against him and he seems unwilling to budge. I decide to just go with it, burrowing into him and staying there while he and his friend talk about some football trade for a pool they're in.

So when my phone starts vibrating in my purse, I don't hesitate to slide it out to read the text:

Was that really you?

My heart jumps.

"No, no, no," Ben mutters, his full attention on me again as he swiftly pries my phone from my hand.

"Nosy!" I smack his face away as he raises his arm high above his head with a grin. I don't doubt he'd like me to scale him like a tree, but I'm not going to.

"He broke that black heart of yours. And now he's *married*. Don't be stupid."

"He's just making sure he has his facts straight before he has me arrested!" I snap, adding, "And I thought you were Switzerland."

Cupping the back of my neck with his hand, he stares down at me with sincere blue eyes. "I am. I'm also a concerned friend. Don't answer him. Nothing in writing. That's my legal advice." He looks over my shoulder and bellows, "Hey, Lina! Come talk some sense into your crazy friend for me."

I glare up at him but he only smiles, dipping down to lay a quick kiss right on my lips. "You're not leaving me like this tonight."

"Like what?"

He tugs my body flush against his and I get my answer, a second before two fierce hands grab hold of each of my forearms. Nicki and Lina, tag-teaming to drag me outside to the porch while my eyes stay locked with Ben's.

"Okay, spill it, MacKay," Lina demands, practically pushing me into one of the few lawn chairs available. Thankfully we don't have an audience, now that the guys have moved their drinking shenanigans inside.

Nicki tries a slightly different approach, taking a seat next to me so that we're eye level. "What's going on with you, buddy?" she asks softly, handing me a beer.

With a groan, I drop my head into my free hand.

And then I tell them about everything. Even the paintball ambush, which thankfully they find more humorous than disturbing. When I'm done, I find myself facing two sets of eyes, one harder than the other, but both empathetic.

"He was sleeping with her almost the whole time you were married?" Nicki asks, her eyes widening in disbelief. "I just don't get it. He seemed so into you. Like, there were no signs that made me think 'cheater.' Not one!"

Lina heaves a sigh. "I don't know what to say about all of this, Reese. Is this healthy? No. Are you going to get hurt again? Yes. Is it worth it?" She pauses, as if to let us both think about it. "No. I mean, that bitch deserves what's coming to her and she's going to get it eventually—don't you worry about that. Karma never forgets. But it doesn't have to come from you. There's really no point in keeping in touch with the douchebag. What you two had is gone and even if you get back together, it'll *never be the same*. You won't ever trust him again!"

"I told you, I don't want to get back together with him!"

Lina's face turns sour. "I need a drink to deal with your stubborn ass. Your turn, Nicki." I watch Lina's willowy frame march stiffly through the door, wondering why my best friend seems so angry at me all of a sudden. We've been through a lot together and she's always been the nonjudgmental constant for me.

"She's just worried about you," Nicki confirms, reaching out to squeeze my hand. "We all are. I know you loved him but the guy's a waste of air, Reese. I wish you'd see that."

I tip my head back and let out an exaggerated moan. "I do see that!"

"Well, then when is this going to end? How far are you going to go with this?"

"I haven't decided yet." That's the truth. I've played a few scenarios out in my head, but I'm not married to any of them.

"Well . . ." A wry smile curls her lips. "At least you have Ben to keep you occupied."

"I do," I agree, smiling as I peer over my shoulder through the window.

To see a platinum-blond hovering and Ben grinning down at her. "Shit. When did *she* get here?" What happened to those litigation guys keeping her entertained? I guess she's not after just any lawyer.

She's after mine.

I take a long draw of my beer as I try to make sense of the tightening feeling in my gut right now. Is it jealousy that he's been with her? Disappointment that that smile's not reserved only for me?

"Well, you'd better get in there before she puts her stripper moves on him," Nicki says, standing. I follow suit and find myself face-to-face with Mason.

"Hey." His face pinches up a bit. "Can I talk to you for a minute?" I look over his shoulder, but there's no Lina in sight. "She's inside," he confirms, adding, "doing shots with Kent and Travis."

"Ooooh . . ." both Nicki and I wail in unison. "Lina plus shots equals pukey-pukey tomorrow. Make sure you have a bucket," I warn Mason, adding, "and hold her hair back." Mason's not going to deal with boyfriend vomit duties very well. This may prove a true test to their relationship.

"Catch you inside," Nicki says with a pat on my shoulder, leaving me alone with my stepbrother. I fall back into the lawn chair and he joins me, to sit silently as I watch a stray cat dart across the street, its eyes glowing against an approaching car's headlights.

"So . . . I think I know what's going on."

"You're *so* clever." I reach up to stroke his head and he swats my hand away, an annoyed frown touching his face.

"You know, when you moved back, I was sure you were trying to swindle Jack out of money. But so far you've done nothing but work and try not to act insane. My dad's really happy, Reese. I haven't seen him this happy in a long time." He pauses. "And he wouldn't be happy if he knew what you were doing."

He's playing the Jack card on me. And it's working, guilt settling onto my shoulders like a dead weight. "Are you referring to what I'm doing with Ben or Jared?"

"Both." Mason pauses. "You know, relationships aren't supposed to be like this, Reese. I don't know if you're going after guys like this because you're a glutton for punishment or because you've just never seen what a decent relationship looks like, but—"

"I'm not *after* Ben," I snap. "And Jared was all heart and no head. That's really the only way I can describe that."

"And were you using your head tonight?" he pushes. "Because I get the impression that you think you have a score to settle with your ex."

"What do you care, Mason? I get that you want to be nice to me because of Lina, but don't suddenly try to be my big brother."

"That's not . . ." His lips purse together tightly. "Don't you ever wonder why your mom is the way she is? What made her so callous? People don't just grow up like that."

"No, I don't, Mason. I try not to think about Annabelle *at all.*" My irritation is growing by the second. Where the hell is Lina? She needs to come fetch her *boyfriend.*

"Well, I think it had something to do with what happened between her and your dad. I think she never got over it, and that makes her chew up good men like Jack."

"And what happened between Annabelle and my dad exactly, Mason? Because I'd love to know and I sure as hell have no idea. Do you?" I learned at a very young age that bringing up Hank MacKay got me nowhere but sent to my room. Annabelle could have ranted about my father to me, but what she chose to do was far worse. She pretended that he didn't exist.

"No, I don't," he admits. "But I know that we'd *all* hate to see you turn into her." He sighs. "I knew she was cheating on my dad before he did. I heard her on the phone, late one night. I just wasn't sure who it was with. Then, when my dad caught them . . ." Mason's jaw clenches. "I hated seeing him cry over her."

A lump spikes in my throat. Jack *cried* over Annabelle? I certainly never saw Annabelle shed a tear over Jack. In fact, I don't think I've seen her cry since the day I watched her set fire to a box of my dad's things in the driveway. She stood there, her arms wrapped around her body tight, ignoring my questions, until there was nothing left but ashes.

"Well, I'm *not* Annabelle and don't *ever* compare me to her." Mason's mouth twists up. "I really hope that's true, Reese."

"All right." I stand, struggling to quash the bubble of pain rising. "I'm going to join your girlfriend for some shots." I round the corner and step through the doorway.

And find Ben with the Twinkie's hand attached to his belt.

Chapter 24

■ ■ ■

BEN

Shit. This *really* isn't helping right now. I peer down at Mercy, at her tits pressed up against my chest, the man-made cleavage through the center. I'm betting Mercy was an A—B, tops—before her implants. "You took the entire night off?"

She shrugs and then offers me a coy smile.

Fuck. I'm halfway drunk and now I have a sure thing rubbing her nipples against me. Where the hell is Reese? She wouldn't have left without her phone and I'm not giving that back until tomorrow. The last thing I need her doing is responding to him. Leaving the party to go meet him. To do what? Vengeance fuck the guy?

I shouldn't care, but I do. I'm just having a hard time figuring out exactly why. I don't like watching my friends make stupid mistakes, but my gut is feeling off about the entire situation. I take a long sip of my beer as I try to figure out if I'm more bothered by her acting like an idiot or her screwing around with another guy when I want to be the one screwing around with her. The woman has turned me upside down. Ben Morris does not concern himself with this kind of shit. Ben Morris goes with the flow. Ben Morris is fucking Switzerland! He can get hot ass wherever and whenever he wants it, no strings attached.

"Are you upset about something?" My eyes find Mercy's double-Ds waiting for me when I look down. Case in point. Though this doesn't appear to be without strings anymore.

I give her my best dimpled grin. "Do I look upset?" *Shit, do I?*

"So what's going on with that lawyer from your office?" she asks innocently.

"Just a friend," I admit, not bothering to correct her on the lawyer piece.

"A friend like me?" Her hand slides down the front of my pants. Mercy giggles as she feels the hard-on I've been carrying around since Reese stalked into the bar in her red dress. "So this is okay? I mean, she could join if she wanted to."

I struggle to keep beer from spraying out of my mouth with my burst of laughter as I picture Reese's face in response to that proposition. It's followed by a rush of blood southward. Damn, that could be hot. I wonder if she'd be into that?

Cool hands slide up under my shirt and then back down to my belt. "Want your gift now?"

Oh, hell. I stall her fingers with my hand. Where is Reese? Her friends are at a table pounding shots of tequila and Jäger, but she's not there. Scanning the crowd, I catch Kacey's eye. I don't know when she got here. I give her a wave. She responds with a nod toward Mercy and then that "what are you doing?" glare.

"I leave you alone for two minutes . . ." I hear Reese's voice—laced with annoyance—coming from my left and I quickly maneuver out of Mercy's grasp to wrap both arms around Reese's body in a close-fitting hug.

"Please don't leave me again," I whisper into her ear. "I'm defenseless against her."

"Jackass," she mutters, glaring up at me. I can't tell, but I think she may be genuinely mad at me. There's definitely a spark of anger in those gorgeous eyes.

So I drop a lightning-fast kiss on her lips and beg, "Save me from her silicone."

She cocks her head to the side, her gaze dipping down to my mouth. "You know you're a pig, right?" The bite is gone from her tone, though. In fact, I feel her leaning farther into me.

"Yeah, but I'm *your* pig tonight."

■ ■ ■

"You weren't lying."

I smile. "Mama bought me two sets."

"I didn't think they even made them for a bed this big," she murmurs, her finger tracing over a grinning Buzz Lightyear. Her gaze roams my room—the plain blackout curtains, a couple of empty beer bottles lining the dresser, and a wall of half-naked football cheerleaders, each poster signed and personalized to me.

"It's exactly as I pictured it." She steps over to read one of the messages and then shakes her head. "So, when do you plan on growing up?"

"Never. Just call me Peter Pan." I don't even notice the posters anymore. They're like wallpaper. I figured I'd toss them when I move, whenever that is. I've actually started scanning the newspapers for a one-bedroom apartment, but the very idea of living alone isn't appealing. That's the thing I like about this house—there's always someone around, always people coming and going. Just like growing up with my brothers and Elsie.

I thrive on that kind of chaos.

She glances coyly over her shoulder at me before her attention drifts to another poster—a Dallas Cowboys cheerleader who I met at a tailgate party and who developed a little crush on me. "So these are all fairies? Where are their wings?"

"Removable," I offer, taking slow steps toward her, her bare shoulders and smooth skin begging to be touched. After the slew of almosts, I can't believe I finally have Reese in my bedroom. I've never worked this hard to get laid in my entire life.

"As are their panties, I'm sure you discovered quickly," I hear her mutter under her breath, her eyes still searching the wall, her jaw working against itself.

"How about you focus less on these women and more on the soon-to-be-naked guy standing behind you. If that really is your thing . . . I'm still wondering."

I grunt as her sharp elbow flies back to jab my stomach, but it doesn't dissuade me from shifting her hair off to one shoulder, giving my mouth access to her slender neck.

"You know, you're a lot different than I thought," she purrs, her body falling back into my chest, her head tilting up to give me a full view down the top of her dress.

I can't help myself from grabbing her hips and jerking that full ass of hers into me, to let her feel how bad I want her. She rocks her hips against me in response; such a simple move and yet it's driving me wild.

"How so?" I've been eyeing her dress for access points all night, so I know that the zipper runs along her rib cage instead of her back. Slipping my fingers up under her arm, I locate the slider and tug it gently. The tautness in the top of the dress immediately gives, the material folding over itself and falling to uncover a matching red lace bra. Another quick move by my fingers and I have that dropping to the floor.

"I don't know. You just . . ." Her words fade in a heavy sigh as I reach up to fill my hands with her tits, trying hard not to squeeze them too tight. I don't know what it is about the way she sighs, but it makes my ability to restrain myself vanish.

I slide my hands down her waist, my fingers working their way under the dress and panties until I'm able to push them into a heap on the floor and she's stepping out of them without my request. Kicking them out of the way, I grab her waist and spin her around to face me. "Good, different?" I ask with a playful smirk as I press her up against the wall and force her legs apart, enough to make room for me as I fit my body between them.

I won't lie. I've been in this exact position with women many times before. But being here now, with Reese, somehow feels new.

Her breath hitches, her arms moving to wrap around my neck and yank me down to meet her mouth, slipping her tongue in and out before I can even catch it. "Yes," she moans, and I'm not sure if that's a yes to my question or to what's coming. Her clawing fingers at my back, my shirt bunching up within her hands, reminds me that I'm still fully dressed. Something I completely forgot about, distracted by the taste and softness of this tumultuous, vindictive woman's lips.

My wild horse.

"Why is it I always end up naked before you?" I feel her cool hands retreat down to the hem of my shirt and slip under to drag it up. I break away long enough to yank it over my head and toe off my shoes, then I dive back against her.

Two hands pushing against my chest stop me.

Biting her bottom lip in a way that makes me want to shove her hands away so I can bite it for her, I heave a sigh. Her fingers assess the ridges of my chest, trailing down to my stomach.

"You love my body, don't you?" I murmur.

Heated eyes lift to meet mine, boring into me with a new intensity I hadn't expected, and I can't stop myself from leaning in, more than eager to feel her skin. Once again, her hands push back to stop me.

"It's been a while for me," she admits, her gaze dropping to my belt buckle, her long lashes fluttering. Is she nervous?

"Since your ex?" I'm pretty sure the answer to that is yes, given what I overheard the other week when I surprised a sick Reese at her home.

A single nod answers me. Reaching down, her fingers make quick work of my belt and zipper, unfastening them until the dress pants I wore to work today are hanging open, showing off the sizeable bulge I have for her under my briefs. I catch her wrists and gently pull them back, allowing me space to step in until the cool metal of her piercing grazes my chest. I bend down to kiss the corner of her mouth. "You just tell me how fast or slow to go then, okay?"

In response, she pulls out of my loose grip. One arm reaches around to dig into my back pocket, seizing my wallet. She retrieves the condom waiting inside and tosses my wallet to the side as if it were trash.

"Well, you seem to remember the basics, at least," I mutter wryly.

"Oh, I remember more than the basics." Her palms slide slowly, all the way up the front of my body as if memorizing its surface, until her hands coil around my neck, her head dipping back to regard me with a smirk. "I just hope you're decent or all this buildup will be rather disappointing."

My head falls back as a loud bark of laughter escapes me. *So do I.* I've never had a problem, but with this girl . . . A sudden case of nerves hits me. "As long as I can get through those cobwebs, I should be fine."

Thanks to the lamp I turned on when we came in, I catch her cheeks changing color. Maybe that's why she decides to slap the condom into my hand and yank my pants and briefs down, barely making the effort to get the elastic around my dick.

My hips pull back in reaction. "Hey! Why are you intent on breaking it!" She's either angry or nervous; either way, my vital body part will not become a casualty. I pin her hands up above her head with one arm before kicking off my pants and briefs.

She opens her mouth to say something but I cut her off with a deep kiss, slipping my tongue in to take complete control of her mouth, while my free hand runs up her inner thigh.

She may be nervous, but she's soft and wet and so damn ready.

"Screw the foreplay," she growls against my mouth, a leg hitching around my thigh to pull me against her. Her hands struggle against my grip but I don't relent.

And I'm torn between laughing and groaning. *Fuck*. Normally, I try to keep my pants on as long as possible because once they're off, I have a five-minute threshold until I need to be *in* something. And I need to be in her. Right now. She's so close. Just a quick maneuver and I'm golden. And then she has to go and say that!

Except, the small mewling sounds she's trying to stifle as my thumb and fingers work against her is enough to hold me back. Breaking free of her mouth to shift my attention to her neck, I take my time inhaling that strawberries-and-cream scent as my tongue trails the curves of her collarbone. Her body's still squirming against my hand, her breathing growing more ragged and uneven. I keep those hands pinned above her head until I lose my reach as my knees hit the floor.

"I need more time for—" She gasps when my tongue catches the first sweet taste of her, my arms hooked tight under her thighs, my shoulders holding her against the wall.

She cries out, grabbing fistfuls of my hair until my scalp hurts. I don't give a shit; this reaction is worth the pain. It's times like these when I'm happy I can bench press almost double my weight, because I have no problem keeping her writhing body still.

My name tumbles from her mouth in a moan as a thump sounds—her head falling back against the wall. "Okay, fine." She resigns herself to the fact that I'm not letting her go. Her fingers slowly loosen their grip of my hair, until they're rubbing my head where it's sore, her thighs falling apart as they relax slightly. And when she comes?

Jesus.

I kind of wish the music weren't so loud because if the guys had heard that, I'd be getting pats on my back for weeks.

The last quiver through her body is barely done when I'm on

my feet. She falls into me as I lift and carry her to my bed. Tossing her gently, I reach into my nightstand for another condom—I'm not about to go looking for the one lying on the floor.

Her eyes are at half-mast as she peers up at me, a perfect balance to her flustered cheeks and the puffy lips I must have given her from kissing her so hard. Downright sexy.

"You're not going to fall asleep on me, are you?" I ask, stretching over her. If she does, I'll die.

A sly smile curls her mouth as one hand cups the back of my neck while the other reaches down to grab me and guide me into her. "If I do, then you're doing something terribly wrong," she whispers, adding, "Just don't hurt me."

"Do you think I'm an amateur?" Hurt her? I'll be lucky to get all the way in her before I lose it. And then I *will* look like an amateur. She feels too damn good and tight. Better than I remember it feeling in a long time. And different. I'm sure it's just the anticipation, dragged out over months and multiple failed attempts.

A deep, throaty laugh spills out of her, her muscles clenching, making her constrict around me.

"How about you hold off on the laughter until after," I say, gritting my teeth. And then I'm kissing her, happy to have her tongue in my mouth again as I push in slowly, sliding a hand under her hips to lift and angle her the right way.

It's not long before there's no trace of humor in her features, her eyes burning into mine, her slick body slipping against mine, her breathing getting raspy as we rock against each other, picking up speed and intensity quickly. Sharp nails dig into my shoulder blades as she demands, "Deeper," and I groan, knowing I won't last another minute like this.

I lift her body and spin around to lie back and enjoy the view of a naked Reese riding me.

Fantastic. This has earned you a whole extra thirty fucking seconds, maximum, dumbass.

When I watch those natural teardrop-shaped breasts bounce like only real ones can and her fingers weave through mine, resting against her thighs, I cut that down to an extra ten seconds, maximum.

And when her first cries sound out not long after, I know I won't even make it that long.

Chapter 25

- - -

REESE

I'm cradled in a set of powerful arms before I'm even conscious. It takes a few blinks and missed heartbeats to focus in on the gorgeous face and the smile staring down at me.

"Time to get up."

"Who let you in here?" I croak, feeling my scowl form, the fact that I'm completely naked and he's fully dressed not lost on me.

"This is my room, remember?" He sets me back down on my feet. "Come on. It's almost eleven."

"Sure, okay." I crawl back into bed and pull the covers up over my body. They disappear just as fast. "Pervert," I mutter.

"We've got to hit the road."

"I think it's better for all parties involved if you give me another hour," I mutter, rolling onto my stomach. This could very well be his way of getting me out of his bed. Right now, I don't care. We didn't fall asleep until well after five this morning.

There's a long pause.

"Stop staring at my ass," I mumble into the pillow.

I feel strong, hot hands run up the backs of my legs. "I can't help it."

"I thought you were in a rush."

"I only need five minutes."

"Don't I know it." I smile, earning a stinging slap across my left ass cheek.

"Are you complaining? Because you sure weren't complaining last night. Not the first or the second . . ." Ben tempers his weight as he lies down on top of me, his mouth against my ear, ". . . or the third or the—"

I turn my head to steal his words with a hard, quick, close-mouthed kiss. Then I roll back and face the other way to hide my wide grin. The one that would tell him how much I'm not complaining about last night.

Last night was . . . unforgettable.

"Well, I could use those five minutes now for something more enjoyable, like brushing my teeth," I lie as his hand slides between my legs and into me.

"Huh, well then what's this?"

I reach around to smack him haphazardly. "You're such a romantic."

"Don't even pretend romance is your thing," he shoots back. His weight disappears suddenly. When I dare glance over my shoulder, his shirt is already off and he's working on his jeans. With the speed of a well-practiced expert, he has a condom on and is back on top of me again in seconds, his arousal pressing up against my thigh as a hand slides under my stomach to force me onto my knees. I don't know that Ben has a favorite position yet but he certainly struggles to last long with this one, I learned last night.

"What are we doing?" *Shit.* I didn't mean to say that out loud. I just . . . I figured that after he got what he wanted last night, he'd already be losing interest.

A big, confident smile splashes across his face. "What does it feel like we're doing?" I can't tell if he knows what I truly meant and is just avoiding the question. But then he stalls to lay a kiss on my shoulder blade. "I'm heading up to the grove today. The tangerines are a couple of weeks early and Mama's got a bunch of orders to fill. Do you want to come? I'm staying overnight."

The grove? A blip of excitement jumps in me. I've caught myself thinking about Wilma and that house often these last few weeks—while staring out at the busy Miami streets, or sitting in Jack's modern but plain suburban home—wondering, hoping to visit again.

Now I have the chance and it's because Ben has invited me.

Two elements that I find equally thrilling.

"I'll let you drive the tractor," he offers in a taunting voice, as if he's trying to entice a child with a candy bar.

I don't answer with words; I simply peek over my shoulder at him, letting him see my genuine smile.

It earns one in return—a soft, boyish one as he looks me over. "But first . . ."

■ ■ ■

"Sorry we're late, Mama." I watch as Ben scoops his mother up and whips her around before laying a kiss on her cheek, just like he did the last time. I'll admit . . . it makes my heart swell. "Reese takes forever to make herself pretty."

Jackass. "Clearly," I mutter dryly as Ben occupies himself with an excited Quincy. He gave me all of ten minutes at home to shower, change, and pack some things for an overnight stay, paranoid that Jack would show up to find him in the driveway. He wouldn't even come in the house. The official story is that I'm staying at Lina and Nicki's this weekend. We've already texted them and Mason to line it up. None of them are answering their phones, but I'm assuming it's thanks to a nasty hangover and Mason playing nursemaid to Lina.

"And here I thought you looked this beautiful just rolling out of bed," Wilma says, walking over to wrap her arms around me in a warm hug. "Should I smack him or will you?"

"Oh, I'll make him pay for that," I promise, feeling all kinds of weirdness and warmth with her gesture. Is this what a normal mom is like? Or did Ben just hit the jackpot? "He's quite a character, isn't he?" I muse.

Wilma's face beams with pride. "He certainly is." There's a long pause and I have the distinct feeling that she's dying to begin asking intrusive questions about my relationship with her son. But she doesn't. Instead she reaches up to touch the underside of my hair. "I love this color. It suits you."

I smile, thinking how different Annabelle's response would be to that.

"Thank you so much for giving up your weekend to help out. The orders are pouring in and I don't have the seasonal staff starting for another two weeks."

"Are you kidding?" I let my senses take in everything around me—the peaceful silence, the house that may be in need of repair but is still stunning, the giant oaks that give the property such a haunting, romantic feel—and I exhale blissfully. "I'm just happy to be back so soon." There's really only one thing that isn't entirely charming about the Bernard Morris Grove, but it's well hidden in the barn, probably sucking back a bottle of whiskey.

"You coming?" Ben hollers, climbing onto the old tractor and sliding on the cowboy hat that was hanging off the back of the seat, a sight that leads to something stirring in my lower belly. I don't have a thing for cowboys. All the ones I've ever met leave much to be desired.

Until now.

"I thought you said I could drive?"

"I lie to get pretty girls to do things. Haven't you figured that out yet? You can sit on the wagon or up here." He pats the piece of metal beside his seat, covering the giant tire.

I climb up and hop onto his lap instead. "Fine. We can both drive."

"This probably isn't a—" he begins to say but I crank the

engine and the rumble of the tractor kills his words. "Okay, you asked for it!" he yells, throwing it into gear, and with one arm wrapped snugly around my waist, he sends the tractor lurching forward down the path.

He takes the same path that he did a few weeks ago in the dune buggy, only at a much slower rate and not quite as far. "I've never been on a tractor before!" I yell back as he turns down a narrower path and cuts the engine. Taking in the orange globes contrasting against the rich green leaves, I ask, "Are these tangerines?"

A hand pushes my hair out of the way and then Ben's mouth grazes over my neck, the heat sending tingles down to my fingertips. "Some sort of citrus, anyway."

I reach back and swipe his cowboy hat off his head. "Is that the technical term?"

He answers me by reaching down and unfastening my jeans.

My eyes widen as I glance around to make sure we're completely alone. "What do you think you're doing?"

"Solving the problem you just created by bouncing on my lap for the last ten minutes."

■ ■ ■

"So?" I hear him say, my head resting on his broad chest. "You want to quit your day job and be an orange farmer, don't you?"

I smile, stretching my legs out around a crate by my feet. There are fifteen of them taking up space on the wagon we pulled out here behind the tractor, which we're now lying on. "Depends. Is the tractor ride a daily perk?" As sore as I am from last night and this morning, the second Ben had my pants off, I couldn't climb onto his lap fast enough. Anyone who might be hiding out here just got one hell of a show.

He chuckles but doesn't answer.

"Do you?" I finally ask.

"Sometimes. It's relaxing out here. I have so many great memories, with my brothers and sister. But . . ." His voice fades.

I lift my head to catch that far-off look in his eyes, Ben losing himself in a thought. "I didn't work my ass off through law school for nothing. And then I'd be dealing with that mess," he says, throwing a lazy hand toward the house. "It would cost a fortune to renovate that place, and what the hell am I going to do with it?"

"Is it just because of that?" Something tells me it has more to do with the mess in the barn.

He opens one eye and peers down at me. "What? You think just because I let you pick my oranges, you get to ask all kinds of personal questions now?"

I'm not sure if he's bothered by my question but, judging by the proud grin on his face, I'm pretty sure his "pick my oranges" reference has nothing to do with fruit. I reach up to flick his ear. "I thought they were tangerines."

"Ow!" he whines, but it's followed up by a smile as he grabs my hand and pulls it down to rest beneath his on his chest. I wait quietly, staring at him until he finally speaks. "I remember noticing the whiskey on my dad's breath when I was around ten. Mama says he wasn't always this bad. Apparently he barely drank when they got married. He was a different man back then, she says. Maybe that's true. All I know is it kept getting worse, until I was embarrassed when anyone came over."

I feel for him. At least Annabelle could usually hold her liquor well. But on those nights when she didn't, I went to Lina's house instead of having her come over. Lina's parents don't even touch alcohol.

"He liked to go out on Friday nights. When I was about sixteen, he started going out and not coming home until the next morning. He never said where he was, and when I asked him, he'd just tell me to mind my own damn business. It drove me nuts, because I knew what it was doing to Mama. She'd come down from her room, her eyes all puffy and with dark circles from lack of sleep. Sometimes I'd walk past her door and hear her crying.

"Turns out Mama knew where he was, what he was doing—or *who* he was doing—all along."

"So your dad had an affair?"

"Well, I wouldn't call it an affair. More like he'd get drunk and fuck anyone who gave him an opening. Pretty much anything he could pick up at the bar. He'd been doing it for years. He was a good-looking man. He got a lot of attention."

Poor Wilma. "Does he still do it?"

Ben snorts. "Doubt the guy can even get it up anymore. He's got more whiskey than blood running through his veins nowadays. But he went into a deep depression after the accident and hasn't had much interest in . . . anything, really. I don't know that he's even left the property in the last few years. He can't drive himself anywhere with only the one arm. Orders his booze by the case, delivered right to the barn."

"Wow." I turn my head to rest against Ben's chest once again, listening to his heart hammer against its confines. "I can't believe she stayed with him."

"Yeah, well, marriage makes people do stupid things, I guess." There's a pause. "Like wasting time on guys who cheat and then marry their mistresses."

I roll my eyes. I knew that was coming. "Well, have no fear. I don't think I'll be hearing from him again, thanks to you." Ben handed me my phone back this morning and there was no follow-up text.

I never responded to Jared, either. I don't know what to say, and I'm taking my new lawyer's advice and not putting anything incriminating in writing.

"I hope not." Suddenly my body is turning and I find myself on my back with Ben's face hovering above me and his big arms on either side of my head. Clear blue skies stretch out beyond.

This. Right here. Right now. I think I could be an orange farmer if it meant relaxed days, peace and quiet, Ben.

Shit.

"You look like you're about to scream," Ben muses, his knuckles finding their way to my cheek to softly graze it.

I think I am. At myself.

Did last night just mess everything up between Ben and me?

Do I want more now?

I peer up to find an odd expression on his face as he studies me. "What is *that* look for?"

"Not sure yet," he answers cryptically, dipping down to lay a quick peck on my neck. "Come on—dinner's going to be ready soon." As if on cue, Ben's phone chirps.

Chapter 26

■ ■ ■

BEN

"She seems like a very nice young lady," my mama offers as I trade an armload of dirty dishes for slices of pie.

"She has her moments," I mutter with a smirk. I'll have to tell Reese that later. I imagine it'll earn a black heart rebuttal or two and a scoff at the "nice young lady" descriptor.

"Oh, Ben," my mama scolds, but I hear the smile behind her voice. "You are incorrigible sometimes." There's a pause and then she says, "I've made Elsie's old room up for tonight as it has a queen-sized bed. Do I need to make up a second one?"

My look of surprise has her chuckling. My mother, the church-abiding citizen, is basically condoning premarital sex under her roof. Because there's no way I'll spend a night in bed with Reese without some good ol' premarital sex. "Don't look at me like that. I'm just so darn happy you finally have a girlfriend."

I open my mouth to correct her when a howl of laughter escapes the dining room. "You used to play the clarinet?" Reese calls out.

"You realize you're giving her an arsenal against me with that damn photo album, don't you?" I chastise my mother with a grin on my face.

"Language, Ben. And I'm sure you've given her plenty of material already." She reaches up to squeeze my chin. "I'm proud of you, clarinet and all."

"Is this *you* in the pink dress, Ben?" comes the next question, followed by, "It is! You've got to be at least ten here!" and then that deep, infectious laugh of hers.

"Don't let that picture fool you, Reese," my mama calls out, her dimples—the ones I inherited—piercing her cheeks. "Ben figured out playing dress-up with the neighborhood girls meant he'd get to watch them change." Shaking her head at me, she adds, "Boy, was Reverend Perkins ever upset when he figured out what was going on."

"Oh, yeah." I rub a hand over my stubble as I recall his daughter, a cute little blond who was way more curious than her daddy could have imagined at eleven years old. A swat of my mama's dish towel against my ass has me dropping the memory quickly.

I watch her with fondness as she rinses the plates off and slides them into her dishwasher. I got away with a lot more than I probably should have growing up but when Mama put her foot down, I always listened. Hearing bits and pieces of Reese's childhood and that sad excuse for a mother only solidifies how good I had it.

When Rob phoned to tell me that Mama had had a heart attack in the middle of his kitchen, I was in my car and driving nineteen hours straight to Chicago without stopping, my own chest ready to explode from fear the entire way. With it being Easter weekend, there weren't any available flights until the following day and I wasn't willing to wait. Thank God she was okay.

Minor as it was, she didn't escape unscathed. I can see it now. She's aged a lot since, moving slower, the lines on her face more prominent. "How are things going here, Mama? Honestly." Between me being tied up with school, then the bar exam, and now the new job, she has refused to shed much light on the situation. She doesn't like putting the stress of the place on me. The problem is, it's already on me. Aside from her, I'm the only one here.

With a deep inhale, she starts scraping the scraps off the plates. "It's a lot for just me, Ben. I'm only fifty-one but I'm feeling so much older lately. Too old to be worrying about money, wandering around out there checking trees for disease, and dealing with drought and pesticides." There's resignation in her voice that I've never heard before. I have to wonder how different it would be if she had a decent man to share the load with.

"Have you talked to Rob and the others? What do they say?"

Her mouth twists with sadness. "Same thing they always say: sell it and leave your father."

"And?"

"What do you mean, 'and'?" A hint of irritation spikes in her voice now. "This place is my life. The Bernard family's life! I can't sell it."

"I know, Mama." She'd be miserable anywhere else. "But he . . ."

"You know what my answer is. It's the same as it's always been: for better or worse. That's what I signed up for."

"Yeah, but does better or worse—"

"Leave it be, Benjamin. It's my decision. It's my business."

Something Reese said has stuck with me. "Are you happy with never having a Christmas under your roof with your kids? Your grandkids? We haven't all been together here in *eight years,* Mama! And it's all because of him!"

She sniffs, and I see the pain poorly veiled. "I'm trying my best. I still see them."

"Yeah, you just have to go to Chicago to do it. No holidays, no birthdays." I set the plates down on the table—the table that *he* made—and lean against it, my fists starting to hurt against the solid wood. I take a calming breath. "Your friends don't even come around anymore. Walking into this house is plain depressing." Her silence unnerves me. Though I don't mean to, my voice begins to rise. "There's like a thick fucking cloud of—"

"Watch your language with me, Benjamin," she says, cutting me off, her tone sharp.

"Sorry, Mama. I just . . ." I groan loudly. "I don't get it! I've tried, but I don't get it."

"Marriage is forever, Ben."

"Yeah. A death sentence, apparently."

A throat clearing turns both of us toward the entryway where Reese stands, holding up a set of owl shakers. "Should these stay in the dining room or come in here?"

"In here, dear. Thank you." My mama quickly collects them from her hand, slightly flustered. "Ben told me key lime is your favorite, so I made one this afternoon. I hope it's up to par."

Reese accepts the plate, leveling me with a wicked smile. "I'm sure it'll be the best I've ever had."

I'm either getting laid again or slaughtered tonight.

It's definitely one of those two.

Chapter 27

. . .

REESE

I'm too smart for Ben.

He's so easily distracted. When I handed him my empty plate after devouring the pie Wilma made—which was delicious; limes and I may have found a common ground—and slid my free hand into his pocket, he assumed it was a prelude to later, grinning down at me slyly. How he missed my true intention—taking the set of keys in his pocket that I saw him deposit there earlier—I'll never know.

And now I'm out the front door and darting across the front lawn, intent on getting the engine started on that dune buggy before Ben catches up to me. I know it's childish, but just picturing Ben laughing as he chases me down makes me feel better.

I've only ever seen one side of Ben—the playful, easygoing guy who's unruffled by anything and confident as all get-out. I didn't realize how much I'd come to appreciate that consistency until it was disrupted by an argument with Wilma. I don't know what they were arguing about but when Ben's voice started to rise, I was desperate to interrupt it. Hence the lame owl saltshaker excuse.

I think Ben has a strange power over me—the ability to balance my chaos. And, the more time I spend here on the grove—in his life—the more I think that his entire world seems to stabilize me. Or at least makes me care less about my own problems. Hearing Ben upset the way I did today, though, and with Wilma no less, was like a kick to my little self-centered universe, pushing it off its axis.

A loud clatter comes from the barn, followed by a hushed curse. A mixture of concern and curiosity—more curiosity—pricks me and I step forward to the window next to the large closed barn doors to peer inside.

And jump back with a yelp as a face appears inches away. The image comes into full view a moment later when Ben's dad pushes open the door to stare at me through red, glassy eyes. Ben obviously gets his height and frame from his father, though this man has long since lost all of his muscle mass, replaced with the lanky skin-and-bone look of a deep-rooted alcoholic. I'm betting that at one time he was quite handsome. Maybe as handsome as Ben. Maybe that's how he managed to interest so many women. Except there's no charming smile, no dimples, and certainly no friendly crystal-blue eyes to win me over. Those are all his wife's contributions to their son.

"I'm sorry," I offer. "I heard a noise and just wanted to make sure you were okay."

"Oh, yeah?" I catch a hint of the slur seconds before a waft of whiskey hits my nostrils. "I'm fine, but that's nice . . . nice of you to check." Taking a quick step to correct his balance, he says, "I heard you were admiring my carpentry?"

I guess Wilma and he do still speak. Knowing what I know, I wonder what those conversations are like. "Yes, the furniture in the house is beautiful," I offer with a tight smile. I've never been comfortable around drunk parents. I'm even more uncomfortable around drunk *fathers*. Especially ones that I know are prone to cheating on their wives. Especially ones that are looking at me the way Ben's father is looking at me right now. I fold my arms over my chest.

He waves his one arm dramatically. "Come in!"

I glance over my shoulder. Ben's not out yet.

"Oh, he'll come find you," Ben's father says. I try not to stiffen as his hand falls to my back, guiding me farther into the barn. The smell of cut wood instantly permeates my nostrils and I inhale deeply. "You can smell that, can't you? Wood—the best smell in the world."

I relax a little as he shifts away from me, stumbling over toward the opposite wall, where a myriad of saws sit lined on tables as if on display, the metal on the tools gleaming. An old tube TV lights up a corner, the sound of the baseball announcer's voice buzzing softly in the background, competing against the crackle of country music over the radio.

"It's very clean in here," I remark, looking at the piles of wood neatly stacked along another wall. And in the center of the room—a giant two-story space with naked bulbs dangling down from the rafters—sit several pieces of furniture in various states of completion. "I always imagined a lot of sawdust in wood shops."

"Used to be." Strolling over to place his only hand on a giant slab of grainy wood, he murmurs, "This was going to be a beautiful coffee table. I could have made thousands selling it."

I let out a low whistle.

He peers up at me. "Would you like me to finish it for you? It's black walnut. Not easy to come by a piece like this."

My eyes widen in surprise with the offer. Jack would love a coffee table like that. I open my mouth, the beginnings of "Sure!" escaping, when Ben's voice cuts into the murkiness with a harsh, "No!" Spinning around, I find him standing just inside the door, his jaw taut with tension as his eyes dart around the space as if chasing ghosts within the shadows. Even the darkness can't hide the ashen color of his skin.

"What's wrong, son? Forget what this place looked like?" The resentment laced through Joshua Senior's voice is unmistakable.

I hear Ben's hard swallow as he steps up behind me, curling his arms over my shoulders and across my chest, hugging me to him. Almost protectively. "Come on, you little thief. I'll let you drive, seeing as you're hell-bent on it."

His words are teasing, but I know not to argue or joke or give him a hard time; the odd softness in his voice echoes like a shriek within these walls. "Okay."

"What's the rush? You haven't been in here in, what, eight or nine years? How long has it been since *the accident*?" Ben's dad slaps the wood table surface. "Don't you want to look around? Relive some memories?"

"Joshua!" Wilma's cry comes from the doorway and when I turn to look at her, her pale face matches Ben's. And I see the tears. There are definite tears welling in her eyes as she looks from her husband to her son—pausing on him, a pained expression furrowing her brow—and then back to her husband. I catch the subtle nod of her head. "Why have I let this go on for so long?" I think I hear her murmur faintly as a mask of resolution slides over her face, a moment before she closes her eyes and squeezes them tight.

And glancing at her husband's expression, I believe he heard it, too. I watch as whatever little spark of fury sat burning in him dies. He hangs his head and shuffles quietly past us and out the door.

Walking slowly forward to Ben and me, she reaches up to lay a hand on his cheek. "It was an accident, Benjamin. We all know that. Even he knows that, whether he wants to admit it or not." Fresh tears find their way down Wilma's cheeks. "But everything after is all my fault."

Ben releases me to pull Wilma's tiny frame into his arms. "None of this was ever your fault."

She steps away, guiding him back to me with a sad smile. "I'm just so happy to have you both here. You go enjoy yourselves.

Benjamin, I'm going to fix this. I'm going to make it right." With that, she turns and steps away, a fierce smile of determination painting her face.

And I'm left standing in the middle of this vast open space, watching a very quiet Ben stare at that old unfinished coffee table with a lost look on his face, battling something privately.

"Ben?" I call out, fighting against the shiver as I hear his name bounce off the high walls.

It seems to break him free of his trance because he turns to me and cracks a grin. "Come on. Let's go." The strain in his voice is unmistakable, though, and there's certainly no twinkle in his eye.

"What happened in here?"

"Ahh . . ." His gaze drops to the ground, his lips tucking into his mouth in a tight purse. "The worst day of my life. That's what." He tries to cast it off with a lazy shrug.

My sneakers scrape against the concrete as I do a circle around the table, running my finger along the deeply defined grain of the wood. "It's beautiful wood. I've never seen anything like this."

"Reese, don't . . ." he starts when my fingers run over a giant splotch, as if someone spilled something on the untreated wood and stained it. I look up to see the pained expression on Ben's face.

"Come on. You're my obnoxious, loud, insensitive Ben! *I'm* the melodramatic one."

"I'm yours?" he repeats with an arched brow, though that teasing lilt is missing.

I gulp. "What's wrong with this table?"

He strolls over, making a point of sidestepping an area on the floor instead of walking straight to me. "You remember what I told you about my dad and the things he did behind my mama's back, right?"

I nod quietly.

Licking his lips, he studies the wood for another long moment. "Normally he'd stay away from the local bars. It's a small town and people talk. Everyone's up in everyone's business. Well, one night he decided the local bar was good enough. The next morning, Mama started getting calls from friends. So-and-so's brother-in-law or someone saw him stumbling out with my football coach's wife. I guess Coach was out of town." Ben snorts as he shakes his hung head. "Mama was mortified. And not even for herself. She knew Coach would hear about it and she was afraid he'd take it out on me.

"When my dad pulled into the driveway that day, I guess she laid into him. Slapped him across the face. Well," Ben grits his teeth, "he swung back. I came home a few hours later to find her hiding in her room with a broken nose and an ice pack. And when I found out what happened . . ." His mouth twists up. "I charged in here, ready to beat the hell out of him. He was already hitting the bottle again, working on that table. I was so angry, I ran at him. I shoved him. Hard." Ben pauses to swallow, a hand running through his hair. "And then, I don't really know how everything else happened. One second he was tumbling back, the next his arm was lying on the ground and there was blood everywhere. Jesus, Reese! The whiskey made it worse. It was pumping out of him like we were in a Quentin Tarantino movie."

My stomach tightens with the visual he's painting. I look at this table under a new light, seeing that stain for what it truly is.

"The idiot had removed the safety mechanisms off all the saws. Said they were a pain in the ass while he worked. He somehow hit the power switch when he fell." Ben's head is shaking. "I was pissed off but I never meant for that to happen, I swear. I called nine-one-one right away. He almost bled out on the way to the hospital. They weren't able to reattach the arm." He sighs heavily. "The one and only thing my dad was *ever* passionate about was carpentry. And with only one arm, he can't do much. So he doesn't. He doesn't do anything but sit in this barn and hate life."

Ben's hand lifts to run along a particularly dangerous-looking saw.

"Is that the one?"

His nod answers me. "He was always a cynical man. Never happy. Not one to spend much time with his kids. After the accident, he hit the bottle even harder and went into a deep depression. He hasn't come out of it yet and he refuses to get help. He blames me for everything. For the accident, for my brothers and Elsie not coming around. But the reason none of my brothers and sister come here is because they hate his fucking guts for cheating on my mama and then hitting her. And for being a drunk. They've already said that they won't step foot on this property while he's here. And they're angry with my mother for standing by him because she's got it in her thick skull that this is the 'for worse' part of her marriage vows. Well, if you ask me, 'worse' is pretty damn bad."

"Is she happy?"

"How can she be?" Bright blue eyes pierce me, his arms thrown up as if in surrender. "They sleep in separate rooms; he's in here all day. He helps her with nothing. They live completely separately and because of him, she doesn't get to see her kids or her grandkids. Is *that* what a marriage is?" He shakes his head. "And she wonders why I want nothing to do with it."

I hazard a step forward to put a hand on his forearm. For reassurance, for comfort. For friendship.

"God." Ben shakes his head, his nostrils flaring. "I still can't stand the smell of cut wood. It makes me want to puke. And the sound of a saw cutting . . ." He squeezes his eyes shut as he shudders.

"Well then, come on." I hook my arm through his and wait for those eyes to open and focus on me. I take slow steps backward, pulling him away from the dank barn and the sharp saws, the lingering memories. He lets me lead him out. "Let's get you out of here."

Chapter 28

■ ■ ■

BEN

"I thought she was die-hard Christian," Reese whispers as I lead her into Elsie's old room. The walls and curtains are still the same color—white and yellow—but all the boy-band posters and cheerleading stuff that made it feel like my older sister's room have long since been packed away.

"She is, but she's also die-hard get-Ben-married," I say with a chuckle, adding, "And you don't have to whisper. Mama's room is on the other side of the house, and a fucking jumbo jet crashing into the house wouldn't wake my dad up once he's out."

I feel her come up behind me, wrapping her arms around my sides to clasp her hands on my chest. "So do you want a church wedding? Because I'm partial to eloping."

"Uh . . ."

She snorts against my back. "Your heart is racing."

Lifting an arm up and over, I pull her around and to my chest, just so I can make her tip her head back and look at me. I love her face angled up like this. "Funny."

"I thought so." Lifting onto her tiptoes, she lays a soft kiss on my lips. It catches me off guard, but not in a bad way. It's just that

I'm always the one stealing the kisses. It's the second time today that she's done it.

Peeling away from me, she slaps my ass. "Bathroom's the third on the left?"

"Yeah." She slings her knapsack over her shoulder and steps into the hall, smiling. When I hear the bathroom door click, I take the opportunity to make my way down the hall to Mama's door to find her room empty. On a whim, I keep heading down the hall, rounding the corner quietly. I've snuck out of this place so many times, I still know how to avoid the loud creaks.

My father's door sits open a crack, enough so that my mama's voice carries out clearly.

"I've given you thirty-three years of my life, Joshua. I've hoped and prayed that you'd come back to me, that the young man I fell in love with, who gave me five beautiful children, was still somewhere in there. But . . ." I hear her ragged sob before she stifles it, pausing before speaking again. "But I know now that he's gone for good, because the Joshua I fell in love with wouldn't keep hurting his own child. Of all our children, Ben is the one who has reason not to come around again and yet he's here."

My dad's rough voice pipes in then with, "Well, he feels guilty."

"Maybe," she admits through a sniff. "But it's also because he loves fiercely. That boy has always had so much love to give and I'm afraid that after what he's grown up with, he's never going to give anyone a real chance. None of them will."

"The others are fine."

"The others are *not* fine, Joshua. Josh's wife left him because he drinks too much and had an affair, and Elsie's turned down that boy's proposal twice because she doesn't know how to trust a man. They just broke up for good this time. Jake doesn't want to marry Rita, who's carrying his child, because he's afraid to jinx it."

Shit, I didn't know any of that.

Mama clears her throat. "I need to do what's right for my

children now. What I should have done years ago." I hear the creak of my granddaddy's rocking chair as Mama stands. "This ol' house is falling apart, and it's not because of loose shingles or leaking pipes or a crooked porch. It's because it's lost its family. Its soul. And without it, there's no point in any of it anymore."

Not a word comes from my father. No argument, no pleading, no apologies. No excuses.

"The Cornells asked if we were interested in selling a while back. I'm going to see if they're still interested."

What? Sell? She just finished saying that she won't sell!

Finally, my dad speaks up. "I thought you didn't want to sell the grove, Wilma."

"I don't." Her voice cracks. "But we can't continue like this and I love my children too much not to make a change." Much closer to the door, I hear her add, "You know, I learned to live with the whiskey, I even forgave you for all the women. I blamed myself for that, for not staying attractive enough to satisfy you."

Hearing that, my teeth actually crack, they're clenched so tight.

"But I can never forgive you for trying to kill that sparkle in my baby's eyes. And I'll never forgive myself for allowing this to go on for so long."

The door opens and Mama steps out, her eyes red and puffy from crying. She sees me and immediately puts on a brave smile as she pulls the door behind her. It doesn't hide her wobbling bottom lip.

"Mama, I'm fine. I can handle him. You're not giving up your home—"

"Hush." She reaches out and grabs my arms. She looks so damn small, but she has a fierce grip when she needs it. "I can do whatever I want. And you aren't fine, Ben. When you trust yourself enough to let yourself experience the kind of joy that a good relationship can bring you, that's when you'll be fine." With a pat on my shoulder, she turns and walks away.

I'm left standing outside of my father's door.

And I hear the muffled sobs behind it.

■ ■ ■

"Your sister had a great view." Reese's back is to me, her silhouette—long, lean legs stretching out of little shorts and a plain T-shirt—as tempting as ever as she stands in front of the window. I smile to myself. This, here, is why I like her so much. She's not trying too hard. Most girls would have packed some frilly black thing. Mercy would have been lying naked on the bed already. Not Reese, though. She doesn't give a fuck. And the funny thing is, she's even sexier because if it.

"She did," I agree, coming behind her to rest my chin on her head as I look out over the darkness. It's hard to see but with a full sky of stars, you can just make out the tops of the trees.

"There's something really special about this place, isn't there? I can feel it when I come here. It's like all that shit out there isn't happening. I can see why your mom doesn't want to leave."

"Yeah." Except she does now. My wheels are churning, trying to figure out how she can stay while getting him away. *Fuck.*

Reese turns her body around until she's facing me. "How's Mama?"

Her calling my mother "Mama" makes me grin. "She thinks you're a sweet girl."

The responding snort I get in return is exactly what I expected, making me chuckle as she breaks free to crawl into bed and under the covers, watching me intently as I peel my clothes off.

"Playing hard to get?" she says, but I hear the hitch in her voice as her eyes drift over me.

"What did you expect?" I lift the blankets to slide in next to her and hit the switch on the lamp.

"Full two-piece pajamas with pockets, just like Mason." She wastes no time, resting her head in the crook of my arm, her own slender arm coiling around my chest. It's . . . nice.

There's a long, comfortable silence before I hear myself say the words out loud. "She's leaving my dad. She just told him. That's it."

Reese's fingers, which were doodling little circles against my chest, stop. "Are you . . . is that good?"

"Yeah. It is. And it isn't. She'll have to sell."

I hear a "shit" under her breath as she swallows hard. "Why?"

"She can't come up with the kind of money she needs to buy him out and the bastard's never going to give the place to her. After all he's done, you'd think he'd at least do that." I hear the bitterness in my voice and, by the sudden tension in her body, I think Reese does, too. "Sorry," I murmur softly. "You don't need to hear all that."

"That's okay. It's what friends are for."

I feel the soft smile stretch across my mouth. It's funny—I have a lot of friends that I've known for a lot longer than Reese, and yet I feel closer to her than any of them. I hadn't realized how connected we've become in such a short period of time. "You know what else friends are for?"

"Causing pain and frustration?" A sharp nail against my nipple has me hissing and swatting her hand away.

She apologizes with her wet tongue covering the sore spot.

Chapter 29

■ ■ ■

REESE

"You squirm a lot in your sleep," Ben murmurs into my ear, somehow sensing that I'm awake.

"That's because you're a leech," I grumble, the soft tickle of his breath grazing the back of my neck. I've never been a cuddler. Normally, I hug the edge of the bed, despising anyone else's body heat. Jared knew it and was fine with it, preferring his own space anyway.

Not Ben. Every time I tried to shift away, an arm or leg managed to lock itself around me and yank me back, until he was molding his body to the back of mine. Never in a million years had I expected him to be the type.

I also never expected to find myself liking it.

"Leech?" With a strong hand against my shoulder, Ben pushes me onto my back, his mouth affixing itself to my breast. It takes a moment and a pinch of pain to realize what he's doing.

"Stop it!" I smack him against the head. "What are you, twelve?"

He lifts his head to check his handiwork with a smirk and then dips down to nuzzle himself in the crook of my neck, sending shivers through my body. "Oh, that's right. I forgot how nasty you are in the morning. Let's see if we can fix that mood." Ben throws the covers off and starts working his way down, his hot breath leaving a trail along my chest, my stomach, my belly button, and farther down.

■ ■ ■

"Hello?" The delicious scent of coffee and baking tells me there recently was life in the kitchen, but it's empty now, save for a plate of scones and jar of marmalade on the table. I help myself to a cup—as great of a wake-up as Ben just gave me, I still need my coffee—and then go in search of him, wandering through the main floor, out to the back veranda. When I pass the foyer and notice that the front door is partially open, I venture out onto the porch.

Ben is standing in the driveway, his arms wrapped tightly around Wilma; her face buried in his chest, her tiny body shaking.

Sirens sound in the distance.

I pick up speed until I'm running. I'm sure my feet are stomping against the gravel driveway, but all I hear is the pounding of my blood in my ears as I close the distance, until I'm skidding to a halt to find Ben's eyes squeezed tight, his jaw visibly taut as his mother sobs uncontrollably.

There's really only one thing—or one person—this can be about.

And when I turn to see the barn doors gaping open, and the body slumped over in the Adirondack chair, the arm dangling lifelessly to the side, that bottle of whiskey lying on the ground next to a small white bottle, it's not hard to put all the pieces together.

A processional of lights and sirens invades the serenity of the family grove as a line of emergency vehicles race up the picturesque driveway. When the paramedics hop out, arms loaded with big black bags, and neither Ben nor Wilma makes a move to address them, I take charge. "He's in there," I say, pointing. They don't need any more instruction than that, but I run over with them anyway.

And wish that I hadn't.

There's no doubt in anyone's eyes that Joshua Morris is beyond saving, his skin an unappealing shade of gray that I've never seen on a human being, the very shape of his face transformed, the muscles lax. By the yellow-tinged stain on his shirt, he had vomited at some point.

The paramedics—a man and woman in their early thirties who have probably seen this more than once—begin with standard protocol, checking his pulse and his pupils, but it's not long before the male glances over his shoulder at the police officer and gives a very clear, single shake of his head.

The female paramedic begins reciting a bunch of personal and medical questions that I can't answer. I admit as much to her and then retreat to Ben, my steps shaky.

"She found this next to him this morning. He must have come back out here, not long after we went to bed last night," he explains in a low, somber voice to a young police officer, handing him a sheet of paper and an envelope.

"Were there any signs to suggest that Joshua Morris was thinking of taking his own life?" the officer asks.

Ben shrugs, his eyes wide with shock as he stares at the ground, Wilma still in his arms. "He's been doing it slowly for years with the booze. You know that, Roger." The cop doesn't look that much older than Ben. Maybe they went to school together.

Wilma finally speaks up, her voice ragged. "Joshua is allergic to aspirin. Quite severely, too. And that was a new bottle that I bought for myself." She sniffs, her voice dipping low as she admits, "He knew exactly what he was doing."

They talk a bit more, the officer asking various questions, a few of them—about their marriage, their finances, potential infidelities, and such—irritating Ben enough that he instructs Wilma in a very lawyerly manner not to answer.

The officer finally turns to me. "Can I have your name, please, miss?"

"That's Ben's girlfriend," Wilma announces quickly, reaching back with her arm to beckon me forward. I comply and find myself tucked under one of Ben's arms in seconds. We steal a glance at each other over her introduction, but neither of us corrects her. It doesn't really matter right now. Still, I don't miss the tensing in Ben's jaw.

"I'm so sorry you had to see this, Reese," Wilma offers as a fresh set of tears fills her eyes. I can offer nothing more than a sad smile as Ben tightens his grip around us, squeezing us to him.

I guess the coroner's office isn't busy on a Sunday morning in the heart of Florida's richest orange groves because an old, wiry man shows up less than an hour later to make the official declaration: Joshua Morris Senior is dead.

And not long after that, still standing in the exact same spot on the driveway, the three of us quietly watch the taillights disappear as the last of the vehicles drive away, his body in one of them.

Wilma releases a heavy sigh, a resigned mask taking over her face. "Well, I suppose I should go call your brothers and Elsie and start making arrangements." Her voice has taken on an almost lifeless murmur.

"I'll be there in a minute to help, Mama," Ben offers.

"Okay. I'm so glad you were here." Patting Ben's shoulder as she passes him, she moves slowly toward the house, her head hung, while Ben wanders over to stand in front of the barn, his arms folded across his chest, his back rigid. And he says nothing.

He simply stares at the empty chair and the bottle lying beside it, until I can't help myself. Closing the distance, I set a tentative hand against his arm and lean into his side. His face is stern.

We stand like that for what feels like an eternity. I want to ask him how he's feeling but I won't. Knowing what I know about their relationship, I can't even guess how Ben might feel right now. Anger? Relief? Happiness? Is there still room for sadness somewhere in there? I finally settle on, "I'm glad she wasn't alone."

His head bobs slowly. "Yeah." His eyes roll all over the barn.

"I want to burn this entire fucking building down. Pour gas all over it and light it up." After a pause, a feeble attempt at a smirk touches his lips. "What do you know about arson?"

I jab a finger into his ribs softly. "I told you, I'm not a criminal. I'm just an occasional idiot who always gets caught."

He starts to chuckle and my insides instantly warm. It's bizarre; I remember a time when the sound of Ben's laughter made me cringe. Now I can't get enough of it. "Not that I have the best ideas, but I don't think setting fire to this place would be a good one."

He heaves a sigh. "No, you're right. I've got a lot to do, with the funeral arrangements and all that. I guess I should phone Jack. Do you think he'll give me the week off? I don't want to leave Mama here alone and I don't know how long it'll take for everyone else to get here."

"Jack's big on family-first. I'm sure he'll agree to it." A whole week without Ben at work? It's understandable. Still, the selfish part of me fills with disappointment.

He kicks at some loose gravel carried into the barn. "I guess we're going to miss those orders."

"Says who?" I stick a hand into Ben's pocket, squeezing his thigh gently as I fish out the set of keys that I know are nestled there.

He peers down at me curiously. "What do you think you're doing?"

I give him my best southern accent as I drawl, "Goin' tangerine pickin'. What else?"

A crooked smirk sets one dimple on display. "You don't have to do that, Reese."

I reach onto my tiptoes and lay a kiss on his cheek. "I know."

■ ■ ■

"I was thinking we could go out to dinner tonight as a family. You, me, and Mason. We've never done that before. What do you think?"

"Uh . . ." I stumble to find the right answer as I stare at the row of tangerine trees, stretching out as far as the eye can see. "Today's not a good day, Jack."

"Oh, okay. I understand. Maybe some other time," he says, his tone reluctant. *Shit.*

"It's just . . ." I close my eyes and take a deep breath. "I probably won't make it back to Miami early enough. I'm up at the grove again."

There's a long pause. "I thought you were with Lina this weekend."

I guess he hasn't floated the idea of dinner by Mason yet. I need to warn the guy before his father ambushes him. "No, I've been up here since yesterday morning. Ben's mom needed help with some early orders and I really like it up here. It's peaceful."

Jack's heavy sigh fills my ear. I can picture him pinching the bridge of his nose.

"So does this mean—"

"Ben's dad died this morning, Jack," I blurt out, wanting to avoid answering the other question. Not that I have an answer.

"What? Is Ben all right? I mean . . . was it sudden? How did it happen? Heart attack? Stroke?" he stammers slightly, caught off guard.

"A fifth of whiskey and a bottle of pills," I admit somberly. "Ben's going to need the week off. He'll phone you later."

"Of course." More to himself, I hear Jack mutter, "Family always comes first."

I hear the big farm truck plodding down the trail behind me. "Look, I've gotta go now, Jack. I'm trying to help Wilma get at least some of this order filled."

"Good for you for helping them."

I smile. Jack always points out when I'm doing something right or good. Sometimes I feel like I'm getting a standing ovation for tying my shoes properly. Today, though, it makes me glad to know that I'm helping Ben and Wilma in some way.

"See you tonight, Jack. Ben's going to drive me home."

I hang up as the truck pulls to a stop, those squeaky brakes sending a tiny shiver down my back. When Wilma and not Ben hops out, I'll admit that I'm slightly disheartened, but the feeling quickly vanishes because I am, after all, happy to see her.

"You're looking a little pink there, Reese. Here, you need this. Don't want to ruin that lovely skin of yours." She hands me one of those giant floppy hats that you see famous people on beaches wearing. "And you must be thirsty." She hands me a bottle of water, which I thankfully accept. I've been out here for three hours and my mouth feels like cotton.

"Hold still." She pulls a can of sunscreen out from who knows where and begins spraying my arms with it as I drink. "I hope you don't have anywhere fancy to go anytime soon, because you're going to have a lovely farmer's tan on your arms."

"Nope. I think I'm good for big events in the near future." Annabelle would disagree, seeing as her charity ball is next weekend. "You really didn't need to come out here. I'm fine on my own and I know you have a lot of planning to do."

"Not really. I've called my children and the priest. Ben's making arrangements for the coffin and the burial. And now what?" She shrugs, leaning over to sift through the baskets that I've already filled on the back of the tractor wagon. "Cook. And wait around, twiddling my thumbs, that's what. I may as well be out here."

And mourning the loss of your husband, who just killed himself hours ago. I don't say that, though. I don't doubt that Wilma will do more than her fair share of crying over her husband. I'm sure she already has. I'm sure she's been quietly crying for years.

"You have a good eye for picking fruit."

I smile, resuming my task. "I had a good teacher."

"You did," she agrees. "I always hoped the football thing was just a boyish phase that he'd grow out of. I was convinced he'd be the one to keep this grove going another generation. But then he got a scholarship and, well, we were all sure he'd make it all the way. Had he not been injured, I'm sure we'd be watching that boy run around in tights on the television right now."

I snort loudly at the thought of Ben in tights, but then I have to admit, he probably looks hot in a football uniform. "I got the impression you always supported football?" That picture on Ben's desk with Wilma's beaming face certainly made it appear so.

"Oh, I did!" Her voice spikes, as if just the *suggestion* of *not* supporting her son is appalling. "I'm his mama. Of course I did. It's his life, after all. I just wanted him to be happy." She adds wryly, "And not make me a grandmother too early."

"Man, I wish I had you growing up," I admit. What would it have been like to have a mother like Wilma? You couldn't possibly *not* succeed with her in your corner.

"I take it your mother and you had a difference of opinion?" The curiosity is thick behind her light tone.

"Annabelle had a very clear picture of what her daughter should be and I certainly wasn't it."

Wilma is silent for a moment. "I'm sorry to hear that, Reese." There's a pause. "What about your father?"

"I barely remember him. He took off when I was five and I haven't heard from him since." It's funny, admitting that to Wilma isn't as painful as it normally is. I shrug. "It's fine. I have Jack now. He's a pretty decent replacement father." I smile as I say that, wondering if he sees me as more than just that wayward girl he rescued.

Wilma reaches up to pluck an extra-large tangerine off as she drifts back to our previous conversation. "When Ben got injured, I thought he'd come back home, but he decided he wanted to become a lawyer. I was surprised, to be honest. He never seemed like one to sit in an office, surrounded by paperwork. He's always liked working with his hands. A part of me wondered if it was the bad blood with his own father that kept him away."

"He comes to visit you regularly though, right?"

"Oh, yes." Her head bobs up and down ardently. "Almost every weekend during the season, which is half the year. He calls me every single day, too. Ben is just about the best son a mother could ask for. Sure, he was a handful growing up, what with all his chasing girls and mischief. But he's the most loyal, honest young man. That's not just his mama saying that. It's the truth. The boy is a terrible liar, even on those rare occasions when he probably *should* lie or just keep quiet. Now, if I could just get him to settle down with a nice girl, I'd be thrilled."

"I don't know that Ben's in any rush to settle down." *Ever.* What would it actually be like to have Ben 100 percent of the time, with no worries? Would he be who he is today? Would he change?

I feel her eyes on me. "He's just afraid that he'll be like his father. He couldn't live with himself if he hurt someone like Josh hurt me. The thing is, Ben isn't capable of hurting a woman like that. His heart is just too darn big."

I know I shouldn't ask, but I'm asking. "Why . . . I mean, how did you put up with it for all those years?" I'm dying to know what would possess a woman like Wilma—who seems so strong and self-sufficient—to stay with Ben's father for so long.

A thick silence fills the air. I glance over to see her sad smile, a far-off look in her blue eyes. "Because I fell in love with a man. And then I held on to the memory of him, long after that man was gone," she murmurs, a soft, sad smile touching her lips. "It wasn't always like this. Joshua was the handsome, intense boy in high school that all the girls wanted to date. I thought I had died and gone to heaven when he walked up to me after class one day and asked me to go to the drive-in with him that weekend. I mean, I was the plain Jane orange farmer's daughter. What could he possibly see in me? I can still remember that first night—the smell of his cologne, the blue of his eyes, his quiet smile, the way it felt to have his arm around me. You'd think he was a movie star or something, the awe I felt. It was ridiculous."

"I was like that with my ex-husband," I murmur softly. Right down to the shock and awe.

A hand reaches out and pats my forearm lovingly. "Ben mentioned something to me about that. I'm so sorry." Pulling back, she goes on. "Joshua and I got married right out of high school and moved onto the grove with my parents. I was an only child and I knew I was going to run this place. Joshua knew he wanted to make furniture, so it was perfect. I was pregnant with Josh Junior within two months. The others followed like dominoes. Did Ben tell you that I had all five children in seven years?"

I nod.

"Joshua had a very healthy appetite." She chuckles. "I guess Ben didn't fall far from the apple—well, orange," she holds up a fruit—"tree in that regard."

Oh my God. I duck my head, appreciating the wide brim of this hat to hide my red ears.

"As you can imagine, with five children running around this place and trying to take over the whole business from my parents, who were older and ready to retire, it was busy around here. Joshua seemed content building furniture and selling it. He was never a really 'hands-on' kind of father, but I knew it was because he had an absent father himself. He didn't know how to play with a child." I watch her pick through the tree for a moment, observing how swiftly she zeros in and plucks the ripe fruit, as if she could do this in her sleep.

"I had no idea he had started drinking in there. Josh was a quiet, broody man to begin with and I was naïve. I didn't know the signs. I didn't grow up around that sort of thing. The only alcohol in our house was champagne on Christmas morning." She heaves a sigh. "I blamed myself for a long time. I figured I wasn't enough for him, that I wasn't attractive enough anymore, my body stretched out with having all these babies. Josh was still in good shape, aging gracefully. I was too preoccupied with the children and work to put on makeup and lace. When he started going out at night and coming home with lipstick on his collar, I was devastated. But I looked the other way. I cried. I convinced myself that every woman must deal with this sort of thing. And I prayed. I thanked God for giving me my life and my children and asked for his help to make me a better wife so my husband didn't need to drink or go to other women anymore. I was stupid," she admits more softly. "When I finally accepted that my husband had serious alcohol problems and I confronted him about it, it only got worse. He lashed out, telling me to leave him be, that he could stop if he wanted to but that it helped him suffer through the monotony of this life. And then he started drinking more.

"And then the accident in the wood shop happened. I assume Ben told you about that?"

I nod again, quietly picking as she goes on.

"I lost Joshua after that. The man I fell in love with was gone for good, leaving me with a memory I didn't want to let go of. Not until last night, when I saw the look on my baby's face, when I realized all that I had lost by believing that if I just held on long enough, we could go back. That everything is worth trying to save."

I hear the first sounds of the dune buggy engine in the distance, the familiar dips as it shifts into gears, each one bringing the rumble closer. It sounds like Ben's got the needle buried.

Wilma smiles sadly. "It hasn't sunk in yet. I'm in shock—I know it. All I can think of right now is that it's going to be so nice to have all my children here, under one roof again. Even under the circumstances." I help her load the filled crate onto the trailer as red and yellow come into view, a cloud of dust billowing.

Her hand, small but deceptively strong, grabs hold of mine. "I don't care what that boy has told you. He cares a great deal about you, whether he has admitted it to himself yet or not. I've seen how he is around women and he's just different with you. I can't quite put my finger on it." She smiles as she pats my hand and then lets go. "Don't give up on Ben just yet."

The dune buggy comes to a skidding halt. "Mama, you disappeared on me." Ben grabs onto the roll bars and hoists his giant body out in a very "Dukes of Hazzard" way, cautious eyes shifting between me and Wilma. "What're you doing out here?"

"I'm helping Reese, of course. What does it look like I'm doing, Benjamin?" she retorts snidely.

"Lorna Parker's waiting for you at the house with more food."

"My gosh. Thank goodness we'll have a full house. I don't know how else we're going to get through all this before it spoils."

"Maybe you should stop making more, then," Ben remarks with a head shake. "The timer on the oven started beeping, so I took out the meatloaf. I dunno if it's done yet, but it sure smells good."

"Perfect. Thank you, son." She pats his cheeks once and then climbs into her truck. She's gone in seconds.

"She seems to be holding up well," I note.

"She's in shock. If you have any requests—cookies, cakes, a leg of lamb—now's the time to ask. The woman probably won't stop cooking for the next week."

"I think I'll have to try that next time I deal with a cata-strophic event." It's a lot healthier than Jim Beam and, after what I've witnessed this weekend, I'm considering swearing off hard liquor for the rest of my life.

Ben rounds the trailer and starts shifting the boxes around, the muscles in his arms straining against the weight. "You've done a lot."

"Remind me when my body hurts tomorrow," I mutter, turning back to the tree. Who knew picking fruit could be so strenuous? But with all that stretching and reaching, I know I'm going to feel it.

Strong hands land on my shoulders and begin kneading softly over the balls and down my biceps. I groan and lean back into his chest.

"What's with this hat?" Ben exclaims, yanking it off my head and tossing it onto the wagon before returning his attention to my body.

"What? Your mom doesn't want my beautiful, flawless skin damaged," I explain, enjoying the warmth of the sun almost as much as I'm enjoying Ben's proximity.

"So . . . what were you two talking about?" I hear the smile in his voice but there's also something else there. Wariness.

"The usual."

A pause and then, "Are you going to make me drag it out of you?"

I close my eyes, wondering what that would entail. "Just that you're madly in love with me and you just don't know it yet."

Ben rests his chin on top of my head as he folds me into an embrace. And snorts loudly. "Even on the day her husband kills himself, that woman's intent on marrying me off."

I reach up to blindly pat his cheek, the reminder of this morning sobering. "How are you doing? Are you in shock, too?"

Ben's arms fall from me as he steps forward to stand in front of a tree, reaching for some ripe fruit on a high branch that I can't reach. "I don't know what the fuck I am, Reese. Confused, that's what." Those square jaw muscles harden as he bows his head. "Mama tells him that she's finally had enough, that she wants to be free, and so he goes and kills himself? He sets it up like a goddamn stage, with the doors wide open and him sitting in the middle. How is Mama supposed to react to that? She's going to feel guilty as hell, that's how! She's hiding it well, but I know she's feeling guilty. Was that a 'fuck you' to her? To me?" Ben's head dips and he takes a deep breath. "Sorry. I don't mean to yell. I'm just . . ."

"It's okay. Yell all you want, Ben."

He reaches up to rest his hands on top of his head as his mouth opens to speak, only to falter. And then he explodes. "I'm fucking ecstatic that he's gone, Reese! How *wrong* is that? I mean . . ." His arms drop so heavily that his hands slap against his thighs. He starts pacing. "When I saw Mama crumpled in a heap like that, I thought she had had another heart attack. I couldn't get to her fast enough. And then I saw him slumped in that chair—dead—and the only word in my head was 'finally'! Finally, after everything he's done to her, after all the pain he's caused her and this family, and how much we've lost around here, the fucker is out of our lives!"

His tone softens a little, his voice cracking. "While my mama is standing there, sobbing over his death, I'm ready to sing hal-le-fucking-leuiah." I can almost see the guilt weighing his shoulders down. "What kind of person does that make me?"

"Normal, Ben. He was a shitty father and husband. Even your mother knows that."

"Really?" He turns to look at me. "What if you got a call that Annabelle died. Would you want to throw a party?"

Good question. Annabelle . . . dead? I've never given it much thought. What would I feel for a woman who seemed incapable of feeling anything for me? "I don't know," I admit with a sigh.

We fall into silence as Ben leans back against the wagon.

Finally I hazard to ask, "What'd the note say?"

He purses his lips for a moment. "That he was sorry for . . . everything. He wishes he could have been a better husband. That he wants her to stay on the grove and be happy again."

A lump spikes in my throat. "How does a person veer so far off course?"

"Alcohol . . . depression . . . fear . . ." He shakes his head. "I don't know."

Why did it take a bottle of aspirin and a death wish for Ben's father to admit his faults? What if he had just said these things years ago? I guess maybe he didn't see what was wrong. Or he kept denying it. Until it was too late. "At least he gave her that."

"Yeah. There was also an envelope with a life insurance policy they took out years ago. A pretty big one, too. One that will pay out, even after a suicide." He smiles sadly. "It'll help her fix the house up."

Warmth spreads through my chest. "That's great news!"

Ben turns to give me a funny look.

"What?"

He says nothing, though. He simply holds a hand out. When I take it, he pulls me in to him. Lifting me up onto the edge of the trailer, he wastes no time pushing my legs apart to slide his body between them. "I know it's been a shitty day, but I'm glad you're here."

"So am I." All I've wanted to do is wrap my hands around that giant heart of his and protect it from any more hurt. Hurt like I saw last night. The kind that you feel when you're faced with the deeply rooted bitterness that Ben has had to face for years. I wonder if it's better or worse than the indifference I see when Annabelle looks at me.

I'm expecting Ben's hands up my shirt in seconds, but all he does is rest his forehead against my chest. And so I coil my arms around his head, press my cheek against his hair, and watch the afternoon sun shift along the horizon in silence.

■ ■ ■

"I should have just called him. I don't know how you talked me into this," Ben mutters, pulling into Jack's driveway that night.

"I told you. He already knows I was with you and what happened. He'll want to pay his respects in person."

Ben heaves a resigned sigh.

"He's not going to fire you!"

"Well, doing it today would be in poor taste, I guess." Ben slides out of the driver's side reluctantly and trails me inside.

Both Mason and Jack are waiting for us in the kitchen. Jack's on his feet instantly, walking forward with a morose expression and his arms out to offer a confused-looking Ben a manly hug. Mason is close behind. "How can we help?"

"Well, I think Reese already mentioned me needing a week off. My brothers and sister are trying to get flights in, but I'm not sure when they'll make it. I can't leave my mother alone."

"Done," Jack states simply.

Ben swallows. "Thanks, Jack. That's a relief. I just drove back to drop Reese off and get some clothes and I'm heading back up tonight."

There's an awkward pause as three sets of eyes flash to me—Mason's filled with curiosity, Jack's with reluctance, and Ben's baby blues with . . . I don't know what that look is, but I've been getting it a lot today.

"My mama sent you her meatloaf as a small token of thanks," Ben adds, handing Mason the box that Wilma packed up. News in the small community spread quickly. By the time I made it back to the house, the fridge and freezer were brimming with food from friends, and Wilma was still cooking.

"Well, tell her that was unnecessary, but it'll go to the same good spot it went last time." Jack's soft chuckle fills the kitchen as he pats his belly.

"Well, I should get going." There's another awkward pause as Ben glances at me. I wonder what he's thinking. Probably the same thing I'm thinking: What's the standard protocol for saying goodbye here? Because I know what *I* want.

I want him to kiss me.

Clearing his throat, Ben finally offers, "Thanks for all your help today, Reese. Mama sure appreciated it. You've got to be tired."

Exhausted, actually. I don't know how she does that day in and day out. I simply nod and watch his retreating back as he disappears out the front door.

And it hits me. I'm not going to see him for an entire week. At least! Is he feeling any of what I'm feeling right now? Or is Wilma wrong? Is this just his regular friendship, with a bit of a personal tragedy kicker thrown in to wreak emotional havoc? And what if he *is* feeling it and he doesn't like it? Wilma's been introducing me as Ben's girlfriend to anyone who will listen, including the priest from her parish who stopped by as we were packing the car up to drive back to Miami. There's a really good chance that Ben is looking to hightail it out of here.

Maybe into someone else's bed.

Shit. Am I developing *real* feelings for Ben Morris?

"I forgot something in the car." It's comes out sounding stilted and obviously untrue. I glance at Jack as I pass by. He's just staring at me. I try not to rush out the door, but I'm pretty sure I've failed at hiding my hurry.

Ben's tall frame is just about to fold into his driver's side as the front door clicks behind me. He stops and watches as I take tentative, stiff-bodied steps toward him, my stomach a mix of butterflies and dread, not sure what's going on in his head. This "thing" between us was easier when I didn't care. Now . . . I'm pretty sure that I do. God, I don't want to be another Mercy, another "friend" that he'll need to gently turn down.

"I just . . ." My voice drifts off as I reach him. What the hell do I say now that I'm here? "I'm really sorry about your dad. About all of it. Not just today."

His head cocks to the side as he regards me. "Reese, are you falling in love with me?"

"No!" I yell with a touch too much vigor. I feel my face burst into flames as he starts chuckling. "Shut up, you asshole."

"Dude! My dad just killed himself today and you're calling me names?" His terrible attempt at humor makes me cringe. "All right already, come here." An arm hooks around my back and he pulls me into a tight hug, my face pressing up against the softness of his T-shirt. All of his shirts are soft and comfortable and worthy of melting into. I inhale deeply, catching that soapy clean smell that I've already missed.

"Are you going to survive a week without me or do you need to keep one of my shirts to tide you over?" he murmurs, his mouth pressed up against my hair. I hear the smile in his voice.

I turn my face away as another burst of heat touches my cheeks. "Maybe just one."

He groans, his arms tightening around me. "So you can use it for some weird exorcism-voodoo shit when I piss you off? Hell no! I'll end up with a nasty rash, won't I? Oh, wait. You called *me* a rash, didn't you?"

I find myself giggling against him as movement in the blinds at the front window catches my eye. *Great. Jack.* I'll have that to deal with when I go inside.

Ben must have seen it, too. "What're you going to tell Jack?"

"I don't know." I pull away and tilt my head back to meet Ben's eyes. "What *should* I tell him?"

His chest presses against mine with his deep breath. With another quick glance back at the window, he leads me ahead of his car and into the cover of the garage doors, set far enough out that no window has a view. He looks down at me, roaming my features and settling on my mouth. "That we're good friends." And then, so contrary to his words, and in a manner so different from the Ben that has kissed me in the past, he dips down and settles a soft, lingering kiss on my mouth, his thumbs rubbing against my cheeks. "I've gotta head out now. It's a long drive back and I'm beat," he murmurs against my mouth, his voice crackling with its low cadence. I feel his lips curve against mine. "I didn't sleep well with all that babbling you were doing last night."

"What?" I feel my brow furrow. "I don't talk in my sleep."

There's just enough light from the corner of the house that I see his dimples. "You do. I just didn't have a chance to make fun of you for it earlier."

Curiosity overcomes my embarrassment. "What did I say?"

He pauses, as if deciding whether to tell me. And then he shrugs. "Hard to tell, with that ass of yours going all night, too. What did you eat, because . . . Jeez!"

"What!" I shriek, pulling away from him to smack his broad chest hard as he bursts out in laughter. "I do not *fart* in my sleep!" I hiss. This may be worse than the puke and the crawling.

"I was the one pressed right up against you all night. I think I'd know."

"Oh my God." I close my eyes as I wince. Of all the guys to do that in front of—if it's even true; Jared *never* said anything—it had to be a guy like Ben? Who will torment me! Does this kind of stuff happen to other women, too? Or is it just me? I shift away from him and start moving backward. "Well, you'd better get going. It's a long drive."

Two strong hands shoot out to grab onto me and pull me until my back is pressing against the garage door. "Don't worry. I still think you're hot." With an infuriating smile, he dips down and levels me with one of his overpowering kisses, this one much more familiar and "Ben," buckling my knees as he crushes his body against mine. My eyes finally open to deep dimples as he lifts a hand and kisses my knuckles. "Okay, seriously, I need to go or I'm liable to take you on the hood of Jack's truck." Slipping a hand on the small of my back, he leads me toward the walkway as he heads back to his car. "Do you think you can stay out of trouble this week?"

"Depends. What kind of trouble?"

He rests an arm on his open door as he smirks at me, explaining in a wry tone, "The kind that involves douchebag ex-husbands."

I open my mouth to speak but I stall on the words as I process this. Is he referring to catfights with Caroline and violent outbursts? Or was that his way of saying he doesn't want me messing around with anyone? I settle on, "Depends. Do you think you can stay away from Twinkies?"

He winks. "I knew you were jealous." And then he climbs into his car without giving me a proper answer. I watch him pull away, feeling irritated and suddenly empty.

With a deep breath, I walk inside.

Jack and Mason are still in the kitchen, Jack carving a sizeable piece of meatloaf and loading it onto a plate. "Have you eaten?"

"Yeah, Wilma wouldn't let us leave until we ate," I explain, reaching into the fridge for the jug of chocolate milk. I screw the top off and am about to lift it to my lips to chug it back when I catch Mason staring at me, his mouth open and trying really hard not to scold me. My arms drops. I reach out and get a glass, making a point of watching him with a "See? I can be considerate!" glare.

"Well, the woman sure can cook," Jack muses, opening the microwave to slide his plate in. "I'm not even hungry and I have to eat this."

I pat his belly affectionately. "Be careful. Wouldn't want to get too plump for Ms. Sexton."

Mason starts snickering from his seat on the bar stool.

"Mason . . ." The kitchen fills with loud beeps as Jack punches instructions into the microwave. "Why don't you go to your room and talk to that lovely girlfriend of yours."

Mason's laughter cuts off short. "You're sending me to my room? I'm twenty-five years old!"

"Yes, that's right, you are. And yet you got caught lying to your father this weekend." Jack stands in front of the microwave, a small smile on his face.

"Good luck, Reese," Mason mutters, grabbing whatever magazine he was reading and his glass of chocolate milk.

"So . . ." Jack takes a moment rifling through the forks in the cutlery drawer, as if there's a "good fork" versus a "bad fork" in there. It's a matching set. "How is Ben's mother taking it?"

"Hard to tell. She kept herself really busy today. Ben thinks she's going to have a hard time once the dust settles."

Jack pulls the heated plate of food out of the microwave and heads toward the breakfast bar. "I can't imagine losing her husband like that is easy."

"It was bad, but it could have been worse." I'd imagine a bottle of pills and some puke is definitely easier to deal with than a shotgun or a rope. If Wilma had walked in on that . . . My stomach tightens with the thought. She's such a sweet woman and she deserves to be happy.

She's also a fascinating woman. Perhaps it's because of the vast difference between her and Annabelle. All I knew growing up was a woman who kept trading up for power and prestige. Wilma is completely opposite, standing by a wretched man for thirty-three years, holding onto the few years of bliss she remembers. Did either of these women make good choices?

"How is Ben taking it? Should he be driving alone?" Jack asks.

I think back to what I just left in the driveway. Ben being . . . Ben. "I think he's okay," I say tentatively, adding, "He didn't have the closest relationship with his father."

Jack nods as he sits down. "And what about his relationship with you? How close is that?" He shovels a mouthful of meatloaf in and chews slowly, his eyes never leaving my face.

"We're good friends," I parrot Ben's earlier words. It's not a lie. We have formed a close friendship. It may not be entirely platonic. Or not platonic at all but, as long as Jack doesn't ask for specifics, it's a solid answer. Plus, if I admit to nothing, then I'm not putting Jack in an awkward position, where he's forced to do anything about it at work.

My logic is sound.

I watch Jack process that as he swallows and fills his mouth again. I always know when Jack is thinking because his eyes remain downcast and trained on a specific spot. Finally, he places his fork on the counter. "I think you two both have very bright futures, and I'd hate for something to jeopardize that."

"Nothing's going to," I promise, though inside I know I'm not as confident as I sound. What's going to happen *when* Ben sleeps with someone else? Curls up in bed with her? Makes her laugh and feel special?

The very thought of it has me clenching my teeth.

Jack makes a soft grunt, as if he can read my mind, see my doubts.

I finish my glass of milk and rinse it out. "I'm heading to bed, Jack. It's been a long day."

"Okay. A package arrived for you yesterday, from Annabelle. I left it in your room."

"Great." What could that be?

"Reese?" Jack calls out after me as I pass him.

I slow reluctantly. I can convince myself of whatever logic I want; deceiving Jack still feels wrong. "Yeah?"

"You understand why I'm worried, right?"

"Because I'm an emotional mess who may accidentally repaint the interior of Warner in a fit of rage?"

A crooked smirk touches his lips as he pauses. "Ben seems like a good guy, but . . . I don't want you ending up bitter like Annabelle." I bite the inside of my mouth to keep quiet, recalling his own son's similar words only days ago. "Just . . ." Jack picks up the glass of red wine he has barely touched since I arrived home. "Keep it out of the office, Reese. I don't want anyone asking questions. It'll look like I'm favoring you." He takes a sip. "More than I already do."

I offer him a tiny, imperceptible nod as I take off up the stairs and to the privacy of my room, to find the giant white box resting on my bed. Tossing my knapsack to the floor, I peel off the tape securing the top. A pile of amethyst-colored satin nestled among tissue paper stares back at me. Unfolding the note card on top, I read:

> *For this Saturday's charity ball. I hope you haven't gained weight.*

I sigh. This event must be really important for her image for her to be going through all this trouble to get her daughter there. I pick the box up and toss it into the corner without even pulling the dress out.

Because I'm not going.

It's eleven by the time I'm crawling into bed when my cell phone rings. My stomach does a flip when I see Ben's name appear.

Oh God, I'm so screwed.

I answer with his line. "You missed me that much already?"

"How'd it go with Jack?" he says over the rumble of his Volkswagen engine.

That's why he called. He's worried about his job. Of course he is. "Okay. You have nothing to worry about."

"Really?" The doubt in his voice is unmistakable.

"Yeah. As long as you don't tell everyone at work that you're in love with me, you'll be fine."

He bursts out laughing. I bite my lip against the urge to ask why that's so funny.

There's a long moment of silence, where I expect him to say goodbye and secretly dread it.

And then I hear him ask, "Sing something to me."

"What?"

"It's a long drive and I'm fallin' asleep. Sing me something before I crash."

I try to keep the surge of warmth from exploding in my voice as I mutter, "Fine," and drop into my beanbag chair. Setting my phone down and putting it on speaker, I pick up my guitar and begin picking at the strings haphazardly. "Any requests?"

"How about . . . 'Achy Breaky Heart'? 'Ice Ice Baby'?"

I roll my eyes. "None. Okay, then." I settle in as I keep picking until a familiar tune surfaces and I find the words to "The Freshmen," by The Verve Pipe, flowing out of my mouth.

It feels good to do this now. Not for show, not for revenge. Just for me.

And for Ben.

"You still awake?" I ask as the last note to that song fades.

"You bet, darlin'. Sing me another." I feel my lips curl up in a warm smile as I pick another song.

By the time Ben pulls into the driveway at Wilma's almost two hours later, my voice is getting raspy and my ass is numb. "It's late. You'd better get some rest," he says.

"Does it feel different now, being there?"

There's a long pause. "I don't know yet. I haven't figured out how I feel about all this." Much softer, I hear him add, "About a lot of things."

"Yeah. I know what you mean." I immediately bite my tongue. Was that too obvious?

"Good night, Reese."

"Good night, Ben." I hit the "end" button before I'm tempted to say something I'll regret.

Chapter 30

. . .

BEN

"*This feels different,*" I admit to myself as I lie in bed, my head nestled within my arms, staring up at the ceiling of Elsie's room.

And it has nothing to do with my dad being gone.

I wish Reese were lying next to me. I'm trying to tell myself that it's because I just sat in the car for two hours listening to her sexy voice. I was grinning like an idiot the entire time.

And then, when I caught Mama in here with her hands on the pillows, about to change the sheets, I hollered at her to stop. She patted my chest with a little smile and left quietly, leaving me to bury my face in Reese's pillow to inhale the scent of strawberries and cream.

And now, here I am, thinking about kissing Reese tonight before I left her, and how much I didn't want to leave her.

To be honest, I was expecting the novelty of Reese to wear off after Friday night; that finally getting her into my bed would have satisfied this intense urge that's been driving me crazy for weeks. I mean, I'm a guy who likes the chase. That's *always* been the case. But it's not the case with Reese.

Quite the opposite, actually.

Now, I just want to hold onto her to keep her from getting

away. And leaving her tonight, thinking about her possibly hooking up with that douchebag ex of hers, had my teeth grinding against each other. I know that part of it is her giving him the time of day after how much he hurt her. But most of it's not, because when I think about her hooking up with *anyone* else, I feel the exact same tight ball forming in my stomach.

Yeah, things have definitely changed. I'm just not sure what the hell I'm supposed to do about it.

■ ■ ■

"How'd you sleep, darling?" Mama asks from her seat on the back porch, one of Grandma's knit blankets wrapped around her as she sips at her tea.

I lean in to lay a kiss on her head. "Out like a light, as usual. You know that." Once my body shuts down, it takes a lot to wake me up. I was teasing Reese yesterday. If she was talking or doing anything else in her sleep, I have no fucking clue.

Mama smiles. "You always were my best sleeper. Such a happy, easy baby."

I set my cup of coffee down on the small end table—another piece made by my father; the house is like a Joshua Morris museum—and settle myself into a chair. "When's everyone getting here?"

"Elsie should be here this afternoon. Rob and Jake will be here Wednesday with their families. Josh, not until late Thursday. He can't afford to lose time with work." My oldest brother—my father's namesake and arguably a chip off the old block—works as a crane operator in Chicago. At least *he's* admitted that he has a drinking problem and is trying to get help. The medical bills, coupled with child support and alimony, mean he's struggling to make ends meet in a shitty studio apartment in one of Chicago's less desirable areas.

"It's gonna be a full house."

"I know." Mama smiles sadly. "It's been a long time since I

could say that." She holds out a plate of cake. "Here, have some of this. We have twenty more waiting inside."

"Neighbors have been good to us." I gladly reach out and grab a piece, stuffing it into my mouth.

"It's delicious, isn't it?"

I moan in response. I never turn down sweets, though I probably should. If I ever stop working out, I'll end up with a gut like Jack's in no time.

"Hayley made it."

"Who's Hayley?" Crumbs fly out of my mouth.

"Don't talk with your mouth full," Mama scolds. "Lorna's daughter. She's coming by to help pick. Yesterday's harvest went over to the packing place this morning. They'll be on the road by this afternoon."

At least that's taken care of. I still can't believe Reese was out there that long, filling those crates. I could kiss her for it. Hell, I could kiss her for anything, but that's as good an excuse as any.

There's a pause. "There's always room here for one more."

I shoot her a confused look.

"Reese, son," she clarifies with an exasperated sigh. "Why don't you invite her to come up and stay with us."

"Well, for one thing, because she works full time. Plus, why would she want to hang out here for an entire week while we get ready for a funeral?"

She takes a small sip of her tea. "Something tells me she would."

Of course. Which brings me to what I haven't had a chance to say earlier. "Mama, you've gotta stop telling people that Reese is my girlfriend."

"Oh, did that slip out accidentally?" She makes a show of dusting crumbs off her hand, her eyes averted.

"Just once or twice," I mock softly, leaning back into my chair to stretch my feet out. "We're just *friends*. I don't need things to get confusing by putting labels on it."

"You think the label's going to change what's going on?" I catch her lips curl into a smile, as if she knows some secret, but she hides it behind another sip. What the hell did those two women talk about out there yesterday? It was a sly move on Mama's part. One minute she's in the kitchen. Then I head to the can and she's gone when I come out.

"How was dropping her off last night? Did your boss say anything about you two?"

"He offered his condolences and told me that family comes first."

"Hmm . . . sounds like a good man," she murmurs.

"Yeah, he is." And I'm starting to feel guilty for what I'm doing with his stepdaughter, especially after our talk. He must have figured it out by now.

"Well, I've booked the funeral for Friday. Pastor Phillips said he can do it. I don't want to bother with a visitation. I don't expect many people . . ." Her voice drifts off and her gaze becomes distant.

"Not for him, anyway." As soon as I see her flinch at my words, I regret it. I've been really careful not to talk like that, not to let any of my feelings come out. It only hurts her.

Reaching out, I take her hand in mine. "I'm going to phone the insurance company today and get everything sorted out. Okay?"

She nods slowly. "I didn't realize how expensive funerals have become."

"Don't worry about that, Mama. I've got money to cover that until the insurance pays out."

"Oh, I can't take your—"

"Don't worry about it. I'm fine."

She peers up at me. "How'd I get so lucky to have a son like you?"

Getting up, I kiss her again. "Because you raised me to be like this. And because I made a lot of money taking care of naked women at Penny's."

"Oh, Ben." She shakes her head but then starts to laugh softly. "I'll be out in the grove. Call my cell if you need anything."

As I'm walking through the door and into the kitchen, Mama calls out, "I'd like Reese to come to the funeral. Do you think she'd come?"

I shake my head with resignation, knowing what the woman is up to. "I'm not sure, Mama. I'll ask her."

■ ■ ■

The familiar rumble and squeaky brakes of the farm truck comes to a stop behind the tractor. Assuming it's Mama, I don't bother turning around.

"Ben?" My name rolls off an unfamiliar female voice.

Turning on my heels, I watch a twenty-something-year-old girl with white-blond hair and mile-long legs slide out of the truck.

Slamming the heavy door shut, she walks forward, her hand out. "I'm Hayley Parker. I'm here to help pick."

I accept it with a quick shake. "Yeah, right. Mama said you'd be by. Thanks for offering."

Sidling up beside me, she slides her hands into the back pockets of her shorts as her blue eyes take in the tree in front of us. "I used to work on a citrus farm, so I have practice."

"Perfect. Then I won't make myself look like an ass by trying to train you." She's pretty, there's no doubt about that, in an all-American-girl kind of way. I've had plenty of them.

Her smile does a flip into a full-lipped pout as she reaches out and lays a hand on my bicep. "I'm so sorry about your dad."

With a nod, I turn back to pluck a few high tangerines.

"You don't remember me, do you?" she asks, joining in to test and pull some fruit off the lower branches.

My hand freezes. *Shit* . . . That sounds like a setup. She doesn't look at all familiar and I'm usually good with the faces of women I've screwed around with. I hazard a glance at her, to *really* look at her. How the hell did I miss the perky set of tits staring out at me from beneath that tight pink T-shirt before? Probably because of those damn legs.

"You were a senior when I started high school," Hayley finally elaborates.

"Did we . . . know each other?" That's my covert way of asking, "Did I nail you?" Because I'd be surprised. Fourteen-year-olds didn't do it for me when I was seventeen.

"No. I mean, *I* knew who *you* were." Her voice trails off as she blushes, her fingers stretched over multiple pieces of fruit as she strolls over to a crate to gently lay them in. "I went to every single one of your games. I had the biggest crush on you back then."

And . . . there it is.

I try to stifle my grin. She's not the only one. I'm not trying to be a dick about it but when you open your locker to find folded love notes spilling out enough times, you can't deny it. "You never said hi?" I tease.

She starts giggling as she moves past me, her arm brushing against mine. "No way! I was a scrawny little kid back then."

And you're not anymore. Is that what she's hoping I'll notice, wearing those tight black shorts? Point made.

"Can you please help me reach those ones?" she asks coyly, standing beneath a branch that extends out above her head. Her hands stretch up enough to lift her shirt, showing off a belly ring.

It instantly makes me think of Reese. Reese doesn't have a belly ring. Why doesn't she have one? That seems to be the standard prerequisite before women move on to the more adventurous locations.

"Ben?"

"Uh, yeah, sorry." Peeling my eyes away from her piercing, I give my head a shake and shift over to gently pull the branch down. There're plenty of ripe fruit within her reach. There's no need for this whole orchestrated move of hers, where she's standing well within my personal space, facing me, a small smile touching her lips, her eyes on me more than the task at hand.

If the girl knows me, then she knows exactly what I'm like. I never bothered to hide that fact from anyone. I have a strong suspicion that if I wanted to get laid right now, this girl is as good as naked.

There's only one problem.

She's not Reese.

Fuck . . . what is happening to me?

Am I actually turning this down?

Yes.

Yes, I am.

"Listen, I'm going to take the truck and head back. I've got some things I need to take care of." Her face crumbles with disappointment, obviously realizing that this eight-year campaign of hers isn't going to come to an epic conclusion in the grove today. Just in case she decides to throw herself at me—because I've had that happen before—I let the branch snap back up in the air as I take several steps backward. "Mama will be back out with the truck soon." I don't wait for her answer before I'm climbing in the pickup and hauling ass back home.

"Did you know that Lorna's daughter has had a crush on me since she was fourteen?" I ask Mama as I jump out of the driver's seat, back at the house. "'Cause anyone can see that."

"Did Hayley find you all right?" She keeps her eyes focused on the planters she's watering.

"Yeah, Mama. She found me, *all right*."

"She's a pretty girl, isn't she?"

"Yeah, I guess." I shake my head. "What's goin' on with you? One minute you're trying to marry me off to Reese, the next you're setting a blond trap for me!"

A slow smile stretches across Mama's face until it's taking up most of the real estate. I don't know that I've seen her this happy in a long time. "But you didn't get caught in it, did you?"

"What the hell, Mama! Did you really want me to?"

The water pouring out from her watering wand dies in a dribble as her smile morphs into an exasperated glare. "I wanted you to see for yourself how Reese has changed you, son. Had you never met Reese, what would have happened out there?"

I'd have that girl bent over the side of the wagon right now— that's what would have happened. My brows spike as I take in Mama's expectant stare. Does she want details?

"Oh, Benjamin." She waves a dismissive hand. "I've raised four Morris boys and dealt with your father for years. I'm no idiot. Those ladies at the drugstore always got a hoot out of me, filling my cart up with condoms for my *active* children."

I smirk, remembering Jake and me walking into each other's rooms the first time, holding out the boxes of condoms we'd each found on our nightstand. We figured out pretty quickly who had delivered them, seeing as our dad didn't give a shit. Mama earned the nickname of the Trojan Fairy. Behind her back, of course. There was an unspoken agreement—Mama didn't mention it to us and we didn't say a word to her. From then on, we'd just leave a note on our nightstands when we were out, and a new box would appear a few days later, along with a note telling us that she didn't condone this behavior and to be safe.

With a heavy sigh, I hang my head as I resign myself to the fact that Mama's right. Reese has done something to me. "Well, I'm not going back out there, so you'd better rescue her with the truck or she'll be grinding the gears of the tractor to get back. I doubt that girl can handle a stick."

Not that kind, anyway.

■ ■ ■

"How are you possibly *bigger!*" Elsie says with a laugh as I throw her tiny body over my shoulder with no effort.

"I'm not. You've just started shrinking in your old age," I tease, grabbing her bag with my free hand and carrying her toward the porch like a sack of potatoes.

She starts playing the bongos on my back with her hands. "Okay, seriously, Ben. Put me down."

"Or what?"

There's a long pause as her impish mind searches for something she has on me. She's a lot like me in that regard. "Or I'll tell this girlfriend of yours that you used to pretend you were Patrick Swayze from *Dirty Dancing* and you memorized all the dance moves."

"Reese has got way worse material on me than that." I drop her suitcase and swing her down off my shoulder to take in her cute face. She looks so much like a younger version of Mama—but with long, curly, chestnut hair—that it's crazy. "And she's not my girlfriend, Elsie."

"That's not what Mom says." She laughs at me as I roll my eyes and shake my head. I think I'm the only one of us that still calls her Mama. Reese is right. I do milk the youngest child thing for all it's worth.

Elsie's smile falters as her eyes dart to the barn. "It's so weird to be back here, Ben. It's been so long. Everything looks the same but it's not anymore, is it?" She was already in college when my dad's accident happened. We talked on the phone a lot after but she never came back. Of all of us, my sister has been gone from here the longest. She flew in to Miami to see me after my knee injury five years ago, when I was high on Percocet and hostility over a future lost. Aside from a trip out West to visit her three years ago, I haven't seen her in person since.

"How is she doing?" I know they've stayed close, even though Elsie has refused to come out here. But still, not seeing your mom face-to-face for almost five years is crazy.

Before I can answer, the front door creaks open. We turn to see Mama step out, wiping her hands on her apron. She's been in the kitchen all day. Whatever she's making, it involves a lot of flour because she's got white powder all over her cheeks and her chin.

That doesn't dissuade Elsie from taking off immediately, running like a little kid into Mama's outstretched arms, the sound of their cries filling the late afternoon air.

■ ■ ■

How's Warner?

I lie back in bed, watching the screen on my phone, expecting Reese to be asleep but hoping that she's not. Since Mama's "experiment" with Hayley, I've pulled my phone out a dozen times to check in with Reese for . . . nothing, really. Just to say hi, to make her laugh, to have her make me laugh. But I could never decide what to say. Normally, I don't know when to shut up.

The indicator changes to "read," making my stomach do a flip. *Fuck* . . . I'm acting like a chick.

A few seconds later:

The law bot came looking for you in my office this morning. I've buried her body under your desk. You'll have to clean that up when you get back.

My snort cuts into the quiet room.

Tell Mason. He's better at cleaning than I am.

How is it up there?

Women are throwing themselves at me. You better get here quick.

I wait and wait and . . . it says "read," but there's no answer coming. I'm expecting some snide remark, calling me a pig or something. But the longer I wait, the more I'm starting to think that was a boneheaded thing to say. I *do* wish she'd just drop everything and race up tonight, but now she probably thinks I'm up here screwing girls.

Does she care, though?

I hesitate for just a second and then type out:

The funeral's on Friday. Mama wants you to come.

I wait. She's read it.

Still no answer.

"Fuck!"

I guess that came out a little too loud, because there's a knock on my door a moment later. "You're not doing anything gross in my old room, are you?" Elsie asks.

"I wish!" I holler back.

"Are you decent? Can I come in?"

"Yeah." I make sure my sheets are covering the vitals as the door creaks open and my sister walks in.

"What's wrong?" Elsie always seemed to like being smack dab in the middle of four brothers. Josh and Rob harassed the guys at school for looking at their "cute little sister," but then she'd turn around and do the same for Jake and me, playing the protective sister. The funny thing is, in the end all four of us were protecting her. She was in the middle of a big Morris sandwich, with brothers chasing off assholes from all angles.

"Ah, nothing. I'm just an idiot."

Crawling onto the bed, she falls back to share my pillow. "Who are you texting?"

"Reese."

"Ah yes. The *friend* who visits your mother with you on weekends and spends the night in the same bed."

I shrug. "This is me we're talking about, remember?"

She rolls her eyes. "How could I forget? All of my senior friends were asking me to hook them up with my dorky freshman brother."

"I wasn't so dorky to them, was I? How's Shelley Armstrong,

by the way? You still talk to her?" Shelley was Elsie's hot best friend in high school.

There's a pause and then, "That wasn't a rumor?"

I feel the wide grin stretch across my face. "At Ansell's party after the homecoming game. It earned me legendary status with the guys pretty quick."

"She lied to me!" Elsie punches me in the arm. "You're lucky I love you so much, you pig."

"Funny. That's what Reese calls me. You two would probably get along well."

I feel her eyes on me. "Is she the reason you turned down Miss Florida today?"

"What?" I feel my brow pinch.

"Hayley Parker? She won the state beauty pageant last year."

"Seriously? . . . Huh." Picturing those legs, I mumble. "Not surprised. She definitely wasn't looking to solve world peace out there today, though—I can tell you that much."

Elsie snorts. "I couldn't believe it when Mom told me you were back within five minutes of her sending Hayley out. That sealed the deal in her eyes. Her little Benjamin's in *love*."

"That didn't mean anything," I deny, though everyone under this roof seems to know I'm lying. "Hell, I just lost my father yesterday. I'm just not in the mood."

She barks out with laughter, sounding a lot like me. "Oh, bullshit! Do you remember when Cheechee died?"

"Of course I do! Man, I loved that dog. He was the best." I still remember the way my stomach hit the ground as I was rounding the bend in the road, closing out a five-mile run, and found his broken, still body lying on the shoulder. He had been hit by a car.

"Exactly. You carried that dog all the way up the driveway in your arms, bawling your eyes out."

"We all cried. Even Josh!" Our oldest brother was never big on showing emotion.

"But you sure weren't crying later that night at that party, when I found you in the back of some girl's car with her head in your lap."

I burst out laughing. "Oh yeah. She was consoling me. You should have seen the look on your face." That was the problem with all of us being so close in age. We went to a lot of the same parties and knew all the same people.

Elsie rolls her eyes. "Well, then don't tell me you would have had a problem getting into the mood with a beauty queen when a man you hate is finally dead."

It's a somber reminder of why she's here, stifling our laughter.

"And what would Mama have done if I had gone for it?"

Elsie starts giggling. "She said she was going to drive out in the dune buggy and beat your ass if you weren't back within half an hour."

Just the image of a fifty-one-year-old Mama racing around in that thing has me bursting out with laughter again.

Nudging in closer, Elsie asks softly, "So, tell me about her. What's she like?"

I heave a sigh. "I don't know . . ." I smile. "She's funny. She has me laughing all the time, even at work when I want to slit my wrists with all the files I'm buried under. And she's smart. Way smarter than me. I told her she should go to law school. She'll ace all her classes if she doesn't piss her profs off too bad. She's really talented, too. Man, you should hear her sing. She has this incredible deep, raspy voice that—"

"I don't believe it," Elsie cuts in, turning to look hard at me, her eyes twinkling. "It's true! My little baby brother's *finally* stuck on a girl."

Oh, Christ. I close my eyes. "Now *you're* starting with me?"

Her head bumps up against mine. "Well, you didn't lead with 'she's hot.'"

"Well, that's a given. I was just trying to spare you. You want to hear how hot she is? Fine! She's got this round, tight ass that I just want to—"

"Ugh, Ben!" Elsie punches my bicep with one of her bony knuckles. It doesn't hurt but I stop anyway, grinning at her until she starts laughing, curling up next to me again.

There's another long pause. "Darrin and I broke up. Did Mom tell you that?"

I can hear the sadness in her voice. "No. But I heard her saying something about it to Dad . . . Are you okay?"

She shrugs. "Yes. No. I don't know. I loved him so much, Ben. And we were so happy most of the time, except for when we weren't and it was my fault. I couldn't trust him. I had no reason not to and yet there I was, constantly checking his emails and his phone, accusing him every time he came home late."

"Of course you couldn't. Look at what you grew up seeing."

"That's just Mom and Dad, not everyone."

"To a kid who sees that day in, day out, it can be *everything*."

"I guess." She sighs. "I don't know if I'll ever understand why Mom didn't boot his ass out years ago. We all would have been better off. I mean, look at Josh. It's like he tumbled right out of the mold. Did you know he was seeing that other woman for two months before Karen found out? Thank God she dumped his ass. He deserved it."

"At least he's trying to get help for the drinking," I offer half-heartedly.

She sits up slowly. "The rest of us aren't much better. Rita wants Jake to propose now that she's pregnant, and he won't. I'm a suspicion freak." She throws a casual hand my way. "And look at you."

"Look at me, what? Hey, I haven't lied or cheated on anyone. I've made zero commitments."

"Yeah." She turns to look at me, the moonlight highlighting the sadness on her face. "And you're going to miss out on all the wonderful things that come with committing. Just think how nice it would be to have one person that you trust so completely." More matter-of-factly, she states, "Reese was here on Sunday. She saw it all. She's a part of this, whether you like it or not. You should ask her to come up for Friday."

I hold up my phone. "I did. No response and I *know* she's read it. Maybe she doesn't want to come. I wouldn't blame her. It's a funeral, Elsie. Not a party."

"What'd you say to her?" Elsie frowns as I let my phone fall into her hand. Scanning the text message, she groans and then flicks me in the ear. "You're such a dumbass." Tossing the phone at my chest, she stands and walks toward the door, shaking her head. "Tell her you barely noticed the girl and that *you* want her to come. Good night." The door closes softly behind her.

I'm left staring at my phone, wondering if Reese is already asleep. Listening to my big sis, I quickly type out:

> I didn't screw around with anyone and I want you to come to the funeral. Please.

And I wait.

Chapter 31

■ ■ ■

REESE

I gape at the screen of my phone as my brain begins to process what my heart has already figured out.

I have a real *thing* for Ben.

A *thing* that made my insides clench up when I read that awful joke he made about women throwing themselves at him; that made disappointment swell when he told me *his mother* wanted me at the funeral, and then made my entire being melt in relief with this last text.

Friends go to their friends' parents' funerals. That's normal. I'm sure Ben will have lots of friends there to support him. That's why he's asking me to come. It's a fucking *funeral*! His *father's* funeral!

And I know that I want it to mean more.

Okay. I'll be there.

■ ■ ■

I stare.

With my chin resting in the palm of my hand, I stare out the glass, over the cubicles, to the empty, dimmed office, picturing that giant guy with his deep, adorable dimples, walking by my office with that big grin, throwing me a wink.

And I keep losing my train of thought as I picture myself hopping on my bike and going to see him. To see how he's doing. To make sure he's not reacquainting himself with the neighborhood's female population.

"Oh God," I groan. "Stupid, stupid, stupid." The cool wood feels soothing against my forehead as I gently bang my head against my desk. Jack was right. Here I am, *already* bringing it into the workplace. What if it means nothing? Then what? What happens when he comes back? What happens when another stripper strolls in? Or I see him flirting with another woman? I feel like I have something to lose here.

Ben has wormed his obnoxious self into my heart. I'm actually starting to feel sorry for Mercy, and all the other girls he has surely left in his wake. The scariest thing is that he does it by being himself—a kind, funny, easygoing guy who sends a text to say hi and calls to ask a girl to sing to him because he wants to. He doesn't hide who he is; he doesn't lie or promise anything. He doesn't play stupid head games. Whether those girls are completely clueless and fall into the accidental trap or stand on the edge and knowingly do a swan dive into it, like I just did, we all eventually fall for Ben's charm.

And now I can't breathe under the weight of those consequences. I need to get out of here.

■ ■ ■

"I got you an *extra*-big piece!" By the giddiness on the waitress's face, you'd think she was serving a movie star.

"Thanks." With a sigh, I break off a chunk and slide the tangy filling into my mouth, letting it melt over my taste buds.

Ben was right. Sometimes, change is good.

"And?" It's so sudden, so close to me, and so unexpected, that I jump. "What do you think? Isn't it the best key lime pie you've ever had?" *Good grief.* She's actually watching me eat. It's beyond irritating.

Maybe that's why I decide to be a complete bitch and say, "I've had better." It's true. I have. At a lovely little citrus grove about two hours north, surrounded by laughter and love and friendship. But when she turns and leaves, a deflated frown on her face, I instantly feel guilty.

"Reese?"

My stomach drops at the sound of his voice. I turn back to find familiar green eyes staring down at me. "Jared?" This is *so* not what I need to deal with right now.

He gestures behind him absently as he explains. "I just stopped by your office, hoping to catch you before you left for the day. Some lady with a big mole said you'd probably be here."

Mrs. Cooke. I told her I was taking a break and then I'd be back. I'm actually planning on working late tonight, to make up for whatever I miss tomorrow while at the funeral. And because I've gotten very little done, since I've been busy fantasizing like a moron.

Sitting up, I self-consciously adjust my shirt as Jared folds his tall body into the other chair. "I don't remember you liking limes," he murmurs, shaking his head, a little crease lining his forehead.

"I don't remember you dressing like a Nordstrom mannequin." Seriously, what the hell is he wearing? A dark green sport coat and what I can only describe as "trousers." I mean, he still looks *good*, but he's never been the metrosexual guy, preferring the "I just picked these clothes up off the floor and don't I still look hot" style.

"Couldn't walk into a law firm looking like a welder, now, could I?" He pauses, glancing around. "Where's your lawyer boyfriend?"

Is that what this little getup is about? Is he feeling inferior to Ben? I grit my teeth against the smile. And then I remember that Ben isn't mine and probably never will be, and the smile runs off on its own. "At his mother's. His father died last weekend."

"Oh." He frowns. I note that there's no "sorry" attached to that. It would be the polite thing to say. Then again, I was usually the one picking up on manners where Jared lacked.

He settles a heavy gaze on me, his face unreadable. "So I learned all about Facebook privacy settings last weekend."

I feel my cheeks burn as I avert my gaze to a miniature palm tree next to our table. I haven't dared look at his profile since last week, preferring ignorance over seeing a picture of a restraining order that I figured he was filing against me.

After a really long, unbearably awkward silence, I realize that he's waiting for my response. So I clear my throat and offer, "I warned you, didn't I? You never can be too careful about the crazies."

He dips his head. "I probably should be fucking furious with you, Reese." Peering up from under heavy lids, he admits, "But I'm not. I deserve it. I deserved having the apartment trashed. I deserve sitting there and watching that asshole suck your face in front of me."

A spike of annoyance jumps inside me, the need to defend Ben overpowering. "Ben hasn't done anything to you." Jared's knowing glare makes me correct that. "Okay, fine. But in his defense, he had no idea who you were."

A smile quirks Jared's lips. "Fair enough. If it were you and me out there and we came across a couple going at it, we would have done the exact same thing. Maybe with a little less *passion*, but . . ." His words drift off in a wry tone.

"What did Caroline say about it?" I dare ask.

"I'm not telling her." He reaches forward to rest his hands on the table, only inches from mine. Something tells me it's a very conscious move on his part.

"And does she know that you're here now?"

"She doesn't own me, Reese." He heaves a sigh. "We haven't talked in a few days. She's staying at her friend's house right now.

I just . . ." His face pinches together as he closes the gap to take my hand. "I knew the day I ran into you here that I'd made a fucking huge mistake. I should never have left you. I want you back."

"Huh." That's all I can manage as I slump back into my chair, all ability to speak gone as a nauseating swirl of emotion rises in my chest. This is not what I expected. *Back?* "Back for what?" I hear myself ask out loud and immediately bite my tongue.

His shoulders sag as if relieved of some huge weight. "Please just give me another chance. I know you want to."

"What makes you so sure?" Because suddenly, I'm not so sure, either.

"Oh, come on." A slow, seductive smile curls his lips as he reaches forward and entwines his long fingers through mine. He knows that smile has the power to melt all of my defenses. I've told him as much a thousand times. "Lurking on Facebook, hunting me down at paintball. The way you walked into that bar in your little red dress, flipping your hair around like you didn't have a care in the world, getting up on the stage. You knew that'd get my attention. And you did. Now I'm giving you what you want." He pulls my hand up to his mouth, until the heat from his mouth is dampening my skin. Just like he always used to do. "I can't stop thinking about you. You know we were amazing together."

It's strange. I've pictured this moment before—though Jared was much more contrite in my version—and it always came with a euphoric high. Now, though, I'm not feeling euphoria. Not unless anxiety and guilt is a part of the emotional package.

"Yeah, we *were* great together. And then you crushed me by cheating on me. And then *marrying* the girl!" I shake my head as I pull my hand away from him. "And now you're ready to cheat on her—your wife—with me?"

Resting his elbows on the table, he begins rubbing his face with both hands. "I can't help who I love and I never stopped loving you, Reese. I just thought I loved Caroline more. But I don't." His hands drop. "Not the same way that I love you. Please, give me another chance. Just . . . come back to my place. Let's talk more."

"We're talking now."

His eyes drop to my mouth with a secretive smile.

I know what he's looking for and I highly doubt talking is a part of it.

I smirk. Funny. If this were Ben, he'd have come right out and said he wanted to take me home to get into my pants. Then again, this would never be Ben because he'd never play with my heart like this.

"I don't think so."

His lips twist pensively.

"What?"

He shakes his head and frowns. "I'm just trying to figure out if you're playing hard-to-get or if you're actually turning me down."

I could really screw with him. I could go to his condo, climb into his bed with him, and take back what was taken from me so long ago. Even if just for one night. If he truly loves me—I'm beginning to wonder if Jared knows how to love—it would hurt him. It would crush Caroline.

But it would kill me.

I stand. "Goodbye, Jared. Don't ever call me again." I'm making a smart decision. For once.

Throwing a twenty down on the table for my order, I turn to walk away.

To see a set of red, watery eyes that match the red hair framing her face. I don't know how long Caroline's been watching, how much she picked up from that. Enough, I would say. Enough that I should feel better about this. This should be a victory.

But all I can feel right now is relief that I'm not hanging on to a memory that I'll never get back. And pity, for her, for being in love with a guy like that.

"He's all yours, Caroline. But honestly, I think even *you*'re too good for him." I walk past her without a glance back.

■ ■ ■

A knock sounds at my door a second before Mason's half-tamed dark mop pokes in. "Hey, Jack and I were thinking we should all go out to dinner tonight . . ." His voice drifts as he watches me stuff the last of my clothes into a brimming knapsack.

"I'm heading to the grove now." After what just happened with Jared, I can't wait another night. I haven't even messaged Ben to tell him that I'm coming. I'm afraid he'll tell me not to and, well, I just need to be there.

I need to see Ben.

"Oh. Okay." He looks down at the bulging white folder held together with a thick rubber band that sits gripped within his fingers.

"What's that?"

He sighs and glances furtively up at me. "Just a case I'm working on."

"Yeah? What's it about?" I ask, pulling the zipper on my backpack. Mason can usually carry on a semi-normal conversation if it's about a case.

"Hey, do you think you can take a look at the suit I laid out for tomorrow? You know me and colors."

"Uh . . . okay?" Mason has never asked me to do that. "Why don't you ask Lina about that?" My hands freeze. "Oh, shit. Did you break up?" In the next breath, I accuse him, "You didn't hold her hair while she puked, did you?" I haven't talked to Lina since last weekend. If they did break up and I'm just finding out about it now, then I'm a really shitty friend.

"No! I mean, yes, I did! And no, we didn't break up." He's completely flustered. "I just . . . I'm asking you because you're here. But if you want your family showing up to the funeral looking like a clown, then fine, I'll just—"

"Okay! Jeez." I stroll past him and into his room, smiling to myself over the term "family." Even with the divorce, he and Jack *are* my family.

"You've got to be kidding me," I mutter as I see the burgundy dress shirt with tiny taupe ducks all over it. "What is this, *Duck Dynasty Goes Formal?*" I yank the shirt and toss it into the trash can. Fishing through his closet, I find a plain navy shirt. "That works." I turn to find him leaning against the door frame, watching me. "Did you actually pay money for that shirt?"

He shrugs. "The guy at the store said it was in style."

"So were 'grandma's couch' floral pants and you didn't see me wearing those, did you?" I pass by him, heading to my room.

"Did you really have to throw it in the trash?"

"Yes. Don't ever shop without Lina or me there again. Ever, or I'll disown you." I grab my backpack off the bed, desperate to get on the road.

"Mrs. Cooke sent a big flower arrangement on behalf of the firm."

"That was nice of her."

"It's supposed to storm tonight. Are you sure you don't want to take the car?"

"Yup. I'll make it before the storm rolls in."

He's standing there, looking at me all awkward. "Okay, well, ride safe or whatever you call it. I guess we'll see you tomorrow?"

"Yeah. Mason, why are you being so—"

My words cut off as Mason reaches out and gives me a tentative hug before almost jumping away and storming out of the room.

Shaking my head, I turn and leave, desperate to see Ben's smile again.

Even if it's only as friends.

Chapter 32

...

BEN

"Pick it up, darling. I'm going alone," Mama orders, taking me out of the round.

I toss my cards down and fold my arms over my chest, smiling as I watch Elsie and Jake try to trump her, fond memories flooding me. Sunday night was always game night at home, out on the back porch. No excuses. In the earlier days, even my dad would come out sometimes. He'd usually be working on furniture designs and end up passed out in the chair, but I knew, by the way Mama stole glances his way and smiled, that she was just happy to have him there.

When we were young, and Mama's parents were alive, it was Go Fish. There was a brief stint of Monopoly somewhere in there, but after Jake and I tag-teamed against Elsie to make her cry too many times, the game mysteriously disappeared. To this day, I don't know where Mama hid it.

We all learned how to play euchre the summer of my eleventh birthday after my grandpa died of a heart attack. My grandma had moved into a home, preferring the peace and quiet over five kids in their teenage years. With us plus Mama, we always had more than enough players. That changed quickly, though, with each Morris kid leaving home as soon as they had an excuse, until it was just me and Mama sitting out on that porch on Sundays, resurrecting Go Fish.

I can't believe it's been eight years since we've all been in one place.

And tonight, while it's Thursday and not Sunday, we're all playing cards under Mama's roof again. The happiness is radiating off her.

"Will you be fine in Ben's old room?" Mama asks Tara, Rob's wife, as she and my brother come down from putting their two girls to sleep in the largest room of the house, with enough space for all four of them.

"Yeah, it's perfect, Wilma. Thank you." Tara's a soft-spoken, brown-haired woman with big eyes. She seems nice but she doesn't talk much. Way too quiet for my taste. And too skinny, but Rob always did like them twiggy. I get the impression that I make her nervous. The two times I've walked into the kitchen with just her there, she's left in a flash.

"You mean *my* room? Ben stole it after I moved out," Rob retorts, slapping me across the back as he walks by.

"And it finally saw some action," I murmur, shooting a wink Jake's way. Of all of us, Rob was the shyest around the girls.

"It saw plenty of action, you jackass," Rob scoffs.

"A hand job from Molly Mumford doesn't count."

"Boys!" Mama exclaims as Jake and I burst out in laughter. Even Elsie can't keep the giggles under control. No doubt, she remembers. The three of us had cups pressed to the wall between Elsie's and Rob's old room, listening to the entire thing.

"I think the best part was when Molly screamed and said, 'It's so sticky!'" I say that last part with a high-pitched squeal, reenacting exactly how I imagine the girl looked, holding my hands up in the air, my face a mask of horror.

"Benjamin James Morris!" Mama calls sternly, throwing her cards down as Elsie and Jake explode with laughter. Even Tara has a hand over her mouth, trying hard to contain her amusement.

"I'm gonna kick your ass," Rob mutters, though it's with a tight-lipped smile.

"Anytime, bro!" He and I are the closest in size, though I've got at least thirty pounds of muscle and two inches of height on him.

"There will be no kicking of any kind under this roof!" Mama warns with a finger.

Rob snorts. "Fine. Let's take it to the barn. It's better for fighting anyway."

Dead silence.

"Shit. Sorry, I didn't mean anything by it," Rob backpedals, his hands up in apology.

"No worries, man." I toss a casual wave his way. "You're right, the barn is a good place. As soon as we sell the last of the tools and wood, we can start our own fight club in there and Baby Boy Morris will kick all your old asses." I've been busy this week, clearing out the saws and other tools. There's a ton in there. Add it all up and it's worth a lot of money.

"Sounds good, man." I feel a light squeeze of my shoulder as Rob passes by again, on his way to check the skies. "I wish that storm wasn't coming. I wanted to take Tara out to the grove."

"You'll have plenty of time over the weekend." Mama turns and beams as Rita, Jake's girlfriend, comes waddling out of the kitchen, a cup of tea in hand.

"What're y'all playing again?" she drawls with that thick Mississippi accent as Jake reaches back to pull her beside him until her belly is resting against his cheek. Of all my brothers, it's strangest to see Jake settled down. He was probably the worst, next to me, for chasing girls. But then he hooked up with Rita at Mardi Gras a couple of years back and things changed quickly. Now he's about to have a baby with her.

"Euchre." He pats his knees. "Come on and sit. I'll teach you how to play."

"Maybe another night. I'm pretty tired." Ruffling his hair—

it's a darker blond than mine—she turns to me and smiles. "Thanks for giving up Elsie's old room for us."

"Just to be clear, I did it for you and that baby, not for this joker." I wink at her.

"I thought you liked the attic! You always liked it growing up," Mama chimes in.

Jake snorts. "What are you talking about? He was *terrified* of the attic! Always crying about ghosts. Wait until the thunder hits tonight. He'll be shaking under his covers, all alone up there." He grunts as the orange I whip at him hits his stomach.

"You're eating that," Mama scolds, wrenching it out of Jake's hand before he can fling it back. She adds slyly, "I'm sure Reese could protect you from the thunder and ghosts if she were here."

"Reese?" Jake and Rob echo in unison, their brows almost jumping past their hairlines.

"Don't tell me . . ." A broad smile stretches across Rob's face. "Benjy has a girlfriend?"

Fuck, I always hated that name. It makes me feel like a dog. Which I've been called many times before, but for different reasons. "Just a friend." I shoot Mama an exasperated look, but she has picked up her cards again and is studying them intently, an impish smile on her mouth.

It doesn't matter. Jake and Rob are already at it.

"What kind of girl could tie this asshole down?"

"What's wrong with her?"

"Do you think she can do basic math?"

"Fake tits or real?" Jake got two slaps across the head and a kick under the table for that question, from every female within reach.

I stand and stretch my hand over my head but manage to get a hand down to block Jake's fist sailing for my stomach. Stepping out of his reach, I wrap my arms around Rita, resting my hands on her belly. Up until my friend Storm got pregnant, I don't remember ever touching a woman's pregnant belly. "When should we tell him about us, Rita?" I say, putting on my best obnoxious grin as I watch Jake's face turn red.

"Get the fuck away from her!" he yells, but he's laughing.

Everyone's laughing. Even Mama's trying hard not to, her head shaking, no doubt over the language. I think she has given up for tonight, though.

And I grin. For so many reasons. It's good to have everyone here.

Almost everyone.

"Where're you going? We're in the middle of a game!" Elsie whines.

"I'm going to see what the mature brother is up to." Josh just got in about an hour ago and he's spent most of that time in the barn.

"Tell him to come back inside," Mama asks. "We're gonna lose power as soon as the storm hits." It's pretty much a guarantee.

I round the corner just as Jake says, "Did Ben actually find someone stupid enough to— Ow! Who kicked me that time?"

■ ■ ■

Seeing the oldest Morris boy standing in the middle of the barn sets my hair on end. It's like bringing Joshua Morris Senior back to life and hitting rewind twenty years. Right down to the piercing, hard eyes.

"Hey," I call out, holding my breath a little as I cross over the invisible barrier between the outside world and my father's realm. I still don't like being in here, even after a week of cleaning and airing the place out and changing all the lights. The dampness in the air with the approaching storm only makes the stench of wood thicker.

Josh turns to look at me, his face blank. Not only is he the spitting image of our dad, he also shares his demeanor. He was the quiet, serious one growing up. A bit of a recluse, preferring solitary hobbies like working on engines. He's the one who taught me how to fix Granddaddy's tractor.

"Hey, Ben," he says somberly. After a pause, he steps forward and wraps his arms around my body, surprising me with a hug. Given our seven-year age difference and our polar opposite personalities, we've never been close. "I'm glad you were here when it happened." Stepping away, he slides his hands into his back pockets, his eyes roaming the vaulted ceiling. "I forgot how big this barn is."

"Yeah. You wouldn't believe some of the shit I found hidden in here." At least fifty empty bottles of whiskey tucked into various corners, along with countless packs of stale cigarettes—I didn't even know Dad smoked—and some dirty magazines from the seventies—probably our granddaddy's—that I shoved into Jake's suitcase as a joke.

"I'll bet," he mutters to himself. "What do you think finally made him do it?"

"Mama was going to leave him."

Josh turns to look at me, the shock on his face readable by anyone. "Really?"

"I heard it with my own two ears. She was done." I hesitate, not sure if I want to admit the rest. "I heard him cry."

Understanding flickers through Josh's eyes as he turns back to the piece of black walnut that's got Dad's DNA soaked into the grain. I had stood over it with a chainsaw earlier this week but couldn't bring myself to start the blade. "I cried when Karen left me, even though I deserved it."

I shake my head. "I don't get it, Josh. You hated Dad for what he did to Mama—so much that you haven't been here in eight fucking years!—and yet you turned around and did the same thing."

"I know." His cheek puffs out as his tongue pushes against the wall of his mouth. "I had it all and I threw it away. I wish I had a good reason, but I don't." He pauses. "I wonder, if Mom had kicked him out all those years ago, if maybe he would have gotten help . . . Maybe none of this—"

"I hear where you're going with this and I don't fucking like it one bit, Josh." I feel my back getting stiff as I stand tall. "Don't you ever try and lay blame on Mama. All she did was love that asshole too much."

"I'm not blaming her, I'm just . . ." His voice drifts off as he walks in a circle. "I'm doing this whole twelve-step thing right now and I'm supposed to say I'm sorry. I've got a whole lotta things to be sorry for. I'm sorry I haven't been here to help. I'm sorry I turned my back on Mom."

"You're not the only one," I remind him, my sudden flare of anger fading fast.

"Yeah, but I'm the oldest. And yet here you are, standing by Mama through it all, still saving the day."

"Not always." I give the black walnut a light kick.

"I'm surprised the idiot didn't lose something sooner, the way he drank," Josh mumbles as a rumble of thunder sounds in the distance. "You know, I always wished I was more like you. Even when you were just a kid and I was almost done with high school." Kicking at a wood-chip remnant, a small smirk curls his mouth. "You were always so damn happy and easygoing. Everything rolled off your back. Everyone loved you. You were so different from *him*. Not like me." He grits his teeth. "It took losing everything—my wife, my kids, my house—to see that." Sliding his hands into his pockets, he turns to look at me with grim determination. "I'm done being like him, Ben. I'm not going to live my life as if I was preprogrammed to be Joshua Morris Senior. I haven't touched a drink in six months; I see my kids every chance I get. I take them places. I talk to them and laugh with them. I let them know that their father loves them. And Karen?" His head dips in submission. "I don't know if she'll ever give me another chance, but I'll do whatever I can to change. I don't want to be lying in a pool of my own vomit in twenty years because I didn't live the life I could have. *All of us* need to take a good look at our lives. If there's been anything about this man holding us back, now's the time to let it go."

I nod quietly as another low, long rumble fills the sky. "We should probably get inside. It's gonna be a big one tonight."

"Yep," he agrees. We both turn and walk to the edge of the barn, standing side by side as we look out on the trees, the tendrils of Spanish moss swaying as the wind picks up and the rain begins to fall, first in random, heavy drops until, within ten seconds, the sky suddenly opens up and sheets of it start pouring down.

A single light crests over the hump in the driveway. Squinting, I mumble to myself, "Is that . . . ?" My stomach does a giant flip as the Harley races up the driveway, its low rumble competing with the thunder above. Streaks of blond and purple poke out from beneath a helmet.

"Who's that?" Josh asks.

I smile, my insides tightening up with excitement. "That's mine, is what that is." And right now, I mean it.

We move to the side as Reese keeps coming, not stopping until she pulls her bike right into the barn, her clothes drenched. I watch her pull her helmet off and brush the hair off that gorgeous face of hers. I've never wanted to kiss a girl so bad in my life.

Caramel eyes peer up at me with hesitation. "You know me and mornings. I just figured I'd be better off coming up here tonight."

"And because you couldn't handle being away from me for another night, of course," I throw back, testing her.

When I see that hard swallow, the pink creeping into her cheeks as she averts her gaze to the ground in a very un-Reese move, I know I'm right.

And I'm damn happy about it.

Her attention flickers to Josh and she sticks a hand out. "Hi, I'm Reese."

"You can do all that hello shit tomorrow." I reach out and wrap my hands around her waist, hoisting her up and off the bike like a little kid.

And then I throw her over my shoulder and march out into the rain. I barely feel it.

Chapter 33

■ ■ ■

REESE

"Ben! Put me down!" I cry out with a laugh as the front door clatters behind us.

I was hoping he'd be happy to see me, but the way he was looking at me out there in the barn, I'm thinking he's going to devour me. I couldn't have asked for a better reception.

"Reese?" I hear Wilma's voice from somewhere in the back of the house.

"Tomorrow, Mama!" Ben's already moving up the stairs.

"Benjamin, you bring that girl down—" The house is thrown into darkness as the lights cut out, distracting Wilma from her scolding, leaving me dangling upside down over Ben's shoulder on a staircase, in the pitch-black.

"Shit." Ben stops to pull his phone out and set the flashlight app before he continues, not putting me down until he has climbed a very narrow set of stairs up to a third-floor room in the attic. "We're sleeping up here tonight," he announces. My feet hit the wood floor just as a dull glow fills the room, the by-product of a small battery-operated lantern that sits on a simple wooden table.

"Wow." I can just make out the space. It's quite large, though most definitely only a fraction of the attic's full size. Everything has been painted white—the floors, the slanted walls, the trim—which makes a nice backdrop for all of Ben's dad's wooden furniture, including a rather stately bed, covered in a colorful quilted duvet. The two large dormer windows must offer ample light in the daytime. Right now, though, they're protesting noisily against the winds and pelting rain. "It's so cozy up here. Very cottage-like."

My knapsack sails through the air past me a second before strong hands grab my shoulders and spin me around. I find myself facing Ben's giant grin. He doesn't hesitate to lay a heavy kiss on my lips and I don't hesitate to lean into it, the feel of his tongue against mine intoxicating. When he finally breaks free, his arms still coiled around my waist, he murmurs in that low crackle, "This was a fantastic surprise."

"Really? Because I've been known to surprise people in rather unpleasant ways," I tease, though inside I'm a basket of live wires. I let my hands rest on his broad chest as I fall into it to inhale his clean, soapy smell. I can't believe how much I've missed it.

He chuckles as he rests his cheek on top of my head. "That's one of the things I love about you."

I'm not sure whose limbs stiffen first but as soon as that sentence—that word—comes out of his mouth, there is definite tension shooting through both of us.

Ben relaxes first, his groan making me curl into him again. "You know what I meant by that, right?"

"That you're madly in love with me, of course." We've joked about it so many times. Now I'd give anything for it to be real. My breathing feels shaky as I force my head back to meet his gaze, hoping he doesn't see the truth I'm struggling to veil.

That I have accidentally developed *real* feelings for him.

But he does. Instantly. Or he sees something, anyway. His knuckles graze my cheek as wariness flickers over his features. "What's wrong?"

I open my mouth to respond—to say what, I have no idea! How the hell am I going to broach this subject without scaring him away?—but I'm saved by an incoming call on his phone. Ben holds the phone up and I see Mason's name. "Did you tell him you were coming?" Ben asks.

"Yeah."

"I'd better get that, then." He drops a quick kiss on my head as he breaks away to answer. "Hey, Mace. What's up? . . . Yeah, she just made it . . . Huh . . . No . . ." He glances at me and then takes a few steps away. "Okay."

I listen absently as I unzip my bag and dump the contents out onto the bed, including the simple black dress for tomorrow that's going to need ironing after sitting rumpled on the back of my bike for almost three hours. I *almost* beat the rain. Thanks to the torrential downpour that hit as I was riding up the driveway, along with Ben's leisurely caveman stroll to the house with me slung over his shoulder, every stitch of clothing on me is soaked through. I'm freezing, and the lower temperature up here certainly doesn't help. I unzip my jacket and toss it onto the back of a chair. My boots and socks come next. I'm intent on getting my pajamas on, even if it's only for the short term.

"Are you sure this is . . ." He heaves a sigh. "Okay . . . yeah, I guess . . . See you tomorrow, man."

I frown. "What'd he want?"

Ben's arm drops heavily to his side, an unreadable expression turning his face eerily calm. There's a long pause as he very obviously drifts off in thought, his eyes rolling over me, my bag, and all the clothes that have spilled out, and then back to me.

"You're kind of freaking me out, Ben. What's wrong?"

I hear the tiny exhale he releases before he tosses his phone onto the table. "He was just worried about you getting here with the storm, is all."

"Are you sure? Because he was acting really weird tonight. He *hugged* me."

Ben smiles as he walks over to where I'm standing. Dipping his face into my neck, he lets his mouth linger there, sending shivers through my body. "What, like a big bear hug?"

"More like he was hugging a porcupine."

Ben chuckles. "Mason's a weird guy. Weird guys do weird things."

"Stop talking about my stepbrother while you're doing that," I mumble, letting my head fall back as the rumble of his voice tickles my skin.

"Fine." He disappears suddenly. I turn in time to see him make a sweeping move across the bed, scattering everything onto the floor.

"Hey!"

"Payback's a bitch."

I smile, a hazy memory of Cancún flashing through my mind. "Have you been drinking margaritas? Because I think that's one of those times where two wrongs definitely don't make a right." Had I not thrown up on him, had we actually slept together that night, would I be standing here right now, wondering how on earth you tell a guy who avoids commitment that you've fallen for him, hard?

He reaches out to grab my hand and pull me toward him, until he's able to push me onto the bed, his fingers deftly unfastening my belt. "Your clothes are wet. You need to get out of them and quick." The guy has undressing women down to an art because somehow he manages to pull every last stitch of clothing off of me in record time and with no help on my part, until I find myself lying naked across the bed with his eyes grazing over my body.

"The attic needs reinsulating," he confirms as a shiver courses through my body. I honestly don't think it's from the cold.

"I'm naked, again. And you're not, again."

Ben yanks the back of his sodden black T-shirt up and over his head before letting it slide down his arms, uncovering the smooth ridges of his muscles. As lightning zigzags through the sky in frequent bursts, filling the attic room with flashes of white light, I watch him undo his jeans and let them fall, pushing his boxer briefs off with them. I find myself lying on a bed and staring at a very naked, very appealing, and very aroused Ben in front of me. My breath hitches with the sight.

"You seem to have a problem," I muse, replaying the old Cancún tape as I prop myself up on my elbows and, though self-conscious, let my legs fall apart for him. Ben's a guy who truly appreciates a woman's body. Not just *a* woman's body. *My* body, it would seem. My plump ass, my soft curves. My biggest insecurities seem to be his biggest turn-ons.

"You have no fucking idea." The sudden tension in his square jaw makes him all the more handsome as he dives into the bed, finding a resting spot between my thighs, his elbows digging into the mattress on either side of my shoulders. The heat radiating from his large body will no doubt counter the chill in the air.

"I haven't stopped thinking about this all week." One of his hands finds its way to my piercing to play with it gently, much more gently than I ever imagined him capable of. "Did you know I turned down a beauty queen?"

A tightness instantly fills my stomach. "Remember that filter you need to work on?" What happens when he doesn't turn the beauty queen down? Or the Twinkie? What will that do to me? To us? To *this*? We'll *lose* this forever! That's what will happen.

I stare up at him and bite my tongue, terrified that my own filter is going to fail me. "Why?"

Curious blue eyes take in my features. It's impossible not to notice the speed and intensity of his heart beating against my chest. Leaning down to graze his lips against mine, he answers simply, "Wasn't into her."

"Not into a beauty queen? Impossible." I take a deep, calming breath. I could read so much into this. The fact that I want to read *only one* thing into it is telling. And terrifying. Why am I doing this to myself? I *can't* pretend not to care when I do. That would be like throwing all of my emotions into a jar and sealing it. Anyone who knows me can predict the guaranteed explosion, the devastating aftermath.

"I know. Shocking, isn't it?" I catch the twinkle in his eye. It fades quickly. "What's going on with you? You seem off."

"I saw Jared tonight," I suddenly blurt out. I guess that's as good a place as any to start.

Ben's hand, now cupping a breast, freezes. I catch the bob of his Adam's apple with a hard swallow. "And?"

"He told me that he loves me. He regrets ever breaking up and he wants me back."

Ben's forehead dips to rest against mine. We lie like that, in complete silence, as the thunder rolls on outside, the storm still increasing in intensity. It's either the slowest or the longest storm I've ever witnessed, most in Florida hitting hard and fast before moving on quickly.

Finally, he heaves a sigh and lifts his head to look out the window, the light stubble dusting his jaw visible with the flashes of bright light. "I should have known this would happen," he mumbles, his head shake almost indiscernible. "Serves me fucking right, doesn't it?"

I frown as he rolls off me, taking all his warmth and affection, and lands on his back. One hand slides behind his head. "Did I just miss something?"

Ben's soft laughter fills the dimly lit attic. "Talk about irony. You know, when Mama and Elsie started riding my ass about me having feelings for you, I kept brushing them off." His head lolls to the side, sad eyes on mine. "Now that I've finally admitted to myself that I want more, I have no chance. Do I?"

My heart feels like it just swelled two sizes. *What? Did I just hear that right?*

Ben *wants* something *more?* I prop myself up on my elbows

as a swirl of confusion and exhilaration rips through me like a tornado. But then . . . "What the fuck are you talking about?"

He throws a hand up and states matter-of-factly, "You're here to tell me that you're getting back together with that asshat, right? That's why you came up here tonight?"

"If I were getting back together with Jared, do you think I'd be lying here, *naked*, with you?" I can't help but sound annoyed with him.

There's a long pause as he processes my words. And then he shrugs as a sheepish smile curls his lip. "I dunno. Figured you were maybe giving me one last ride before you took it away?"

"No, you . . . Ugh!" I roll my eyes as I fall back onto the pillow. This couldn't have possibly played out better. Not five minutes ago I was terrified of Ben seeing how I truly feel, and now he's gone and confessed that it's not one-sided.

This changes *everything*.

"So, you're saying that you're not getting back together with him?" he asks cautiously.

"No!" Suddenly I feel like laughing as the tension slides out of my body, making way for the rash of butterflies that have taken flight.

Beside me, I hear a quiet mutter of "Thank God" escape his lips, followed louder by, "Why not?"

"Because of this jackass I picked up in Cancún. That's why." And there it is. Not exactly romantic, but Ben and I have never been about waxing poetic.

"Seriously? Wait . . . *I'm* the jackass, right?"

When I sigh with exasperation, he rolls onto me to assume his previous position, the wide grin back on his face. "So, what does this mean exactly?"

I chew the inside of my mouth as I consider my next words. We've always been about blunt honesty. There's no point changing now. "It means I want your womanizing mama's-boy football-player butt all to myself and if I catch you with any Twinkies or beauty queens or anyone else, you'd better run far and fast because I will hunt you down."

His fingers brush wayward strands of hair off my face. "You know I'd never even consider this if I thought I could hurt you like that, right?"

I can only manage a nod, but it's enough. For all the faults that people could find in Ben, they'll never find someone with a bigger, kinder heart than his.

And just like that, something monumental has changed between us.

He leans down and captures my mouth with his in a deep, needy kiss that has my head sinking into the pillow, on the cusp of gasping for air. I'm marginally aware as he reaches into a side table to grab a condom. Tearing it open and sliding it on with ease—one-handed, no less—he pushes into me smoothly, all while never breaking his kiss.

My body is long past ready to accept him.

All of him.

Chapter 34

...

BEN

I don't believe it.

I, Ben Morris, have a girlfriend. At least, I think I do. Aside from the loose threats of bodily harm, we didn't get into the specifics.

I roll my head to study Reese's still form as she takes long, slow breaths, her head nestled in the crook of my arm, her hot, naked body suctioned to mine. She's like a sleeping dragon, so peaceful in slumber, so fiery when conscious. And I can't wait for her to be conscious again.

Tonight was . . . enlightening.

I went from being a cocky ass that was sure he had her, to feeling my guts tumble out thinking she was going back to her ex, to utter fucking rapture as she laid it all out on me.

Reese wants me and only me.

If I had only known back then, when I watched that purple-haired girl slide off her chair in her drunken state . . . I smile to myself, unable to keep my arms from tightening around her little body.

Josh's words from earlier are sinking in. Letting my dad's faults and errors dictate how I will live my life is the worst mistake

I can make. And like it or not, it's what I've been doing. Letting a girl like Reese get away because I'm afraid that I'll be like my father will only lead to a miserable, lonely life. The ironic thing is, I don't know that I would have appreciated that had she not already been here, within reach. Showing me what I have to lose.

I lean into her, unable to keep myself from placing a soft kiss on her lips. She lets out a feeble groan in response but otherwise doesn't stir. I'm tempted to wake her up, but I won't.

Tomorrow's going to be a long day for *all* of us.

That reminds me . . . I shift her off of me as gently as possible and then sit up, earning a small mewl of protest. Reaching down to the backpack leaning against the wall beside the bed, I quietly unzip the outer pocket that Mason described when he called earlier. Inside sits the stack of envelopes, bundled tightly with an elastic band.

Answers to the questions she's been asking all these years.

I don't know what Jack and Mason are thinking, having me be the one to do this. Mason said they were planning on showing her everything tonight at dinner. That's nuts. I don't see how you deliver this kind of news over a plate of fries. Then again, I guess there's probably no good time to lay this on a girl like Reese. Doing it when she's up here, in a place that I can tell she loves, away from civilization, with me to rein her in, may be the best option.

I just hope she sees it that way, too.

Chapter 35

...

REESE

"I can't believe how much you all look alike," I say, taking in the row of Morris children standing and watching two little blond girls tease Quincy with a ball. The hound's attention sways back and forth between the girls and the crowds of people as if she can't decide if she'd rather have the ball or the scraps of food that are bound to fall from the small paper plates.

"Yeah, we get that a lot." I instinctively fold into Ben's side as his arm settles over my shoulders, squeezing me tight to him.

"But you're the best-looking, of course," I add wryly, beating him to it.

"I am. Don't forget it," he chuckles and I fight the urge to kiss him. We've been very careful with all public displays of affection given Jack is floating around. At some point, we're going to have to break the news to him that Ben and I are together and we're *far* past just friends. Though I've decided that I'll throw a fit and threaten to quit if Jack doesn't let Ben stay at Warner, I honestly don't know how the hell we're going to work together. The guy can't be in a room with me without touching me in some manner, and it doesn't seem to matter who else is there.

He proved that early this morning when he pinched my ass as I was meeting his entire family for the first time.

I had wondered what being in a room with all five Morris children would be like, and whether Ben was an anomaly or part of a matching set. When I was finally allowed out of the attic and into the bustling sunroom, I found out quickly. The entire Morris clan plus affiliates were there, grazing off a table laden with pastries and fresh fruit and deliciously scented coffee.

Laughing. Smiling. Filling this big, sad old house with what it so desperately craved again.

A family.

Within five minutes of introductions—leaving me red-faced after Ben's brother Jake felt the need to comment on the disruptive noise over their room last night—I could see that their ties went much farther than physical similarities. The very idea that these five children and their mother haven't been under this roof in eight years seems unfathomable. Any outsider watching wouldn't buy it. Then again, they also probably wouldn't believe that the man whose physical attributes can be seen in each and every one of his boys cast a gloom over their lives dark enough to make them abandon each other.

The service for Ben's father was held in an old white church ten miles away and was solemn, as expected. What wasn't expected was the crowd of people in attendance. Though Joshua Senior may not have made many lasting friends, the Bernard and Morris families certainly have. Those people packed the church to pay their respects, over two hundred of them returning to the grove with the family for a late lunch.

"What do you think's going to happen now?"

Ben frowns. "What do you mean?"

"I mean tomorrow and next week, and next month. Look at everyone." I gesture toward his family—Jake standing behind his girlfriend, his arms coiled around her belly; Rob and his wife laughing at their kids; Elsie and Josh linked arm-in-arm and smiling. Granted, I didn't know them before, but they all look so content. And Wilma . . . The woman has been dabbing at her eyes with her handkerchief all day. During the service, I know those tears were meant for the loss of her husband. But mostly, it wasn't sadness I saw.

It was gratitude, and relief.

"This house is meant to be filled with noise. Wilma's meant to see her children. Her grandchildren should be running around, laughing and swinging on that big old swing. Even Quincy's in heaven right now!"

Ben chuckles. "She's going to end up in dog heaven soon. She's too fat for all this excitement."

"But what happens after today?" I press. "Please tell me you guys have talked. Something has to change. For Wilma's sake, for this grove's sake . . ." A lump in my throat is forming, as I think about how sad and lonely Wilma will be once everyone's gone. As much as I loved the grove before, now that I've seen it at its best—alive—I can't bear to see it so quiet and empty again.

Ben sighs. "I'm not sure yet, Reese. Everyone's got a life somewhere else now. We'll see what happens."

"You need to make it happen, Ben. At least for holidays and birthdays and . . ." A thought hits me. "Jake and Rita should get married here. You need to tell him that."

"Sure!" Ben's face splits out in a wide grin as he cups one hand over his mouth and hollers, "Jake! Reese thinks you and Rita should have your wedding here!"

"Ben!" I'm not fast enough shoving my fist into Ben's ribs to cut off his words and, by the flat glare his brother gives him, Jake isn't impressed by them. If Rita heard them, which I'm sure she did, she doesn't let on, intent on keeping her focus on the two little girls.

"Benjamin, would you stop harassing your brother," Wilma scolds. We turn to see her closing the distance, trailed by Jack and Mason. I instinctively shift away from my comfortable nook against Ben's body at the same time that his arm slowly retracts from my shoulders, until just his hand is settled on my back.

"Ben, Jack was just telling me how impressed he is with you at work," Wilma explains, smiling up at her son, her face full of pride.

"I proofread like a boss," Ben mocks good-naturedly.

"Though I don't know why you bothered with law school, given you had this place to fall back on. It's breathtaking here," Jack offers, his hands lifting in gesture of our surroundings.

"It is," Ben agrees.

"Maybe you and Mason can come with Reese another time. I'm expecting her up here quite a lot."

Good Lord, Wilma. Ben's deep inhale next to me tells me he's thinking the same thing I am.

I think all of our eyes—Mason's included—are locked on Jack, waiting for the reaction, wondering what it might be.

Those gray eyes soften with a genuine smile as he dips his head, as if acknowledging something silently. Maybe he is. "We'll gladly come visit with her sometime. I wish we could stay longer today, but we'll be leaving shortly for Miami." Turning to Wilma, he offers, "Again, we're very sorry for your loss. If there's anything we can do to help, please just let Ben know."

Wilma glances at Ben and me and winks as a woman calls her name from the front porch. "You already have. If you'll excuse me, it sounds like I'm needed in the kitchen." She reaches out to shake Jack and Mason's hands. "Thank you for coming today." With that, she turns and hurries to the house.

"Well, Reese's Pieces, I suppose we'll see you by the end of the weekend, hey?" Jack says, a loving smile on his face. He steps forward, gripping my arms with his hands. "And remember, we're always here for you." Worry flitters through his eyes as he turns to level Ben with an unreadable look. "Take care of my girl this weekend."

"I will."

He slaps Ben's shoulder once. "I know you will."

I feel the deep furrow in my brow as I watch them leave. "Okay, see that? Now Jack's acting weird, too. Don't you think?"

"Well . . ." Ben draws that out as he turns to settle a long, hard look on me. So long, it starts to make me squirm.

"What?" I snap.

Gritting his teeth, he gives a cursory glance around the lawn. "I think I've shown my face long enough here." Dropping his gaze to me again, he says, "Let's go for a ride."

Chapter 36

■ ■ ■

BEN

"I love this time of day up here!" Reese yells over the roar of the engine as she kicks the dune buggy into fourth gear and swerves to avoid a pothole in the trail, the late-afternoon November sun beginning its descent over the horizon.

"Can we not add to the funeral count this week?" I yell back, gripping the roll bar with white knuckles. The woman is a maniac behind the wheel. I don't know how she hasn't crashed her bike yet and I'm starting to think that I don't want her on it anymore, because it's only a matter of time before she does. The only reason I handed her the keys is because I knew she'd need to have a bit of fun before I drop a giant bomb on her head.

"Left up here." I point and hold on as she whips around the corner, setting my granddaddy's old yellow truck in our sights.

We come to a skidding stop, a dust cloud billowing out behind us and Reese's radiant smile making me second-guess this plan. Maybe I should just pack her up and take her back to our attic room. But, no. That won't change anything. She needs to know this and I've always been the "tear the Band-Aid off" kind of guy. If she ever found out that I'd sat on this kind of news instead of letting her know right away, she wouldn't trust me again. The very idea of that makes my stomach tighten.

I yank the keys out of the ignition—if she's gonna run, it'll have to be on foot—and climb out of the dune buggy. Picking up the walking stick, I go through the same process I've done for years, rattling the truck to scare off anything living in it.

Reese, having changed into jeans and a T-shirt, hoists herself up onto the tailgate. Such a rare, peaceful smile rests on her lips. I don't know that I've ever seen it on her before. It forces my body still, to just stand there and stare at her for a long moment.

I hate that she's about to lose it.

"Why are you looking at me like that?"

I hesitate. And then I reach back and pull out the stack of envelopes that's tucked into the back of my jeans.

Reese's eyes narrow. "Mason had those yesterday."

My thumb flips through the stack—five white envelopes and a yellow one. The yellow one, I'm supposed to hold on to until the end. "Were you and Mason talking about your father recently?"

"Yeah. Last week." Her eyes dart to the envelopes. "Why?"

With a sigh, I stroll over to sit next to her on the tailgate. "Mason told Jack about your ex. How the guy's living in Miami and remarried, and how you've been in touch with him. Mason's worried you're on a mission to punish him."

Reese's head falls back with a loud groan. "Dammit! I told you that guy can't be trusted!"

"Just . . . hold up, Reese. Let me finish." I pause. "Mason was worried; that's why he said something. And of course Jack was worried, too. He's been worried about you since he picked you up from Jacksonville. Worried that you were going to turn out as bitter as your mother after being hurt so bad."

"I'm not Annabelle!" Her cheeks are turning red with anger, making me hold my hands up in surrender.

So far, this isn't going well.

"*I* know you're not. But, just listen. Whatever you and Mason talked about . . . well, he thought it was a good idea to find your father so you could get his side of the story. See what kind of guy leaves his five-year-old in a diner and why. Maybe he had a good reason. Maybe he's just an asshole and your mother is right to hate him. But it's good to know, don't you think?" Knowing what my father was and, more importantly, what I am not has helped me make some important decisions these past few days. Including the one that led me to sitting here with Reese. "Jack agreed with him. So he called the firm's private investigator on Monday morning and asked the guy to look into it." I take a deep breath. "He found him, Reese. He found your father. Turns out it wasn't so hard, after all, if you knew where to start looking."

I watch as the blood drains from Reese's face, until her normally pink cheeks are stark white, making her caramel eyes look a sickly yellow. "Well, where is he?" It comes out in a snap, though I know what sounds like anger is actually fear. Her attention darts to the stack of envelopes in my hand. One of them has a stamp of "Return to sender" on it. The others were never even mailed.

I slide the first one into her shaking hand.

Clearing her throat, she slowly lifts the seal. "These were opened already." The accusation in her tone is thick. "Did you read these?"

"No." Mason admitted that he and Jack had read them first, not wanting to just hand something over to Reese that could devastate her.

With a deep breath, she pulls out the first letter, a single lined sheet of paper with similar but slightly neater handwriting than Reese's.

There's not much else I can do, so I just sit quietly next to her, feeding her a new envelope every time she finishes the last.

Watching the tears start rolling down her cheeks.

And when I hand her the yellow one, the one holding a copy of the official report inside, the telltale stamp on the front, she turns perfectly still.

Her voice is raspy as she whispers, "After all this time, I'm really just like her, aren't I?"

Chapter 37

∎ ∎ ∎

REESE

Ben's Jetta pulls up to the ostentatious white house straight out of Greek mythology, its row of columns and the enormous three-tier water fountain in the center of the circular driveway plain ridiculous. Husband Number Four comes from money and loads of it.

"Well, this looks cozy," Ben observes with a smirk.

"Wait until you see the inside," I mutter. "It looks like a morgue." Thanks to the sprawling layout and lack of furniture, it's also the ideal house for a lavish charity ball.

The car door opens and the valet offers me a hand that I accept only after scooping up the layers of my satin dress. Lina and Mason drove up to the grove this morning with it, so I'd have time to get ready before heading to Jacksonville. Thankfully, it fits as well as if it were custom-designed to my body. Based on the price tag I found in the box, it may as well have been.

Ben comes around the car—looking every bit like a Ken doll in a sharp black pearl tux that he rented last minute—and offers me an arm. If we were here under different circumstances, I'd probably already be scouting out locations to drag him off to by his tie, he looks so appealing. "When did you see your mother last?" he asks, taking the steps in unison with me, slowly. Warily.

"Right after I married Jared. Number Four wanted a big mending-fences family brunch."

"So, what, like . . ."

"A year and a half ago."

He shakes his head in disbelief. "And how'd that go?"

"Terrific. Annabelle told me I didn't have what it took to keep Jared interested and he'd leave me."

And now I think I know why.

Ben speaks to the man with the guest list while my eyes roam over the crowd of finely dressed people of all ages. He's been doting on me since yesterday afternoon, while keeping my mind occupied and cracking stupid jokes to try and make me laugh. Odd, given we just put his dad in the ground. It should be the other way around.

We step into a buzz of music and conversation and laughter— both fake and genuine. The beautiful O'Hara staircase reaching the second floor is closed to guests and lined with a small orchestra of violinists, playing soft classical music while a photographer captures them. Servers in tuxes float through the crowd, balancing silver platters of appetizers and champagne with ease.

I can't help but think that all the money that went into this party could have been better served going straight to the charity. This is Annabelle at her finest.

I never enjoyed these pretentious parties, preferring one of Jack's summer backyard barbeques where I could show up in jeans and a T-shirt. Then again, the look on Ben's face when I descended Wilma's stairs in a dress that cost half the price of my Harley makes it worth it.

Ben stops a server with a hand on her elbow and his winning smile. "Excuse me, can you please tell us where Mrs. Donnelly is?" That's Annabelle's latest last name. It's getting hard to keep track of them.

The young woman blushes as she looks up at him. "Entertaining in the conservatoire."

Ben shoots a questioning look my way.

I respond with an eye roll and a quiet hiss of, "It's a green-house with a piano in it." I think I catch a smirk from the server as she continues on, but I can't be quite sure.

We find our way to the "conservatoire"—an enormous glass room in the back of the house, overlooking an Olympic-sized pool. Though it's minimally furnished on normal occasions, tonight it has been cleared of everything except a black grand piano and the stench of old money. That's where I find Annabelle, amidst a small circle of supremely polished people. She looks as poised and radiant as always in a long, fitted, royal-blue dress that pools around her ankles, her pale skin appearing all the more milky-white next to the vibrant color.

Ben offers my waist a little squeeze and prods me forward. I fight the urge to touch my hair—an understated but elegant side bun that Elsie did for me, showing off the black-cherry layer as I make my way forward.

Ian sees me first. He offers a smile, but it's wary. I'm not stu-pid. To him, I'm the estranged daughter of his trophy wife who, if anyone bothered to do a bit of research, could probably cause some political embarrassment for him, especially around election time. God knows what she's told him about me. At least my rec-ord is sealed.

Annabelle turns. With her tall frame, hourglass figure, and perfect features, she has always been a stunning woman. I can't deny that she still is, though getting a better look at her—at the shape of her eyes, the lack of a single wrinkle or flaw, the very full breasts—I'm betting she's had plastic surgery since I saw her last.

Those cold azure eyes float over the length of me, of my gown, of my hair, of Ben next to me, and I see a flash of something—surprise? Triumph? Suspicion? "I didn't think you were going to make it, Reese," she says in a breathy voice, leaning forward to peck my cheek, much like I'd imagine a chicken pecks at a piece of corn. I mentally compare that to the kiss Wilma planted on me—warm and loving and so . . . motherly.

"I didn't think I was going to either," I admit. Up until yesterday, I had my mind made up.

And then I learned the whole story.

Coming here tonight to confront her may be considered poor timing by some. But I think it's the perfect moment. She'll be sober, for one thing. I can guarantee that her glass is straight Perrier. She won't risk getting drunk with all these people here.

But mainly, she'll be so concerned about how *I'm* going to react—in front of all these spectators—that she won't have a chance to throw a fit.

Turning to Ben, Annabelle purrs, "Hello, I'm Annabelle Donnelly," and holds her hand out limply as if she's expecting him to kiss it.

"Ben Morris. It's a pleasure," he answers with a high-voltage dimpled smile as he smoothly accepts her hand. As much of a foot-in-mouth jackass as Ben can be, he seems to have a way of making a woman react. Even now, Annabelle's eyes scan his body quickly before letting go, a demure smile on her extra-pouty lips. Plumper than I last remember.

"I need to talk to you," I blurt out.

"Sure. Perhaps after the ball?"

"We're not staying long."

"Oh. Well, I hope you'll at least stay for some family pictures. Ian's children flew in to be here. The photographer is setting up in the library." To those who don't know her, Annabelle looks unperturbed. That vein in the side of her neck is pulsing, though. She's on edge.

Her delicate shoulder begins to curl back toward the circle, already dismissing my presence, until I say, "I found Hank."

Every part of her freezes. Her fake smile, her enhanced body, her breath. For one very long moment, Annabelle looks like a statue.

"Excuse me, everyone," she announces, setting her flute onto a passing server's tray, before she begins her slow, feline stalk past me, her four-inch heels clicking against the marble floor.

"Do you want me to come with you?" Ben whispers into my ear.

"No. I'm good."

"Okay. I'll be here if you need me," he whispers, laying a kiss on my temple before he reminds me, "You're just here to talk."

"Yup," I answer with a tight smile, hoping I can keep my promise. We exit the room and head to the left, down a quiet hall that has been roped off to guests. To anyone witnessing this, we probably look like a strange processional of Holiday Barbie dolls. Certainly not like mother and daughter.

Annabelle pushes through a set of solid double doors, leading me into what appears to be Ian's office, a masculine-looking room of floor-to-ceiling drapery, dark cherry wood, and black leather. When those heavy doors close behind me, the lively sounds of music and laughter vanish completely.

And now it's just Annabelle and me.

She clears her throat. "What is it you'd like to talk about, exactly?"

There's no point dancing around this. "Did you know that my father was trying to find me?"

She clears her throat again. "I assumed that he would have, eventually. Not that I've spoken to him again after he left us."

"No, Annabelle. Not *us*. You! He wanted to take me with him to his new life, with *MaryAnn*. That's where we were the day you reported me kidnapped. You knew exactly where we were. You knew I wasn't in any danger." I see the flash of pain in her eyes and I smile, though there's no pleasure in it. "Didn't think I'd ever find out, did you? Lucky for me you went on to marry a guy like Jack, who cares enough about me to start asking questions, even sixteen years later."

Bowing her head, she seems to take a moment to breathe,

her chest rising and falling heavily several times. "How is he?" she finally asks in a hoarse whisper. "Hank."

The lump that's been sitting at the base of my throat since yesterday flares, knowing that I'll never get to see him again. "He's in a Tallahassee cemetery. He was run off the road on his Harley by a truck driver who hadn't checked his blind spot before changing lanes, about eight years ago."

My words slap her across the face as forcefully as if I had hit her with my palm. Whatever color was left in her cheeks vanishes, leaving her gray-skinned, her mouth hanging open.

When Jack called the firm's P.I. about Hank MacKay, the investigator started out with the routine checks—police reports and obituaries. That quickly led him to the death report and to the next-of-kin, his common-law spouse, MaryAnn Seltzer.

It all sounds so easy.

Hank had written several letters to me, hoping he'd one day have a place to send them. After his death, MaryAnn gave the letters to Bethany MacKay, my father's sister. An aunt who I didn't even know existed. Who lives twenty minutes away from me. MaryAnn had a hunch that one day Hank's long-lost daughter would track the MacKay family down.

"You met my dad one night at a Miami bar where his band was playing. He had just broken up with his girlfriend. You were watching him play the guitar. And then, when some girl tried to cut in front of you, you dumped a beer down the back of her shirt. You pretended it was an accident but my dad saw you intentionally pour it." I smile at that. It's something I would do, except I wouldn't hide it. I'd own up to it with pleasure. "He said you were the most beautiful woman he had ever seen. You started dating right away. He'd drive an hour into the city every chance he got. Then, six months later, when you found out that you were pregnant with me, you got married. Neither of you thought twice about it."

I begin retelling all that that first letter explained in great detail, stories that I'd never heard from Annabelle. As I do, I see the emotions threatening to break through her mask. "You moved into a two-bedroom apartment in his hometown, where he worked as a mechanic in his father's garage. You stayed home with me." I step farther into the room, my eyes taking in the painted portrait of Annabelle that sits over the fireplace on the wall, in a sexy slip dress and a fur stole. "You *hated* it. You hated being stuck with a baby at home. You were bored with small-town life. You wanted to move to Miami but Hank wasn't willing; he was the only one bringing in a paycheck. Plus, he was going to take over the business from his dad.

"You two fought a lot because of it. You fought a lot in general. You had a huge argument one Friday night when I was about three and the neighbors called the cops. Hank was so mad, he took off for a few hours. When he came home, he found you passed out on the couch. I was sitting in a pool of spilled vodka, crying. That's when you claimed you were suffering from post-partum depression, and that you were going to get help. After that, he started taking me everywhere with him, until you got better."

From what Hank learned of her parents—who I apparently met, though I don't remember—Annabelle was raised in a middle-income household where hugs were meaningless and image was everything. That she fell in love with my dad—a blue-collar, guitar-playing, Harley-riding, tattooed guy—was against everything she'd learned growing up. But it also proves that Annabelle once knew how to love. How to let her heart win.

My dad began bringing me to the garage. He knew it wasn't an ideal place for a little girl but he could see a change in me right away: how much more I laughed and smiled and talked around him.

"Things didn't get better. You were still so miserable, stuck in that small town with a little kid in your early twenties. You started resenting him for all of it. He figured he was going to come home one day and find you gone." And he started wishing for it, he had admitted in his letter.

"You two drifted apart. And then my dad ran into Mary-Ann—his ex-girlfriend before you, who had broken up with him when she went away to college. Things just kind of picked up where they left off." I turn to take in Annabelle's face. "He cheated on you." I'm surprised she never told me. I would have thought that being able to blame Hank MacKay would have given her satisfaction. I also would have thought that she might reveal the truth, knowing how much pain I felt in a very similar situation with Jared. An eerily similar situation. Sure, it was a much shorter relationship and we hadn't created another human, but still, that kind of heartache could have found us some common ground, something we finally shared.

But instead, her pride kept her silent for sixteen years.

You would think that with that much time passed and three husbands later, Annabelle would be indifferent at the very least. But when I see her eyes brim with tears and her jaw visibly tighten, I know that she is far from indifferent.

I see firsthand how badly my father had hurt her.

When I read through the candid account of what led to my parents' breakup, something happened that I've never experienced with Annabelle: I felt for her.

"They were together for six months before you found a receipt for a necklace he had bought her. You confronted him. He admitted it and asked for a divorce."

It feels weird, running through the events of my parents' history with the woman who lived it. But she's spent so much time running from it, and dragging me down with her. It's time we both faced the past—the thing that's gotten us here.

"He told you he was moving to Tallahassee. MaryAnn had inherited her grandparents' ranch. He wanted to take me with him." That my dad had refused to move, to give up the garage for Annabelle—the mother of his child—but was more than willing to walk away from it all for another woman, must have been devastating for Annabelle.

It would certainly crush me.

"You stormed out of the apartment in a rage. He packed me up in the truck and drove to her ranch. He wanted to see how I'd like it there." I feel the sad smile touch my lips, thinking back to the fleeting memory of chasing a chicken. One of my few memories of that weekend. "Apparently I *loved* it there. I got along well with MaryAnn." The smile drops off. "After a few days, when he hoped you had calmed down, he packed me up and we started heading back. We stopped at a truck stop just outside of Gainesville to have dinner. That's when my dad called you and you told him that you had reported me kidnapped. That you were going to make him regret the affair."

A single tear slides down Annabelle's flawless cheek.

"He didn't know much about kidnapping except that, with his record, there was a good chance that he'd do time if he was convicted. So, he panicked and did the only thing he could think of—he left me in the diner."

I must have read that part of the letter fifty times, seeing the night not through the eyes of a confused five-year-old girl left alone but through the eyes of a heartbroken, frightened twenty-eight-year-old father, terrified of spending years behind bars. When I saw his truck pull away, I thought he had left. But he hadn't. He had parked in a dark corner at the far end of the lot, shutting off his lights. And he had waited. For two hours, he sat and watched—gripping the steering wheel tightly, feeling like someone had reached in and torn his insides out—to make sure no one tried to take me. When the police car finally pulled in and the officer sat down with me, he left.

And he regretted it every day after.

When my grandparents came by to visit me a week after the incident, as requested by their son, we were gone, with no forwarding address.

"Why?" It's ironic: for sixteen years, that same question sat on my tongue, only it was intended for Hank MacKay. Now, the real answer belongs to my mother. "Why would you use me to hurt him like that? Why would you not let me have a father who loved me in my life?"

Annabelle's silky blond hair sways as she shakes her head, her voice hoarse and barely audible. "Because he wanted to take you—something we created together—to *her*. I knew you'd like her more."

"But you've never even wanted to be a mother, Annabelle!" I'm struggling to control my voice now.

"That's not true. I just . . . I didn't know how to be *your* mother. You are *so* much like him, Reese." Her voice wavers as she squeezes her eyes shut. "You're *all* Hank. You're obsessed with rock music and motorcycles. I could never keep you in a dress for more than five minutes. Everything about you is your father and every time I looked at you growing up, it reminded me of him. And it killed me." She hugs her chest as if suddenly cold. "I thought you'd be too young to remember, that you'd forget about him. Or maybe you'd begin to resent him, too." She brushes another stray tear away. "But you didn't. You just seemed to resent me more."

I watch this woman quietly, seeing her in a new light for the very first time in my life. A sad, desperate light. "And did you forget about that hurt when you cheated on Jack? When you left Barry for Ian?" There's no malice in my voice. I already know the answer to that, but seeing her bow her head is confirmation.

Annabelle hasn't let herself fully love anyone since Hank MacKay. Jack . . . Barry . . . even Ian. They're all substitutes for him—successful husbands who can fill all the other voids in her life except the one that matters. The one in her heart.

I release the breath I've been holding, and suddenly things seem lighter. I came here tonight to put it all out in the open. Not because I thought it would change our relationship.

Annabelle and I will never be close. But, thanks to this, I can begin to understand why. It's nothing I did. It's nothing I can change. What I *can* change is making sure I never end up as bitter a woman as her.

When I read that first letter, the one with the "return to sender" stamp on it and the only one that recounted the ways my parents hurt each other terribly, I panicked, my own doom flashing before me.

But since then, I've realized that I'm not really *just* like her. I'm *a lot* like her. If I had gone back to Jared's condo with him, had finished what I had started, had hurt him, hurt Caroline . . . then I wouldn't be able to claim any difference between us at all.

But somewhere along the way, I let myself care again. Maybe even love again. Unintentionally, unexpectedly, I fell for Ben.

And now, I just want to go be with him.

"Here." I hold out an envelope.

She eyes it warily. "What is it?"

"Maybe some closure for you." Aside from the initial letter, most of the rest were more like journal entries, about things in Hank MacKay's life that made him happy—his son with Mary-Ann, the modest home they shared, the trucks he restored and sold to supplement their income—and the things that made him regretful. Cheating on Annabelle, having married her when he was young and stupid but knew he was still in love with someone else. But mostly, for ever leaving me.

The last letter was from MaryAnn, and talked about how Hank had contacted a lawyer to better understand the risks associated with the outstanding warrant out for him. While the lawyer thought he could get the kidnapping charges dropped, the child abandonment case would stick. Hank was considering turning himself in, hoping that it might lead to finding me again.

Among those letters, though, there was a heartfelt apology to Annabelle. Whether it's enough to melt the protective layer of ice remains to be seen. I leave Annabelle with it, the only thing that may ever open her eyes.

And I go in search for what opened mine.

I find him in the grand foyer with a satay skewer in his hand and circled by three young women in Cinderella ball gowns. The oldest one can't possibly even be legal, and yet they're all very familiar with the batted-lash approach.

I sidle up to his side and loop my arm through his. "Ready to go, or do you need some more time with your jailbait?"

His grin doesn't falter with my words. "Sorry, ladies. The boss is here." Their matching pouts are the last thing I see as I tug Ben out of the house, barely giving him a chance to deposit the remnants of his food onto a tray.

He hands his ticket to the valet and then pulls me into his chest. "Feel better?"

I heave a sigh. "Not yet, but I will." I haven't come to terms with any of this. Right now, I'm not sure that I'll ever stand face-to-face with Annabelle again.

"Good."

I've never used the word "dashing" to describe a person but right now, staring up at this blond man in his tux, his dimpled smile and blue eyes twinkling, that's the only word I can possibly find to describe him. And it's not even because of his physical beauty. Everything about him is appealing. Even his big, obnoxious mouth.

"Can we go now? Or do you feel the need to cause some chaotic scene to end the night off in Reese style?"

I press my cheek into his chest to listen to his heartbeat as I smirk. "I have no idea what you're talking about." I stare out at that tacky water fountain—a statue of a Greek goddess standing in the center of a small pool, surrounded by three-foot-high sprays of water and illuminated by blue spotlights.

And ask suddenly, "How cold do you think that water is?"

Though it's an unusually warm November for Florida, it's night-time now and the temperatures have cooled off.

"I'm guessing ball-shrinking cold."

"Care to place a bet?" Before he even has a chance to answer, I pull away from him and run down the front stairs, kicking my sparkly heels off and leaving them on the steps. With one last look at Ben, who's both grinning and shaking his head, I sit down on the edge of the pool, gather up my gown, and spin around to plunge into the water.

"It's not that bad!" I lie, gritting my teeth as I wade into the knee-deep water until I'm standing next to the statue. "What do you think? Is this Annabelle's fountain of youth? Is this Aphrodite? Should I beg her to make me look younger?"

The team of valets and a few party patrons watch me with a mixture of shock and amusement.

Ben takes the steps down with a broad grin, my shoes now dangling from his hand. "Nope. You're not allowed to change a damn thing about you."

"Well, I think you and she have some things to talk about," I tease with a wink. "Why don't you come in here?"

His head falls back with a loud bark of laughter. "Hell no!"

"Wuss."

He regards me for a moment, his tongue running over his teeth slowly as he ponders something.

And then he kicks off his shoes, tosses his tux jacket onto the ground, and steps into the fountain. "I'm going to make you regret calling me that," he warns with grim determination as he stalks toward me, the water no match for his powerful legs. I quickly scramble away, trying to dodge the cascades of water shooting up from the pool, but he's too fast and his strong arms seize me in a backward hug.

"I don't have a change of clothes, Ben!" I remind him with a squeal.

"Neither do I, but you insisted, so I guess we're in for a really interesting drive home, aren't we?"

From my peripherals, I see a small crowd forming on the steps and flashes of camera lights go off, no doubt the invited media for the event. If Ben sees them, he certainly doesn't care. Or maybe he does, and that's why he hooks one arm around the backs of my knees and lifts me up into a cradle.

"Ready?"

"No!" I howl with laughter as I squeeze his neck tightly. "Don't you dare let me fall into this water! It's fucking freezing!"

A strange look passes through his blue eyes. "Let you fall? Reese, you should know by now that I'd never let that happen." His one arm pulls me in to lay a highly inappropriate kiss on my lips, given we have spectators.

And then he starts running through the ring of water sprays. Drenching us both as we laugh and laugh.

Epilogue

■ ■ ■

BEN

"Damn, I can't wait to get this tie off me," I mutter as my fingers curl under the collar of my shirt, already damp beneath the suit jacket. I'll be stripping down to nothing as soon as the pictures are over, if I have my way.

"Stop whining. At least it's May. She could have picked July," Jake reminds me, adding quietly as he wipes his brow, "and we're all suffering with you."

A quick glance at Rob and Josh confirm a light sheen of sweat on their faces. The four of us are standing in the shade of one of the oldest oaks on the property. Rows of white chairs, filled with family and friends, face us. A makeshift altar—an archway covered in orange blossoms—is situated next to us.

Just inhaling the scent calms me.

"You guys have done a ton of work on the house since Christmas," Rob muses, his eyes roaming the big old plantation-style home in the background.

"It was a big insurance policy. Enough to cover the critical stuff." I nod to our oldest brother. "Josh did a lot, too." Josh quit his job shortly after our dad's death and moved down to be with Mama. The money from the sale of the woodworking equipment is more than enough to cover child support and alimony payments for the near term. He, in turn, has been a huge help around here, converting our dad's wood shop into a packing facility and getting that up and running, to minimize off-site fees. He just celebrated his first year of sobriety last week and, though Karen doesn't appear to be ready to reconcile anytime soon, she came down with their two kids this weekend for the wedding.

I've gotten to know my big brother better now, as an adult, than I ever knew him as a child. I've even come to appreciate his quiet demeanor and I think, by the small smiles and chuckles, he has come to appreciate me for who I am.

"It's almost time!" Mama gushes, rushing up to us with her three-month-old grandson in her arms. "You want to see Daddy one more time, Jake Junior?"

"Couldn't be more original, could you," I mock, looking down at the little baby in his tux, the front of it covered in drool. Okay, I'll admit it—he's cute. He'd be even cuter if he didn't cry so much.

"Shut the fuck up," Jake throws my way in a mutter as he leans down to kiss his son's forehead.

"Hush now!" Mama scolds, pulling Jake Junior to her chest.

But I'm not done yet. Getting under my brother's skin is too damn fun. "Did the doctors tell you when he'd grow into that head of his?" I watch the poor kid struggle to lift it. "Or will he always look like a bobble-head?"

I barely get my arm down in time to block the kidney shot Jake delivers to me.

"Are you making fun of the bobble-head again?"

My heart skips a beat with the sound of Reese's voice. I turn in time to see her floating forward through the grass, her old blue Yamaha guitar slung over her back. I take all of her in, including the plunging neckline of her dress, which gives me a good eyeful of those tits I have my hands on every opportunity I get. The dress is long, reaching all the way down to the ground. That's kind of annoying. I really like seeing her legs. But, when she turns around and I see the open back, I figure that makes up for it. "I thought you weren't supposed to wear white to a wedding?"

She shrugs. "You can if the bride makes you wear it."

"Did Rita also pick the dress out? Because if she did . . ."

Her wide lips—painted red today—curl up into a slow smile. "You like it?"

"Yeah. In fact . . ." I reach down and rope my arm around her body to get a good grip on that ass I love so much as I pull her up against me.

"Benjamin!" Mama's loose hand swats at my shoulder. "Not in front of the guests." Heaving a sigh of exasperation, I catch an "honestly" under her breath.

"Yeah, Benjamin. *Honestly.*" Reese's caramel eyes twinkle as she spins out of my grip and takes a step back to where the microphone is set up. Based on what she must have just felt, she knows I'm going to be hauling her up to the attic—claimed as our weekend headquarters—the second those pictures are done.

"I love the orange blossoms," she says to Mama, smiling. "Nice touch."

"We can do the same for you and Ben."

I clear my throat roughly, shooting a stern look Mama's way, but she shifts her focus to her grandson, cooing softly as Reese's head falls back with that loud, throaty laughter.

"Only if you can cover the roll bars on that dune buggy, too, because I plan on coming down the aisle in style." She winks at me and I can tell she's teasing. Thank God. I'm in no rush. I know she's in no rush either. We've got a really good thing going right now.

"How much longer is this going to take?" I mutter under my breath, tucking at my collar as Jack makes his way over with a glass of lemonade in hand.

"Reese, you look beautiful, even with that beat-up old thing slung over your shoulder." He leans in to add a kiss on her cheek before turning to Mama. "Here you go, Wilma."

"Thank you, Jack," she answers with a coy smile.

And . . . Wait, what is that? Is Mama blushing?

I feel the deep furrow in my forehead when I look from them to Jake, who's too busy making googly eyes at his bobble-head kid to see anything else, and back to them. It isn't until I look at Reese, to see her gaze on her stepfather and Mama, her smile secretive, that I clue in.

"Aw, hell no!" My outburst pulls everyone's attention to me, Mama's face suddenly full of worry.

"What's wrong, dear?"

"What's wrong is that I have a strict policy against my girl-friend's stepdad putting the moves on my mama!"

Mama's face turns the color of eggplant to match her dress. If she didn't have a baby in her hands, I think I'd be getting a proper beating right now, right on my brother's wedding altar. *Fuck it*, I don't care. *Jack and Mama?*

Josh lets out a loud snort. Jake and Rob follow closely with chuckles. Even Reese can't keep it down. And it finally clicks. I throw my arms up in exasperation. "Am *I* the only one who didn't know about this?"

"How did you ever pass the bar, man?" Jake ribs.

Mama rolls her eyes and turns around to walk away, but not before I catch her shooting Jack a wink. *Shit.* I had no idea! Jack and Mason have made some day trips up here to help with harvesting. Then Mama invited them for Christmas. And Easter.

I thought they just liked the grove!

"Well, I guess you've been too busy blatantly ignoring *my* policy to notice," Jack muses.

"I wouldn't say 'blatantly,'" I mutter. *Fuck. He has me there.*

Jack's bushy gray eyebrows spike at that. "No? Maybe we should ask Mason about that."

"I warned you—Jiminy talks," Reese murmurs as she adjusts the microphone stand, her cheeks now taking on a hint of color as well.

"Uh . . ." I'm not sure how to respond to that. We've been *really* good respecting Jack and keeping our relationship under wraps in the office, Reese working on Natasha's cases while I take on cases of my own and use two other paralegals. In fact, I'm pretty sure no one has a clue. Then again, maybe everyone knows and we're fooling ourselves.

And, except for one night a few weeks ago when we were working late and I couldn't help making her reenact a fantasy I've had burning in my head for months now involving Reese and my desk, we've kept our hands to ourselves.

What the hell was Mason doing, anyway, coming into the office after midnight?

I'm betting he won't be doing *that* again without calling ahead.

"So we'll call it even, then?" Jack offers with a smirk as he walks toward his seat.

I dip my head as the sheepish grin takes over, just as Reese's phone beeps with a text from Elsie. "It's time!" she announces, tossing her phone haphazardly onto the ground a few feet away—she's going to forget it there and then go ape shit looking for it later, guaranteed—before her fingers strum the first chords. When her mouth opens and the words to the song come tumbling out in that deep, raspy voice of hers, Jake has to elbow me in the ribs again to get me to turn around and face the aisle. I last all of five seconds before my attention's back on Reese.

I don't think I'll ever get sick of hearing her sing. Or talk. Or laugh, or bust my balls, or tell me I'm a jackass. And I don't see how I could ever get sick of waking up next to her in the morning, or pulling all her clothes off of her at night, because I haven't yet. It's the exact opposite, actually. I just want her more. She's everything I never knew I wanted. She's everything I never knew I could have.

She just . . . fits with me. So perfectly.

I'm vaguely aware of the processional coming down the aisle. I probably should be paying attention to the bride.

But I'm too busy staring at my Reese.

ACKNOWLEDGMENTS

Writing this acknowledgments page is bittersweet. A year and a half ago, I wrote *Ten Tiny Breaths*. The secondary characters in that book were just that: secondary characters; people with lives and back stories of their own, but not main characters. Until you all began asking for their stories.

Five Ways to Fall is the last planned novel in this series. I've had a blast over the past year and I hope you have, too, seeing the *Ten Tiny Breaths* characters (and new characters along the way) come to life. I feel like my writing career has come to life along with them, and I have many people to thank for that.

Always first and foremost, to my readers—your messages, your tweets, your posts, your everything are greatly appreciated. You tell me that you have your sister/daughter/friend/cousin/mom reading the series and that makes me all giddy inside. Without you reading and spreading the word, I would not be able to do this. At least, not well.

To the bloggers (my readers on steroids)—every time we have a cover reveal or a release day or a tour and I hear from Inkslinger PR about how many of you reach out, asking to participate, I'm amazed. I keep wondering, "Why do these wonderful people want to help me?" And then I remember . . . because you are all so incredibly generous with your time and your passion.

Special thanks to the *Five Ways To Fall* street team—my first ever street team!—for all the love, support, and excitement you have brought to this book release: Michelle Kampmeier, Megan Toffoli, Autumn Thibault, Jennifer Harried, Lori Wilt, Kathryn Grimes, Bianca Janakievski, Jessica Hurtado, Christine from I Heart Big Books, Natalie Gomes, Rachael MacDonald, Nicole Martin, Leah Smith, Samantha Sideslinger, Holly Baker, Emily Kyle-Cooper, Jenn Benando, Lisa McCarthy, Carol Evans, Katie Pruitt-Miller, Jessica Sotelo, Bella Colella, MJ Fryer, Katie Murphy, and Denise Sprung.

To Candice S. Ly, the winner of the book-naming contest that we held to name *Five Ways to Fall*. It is the perfect name for this novel, and I hope you love seeing it in stores this summer as much as I will.

To Jessica Lynn, for naming Reese's mother. If you hadn't given me "Annabelle," then I couldn't have come up with "Annabelle Lecter," and, well, that's just pure genius.

To Heather Self, a.k.a. The Self, for your invaluable C.P. opinion when I was struggling with that dreaded opening chapter. And the second chapter. And the third chapter. . . . You listened to me ramble for an hour on the phone even though none of what I was plotting actually made it into the book. That's a true friend.

To Autumn Hull, for always jumping at the chance to read my books (even though I never ask because I hate asking) and for providing stellar input. And for that sexy maiden name.

To K. P. Simmon and Inkslinger PR, for continuing to walk with me along this incredible journey (translation: helping me figure out Western Union while stranded in a foreign country, introducing me to Chick-fil-A). You also know a great deal about books and PR and stuff. Like, a lot of stuff.

To Stacey Donaghy of Donaghy Literary Group, the best agent in the whole wide world. Sometimes I wonder how I get any books written, given how much time I spend laughing with you.

To Sarah Cantin, for not giving up on me with this book while the squirrels were running rampant in my head. Ben and Reese thank you for pointing me in the right direction.

To my publisher, Judith Curr, and the team at Atria Books: Ben Lee, Valerie Vennix, Kimberly Goldstein, and Alysha Bullock, for getting yet another beautiful book into the hands of readers with your magic. Number four!

To Paul, Sadie, and Lia, and all my friends and family, for putting up with me. Still.